OH, HEC!

Paul Davidson

FOURTH BASE PUBLICATIONS
WATFORD
Published in association with Pathfinder Paperbacks
www.pathfinder-paperbacks.com

OH, HEC!

All characters in this publication are entirely fictitious
and any resemblance to real persons, living or dead, is purely coincidental.

ISBN 0-9543816-0-2

First Published 2002 by
FOURTH BASE PUBLICATIONS
32 Fourth Avenue
Watford
Herts WD25 9QQ

Printed in Great Britain for Fourth Base Publications
by Biddles, Guildford

OH, HEC!

To my dearly beloved Maureen, sorry Carol,
without whose help and support this would not have been possible.
Also a big thanks to Mum June
and all my friends and colleagues too numerous to mention,
who gave me the necessary inspiration.

About the Author

Paul Davidson is forty-eight years old and his one major ambition is to live until he's fifty. He lives in Hertfordshire with his partner Carol, his expansive sports programme collection and a large collection of fuchsias. His one claim to fame is having a four-page article printed in Lithuania's top basketball magazine. He spends what spare time he has watching Queens Park Rangers and Harrow Borough football clubs and following the London Towers basketball club around Europe.

Contents

Oh, Hec!

Hector Blenkinsop was a sad man. Football was not only his life; it would probably be the cause of his death too.

Hector was what is known in football terms as a groundhopper. This meant that no matter how small, how difficult to get to, or whatever the weather was like, every football ground in the kingdom had to be got to, by Hector, to see a game of football. Hector used to dream of going to every ground in the world, but had once got his hands on a used copy of the *European Football Yearbook* and calculated that he would have to go to a different ground every twenty-eight minutes of his probable remaining thirty-five years on the planet in order to visit all the grounds in Europe, let alone South America and Africa, and so on.

Anyway, places like that were not proper football countries and so did not really count. Hector had only ever been abroad once, to France for a few days, and had gone to a game at Lens while he was there. He didn't like it. He couldn't get his usual three pints of the local bitter in the rather strange bar he went to before the game; he couldn't get the person in the refreshment hut to understand that he only wanted a meat pie and a cup of Bovril at half-time. Worst of all, he could not understand the programme.

At least they did a programme. Hector's worst fear was that he would get to the game and find that they did not do a programme. This thought had actually kept him awake most of the night before the game. He had heard terrible tales of faraway places like Italy and Spain that did not bother with programmes even for the biggest of games. A friend of his had once been to a game at Panathinaikos in Athens while on holiday there and swore blind that they hadn't done a programme.

This was what was wrong with the Common Market as far as Hector was concerned. He always called it the Common Market; to him the euro was something that would never concern him. He could not envisage the day when he would have to pay in euros to get into a Mugglesfield's Breweries League game (or whatever the Northern Premier League was called that particular week). His one trip to France had been enough to convince him that home is definitely where the heart is. Hector did not like foreigners in general. He had stopped going to league football a few years ago when he found he could not pronounce the names of nearly a third of the players in the league. When he heard that a Premier League match had taken place with not one English-born player involved, including the managers and coaches (even the referee and linesmen had come from Paraguay as part of a FIFA experiment), he decided that that was that. Off he went into the depths of non-league football to which he would dedicate the rest of his life.

Programmes meant everything to Hector. His tiny one-bedroom flat was full of them. Every single nook and cranny was stuffed solid with them. Boxes, bundles, suitcases – even the odd milk crate – were so full of them that he had no room for much else in the way of material possessions. His prize collection of tea mugs from all the ninety-two league grounds was in a terrible state, stuffed in two packing cases in the hall. Ever since regular promotion from the Conference had occurred, he had started to get confused as to what ranked as a league club and what didn't, and his collection suffered. As he had visited Macclesfield to see a Hepplethwaite's Tractors Cheshire Senior Cup match in 1991, did that mean it counted as a league club since they had been promoted, or not? He had once been to Hereford United to see a fourth division game against Hartlepool; could he count this as going to all the Conference teams now, or did he have to go back again and see a non-league game there to make it count? Hector wasn't sure. He hoped not. He was not keen on places like Hereford – too rural. Hector had been brought up in the big city and wasn't a fan of the countryside. Too many strange smells, dodgy bus services and intimidating locals with strange accents. Anyway, his Hereford mug had got broken, along with his Luton Town League Cup winners mug and his 'Yo Baggies' limited edition souvenir mug from West Brom. He kept all the broken pieces, of course, in an old shoebox under the sink.

Hector never threw anything related to football away. One day it would be valuable, he told himself. He didn't really believe it, but he had to believe in something. He'd given up on religion in 1972, when his favourite team got relegated. Even though he had promised God, in a one-off prayer of despair the night before the fatal final game, to give up his perceived future life of sin and debauchery and become a monk if God let his team stay up. Hector never actually found out what a life of sin and debauchery was and tended to blame this on that one twenty-four-hour period in his life.

Programmes were the key to everything in Hector's life. If he was going to one of the more obscure teams in the Inglethorpe's Extra Strong Cider Western Junior Intermediate League or somewhere, he would always ring the club secretary the night before to make sure they were doing a programme for the match. No programme meant that he hadn't really been there. All his nightmare moments revolved around programmes. He still had terrible memories of grounds he had visited where 'the man who makes the programmes is ill and won't be coming today'. Or 'we usually do a programme, but seeing as it's a cup match tonight we didn't bother'. Nowadays he had to be sure, so he always rang the night before. No programme meant no visit. There was always somewhere else to go. Preseason friendlies were his worst time of the year. Almost no one did a programme for a non-league preseason friendly, and Hector got so depressed about it that he started producing his own ones on the company computer when his boss was out. He realised that this was a sad thing to do, but it kept his programme collection neat and tidy and that was all that really mattered in Hector's sad little world.

Hector had been to nearly two hundred and fifty non-league grounds. He used to think that that was a lot, until he met two other hoppers in the bar at Kibblesworth Miners Welfare FC one soggy February night, who had been to over five hundred each. When they told him that they knew of a man who had been to over a thousand different grounds, Hector had come close to quitting. He was so depressed, he committed the cardinal sin of leaving a game before the end and slunk back to his B&B in a grimy backstreet two villages away. He even considered ending it all, but whilst having a couple of pints of 'Grandmother's Old Throatwarmer' in the Rat and Ferret next door the following lunchtime, he did some calculations. He worked out on the back of a beer mat that if he went to at least one new ground a week for the next twenty seasons, he could reach a thousand grounds before he died. Then maybe people would talk about him in hushed and reverent tones. This spurred him on and gave him a new meaning in his life. (Little did he know that people spoke about him in hushed tones even then, but only ever behind his back!)

Hector did not have a car. No true hopper has a car. This would take all the fun out of it. Besides, using public transport gave hoppers something else to talk about other than football. 'Couldn't believe it when the 1.35 to the cemetery gates was cancelled. Had to get the 1.17 to Llandrindod Wells and change at the town hall. Bloody disgrace! Only had time for two pints when I got to the ground. It's just not good enough.' Or, 'Nearly missed the train; tripped over three trainspotters on the platform as I was running for the 12.24. Sad bastards, why don't they get a life!'

Hector spent a good deal of his life waiting for buses and trains. To pass the time he read science fiction novels. He had been doing this for years and had read nearly every one that had been published. He had been banned from his local library after an unfortunate incident with an assistant librarian. (He was secretly very proud of this; it was the only time he had been banned for anything in his life. It made him feel a bit of a rebel.) He now got his supply from second-hand bookshops and car boot sales on Sunday mornings. He loved car boot sales. You never knew what would turn up. He once bought fifty copies of Charlie Buchan's *Football Monthly* for one pound at a car boot sale. They were now kept under his bed where they had congealed into one solid lump of soggy paper and had taken on a secret life of their own. He had recently bought four old copies of *Wisden*. He didn't know why – he didn't like cricket – but he was sure they would be valuable one day so he had put them on top of the wardrobe.

The top of Hector's wardrobe was very similar to the inside of the Tardis. It didn't seem to matter how much you stuffed up there, there always seemed room for more. The truth was actually very simple. As Hector pushed more magazines, papers and books on the top, so the ones at the rear fell down the back towards the floor where they decomposed into a fungus that, had Hector but known it, was more valuable to mankind than his entire collection. It was a miracle cure for athlete's foot.

He read at the rate of more than one book a week. This was a lot of science fiction. Poor Hector's brain could not cope with such a large amount of fantasy and often caused him embarrassment. It was not at all rare for a railway booking clerk or bus driver to hear, when asking Hector for his required destination, the answer, 'Any one of the distant moons of Sagor, please' or maybe 'The planet Thandoor in the galaxy of Anthrax the Invincible'.

He had moments in his life when his two greatest loves, football and science fiction, had become so intertwined as to cause him to confuse the two. Once at a particularly tense moment in an FA Trophy tie at Harwood Borough FC, the third great love of his life, he had yelled out at the top of his voice, 'Give it to Gragnorth the Virgin Slayer!' instead of his all-time favourite player, Lenny Easterby. This was the main reason why people spoke about him in hushed tones behind his back. He often introduced himself to people whom he met as Prince Hector the Valiant (this was another reason). But by and large he kept the two worlds apart.

During the day he was a generally mild-mannered stock control assistant, but God help anyone who did not have the correct paperwork. Hector thought a great deal of his stock control paperwork. From nine to five thirty

Monday to Friday, it meant nearly as much to him as football programmes. He had goods received notes under his desk dating back from 1974. He remembered the good old days before computers when stock control was done with pencils and rubbers on endless sheets of paper, taking several weeks. He still had a copy of the very first company stocktake he had done in 1972 stuffed in his bottom drawer. He did not keep it because he thought it would become valuable; he kept it because he was sure that one day, when the computer system broke down permanently (instead of just for an hour or two every day), the managing director would come to him and say, 'Hector, you must save our company. Can you remember how we used to do things before computers?'

Then he would show them. He would show the warehouse staff who laughed at him every lunchtime as he carefully unwrapped his prawn sandwiches. Hector always had prawn sandwiches for lunch. He didn't know why, he just did. He didn't particularly like prawn sandwiches, but he did like having a routine. He had once, in a fit of rebelliousness, ordered a cheese and pickle sandwich at the bakery in the high street where he called in every morning, but it just did not taste right. For a whole week back in 1987 there had not been any prawns and he had had egg and tomato, which he found he rather liked, but on seeing prawn sandwiches back on the menu the following Monday he had gone back to his old habits.

He would show all of them one day. The girls in accounts who sniggered at the multicoloured tank top that he wore every workday. The lads in the workshop who laughed at him for wearing his treasured 'Harwood Borough Wembley 1984' scarf. He had worn it with pride every day since that fatal Saturday in April 1984 when they had thrown away a three-goal lead in the second leg of the FA Trophy semi-final to Tellisford Town and missed out on a Wembley appearance by three minutes. He was proud of that scarf. His dear old mum had knitted it especially for him during the week before the second leg and he would wear it every day until Boro really did qualify for Wembley. It did not matter to Hector that, in the years since then, they had only got past the third qualifying round once and that was when their opposition had been thrown out of the competition for fielding an ineligible player. He knew they would get there one day. His one and only visit to a bookmaker's every year was to put a ten-pound bet on them every August to win the FA Trophy.

One day he would show them all, he thought. One day.

This was not to be that day. This particular Saturday saw Hector sitting on the 357 bus from Glastonbury to Shepton Mallet on his way to see a Thruckett and Threlwall Gas Fires Western Combination League Division One game between Shepton Mallet Rangers and Cullompton Farmers Institute. This was going to be a big day for Hector. He could cross off the first division from his list. He would have done them all. He had the sort of excited feeling in his stomach that only true hoppers get when they go to the last ground in a league. It is rather like the feeling normal people get when they get home and find the house has been burgled, only they recognise it as total despair.

He was wearing his favourite anorak, the one he kept for special occasions. It was a sort of reddish brown colour with a furry yellow lining. He had been with Mary when he had chosen it and it still reminded him of her. Ah, Mary (or Hairy Mary as everyone at Boro called her due to the three huge hairy warts she had on her massive forearms). She had been his one and only girlfriend, before she had left him for the assistant librarian who had banned Hector for assault with a deadly paperback six months before. He was clutching the two-handled shopping bag that all hoppers carry to games, containing all the requirements for his big day out.

He had his railway timetable and his photocopy of the local bus service map that the local tourist board had sent him in 1988. He had his *Non-League Guide*, the nearest thing he had ever had to a Bible and, like an electrician's screwdriver, a thing that never ever left his sight. It stood on his desk all day at work. At night it was on his bedside cabinet in case, as had happened before, he woke up in the middle of the night and could not remember which division of the Grimshaw's Masonry Nails North-Western Alliance League that Todmorden Tuesday played in. He had his lunch, consisting of three strangely shaped cheese sandwiches hacked from an uncut loaf (the bakery didn't do sandwiches on Saturdays). He had a small pair of binoculars given to him as a present by Mary on their one and only Christmas together in 1991. He had two stopwatches, obviously. No true hopper would take the word of the local paper over such crucial points as the timing of substitutions and so on, even if you could get such information. And what would you do if the battery in your stopwatch ran out? Hector took no chances; the second one was an old clockwork one he had inherited from his favourite uncle, Ron, that somewhat mysteriously was divided into three-minute segments. He had his plastic raincoat, more essential baggage for hoppers, and of course his obligatory paperback. This one was entitled

Below the Kingdom of the Krells and he had already read it four times. It was one of his favourites and he had chosen it especially for this auspicious day. What he hadn't known at the time was just what a memorable day this would turn out to be.

The bus rattled on towards the ground. The weather was set fair; he had checked that a programme was being issued. All was well in Hector's world. Somewhere though, something was wrong. He didn't know exactly what, but something did not feel right. He found the ground all right; it was a five-minute walk from the bus stop and was actually signposted from the main road, a very rare event in Hector's experience. There was no one about, but then it was rather early. He walked through the open gates into a reasonably pleasant little ground. There was one fairly new-looking covered stand, with low old uncovered terracing opposite and a pathway behind the goals. Eight old rusting metal floodlight pylons loomed skywards, four on each side of the pitch. In one corner of the ground stood a rather ramshackle wooden building with a big sign on the outside proudly proclaiming, in bright red and yellow letters: WELCOME TO SHEPTON MALLET RANGERS FC, PROUD MEMBERS OF THE THRUCKETT AND THRELWALL GAS FIRES WESTERN COMBINATION LEAGUE. *At least I'm in the right place*, thought Hector as he noticed that if you looked carefully at the sign you could read the names of the last two sponsors of the league through the paint. I suppose the one advantage of leagues changing sponsors every season, he ruminated, is that at least the sign gets a fresh coat of paint each year. *Pity the rest of the ground doesn't*, he thought wistfully.

'Can I help you?' boomed a loud friendly West Country voice from behind him. 'Are you here for the game?'

'Yes,' said Hector. 'What time's kick-off?'

'About three,' came the reply, 'when everyone's here.'

This was not too unusual to Hector; he had once been asked by a club official what time he would like the game to start at a very minor fixture deep in the heart of industrial Lancashire.

'Bar will be open shortly, if you'd like a pint,' said the friendly voice. 'I'll come in and get your admission money when someone else gets here.'

Hector retired inside the building and, following the faded sign saying ME BERS ON Y – G ES S MUS SIG IN, made his way to a fairly large room with the most mismatched collection of chairs and tables he had ever seen. Every single one was a different size or height, or both. Many table legs seemed to be supported by a folded beer mat, a standard ploy for most non-league bars.

One, he noticed, rather bizarrely had a beer mat under each of its four legs. Most of the chairs were covered in the obligatory red plastic, although there were various shades of green and blue, and a very old and obviously much used tartan settee sat in the corner by the stage. The stage itself was about four feet square and would probably have accommodated two people in comfort. The traditional sparkly disco ball hung rather limply above it, although more of the panels were missing than were still there, and sparkle it most definitely did not. A fluorescent pink poster hanging behind what obviously doubled as a stage and dance floor announced 'For one night only at SMRFC, the Wadebridge and Bodmin Big Band'. *Where the hell did they all go?* thought Hector as he ambled to the bar.

Behind the bar were the traditional souvenirs that can be seen in hundreds of such clubhouses the length and breadth of the country. There was a large wooden shield with 'Shepton Mallet Rangers Player of the Year' painted on it in faded gold paint. Three of the small metal shields round the outside were missing and the last engraved one said simply 'Poor Johnny Poges – 1971'. There were the standard foreign pennants hanging in a line, none of which bore the name of any team anyone had ever heard of. Hector was convinced that somewhere there was a firm that specialised in making souvenirs from non-existent teams especially for clubhouses. There was one huge pennant in the centre that read 'Isle of Man Junior Tournament 1963' and of course one that said simply 'Leyton Orient'. There was a trophy of a footballer with one leg missing that was so badly covered in grime it was impossible to read what it had been awarded for. And finally there was a large tarnished silver cup on a shelf, from which a tattered and faded red and yellow rosette hung with 'Wembley 1965' across it.

Hector waited. He paced up and down the bar looking at the various beers on offer. He thought he might try 'Old Griswalds Plunger' for starters. He had never seen a review of 'Old Griswalds Plunger' in a CAMRA bulletin (all true hoppers are members of CAMRA) but that made it all the more special. He noticed how his feet stuck to the carpet as he walked. He was not surprised and he wondered if it was the fault of the carpet or his very sensible, if rather tatty, tan-coloured walking shoes.

He still waited. He thought he might buy a small bag of the temptingly sounding cheese-and-onion-flavoured pork scratchings.

He still waited. He looked at the other posters around the walls. None of them were dated after July 1993, and one even announced the forthcoming attraction of *The New Rock and Roll Sensations – The Wurzels*; it had no date on it but he could guess: he had copies of their albums at home.

Hector still waited. He tried making little coughing noises. He tried rattling one of his pens against a large chipped yellow glass Skol ashtray on the bar (all hoppers carry a vast collection of pens, in all colours of the rainbow, usually in their top pockets but with at least one spare in every other pocket).

He waited some more. He got fed up with waiting and wandered outside.

Nothing. No one.

Even the man with the friendly voice wasn't there. He wondered about that. He hadn't actually seen anyone, just heard the voice. Maybe he had dreamt it. The ground looked different somehow. Newer, more paint. And where were the floodlights? He was sure that there had been floodlights. And the main stand. Wooden and newly painted, it had been one of these new metal pipes and bucket seats jobs when he had got there, he was sure. Now he came to think about it, where were the gates he had come in through? Where was any kind of entrance? There was nothing but an eight-foot-high fence all around the ground – no entrances at all. Hector was worried now; he had come across this kind of thing in his books. Whole planets and galaxies disappeared in his books, but this was real life. This was Saturday afternoon at the football game. Nothing strange could happen here, could it?

He turned and walked back towards the clubhouse. No longer old and ramshackle, it looked new and glistened with a coat of varnish. The most striking thing was the sign. Still bright red and yellow it no longer said WELCOME TO SHEPTON MALLET RANGERS FC, PROUD MEMBERS OF THE THRUCKETT AND THRELWALL GAS FIRES WESTERN COMBINATION LEAGUE; it just said SHEPTON MALLET FC.

He heard voices coming from inside the club and he went in. He was stopped by a man sitting at a table outside the bar.

'You're not a member,' he growled. 'That will be three pence.'

Hector was stunned. He opened his mouth but nothing would come out. He put his hand into his pocket and was staggered to pull out a handful of pre-decimal money. He blindly gave the man a threepenny bit and signed his name in the register handed to him. He walked into the bar. It was packed. People were everywhere. All the chairs were occupied, all the tables were full of beer glasses and a bloke in an ill-fitting tuxedo was belting out Frank Sinatra classics on the stage. He was accompanied by a pimply youth of about eighteen with a six-string guitar, above whom twinkled a sparkling ball of light. He made his way to the bar. People were everywhere. He heard two men wearing large red and yellow rosettes moaning about prices.

'I don't care who we are playing,' said one. 'Four bob is too much to pay to see a bloody football match.'

'And six pence for the programme,' said the other. 'Even if it is a souvenir special, it's not right. Who wants a programme with photos in it anyway? It will never catch on.'

That's it, thought Hector. *The programme. That will tell me what on earth is going on.* 'Where did you get that programme?' he asked the second man.

'Outside by the entrance,' he said, 'but he didn't have many left.'

Blindly Hector rushed for the door. He charged past the man with the signing-in book, gasping that he had to go out, and burst outside into the fresh air. He ran straight into a large man dressed in a very formal but somewhat old-fashioned double-breasted suit.

'Go easy, young man,' he said. 'You'll hurt someone dashing around like that in a crowd of this size.'

Hector stared. All around there was a seething mass of people. Most were wearing big old-fashioned red and yellow rosettes; some were carrying big wooden rattles, like the ones he remembered from when his dear old dad had first taken him to games when he was a kid. Everyone looked weird. All the young men had neat pudding basin hairstyles and strange plain-coloured clothing, except for one very tough-looking group, who had very short hair and wore strange long green anoraks with furry linings to their hoods. Hector made a mental note not to get too near them. He was not sure what they were, but he was sure that they were not here for the football.

The most memorable thing about the crowd was that no one was wearing a replica shirt of any kind. He could not remember the last time he had gone to a game and no one wore replica shirts. Actually, he thought that the general appearance of the people was very good. Whoever they all were, they bore a strange resemblance to Hector himself. Some were even clutching plastic raincoats, he noticed reassuringly. For some strange reason this quite unnerved him. The only other time in his life he had been in a crowd of people that looked like him was when he had been on an ill-fated official hoppers' trip to the north-east one Easter. He and thirty-five clones had spent two nights on camp beds in an old Nissen hut on a disused airfield just outside Sunderland. Hector was almost starting to get nostalgic when he remembered the job in hand.

He tried to concentrate, but it was difficult. He was just starting to remember some of the details of those two nights. He was just starting to remember the terrible smell.

There had also been a fleeting incident in his local police station when he, four tramps and three local drunks had all taken part in a police identification line-up for an infamous local flasher. He still could not understand for the life of him why the police had asked *him* to take part, but he had to admit, they had all looked like someone he knew, but couldn't exactly place.

He pulled himself together. He saw the entrance. He saw the programme seller and made a beeline straight for him.

'Six pence,' said the man. 'Special souvenir edition.'

'Give me five, please,' said Hector, offering the man half a crown.

'I've only got one left,' he said and gave him two bob change.

Hector tried to look at the front cover, but as he was now standing in front of three turnstiles which had appeared in the fence and were disgorging bodies at him at about ten people per second, he turned around and headed back into the clubhouse. With the programme firmly folded inside his jacket, he pushed his way up to the bar, bought a pint of 'Old Griswalds Plunger' for four shillings and made his way to where he remembered the old tartan settee had been by the stage. It was still there, but was brand spanking new. It had a brass plaque screwed to the wall above it with the legend 'In memory of our founder, Hamish Mcsporran, a great man with a strange taste in furniture'. It was empty. Hector sat down. He pulled the programme from his jacket, lovingly smoothing out the creases and took a large swig from his glass. He took a deep breath and his eyes widened as he looked at the front cover.

FA AMATEUR CUP
SEMI-FINAL SECOND LEG

SHEPTON MALLET FC
(Western League)
v
FC MINOTAUR
(Northern League)

Saturday, 15 April 1965

Hector rubbed his eyes. He took another large gulp of his beer. He looked again at the programme cover. It was still the same.

Saturday, 15 April 1965. He could not believe it. He must be dreaming. He pinched himself. It hurt. He was not dreaming. *Oh, wow*! he thought. *I always knew something like this would happen to me. I've gone back in time; it really is 1965. Got to concentrate – what do I do now*? 'Buy more beer,' he answered himself. He was still a hopper after all, whenever it was.

He bought another pint, sat back down and opened the programme. The bright red cover had a glossy finish, but the pages inside looked as if they had been printed with a John Bull printing set. *Wait a minute*, he mused, *it's 1965; they probably have been printed with a John Bull printing set.*

The writing was a bit skew-whiff and difficult to read, but the gist of the editorial was that tiny Shepton Mallet FC had been drawn to play mighty FC Minotaur from the all-powerful Northern League in the Amateur Cup semi-final. 'Shep' as they were referred to had somehow managed to win the first leg in the north-east two–one the previous Saturday and were now just ninety minutes away from Wembley.

The heroes from the previous week were star player and inside left Stanley Bowler, who had scored the first goal; centre forward Pat Givens, who had scored the second with a powerful header; and goalkeeper Jackie McSporran, who apparently had saved almost everything the northern side could throw at him. The club thanked the almost fifty people who had braved the charabanc trip lasting nearly twelve hours each way to the north-east and hoped they had had a good time. It also announced that the mayor of Shepton Mallet himself was coming to today's game and had decreed that the team would be honoured with a civic reception whatever the result of the second leg.

Hector himself was not really a great student of non-league football history and had no idea what had happened in the 1965 Amateur Cup final. He did remember seeing an old silver cup behind the bar with a 'Wembley 1965' rosette clinging to the side.

He looked over at the bar. It was gone. *No surprise there*, he thought. A thought struck him. If he could place a bet he could make a killing. He did not know what the score was going to be, but he did know who was going through to the final.

He drained his glass and stuffed his programme back into his inside pocket. Picking up his bag, he made his way, less hurriedly this time, towards the exit. The ground was even more packed than before. There was a brass band playing in front of the stand. People stood three deep behind both goals and the open terrace was a mass of swaying happy people waving home-made

banners and rattles. *No bookies in here*, he thought. *Wonder if I can get out…*

Just then a huge roar sounded and out of a little wooden tunnel by the side of the stand came the combatants for the afternoon's entertainment. The band played, the people cheered and the two teams lined up on the halfway line and were introduced to the mayor, a small, dapper little man with a moustache and a huge grin, all gold chain and teeth.

Too late, thought Hector, *I can't miss this*. It suddenly struck him that if he could get out afterwards and find a bookmaker's he could make a bomb on the correct score for the 1966 World Cup final. That was something to contemplate. He tried to think of other things he knew would happen. He couldn't think of any. Maybe later.

He pushed and shoved his way to the front of the crowd behind one goal (he always liked standing behind the goal, although he didn't know why; he was a bit short-sighted and sometimes could not properly see the other end).

Introductions over, the game kicked off. The Minotaur players were massive. Dressed in plain white shirts (no advertising in this day and age), plain black shorts and white socks, they looked like they would flatten the home side with no problem. The home players were a strange sight to behold. They were all different sizes and shapes. Tall thin ones, short fat ones. The fullbacks looked like two little barrels on legs. They had on red shirts with dark yellow shorts and socks, although the two different shades of yellow clashed alarmingly. Blood and gold, the programme had said. *I hope it's not their own blood*, thought Hector. He hadn't seen a team line up with five forward since he was about eleven years old and it took him a few minutes to adjust to this idea.

It was all FC Minotaur on the pitch, but somehow Shepton Mallet kept the score to a goalless draw at half-time. Off went the players; back came the band. Deep stirrings were going on inside Hector as if he remembered all this from his youth. He couldn't move; he was pinned against the barrier. This he definitely remembered. How on earth could anyone put up with this? It was dangerous. No one seemed to mind though; they all seemed to be having a great time.

Five minutes after they had gone off, back came the players. *Christ, I don't remember that happening before*, thought Hector.

He was now standing just to the side of the goal that the Minotaurs were attacking. He would see some action this half, he thought. He knew he wouldn't see a goal though. It was going to finish a goalless draw; he just knew it.

Bowler, Shepton's star player, had not come out for the second half. He had been hurt twice by vicious tackles in the first half, which had amazingly been waved on by the referee, and obviously could not continue. There were no substitutes. Down to ten men. Now Hector knew there would be no score. Shepton Mallet without Bowler would not score if they played on for an extra ninety minutes. The crowd was worried, but not Hector. He had seen the rosette. He knew they would win in the end.

The second half started where the first had left off. Wave after wave of Minotaur attacks swept towards the home team goal. McSporran, the goalkeeper, was magnificent. Over six foot – massive for those days – with bright ginger hair, he coped with everything the northerners threw at him. In front of him a giant centre half by the name of Simon Wicker cleared everything McSporran couldn't get to. It was very strange to Hector to see players passing back to the keeper and the keeper not only pick it up, but also wander aimlessly around his area bouncing the ball on the ground for an age before booting it way upfield.

It started to rain. There was no cover except in the stand. No one seemed to care. Hector managed, at length, to get the plastic mac out of his bag – not easy when your arms are pinned to your sides. He might have been pretty squashed, but nobody could contort themselves into a position in which to perform a tricky manoeuvre like getting into a pacamac like Hector could. His mum had made him wear a vest until he left home at the age of thirty-six. At the time, he thought going out without a vest was the bravest thing he would ever do. He was wrong. He did know, however, that not wearing a mac when it was raining was stupid. Not wearing either would very probably kill him, he thought, so he put up with the inconvenience and clambered into his polythene wrapping.

The rain streamed down; the time ticked on. Hector thought that they must be into the last minute by now, although he could not reach either stopwatch to check. Not long to wait now.

Wicker went in for a tackle on Lumsden, Minotaur's granite-like centre forward.

There was a huge crash. They both went down like a pair of rutting rhinos. McSporran leant down and picked the loose ball up. There was a whistle. The referee was pointing at the penalty spot.

The crowd was stunned; there was almost total silence. Wicker tried to protest, but the referee just waved him away. Lumsden put the ball down and walked back about ten paces. McSporran stood on his line, glaring at the

huge monolithic-like figure bearing down on him. Lumsden charged forward. His white shirt billowing out made him look like a huge three-masted sailing ship turning into the wind. He struck the ball hard.

It was roaring straight towards the top right-hand corner of the goal, right in front of Hector. The world seemed to stop revolving and time slowed down. Hector saw the ball heading towards him. It seemed to be travelling much slower now. He could see the yellow laces slowly revolving. He could see little bits of mud stuck on the dark brown panels. And he could see it going into the net.

This can't happen, he thought. *I've seen the rosette. There was no away goals rule in these days, and Shepton couldn't possibly hold on for an extra half an hour with ten men.*

In an automatic reaction he ducked, just as the huge left hand of McSporran loomed across the goal, his arm stretching to its very limit. As the ball was just crossing the line, the giant keeper's hand touched it just enough to divert its path. The ball hit the square wooden post with a thwack. So did McSporran, but with more of a heavy thud, head first.

The ball bounced out towards the waiting Lumsden. McSporran was lying in a heap at the base of the post; he was not moving a muscle. Hector could not even tell if he was still breathing. Lumsden lumbered forward to the ball, ready to strike it into the unguarded net.

Suddenly Hector knew what he had to do. He had waited all his life for a moment like this. He ducked under the railing and ran towards the goal. Lumsden had reached the ball now. He pulled back his right foot. Hector tripped over a newspaper cameraman and fell forward on to the pitch. He fought desperately to regain his balance. The ball had left Lumsden's foot now and was on its way into the goal.

Hector leapt. He caught his foot on McSporran's head and fell forward again. He was not going to make it. He was still falling. The ball smashed into the side of his head and bounced over the bar.

He had done it. Probably. He wasn't really sure what he had or hadn't done. All he knew was that he had to get out of here.

He felt giddy, but he pulled himself up on to his feet and ran for all he was worth. Time was speeding up again now. He could hear nothing specific, but he knew there was a row going on somewhere behind him. Some arms grabbed him and hauled him over the railings at the side of the pitch.

'Quick,' a voice called, 'before the coppers get here.'

Arms were pulling him. He had hold of his bag and he was not letting go of that for anything. No hopper ever let go of his bag. His head began to ache; he couldn't focus on anything. He was being dragged somewhere but he did not know where. He was being stuffed inside a cupboard or something, he had no idea what. The doors were slammed shut. Outside he could hear raised voices all around. People were shouting, but Hector could not make them out. He felt very groggy now. He just wanted to lie down and let his head clear. He closed his eyes.

When he opened them, he could see or hear nothing.

He tried to move. He was very cramped, but he could just stretch his arms out and he felt a rough wooden surface. His eyes were getting accustomed to the light now. He could make out what looked to be a very old large lawnmower next to him. He was in a shed. With a lawnmower. *How strange*, he thought.

He gently stretched out his legs. They hit a rough surface. *Can't stay here all day*, thought Hector. *I can't hear any more voices, I must have blacked out.*

He kicked his legs forward. The doors rattled. He tried again. The doors burst open and in flooded the daylight. It was so bright; Hector could see nothing again. He clambered out and stood up. The world came slowly into focus.

He was alone. Completely alone. He was standing outside a dilapidated groundsman's shed that looked as though it hadn't been opened in years. Where had the crowds gone? He could not possibly have been unconscious for that long, could he?

He looked round. It looked different. The main stand was metal again, with bucket seats. There were eight rusting floodlight pylons around the pitch. He was back where he had started. More to the point, he was back *when* he had started.

A voice yelled out to him, 'Oi, what are you doing over there?' A large old man in an ancient brown suit was lumbering towards him across the pitch. 'Are you all right?' he asked. 'Where did you spring from?'

Hector had temporarily lost the power of speech. He just pointed at the old hut.

'How long have you been in there?' asked the man. 'Wait a minute,' he said, 'I remember you; you were here early and you went in the bar. I wondered where you had gone.'

'I got shut in there,' croaked Hector, pointing at the shed.

'Christ,' said the man. 'I don't know how you managed that. I don't suppose it has been opened for donkey's years. We have a brand new metal shed round the back of the stand that we use now. Did you see the game?'

Hector shook his head, he was not sure what he had and had not seen.

'Missed a good one,' he said. 'Beat them buggers from Cullompton three–nil; you would have enjoyed it. Come over to the clubhouse and have a drink; you look as if you could do with one.'

The man helped Hector across the pitch and into the clubhouse.

While he was pulling off his now rather torn pacamac, Hector noticed that the sign outside the clubhouse read: WELCOME TO SHEPTON MALLET RANGERS FC, PROUD MEMBERS OF THE THRUCKETT AND THRELWALL GAS FIRES WESTERN COMBINATION LEAGUE. *Must get a new mac*, he thought to himself as he stuffed the old one back in the bag. It wouldn't do to get caught without one.

They went into the bar. It was all exactly as before. Completely deserted. Hector sat down on the faded settee. The man brought him a large brandy.

'That used to be my grandfather's seat,' he said. 'He founded this club in 1911. They put that there for him just before he died in 1959. Lovely man apparently; strange taste in furniture. It used to have a brass plaque above it, but it fell off years ago now.'

Hector was aghast. This must be a McSporran he was talking to. He looked at the man. He was tall and he had a few strands of wispy ginger hair across his balding pate. Hector looked towards the bar. He could see the cup; the rosette was hanging limply from the rim. It still said 'Wembley 1965'.

McSporran saw him staring at it. 'Those were the days,' he beamed. 'We had a great team then. I was the goalie, you know. I could tell you some stories about that season that would make your hair fall out,' he said. 'We went to Wembley for the final. Paid for the floodlights that cup run did. I've got all the press cuttings upstairs – would you like to see them?'

Hector nodded enthusiastically. He wished he hadn't; his head still hurt.

McSporran eased himself up and went out behind the bar. He was back a few minutes later with another brandy for Hector and a pile of newspapers six inches thick.

'What happened in the semi-final?' asked Hector, his voice now functioning properly due to the input of brandy into his system.

'Now that *is* an interesting question,' McSporran answered. 'No one to this day really knows. Minotaur, the lot we were playing, got a penalty in the last minute and I pushed it onto the post, but knocked myself out in the attempt, leaving their centre forward with an open goal. He swears the ball was on its way into the back of the net when it suddenly reared upwards and over the bar. We all think he must be mad and just miss-kicked it. He still says to this day that it was a ghost. Strange thing is, some people who were there swear that something ghostlike flew across the goal at that moment and deflected the ball, got some funny pictures in the papers too. No TV in them days, of course, to look at replays. Everything happened so quickly nobody really knows what went on.'

'Can I see the pictures?' Hector asked and the old man nodded and handed him a copy of the *Shepton Mallet Bugle* dated Monday, 17 April 1965.

The headline screamed MIRACLE SAVE SENDS SHEPS TO WEMBLEY. The picture accompanying it must have been taken by the photographer Hector had tripped over, or at least thought he had. He wasn't sure what had happened now. It showed McSporran lying slumped on the ground and Lumsden with one arm half raised in triumph, looming over him with a strange look on his face. The ball was not in shot but across the goal was a very blurred, almost translucent, image of what could only be described as a human figure flying forward, with what appeared to be a cape billowing out behind it.

Christ, thought Hector, *it looks like bloody Batman*. Then he noticed the very sensible-looking shoes it was wearing and it also appeared to be clutching something to its chest. You couldn't make out what it was, but it had two large handles on it.

'Bloody hell!' burst out Hector. 'I really did do it.'

'Sorry?' said McSporran.

'Oh, nothing,' replied Hector.

'That was the picture that caused all the controversy,' said McSporran. 'Some say it's a ghost, but most people think it was just a double exposure. Whatever it was, the referee never had time to restart the game and by the time I came round I was being carried off the pitch shoulder high. There was a hell of a commotion going on in the crowd on the far side but I always assumed it was some Minotaur fans complaining.'

I think I know what it was, thought Hector to himself. He drained his glass, handed the paper back to McSporran and stood up. 'I must be on my way,' he said. 'I've got a long way to go home.'

'Shame you missed the game,' said the old man. 'It's a long way to come to see nothing.'

Oh, I don't know, thought Hector as he strolled out of the club and towards the gates. As he was going through them, he turned. 'What was the score in the final?' he yelled at the figure in the clubhouse doorway.

'We lost two–nil to Islington Town; both of the damn goals were my fault too. I dropped a cross for the first one and then dived completely the wrong way for a penalty!'

Hector smiled. He waved and then turned and walked back to the bus stop. He didn't have long to wait, but he got a very strange look from the driver when he tried to pay him with an old sixpence. Luckily he had his emergency five-pound note in the secret pocket of his anorak; he never went out without his emergency five-pound note. He half expected it to have turned into an old white fiver. *Might have been good if it had*, he thought, *it would have been worth a fortune.*

He climbed the stairs, sat down and pulled his book from the bag. He looked at it. *Somehow it would never be the same*, he thought. He threw it in the bin at the end of the seat. He reached inside his jacket. It was still there.

He pulled out the programme. *A few creases, but in pretty good nick for a thirty-four-year-old football programme*, he thought. He leant back and took a deep breath. *Typical! If only I could tell people about it*, he thought to himself, *but they all think I am mad enough already.*

Never mind. He would be home in a few hours. Back in his flat. Maybe he would have his favourite for supper. Cold baked beans and a lump of cheese. He couldn't have much else really; he had nothing else in. He remembered his sandwiches. They were still in the bag. A bit squashed, but so what? He pulled one out.

He opened the programme and started to read.

Hector's Romance

Hector sat at his kitchen table. He was worried that both of his much loved house plants appeared to have died. He did not understand that the fact he had blocked up two thirds of the kitchen window with football posters did nothing for the natural lighting of the room. The fact that he would water them twice a day for four weeks and then forget about them for another four probably did nothing for their health either. Still, it worried him. If he could not cope with looking after a couple of house plants, what chance did he have of organising his life?

For Hector was in love. Or at least he thought he was. As he had never been in love before, it was a strange and new experience for him, so he wasn't sure, but thinking about it – and he did that often – he figured it couldn't really be anything else.

It had all started several weeks before, one Saturday morning at the station, as he bought his ticket to yet another obscure destination to watch his beloved football. Instead of the usual gruff welcome from the ticket office clerk, he was greeted with a bright and cheery hello from a very attractive (at least *he* thought very attractive) middle-aged woman.

'You're n–n–new,' stammered Hector, the master of the obvious.

'Yes,' said the woman, 'I'm filling in for Harry; he's my uncle. He's had an accident – fell off a ladder, the silly old fool.'

'That's a shame about the ladder, I mean, not him being your uncle,' said Hector. 'I hope he's okay.'

'Should be,' replied the woman. 'Going to be off a long time though. Still, shouldn't be climbing ladders at his age. Where would you like to go?'

Hector did not answer. He suddenly had a vision of this new intruder into his life climbing a ladder in her flowery cotton dress and was quite speechless.

'Come on,' she said, 'you must be wanting to go somewhere.'

'Er, day return to Grimethorpe, please,' Hector said, pushing the vision to the back of his mind and regaining the power of speech.

'Grimethorpe – that's not a very nice place. Why would anyone go there on a nice sunny Saturday like this?' she asked.

'Football,' said Hector proudly. 'They've got a team in the Laminex Macintoshes Northern Intermediate League. Division Three,' he added as an afterthought. 'I've never been there, you see.'

'Oh, football,' she said nonchalantly. 'I quite like football; I watch it on TV. Mind you, I wouldn't have thought that they play it in a place like Grimethorpe.'

'Play football everywhere,' said Hector in a knowledgeable manner.

'Anyway, it was nice chatting to you, but you will miss your train if you don't get a move on,' said the woman.

'Right,' said Hector. 'Okay, best be off then.'

'See you again,' she replied.

I hope so, thought Hector, secretly wondering if he could get a later train so he could carry on the conversation. He decided against this drastic step and ran down the tunnel to the platforms.

The rest of that day was just not quite right for Hector. He got to the ground all right. He got into the clubhouse with no trouble, but instead of having his usual three pints of local bitter before the game, he spent over an hour drinking just one. In this case Packet & Randshaw's excellent Aardvark Bitter. His mind just wasn't in it. He found that he had read the same page of the programme three times and still did not know what it was about and this worried him. It was that woman; he could not stop thinking of her. He watched the game, but he didn't have his heart in it. He completely missed two substitutions and when a passer-by asked him on his way back to the station what the score was, he had to stop and think for several seconds before he could remember. This was very worrying. This had never happened to Hector before and as he sat on the train on the way home he really started to get quite worked up about it.

Hector had only had one relationship with a woman before. Relationship was probably the right word, affair certainly wasn't. Affair would suggest some sort of sexual liaison. Not only had Hector never contemplated sex with Mary, the object of his affections, it was unlikely that anyone else ever had either. She was built like a battleship and probably in the same dockyard. She was about five feet tall and more than six feet round. She had huge hairy arms that hung from her side like two raw sides of beef. It was said that she had more hair on her arms than on her head, but never anywhere where she was likely to hear – people just were not that keen on hospital food. Most people were terrified of her, but she seemed to take an almost matriarchal attitude towards Hector. They had met in a bus shelter in the rain and Hector had been so startled that a woman had started speaking to him that he said nothing for several minutes. This had not deterred Mary: she liked talking. The fact that Hector had not run away or thrown himself under the nearest passing car indicated that he obviously liked her, and before he knew it he had agreed to go out with her the following Monday night.

This was a very worrying period for Hector. He had never been out with a woman on a date before and he did not have a clue where to go. They ended up in the local Chinese restaurant after having had a few pints in the Rat and Sideboard on the way. Hector was a bit disturbed that Mary had quaffed down five pints of mild while he had only got through two pints of Chuzzlewhit's Maestro. He had never seen a woman drink pints before; he thought all women drank small delicate glasses of Cinzano and lemonade like they did on the telly. This was a totally new experience for him and he wasn't sure he liked it.

He didn't say much, he didn't have to – Mary talked enough for the entire pub, most of whom seemed to watch her every move. Hector was not used to all this attention and it unnerved him. He didn't take in too much of what she told him; he doubted if the latest model computer could cope with the amount of information – if that was the right word to use – that she poured out at him. He did gather that she had also worked in stock control, but she had been unjustly sacked after a scandal to do with building computers. Of course, it hadn't been her fault (nothing appeared to be her fault, Hector noticed); she had just been made the scapegoat. Now she worked for the local council, although what she actually did seemed a bit of a mystery. People other than Hector would have thought that she probably doubled for the road builders' steamroller when it broke down or worked on a building site as the demolition ball, but Hector was far too nice to think things like that.

Before he knew it, she had wolfed down about six different courses of Chinese, including two huge bowls of prawn crackers, and he was waving her goodbye at the bus stop. Hector had never seen teeth move that fast – it was like watching something gruesome on the Natural History channel on Sky TV. Hector had Sky for the football but liked to flick around the channels when it was a boring game. It annoyed him that he had to pay for so many channels he didn't want, but that, he thought, was a bit like life: you had to put up with all the crap to get the good bits.

All the way home Hector felt strangely subdued. He had promised to take Mary, in a weaker moment, to see his favourite team, Harwood Borough, the following Saturday and he just knew he would get some serious stick from his mates in the clubhouse. She had been very enthusiastic about going, saying, at considerable length, that she had always liked football even though she had never been to see a game live. She professed to be a Manchester United fan (surprise, surprise) but when Hector had tried to get the conversation around to the game itself, the only subject he ever felt really comfortable talking about, he found that she knew nothing about the sport at all. Other than that David Beckham had nice legs, of course. *Typical woman*, thought Hector to himself. *What do any of them know about football?*

When the following Saturday arrived, all Hector's apprehensions and misgivings were realised. The conversation in the bar stopped dead when he walked in with Mary and did not restart until she was sat down in the corner with a pint of lager and a bag of pork scratchings. He turned red with embarrassment when she was rude to his old friend Tony Jupiter who sold the raffle tickets, and Hector tried to drag her – most unsuccessfully – to the turnstiles. People looking on thought it looked a bit like a small child pulling a huge obstinate donkey and they probably weren't very far wrong.

More embarrassment was to come for poor Hector when Mary refused point-blank to sit in the stand for the game, instead insisting on standing with Hector's mates where they all usually gathered.

She soon picked up that the players, referee, other spectators and, in Mary's case, most of the local residents could hear her when she yelled at the linesman for offside. She didn't know why she was yelling for offside – she did not have a clue what it was – but everyone else always did so she thought it was the thing to do. She found she liked yelling at the linesman and soon started screaming the first things that came into her head at him. Some of this was football related but most was just verbal abuse. The linesman was obviously embarrassed and stopped coming up the pitch as far as she was standing after about twenty minutes. This made most of the decisions he made pure guesswork but, Hector quietly noticed, it did not seem to alter the game one bit.

The second half started much quieter after the linesmen changed sides after half-time, but Mary simply turned her abuse to the referee. Not being completely stupid, for a referee anyway, he had not come down to the corner where they all stood since the first couple of minutes of the game. He was giving that part of the ground a wide berth, but this did not deter Mary – she just upped the decibels to a level approximating to Concorde taking off.

With twenty minutes to go, Hector had suffered enough. His mates were in fits of hysterics at Mary's antics and just kept poking him in the back and saying things like, 'On a promise tonight, are you? At least you won't be able to miss her if it's foggy!' Or 'Rather you than me, mate.'

He managed to manhandle Mary towards the exit and told her he had to leave as he was going out that night and had to get ready. He had a terrible job getting rid of her at the bus stop and although he managed to creep back into the ground for the last few minutes, he stood underneath the floodlight pylon where no one could see him and ran hell for leather out of the gates at the final whistle.

This sad encounter was re-enacted every other Saturday (and occasional Tuesday) at all Harwood Borough's home games for the next four months as Mary became more and more involved in the club. She loved it and would meet Hector earlier and earlier until they started arriving before the bar opened. All Hector's mates thought it unbelievable fun and would buy her pints of lager just to see how quickly she could drink them. She would always offer to arm-wrestle any of them for a pint but none of them was that stupid. She did once take on a fan from their local rivals Wandlestone at a cup-tie. He was built like a brick shithouse and had about the same IQ. They took him away screaming in an ambulance and for the first time in living memory the Harwood Borough fans got no abuse from the Wandlestone mob all afternoon. Mary must have got through about twenty pints in the bar after the game, as she was treated like a hero by all and sundry.

Hector could take no more and started to find excuses why he could not go to their games any more. Mary, for all her outward bravado, did not want to go on her own and so peace reigned back at Dukesmead, Harwood Borough's ground, once more. People still talk about Mary at some games to this day, although in very hushed tones just in case she should suddenly reappear.

Hector started to take Mary to the local library instead. She was much quieter there and it was the only place other than football grounds where Hector spent a lot of time, and he was hugely relieved when she ran off with one of the assistant librarians after he had banned Hector for trying to disembowel him with a paperback. Hector had snapped when he had caught the man attempting and failing miserably to get his arm round her for a cuddle, round the back of the adult section, and had set about him with the nearest available object. The fact that this was a copy of one of Hectors favourite science fiction novels, *The Revenge of Nathnagar*, made it all the sweeter for him. He did not know why he had attacked him – he had no real feelings for Mary other than total blind fear – but something inside him just seemed to snap. He became the first person ever to get a life ban from the entire county's network of libraries, a thing he was secretly quite proud of, although for months he brooded about it. He had got quite attached to Mary in a funny way. It was the same way that a boy likes a big daft puppy, but all in all he knew he was better off without her. Life could resume as normal. He got a lot of stick at the next couple of games he went to, but it did not take too long before things were back as they were before.

This though was different. Hector had never thought of Mary up a ladder. Down a mineshaft maybe, but not up a ladder.

The following Saturday he put on his best shirt and tie, a thing he had never done to go to a football game before in his life and got to the station ten minutes earlier than he needed to in the hope that she was still there. She was, and what was more she remembered him. His heart leapt when she asked him what game he was going to and for a full minute he couldn't remember. Having got his ticket, he summoned up the courage to ask her name.

'Maureen,' she said. 'Maureen Mansikevicus. What's yours?'

'Hector,' he mumbled. 'Hector Blenkinsop.'

'That's nice,' she said and smiled at him.

It was as if the sun had just come out inside Hector. He hadn't seen a smile like that since… Well, he hadn't *ever* seen a smile like that. All too soon it was time for the train and Hector ambled very slowly towards his platform.

This went on for the next four Saturdays. Twice he didn't need a train ticket as he was going to Harwood Borough, but he bought one anyway. Each time, Hector found out a little bit more about her and she a bit more about him. She lived quite close to Hector in her own little flat (Hector imagined it to be all pink frills and smelling of flowers; it was actually a peculiar shade of green and smelt of mothballs and damp washing) and was hoping to get a job in the station full-time. She never mentioned a boyfriend, but he was far too shy to ask. He noticed she had no rings on but he knew that this could mean nothing.

He started to go to the station on his way to work in the mornings even though it was almost a mile out of his way. He would walk slowly past the ticket office to the kiosk and buy a paper, hoping to get a glimpse of her. When he did, he would smile and wave and she would smile and wave back. This would make Hector's day. One day after seeing her, he even let someone bring some stock items into the warehouse at work, without a docket. Mind you, he was in a foul mood all day if he had missed her. This went on for several weeks until the fatal Saturday morning.

'Hello, Maureen, how are you?' he said brightly.

'Okay, I suppose,' she said rather miserably. 'Where to today?'

'Oh, er, Great Shelford, actually. What's the matter? You seem quite down today?'

'Harry's better,' she said. 'He comes back Monday. I know it's rotten to feel like that, I'm glad he's better, but it means I'm out of work again.'

Hector was absolutely dumbstruck. He didn't know what to say so he said nothing, just stood there with his mouth open.

They both stared at each other, neither of them saying anything, until they both blurted out at once, 'I don't suppose…'

'Go on,' said Hector. 'After you.'

'I was going to say, I don't suppose you fancy going out for a drink some time?'

Hector was completely taken aback. It was exactly what he was plucking up the courage to ask her. 'I'd love to,' he gasped with a suddenly very dry throat. 'When?'

'Any time,' she replied. 'I've got plenty of time on my hands now.'

'How about tomorrow lunchtime?' he asked hopefully.

'Fine – how about if I meet you in the Rat and Sideboard about twelve thirty?'

Hector was gripped by awful memories of Mary and said, 'Make it the Palm Tree and you're on!'

'Great, that's a date then,' she said and smiled.

Christ, a date, thought Hector and he wandered off towards his train with his heart all aflutter and his head full of determination to make this the best date ever.

Hector hardly slept a wink that night. He kept having visions of pouring his drink all over Maureen or something equally ghastly. When he did eventually drift off he dreamt that Maureen had slowly started to turn into Mary in the pub and she was pouring pints of lager over her own head and laughing. Everyone was looking at him. He woke up in a cold sweat.

Dawn eventually came and Hector was up with it. He got dressed and went for a walk to the paper shop. He got back home. He went back to the paper shop – he had forgotten to get a paper; he was thinking about

Maureen. He made some breakfast. He forgot to eat it. He cleared it away and then made it again. This time he made himself eat it and he read the paper – the sports pages anyway; he never read the rest. He put on the TV. Endless reruns of yesterday's Premier league football or tractor-pulling from Holland. He wasn't interested in either so he switched it back off. He sat down in his chair with the paper and promptly fell fast asleep.

When he woke up it was gone twelve o'clock. He panicked. He leapt up, put his foot in his abandoned cereal bowl, skidded across the carpet and smashed into the door frame. His glasses fell off and he trod on them getting up, breaking them in half. He rushed to the kitchen and cut his hand quite badly on the scissors trying to cut some plaster strip to hold his glasses together. He fixed the glasses, at least temporarily, stuck some more plaster on his cut hand and got ready for the big event.

He put on his best shirt, a blue and yellow striped one, and his favourite tie, from Harwood Borough. Unfortunately, this was red and white stripes and he looked a bit like an explosion in a sweet factory, but if there was one thing Hector did not have it was any sort of dress sense. He put three pens – good ones, not cheap biros – into his shirt pocket. You never knew when you might need a pen, that was his maxim. He remembered his trousers (another nightmare he had had during the night); he chose the grey flannels he occasionally wore to cricket in the summer and then grabbed his best jacket. It wasn't really a 'best' jacket, it was a bit of a scruffy old blazer, but it was all he had apart from anoraks and he wasn't meeting Maureen in one of those. He finished the ensemble off with his best sensible shoes, a tan pair of brogues, and shut the door and ran down the road. He did not want to be late and it was almost half past already.

He skidded round the corner and there, standing outside the pub, was Maureen. She looked lovely. She had a blue and green floral print dress on and a light blue cardigan over the top. She was quite the loveliest thing Hector had ever seen. And she was laughing. Hard.

Hector stopped. He started to sweat. He wiped his hand over his face and looked at Maureen, She was laughing even harder; she was almost doubled up. Tears were rolling down her face. Hector did not know what to do so he started laughing too. A nervous, quiet type of laugh, but definitely laughter all the same. She walked towards him, still laughing. Hector thought she looked even lovelier but wondered why she was laughing at him. She stopped right in front of him, pulled a hanky out of her bag and licked it.

'I don't know what you have been doing,' she said, 'and quite frankly I don't want to know, but if we are going in there together we had better get you cleaned up a bit.'

She pulled a compact mirror from her bag and held it up for Hector. What he saw amazed him. His glasses were straddled across his face at a weird angle, held together with a huge blob of pink tape. He had a purple bump the size of a grape in the middle of his forehead, although when he gingerly touched it, it felt about the size of a unicorn's horn. He had streaks of blood from cheek to cheek where he had wiped his face and he could see more blotches of blood on his collar.

'I, er, fell over,' he stammered, 'hit my head, broke my glasses.'

'Never mind,' said Maureen, 'let's get you inside and get a drink inside you and you can tell me all about it.' *My God*, she thought, *what have I let myself in for*? Little did she know it at the time, but she would be asking herself the same question for the next twenty-five years.

All things considered, the day went very well for Hector. Bearing in mind that he had turned up looking like one of the losers from *Ben-Hur*'s chariot race, he couldn't have complained if Maureen had left him there and then, but she wasn't like that. For some reason that she never really knew, she quite liked Hector. It could only be that she felt sorry for him, but so what? Hector certainly wasn't going to complain.

She cleaned him up, sat him at a table in the corner of the pub out of the way, bought him a pint of mild and bitter (this really impressed him; he had never been bought a pint by a woman before) and they started to chat. Hector was very relieved to see that Maureen did not drink pints. Instead she had a dry white wine, which Hector thought was the ultimate in sophistication.

As they started to talk they seemed to hit it off straight away. Not only did Maureen watch football on TV, she really knew what she was talking about. She had gone to Arsenal on dozens of occasions when she lived in north London years ago and, although she had not been since, she kept up with all the new players and everything. Hector could not believe that a woman could know so much about football and it changed his entire philosophy about the female sex, built up over many years, in about half an hour.

They talked and talked for hours. She was not interested in Hector's other great love, science fiction, but at least she did not try to denigrate it. She liked eating out (Hector later found out why when he came into contact with her kitchen) and other than that just stayed in and watched TV. Hector

told her all about his job and his past life, what there was of it. He told her of his one and only holiday abroad in France, which he didn't really enjoy, and she told him of some of her trips with old boyfriends that secretly made Hector very jealous.

The two most important things she told him were that she did not have a boyfriend at the moment and hadn't for a few years, and, probably more importantly, that she had a car. It was, she said, only an old Vauxhall Nova that she called Cyril, but Hector could not have been more impressed if she had said she was the pilot of her own Learjet. A car. Hector could hardly believe it. He had not had many dealings with cars. The type of person he met at football did not in general own cars. As he very rarely met anyone else, other than people at car boot sales that he frequented looking for second-hand science fiction books, he had had very few dealings with the more mobile sections of society. She also said that not only did she have no children of her own, but she had no intention of having any, preferring instead to have any she came into contact with ground up and cooked on the barbecue. Hector was very pleased at this; he was absolutely terrified of children and thought that they should be kept out of the way of the general public until they were at least twenty years old.

They left the pub and went for a pizza, which Hector insisted on paying for, and carried on talking in Pizza Hut until it got dark outside. Hector walked her to her flat and they stood outside still talking for nearly half an hour. After they had made arrangements to meet up again in the pub on Wednesday night, Maureen gave him a little kiss on the cheek and let herself indoors. Hector walked the half mile or so back to his own flat as if he were walking on clouds. He was so carried away with the way things had gone that he forgot to watch the Spanish football on Sky, and it was the Madrid derby too, watching instead a romantic drama on ITV. Now he knew for definite that he was in love.

Wednesday night went very well. Not only was Hector not bleeding profusely, but he made a conscious effort to dress more conservatively. He had caught sight of his reflection in the Pizza Hut window on the way home on Sunday night and had been quite startled by the sight. They had a few drinks and went for a Chinese meal. Hector had a panic attack in the restaurant when Maureen admitted to him that she knew nothing about Chinese food and asked Hector to order for her. He coped rather well though, considering he had only ever had a few Chinese meals himself and one of them was the debacle with Mary when he got very little to eat at all.

Maureen asked if she could go to football with Hector on Saturday to which he readily agreed, although he thought later that it might be prudent not to go to Harwood Borough as it might bring back unpleasant memories of Mary. He knew that Calverton Town were at home in the Russett and Pringlethorpe's Farm Equipment East Midland Senior League Division Four, a ground he had meant to visit for years, and Maureen thought it was a splendid idea. She even suggested that they take the car, as it had not had a run for ages. And so the stage was set for the big day.

The day started off well enough. Maureen was five minutes early picking Hector up but he was ready. He had in fact been ready since about half past six in the morning, such was his anticipation. They set off up the motorway for the hour or so's drive in good spirits and it wasn't until Maureen suggested that Hector might have a look at the map to see which junction to take that things started to go wrong.

Although Hector had seen many maps in his life, he had never before been asked to read one. He couldn't find the right page, let alone the right junction, and they went twenty miles out of their way before Maureen pulled into a motorway service station to ask directions. This was yet another new experience for Hector. motorway services. He had never been in one before and while Maureen went to ask the inevitable AA man waiting outside for directions, Hector ventured inside the main building. This was a mistake and it took Maureen nearly twenty minutes before she found him wandering around the car park on the wrong side of the motorway desperately looking for the car.

The next problem was Maureen's confusion of northbound and southbound, and when they eventually set off, it was in completely the wrong direction. After twenty minutes Maureen realised something was wrong as the promised turning had not materialised and, suspecting what the problem was, she took the opportunity to turn around at the next junction. Heading now in the right direction, they were, however, about an hour behind schedule. Half an hour before kick-off they pulled into Calverton High Street and directions to the ground were quickly got from the local petrol station. The ground was found with almost fifteen minutes to spare, but then came the real problem: it was deserted. They bounced almost literally into the small rough car park to find no other cars at all, just a very beaten-up old ice cream van that looked as though it had been there for about ten years without moving. It had actually been there for nearly fifteen years and was often used as emergency accommodation by the club secretary when he was thrown out by his wife for coming home drunk after matches.

They sat for a couple of minutes staring at the totally vacant ground before Hector leapt from the car in a vain hope of finding out what was, or rather wasn't, happening. The gates were locked and there was not a soul anywhere around. Hector ran up the short driveway that led to the ground from the main road and into a newsagent's shop just round the corner. He stood open-mouthed as the man behind the counter told him that they were actually playing a county cup match about ten miles away at Barton Hartshorn.

Hector then realised his mistake. He had been so carried away with the thought of spending the day with Maureen that he had forgotten the cardinal rule of all groundhoppers: always ring the ground first to make sure that the game is on. He ran back to the car convinced that Maureen would never talk to him again when she knew what he had, or rather had not, done.

Maureen, however, was made of sterner stuff. She had been promised a game of football and a game of football she would have. Showing a resourcefulness that Hector was totally in awe of, she grabbed the map, made a few quick calculations, stuck the gearbox forcefully into first gear and screamed off up the gravel drive to the main road. This sent a spray of small stones flying into the old ice cream van that shattered the last unbroken window. The club secretary would be lonely *and* cold tonight. Driving at speeds Hector had not imagined it was possible to do when not on a motorway, Maureen threw the little car round some nasty-looking bends towards Barton Hartshorn. As they approached the village at breakneck speed, they had their first bit of luck of the day. Half buried in a hedge at the side of the road, about half a mile before the village itself, Maureen saw a battered old board announcing the whereabouts of Barton Hartshorn United Football Club. She stamped on the brake pedal, sending Hector flying forward and a plume of grey smoke billowing up the road from the tyres. She slung the car round ninety degrees through the entrance gates and crunched to a halt about six inches from an old Ford minibus.

'Come on,' she said, clambering out of her door, 'it's only ten past.'

Hector did not move; he couldn't. The last twenty minutes had been quite the most astonishing of his life. Maureen had changed from a quiet and fragile little creature into a manic homicidal maniac before his very eyes. He had never travelled at speeds like that, especially down country lanes. Admittedly he had had his eyes closed for most of it so had not seen Maureen knock the local vicar into the Great Ouse, nor had he seen the panic in the eyes of the local bus driver as Maureen had appeared out of nowhere on the wrong side of a double bend, only to swerve clear at the last moment. He would also never know why six of the local dairy herd would never give any more milk – probably just as well. This was a side of Maureen he had not envisaged and he was not sure he liked what he had seen. *Mind you*, he thought, *she does appear to have got us to a game*. He clambered out of his door and followed Maureen to the turnstiles. He was relieved to find that the turnstile operator had quite a pile of programmes left and even more relieved to find out that there was no score.

The game was a good one. Hector and Maureen sat quietly on an old bench behind one of the goals for most of it and Hector was so relieved to see that she had left all her aggression in the car that he almost forgot about the ordeal of getting there. Barton Hartshorn won the game three–two with a wonderful late goal from centre forward Gavin Kellan to cause a cup upset. They were from the equivalent of three divisions below their near neighbours and intense rivals and both Hector and Maureen enjoyed a good hour in the bar afterwards celebrating with the home fans. Hector was very relieved that Maureen only drank Coke in the bar. *If she could drive like she did when she hadn't had a drink*, he thought, *what the hell would she be like with a couple of white wines inside her*? It just did not bear thinking about.

The journey home was much more sedate and they only got lost once. They stopped at a very pleasant little country pub and Hector had a nice pint of Charlie's Very Peculiar, one of his favourite beers, whilst Maureen got directions back to the motorway. On the way home, Maureen asked him if he would like to go back to her place to have a bit of supper and watch *Match of the Day*. Hector, despite his reservations about what he thought was an obvious split personality, readily agreed.

It was soon after this that Hector had his illusions about her flat destroyed. What he had thought of as all pink frills and lace curtains was in fact a very practically laid-out flat with all the walls a strange green colour. When Maureen saw him staring at the walls she explained that her brother-in-law had painted it for her when she had moved in, and as he hadn't charged her anything she did not like to complain about the colour. She had a signed picture of Ian Wright above the bed, which impressed Hector immensely, and a large toy monkey complete with Arsenal hat and scarf sitting in the chair by the window. The only other sporting artefact in the room was what Hector thought he recognised as a miniature baseball bat with 'Montreal Expos' painted on it, perched on top of the portable TV. Hector had never heard of Montreal Expos and guessed it must have been some sort of exhibition she had been to. He made a mental note to ask her about it later.

The flat itself was very small, only a studio type, and half of the room was taken up by a pine table and chairs. The kitchen was immaculately clean, which was, had Hector only known it, a bit of a miracle. Maureen had spent most of the previous day washing up and putting things away, something she was not too good at, so on this particular evening everything was clean and tidy and in its place with its top screwed on properly. They sat at the table and had scrambled eggs on toast and coffee for supper. They shared a bottle of white wine during *Match of the Day*, for which Hector displaced the monkey on to the floor, while he sat on his chair and Maureen watched curled up on the edge of the bed. Hector didn't really like white wine, but he wasn't going to complain; he was having a wonderful time – all memories about the drive from hell were temporarily dislodged from his mind.

They talked for about an hour after the programme finished and parted at the front door with a fleeting kiss having arranged to meet back in the pub on Wednesday.

Hector hurried home and, with joy in his heart, slumped in his chair and sat back to read the afternoon's football programme for the first time. The day's excitement began to take its toll and his last thoughts before he dozed off were that he would have to invite Maureen back here one day, so would have to get the flat cleared up. Whether it was this terrifying thought or the lump of slightly dubious cheese he had consumed while reading the programme, he would never know, but at one o'clock he suddenly woke up with such a start that he fell off his chair. All he could remember was seeing this big red bus hurtling towards him at breakneck speed with the driver just a grinning skull inside a black hood. It took him several minutes to regain his composure and he retired to bed still quite shaken. He could not sleep for hours, seeing hedges and fields flying past his eyes at incredible speed every time he closed them and it was almost dawn when he finally nodded off.

He was still up quite early though and managed to get a copy of a book called *Doing Up a Dump* at the car boot sale he went to occasionally. *This will come in very handy*, he thought as he got the bus back home to start clearing up his flat, a task that to him would be a bigger engineering nightmare than building the pyramids ever was to the ancient Egyptians.

That evening, the end of day one, he had thrown out – nothing!

This was mainly because he just had to read everything he picked up and he couldn't bear to throw anything out that he thought might one day become valuable, which to sad old Hector was just about anything related to sport. He did, however, tidy lots of piles of papers and magazines and could not believe that the carpet under a pile of *World Soccer* magazines next to the wardrobe in his bedroom was a completely different colour from the rest of the room. He even took all his clothes out of the drawers and refolded them. Mind you, you wouldn't have known it by looking at them – there were more creases in them after they had been refolded than there were before, and that took some doing.

He found some wonderful things he had completely forgotten about. He found a 1948 Arsenal versus Burnley programme which he thought he would give to Maureen as a present (he hadn't quite got the hang of romance yet, but at least it was a start). He found a lump of plastic pitch from Queens Park Rangers from the early 1980s, which at first gave him a bit of a start as he had thought it was a particularly virulent form of mould, and he found three of his dad's old football medals. His dad had always told him that they would be worth money one day, but when he had taken them to be valued they had almost laughed in his face. Hector had taken them home with the intention of putting them in a little frame as his father had thought so much of them, but as with most things in Hector's life, he had never quite got round to it. His dear old dad would be turning in his grave at the thought of Hector clearing up his flat for the sake of a girl. Leastwise, he would if Hector had buried him. His mortal remains were actually in a large pot on Hector's kitchen window sill buried under a large red rose. Hector sometimes talked to him while he was washing up, although God knows what he would do if he got a reply. His dad always warned him about girls, which was probably why he had not had much to do with them in his life so far.

It was the following Friday that disaster struck. Hector had had a very enjoyable evening in the pub on Wednesday with Maureen, who had announced that as Hector had been round to her flat the previous weekend it was about time she saw where he lived. Hector froze solid and did not speak for several minutes, relying on grunting noises and at one stage pretending that he was choking on his crisps. There was no stopping her though, whatever excuses he made when he had regained the power of speech. She was coming round on Saturday morning before Hector took her to Harwood Borough's game against Cookham. Hector had thought it would be nice to take Maureen to see Boro, figuring quite rightly that if his friends saw him with someone about as opposite to Mary as you could get, then they would stop the mickey-taking about those terrible days.

He took a day's holiday from work on Friday to clear the place up once and for all and it was this that led to his undoing. The day started well enough and by five o'clock in the afternoon he had surprised himself by the amount of old newspapers and magazines that lay in piles by the back door awaiting the attention of the dustmen. Most of his programme collections had been tidied too; he was not throwing any of them out for love or money – a man must have some principles. If Maureen had any long-term intentions for Hector then it had to include his programmes or the deal was off!

He had managed to pile all the old broken bits of coffee mugs that had once been his prize collection from all ninety-two league grounds but had suffered hard times of late, into one cardboard box that he dumped beside the dustbin. He was astounded by the amount of room these actions gave him in the flat and he thought to himself that he was starting to win the battle. It was at this point that he made the decision that was nearly to cost him his life.

I have written before of the strange life forms that lived, if this is the right word, both under Hector's bed and behind his wardrobe. Life forms that Hector was completely oblivious to. He was so pleased with the way things were going that he decided to move the wardrobe and clear out all the mess from behind it. It was a struggle to get the thing to move in the first place. The subcultures that had evolved over the years from the piles of debris that fell down the back of the wardrobe were quite cosy in their own little private universe and had no intention of moving. The more he pulled at the front of the wardrobe, the more it refused to move.

Hector sat back on the bed and thought about things. He was not about to give up and reasoned that he was just going about it the wrong way. He put both feet on the side of the wardrobe and pushed. It moved slightly. He tried again. It moved some more. After a few minutes he had made it wobble quite severely. Light was beginning to seep in behind the wardrobe as it wobbled and this was having a very funny effect on the organisms behind it.

They had never been in contact with anything other than complete gloom throughout their existence and they reacted very strangely. They started to expand quite rapidly. They made strange noises. They expanded some more. They made more strange noises.

By the time he realised what was happening it was too late. The wardrobe was moving all by itself now and, rather alarmingly, it was moving towards Hector, who was by now half lying on the bed. He put his body between the wardrobe and the bed and heaved. It was no good; he could not stop the wardrobe marching inexorably forward. It started to topple over and from inside it burst not only most of Hector's clothes but several hundredweight of football programmes, scarves, hats, pennants and posters he had crammed into it over the years. Not only was he trapped; he was being slowly forced down between the wardrobe and the floor under the bed.

If Hector had no idea what was causing the problem with the wardrobe, then he had even less of an idea what lurked under the bed. It was in fact a life form completely unknown to mankind that had evolved from a combination of old football magazines, lost unwashed socks and the remains of about five hundred Chinese takeaways that Hector had consumed while lying in bed after a few beers at Harwood Borough. It was smelly, it was greasy and it was angry. It had lain still for years squashed under the bed and was now in danger of being squashed even more by Hector's body. It started to fight back and pushed at him for all it was worth. It too started to expand and poor Hector was in grave danger of suffocation and he started to black out.

What exactly happened next will always remain a mystery, luckily, but it appears that it basically went like this. The life form behind the wardrobe reacted with the fumes given off by the life form under the bed and started to bubble and expand. It reacted with one of the posters that had fallen on it and took on the appearance of a larger than life 3D action figure of Denis Law. The life form under the bed reacted even more alarmingly to the daylight it was now being subjected to and, seeing as it was partly made of old football magazines, took on the form of a misshapen Charlie Buchan with monstrous 1950s-type football boots. It was these grotesque boots that pushed Hector, the bed and four plastic bins full of programmes out of the way in its desperate search for more room. Hector was lifted up and then thrown back on the bed, losing consciousness as he felt himself and the bed rushing towards the ceiling. His last thoughts were, why were two gigantic old footballers having a kick around in his bedroom and where on earth was the ball?

Just as he blacked out completely, the two expanding life forms came into contact with each other for the first time, head to head as it were, and exploded. The air that made up most of the contents of both figures escaped with a huge roar that for all the world sounded like 'Goaalll!'

The massive rush of air as the two gargantuan figures collapsed in a bizarre unworldly goal celebration forced the unconscious Hector and mattress out through the bedroom door, onwards through the door to his flat, luckily left open to take out the rubbish, and down the stairs towards the front door.

At this moment Maureen was standing outside with her finger on the doorbell, having come round to tell Hector that she could not make it in the morning after all, as Uncle Harry had fallen off his ladder again. Hector's lifeless body flew down the stairs on the mattress and crashed into the other side of the door with such force that it shook the door open as it bounced off it and Maureen stepped back in horror at the remarkable sight that confronted her.

She could see Hector, unconscious and wearing what looked like a protoplasmic football shirt of glowing and pulsating multicoloured stripes, with what at first glance looked like a dead beaver on his head. This turned out to be next-door's cat, which had been swept up by the mattress on its nightmare flight down the stairs and was lodged firmly on top of Hector's head with its claws sunk deep into his scalp. Her first reaction was to be sick at the sight of this apparition from a *Ghostbusters* film, but she could see that Hector was hurt and she was not sure that he was still breathing. After prising the terrified cat from his head, leaving some very nasty scratches that would have to wait, she took a deep breath, plucked up all her courage and started to give Hector the kiss of life.

Hector, whose last vision of life had been of a pair of ghastly spectres playing some sort of macabre football game, chose this very moment to start to come round and assumed he had died. All he could see was an angel framed in a bright light bending over and kissing him. As his wits began to come back to him he realised it was his Maureen standing in the doorway and he was happy. She was kissing him. It did not matter for a few moments if he *was* dead: she was kissing him.

When he started to realise where he was and that he was still alive, he started to scrape a curious mixture of what would pass as bubblegum and blood from his face and gulped in large quantities of air. He had no idea what had happened and he never would find out.

Upstairs the two ungodly organisms had dissolved into one another and all that remained was a stain on the carpet that resembled a small patch of chicken tikka. Apart from the wardrobe lying at a curious angle across the base of the bed with its contents strewn across the room as though it had been caught up in a hurricane, everything else was the same as it had always been.

'I was clearing up,' he gasped.

'It looks like it,' she said.

She helped him upstairs into his favourite chair and then managed to drag the mattress back into the bedroom. She straightened the wardrobe, made the bed the best she could and then went into the kitchen and made a cup of tea. She found some TCP in the kitchen cupboard and cleaned the scratch wounds on his head. Miraculously this was the only physical damage he had suffered, although he would never be able to look at a picture of Denis Law again without feeling the urge to vomit.

'If this is the mess you get into doing a simple bit of clearing up,' she said, 'I'd better give you a hand. I can't make tomorrow after all, I'm working at the station again, but I will be here first thing Sunday morning with my bleach gun at the ready and we will sort this place out good and proper.'

Hector finished his tea and dragged himself into his bed, with a little help from Maureen.

'I'll let myself out,' she said sweetly. 'See you Sunday morning.' She gave him a peck on the cheek and left, shutting the bedroom door behind her.

Hector lay back on his pillow. He smiled to himself and snuggled down under his duvet. Maureen had saved his life, or so he thought, and nothing but nothing was going to change his mind.

He closed his eyes and drifted off to sleep. Now he *knew* he was in love.

Hector Abroad

Well, the big moment was here. Hector was looking out of the front window of his flat, waiting for Maureen to chug round the corner in her little car to take them to the airport.

Hector was going abroad. Well, maybe not abroad properly, to Ireland actually, but it was still abroad to Hector. And he was flying there. *On a plane, for Christ's sake*! This thought gripped him as he stood there waiting with a sense of almost total panic as well as excitement. How he had let anyone talk him into flying, he would never know. To be honest he could not remember whose idea it was; only that it seemed like a good idea at the time.

It was about six weeks ago now. Hector and Maureen were sitting in Harwood Borough's social club having a drink on a Friday night, as they had been doing now for a few months, when someone announced that Boro had fixed up a couple of preseason friendlies in Ireland. Most of the small amount of people in the club said that they were interested in going over to see them, including Hector's three best friends, Billy Smallwood, Neville Prince and Kevin Loony. Hector thought later that he just got a bit carried away with it all (although it was probably the six pints of Cardinals Double Flatulent that he had drunk). When Maureen said that she had always wanted to go to Ireland, the deal was done. There was no getting out of it now.

Within two weeks it was all sorted. Maureen would drive herself, Hector and Billy down to Bognor Regis International Airport on the Friday afternoon where they would meet Neville and Kevin and fly off to Ireland. Even though he knew nothing about aeroplanes and airports, Hector knew it was a strange place to go from, but Neville had got some cheap flights through someone he knew who worked in a travel agency. Neville spent most of his life flying here and there watching sport so Hector trusted him. What he did not trust was the aeroplane and the pilot that would take them.

On arrival in Ireland, if they survived the flight, they would get a taxi to the hotel where they would meet up with the players and the other people on the trip, before the first game at nearby Buggleskelly Wednesday on the Saturday afternoon. Sunday would be spent sightseeing before a coach trip on Monday out into the Irish countryside for a game with Ballygobackwards Town in the evening. The return flights to Bognor Regis were booked for early afternoon Tuesday.

And so Hector waited. He had packed what he thought he would need for these momentous few days in his brand new bright red case that Maureen had made him buy specially for the trip. When Hector had shown her the old brown bag he was going to take, Maureen had said that she would not be seen dead at an airport with anyone carrying that old thing around. Hector briefly thought that he might be able to get out of the trip because of this, but she had whisked him straight down to the local Argos and he was now the proud owner of the most garish suitcase in Christendom. To make it worse Maureen had insisted on tying a bright multicoloured strap round it so it couldn't get lost. *Huh*, thought Hector, *I bet it does*.

And then it was time to go. Maureen's little green Nova came round the corner and they were off. They picked up Billy and the journey to Bognor was completely uneventful. The airport was well signposted (Hector had been afraid that he would have to navigate and that had not helped with his worrying), as was the long-term car park. They parked the car, loaded themselves and their luggage into a big pink bus shaped like an elephant and arrived at the terminal. Billy (who knew about these things) said how tiny it was; Hector thought it was huge. They checked in, or rather Maureen checked them in, and, having got rid of the luggage, made their way to the bar. This was the point Hector had looked forward to; he intended getting as many pints down his throat as possible before he had to get on the plane. Maureen had already warned him that he mustn't get on the plane drunk, but he had a plan. It failed dismally.

He tried for half an hour to get Maureen to go off looking round the shops he was told were scattered liberally about airport terminals, and she might well have gone if there were any. There was only a small cigarette kiosk, an even smaller duty-free shop and a strange shop that appeared to sell nothing but souvenirs of London and Belgian chocolates. They sat and had a couple of drinks while Billy went off plane-spotting.

With the flight due to leave in less than half an hour, in rushed Neville and Kevin. Kevin had turned up half an hour late and Neville was not happy. He was not surprised, just annoyed. They had also had trouble at check-in as Kevin's ticket was made out to Belgrade instead of Ireland. Amazing as Budget-Air did not fly to Belgrade, but typical of Kevin, Neville told Hector later. Still, they all had time for another quick drink before they made their way to the plane. Hector was shocked when he saw it sitting by the side of the terminal. It had propellers. Hector thought planes with propellers had gone out with flared trousers, although he still had some tucked away in the bottom of his wardrobe (flared trousers, not propellers) in case they came back into fashion. His first reaction was to run, but Maureen, smiling sweetly, had her nails dug into his arm and was not about to let go. She marched him up the little gangplank and into the aircraft. He could not believe it was so small. They looked bigger than this on TV. To make it worse, Maureen insisted he sat by the window so she could block his escape route out of the plane.

The passengers filed in. There were only about twenty seats and nearly half of them were empty when the stewardess pulled this massive metal bar across the door. *This is it*, he thought, *no escape now*. Suddenly a roaring noise filled the cabin. He was convinced that the plane was about to blow up but Maureen explained that it was only the engines starting. By twisting his neck round nearly one hundred and twenty degrees and bending as far back as he could, Hector could just about see out of what passed as a window. The propeller was indeed turning very fast. The plane lurched forward and Hector hoped that the other one was turning too.

The plane bumped its way for what felt like about three miles while the one stewardess did the curious safety dance at the front of the cabin with what looked like the seat belt out of Maureen's car and a child's rubber ring. She completed this ritual with all the enthusiasm of a man preparing to face a firing squad. Hector had seen various versions of this scenario many times in comedy programmes on TV but it fascinated him to watch one live even though he could not hear a word she was saying. Then they stopped. Hector thought there was something wrong, but before he could say anything, they suddenly shot forward and Maureen gripped his hand tightly. They hurtled along the runway picking up speed and Hector was pushed so far back in his seat he thought he would end up sitting on Neville's lap behind him.

And then it happened. All of a sudden the plane seemed to stand on its tail and shot upwards. Hector had never been so frightened in his life (except for when he was once cornered in the bar at Wandlestone by a couple of Neanderthal-looking home fans after a particularly scrappy local derby that Boro had won with a disputed penalty in injury time). His ears popped, then they popped again. His stomach was not so much left on the ground but left back in his flat. He thought he would not survive much longer; his heart was pumping so hard it must explode any minute; but just as he was about to scream, the plane levelled out, the roaring noise cut down by half, and his heart resumed only beating twice as fast as it should. He turned to look at Maureen and tried to smile. Maureen said later that he only needed a cowl and a scythe and he could play Death in any miracle play without any make-up. She patted his hand and he closed his eyes. Sleep was out of the question but somehow he thought it would go quicker if he had his eyes shut.

Suddenly he heard a voice through the darkness. It was a woman's voice and appeared to say that it was the captain speaking. Hector could not believe it; he knew about women drivers (he had been out with Maureen a few times) but a woman pilot! There was no doubt about it – his worst nightmare was coming true. The voice said that they would be flying at about thirty thousand feet (Hector thought this was a lot but hoped it was high enough to miss any mountains they went over) and that the flight would take about an hour. He looked at his watch: fifty-eight minutes of blind terror to go. She thanked them all for choosing Budget-Air (*I bloody well didn't*, thought Hector) and hoped they enjoyed the flight (*Yeah, right*, he thought).

About a minute later the stewardess appeared in the aisle with a plastic tray that apparently contained his lunch. Now Hector had eaten extensively on British Rail but he had never quite experienced anything like this. There was a cellophane bag with plastic knives and forks in it that was almost impossible to open, two very small sandwiches with the crusts cut off on a paper plate and a small round pot containing what Maureen told him was strawberry cheesecake. But it was like no strawberry cheesecake Hector had encountered while on terra firma. The base was solid and his plastic spoon snapped while he was trying to break it up. The topping was made of some sort of indigestible rubber compound of a sickly red colour that looked about as appetising as four-day-old porridge. He gave it up as a bad job and settled for a scalding hot cup of coffee that slopped about in his cup as the plane ducked and dived.

Hector was just getting used to it – I wouldn't say enjoying it – when the plane hit a pocket of turbulence and dropped quite suddenly. That was it for Hector; his stomach, which had finally caught up with him, dropped away further than the plane and, no matter how much Maureen told him everything was okay, he spent the rest of the flight bent double with his head in his hands waiting to crash.

About four weeks later, or at least it felt that way to Hector, Maureen grabbed his arm and said, 'Okay, all over, let's go.'

He could not believe it; they had landed perfectly safely and Hector hadn't felt a thing.

They all made their way to the terminal and waited by the luggage carousel. To Hector's amazement the first case to come out was his, followed by Maureen's. Billy's then arrived, followed by Neville's but there was no sign of Kevin's. They waited for about fifteen minutes before Kevin went to the lost luggage desk to report it. They were pretty sure it had never been loaded on to the plane in the first place but took the phone number of the hotel they were all staying in and told Kevin they would have it delivered there as soon as they could get it over from England.

They found a large taxi and all piled in and arrived at the hotel soon after. It was not quite what Hector had imagined. For some reason he thought that a football team travelling abroad would be staying in the local Hilton at the very least. Five star this hotel was not. It was called Paddy's and was on one of the main roads in Dublin. Underneath it was a pub, so it wasn't all bad, with about five storeys of hotel above it. The rooms were surprisingly clean and spacious and Hector and Maureen's even overlooked the river instead of the main road. They unpacked, which went well until Maureen tried to close the curtains and the entire curtain rail came down in her hands. A call to reception promised a handyman as soon as possible to put it back up. The TV worked well and Hector was absolutely fascinated by the different channels, as he had never seen 'foreign' TV before. He thought it a bit strange that he could still get BBC and assumed that every country in the world got it. He would have sat there watching RTE all evening if the others had not come banging on the door on their way to the pub downstairs to wait for the main party.

Hector thought the pub was great; Maureen was not so sure. It was just like pubs at home used to be years ago with a wooden floor, plain wooden tables and chairs, and no jukebox blaring out. Hector noticed that of the fourteen pumps behind the bar twelve were for Guinness with one each for lager and bitter. *When in Rome*, thought Hector, and ordered his very first pint of proper Irish Guinness. It was not to be his last. The team, officials and about six other fans arrived around an hour later and after they had all checked in, the bar filled up with everybody intent on having a good time. About an hour after this a fiddle band started playing; Hector was having a great time.

At some stage during the evening a small swarthy man thrust an old bobble hat under his nose and one of Hector's friends told him to put some money in it. Hector thought it must be for the band, who were terrific in his opinion, and willingly put in a handful of change. The man pinned a small Irish tricolour on Hector's shirt and left. Hector wasn't sure what time the bar shut, but he knew he had had a good time. Maureen guided him up the staircase and into their room before he fell fast asleep in the middle of getting undressed. Maureen managed to get him into bed and he slept the sleep of the contented, although she had to get up about five times in the night to turn him over so he did not snore like a pig.

Hector woke early, feeling dreadful, spent half an hour in the toilet, drank about four pints of water, clambered back into bed and went back to sleep. He awoke again mid-morning to find Maureen sitting reading by the window and noticed that the curtain rail was still on the floor by the side of the window. He had missed breakfast, she told him, but so had most of the rest of the party, which pleased him. They were meeting downstairs to go to the ground in about an hour and it took Hector all of that to get washed and ready. Maureen was not going to the match with them, preferring instead to do a bit of sightseeing on her own.

Downstairs a lot of people looked pretty rough and Hector wondered how he compared to most of them; he certainly did not feel too good. He noticed that one or two of the players didn't look too sharp either and wondered how that would affect the game. Two battered old minibuses pulled up outside and they all managed to clamber inside and off they went to the ground at nearby Buggleskelly. Nobody seemed to know what to expect at the ground but they were all pleasantly surprised. Harwood Borough's press officer, Terry O'Booth, who had originally come from that area, had arranged the trip over and was waiting outside to greet them all. They walked in with the players and found a nice little ground with a big old wooden stand along one side and a few steps of covered terracing behind both goals. There was just a large grass bank opposite the stand with a tea hut in the corner. An official from the home team showed the players to the dressing rooms, while Terry O'Booth guided the rest of them under the wooden stand and into the surprisingly large bar area. Hector, like most of the others, did not really feel like drinking, but by halfway through his first glass of Guinness he was feeling a lot better. So much better, in fact, that he forced down another three pints before it was time to go outside and watch the match.

There was what Hector thought was quite a good crowd for the match, probably around three hundred. The game started badly for Boro, which no doubt had something to do with the night before, and they were one down after about ten minutes. Just before half-time, however, Ned McFraser nodded in a good cross from Lenny Easterby and two goals from Matt

Zanardi in the second half won the game three–one for the visitors.

Back in the bar afterwards the Guinness really started to flow, especially when the players came in from the changing rooms. Hector remembered that Maureen had asked him not to drink too much after the game as she wanted them to go out for a nice meal when he got back, so he didn't go too mad. Still, he must have put away five pints before everyone piled in the buses and started back for the hotel. Not surprisingly everyone headed straight for the bar as soon as they returned, Hector included, and Maureen had to drag him out half an hour later. Hector was glad that she did as they found a nice little Italian restaurant about half a mile away and had a very good meal. Maureen even let him put away quite a decent bottle of red wine to compensate for tearing him away from his friends. They stopped at a nice-looking little pub on the way back for an hour but did not go into the bar when they arrived back at the hotel. Hector received one of Maureen's stern looks when he suggested it.

Next morning he was very pleased they hadn't finished up in the bar, as he and Maureen were almost the only ones who made it down for breakfast. They both put away mounds of fried food and toast and then sat down in the reception area to await the arrival of the rest of the party. Billy, Neville and Kevin eventually arrived, none of them looking too good, with Kevin complaining that his luggage had not turned up until eight that morning. Someone had found it going round and round on a carousel all by itself in Stavanger. Had this been anyone else's luggage this would have been surprising, as there are no flights from Bognor to Stavanger, but, as it was Kevin's, everyone seemed to accept it as par for the course.

They all had a lovely day sightseeing, with a big pub lunch thrown in. Hector took hundreds of photos of the cathedral, the castle, the docks, the buses, the trains, the shops, the houses and just about anything that either moved or didn't. They travelled more or less from one end of the metro system to the other and crossed the river that ran through the middle of Dublin about four times on the trolleybuses. Hector really liked the trolleybuses; he had heard about them from his dad when he was a kid but had never seen one, let alone been on one. Needless to say, he took about twenty photos of them.

They got back around six in the evening and an exhausted Maureen went for a lie-down upstairs. The rest, of course, headed back to the bar where, apart from a quick trip next door to a kebab shop, they spent the rest of the evening until closing time. Maureen had joined them in time for the kebab and even forced down a few halves of Guinness herself afterwards.

The kebab must have helped as Hector felt fine next morning and made breakfast with twenty minutes to spare. Maureen, strangely enough, ate nothing, just drank about four cups of coffee, nibbled on a slice of toast and then said she had had enough. Hector suspected she had a bit of a hangover, but he knew she would never admit it so he did not press the point. They went back to their room to get their things after the meal and Hector noticed that the curtain rail was still lying in the same place. *So much for as soon as possible*, he thought.

The two of them went shopping after breakfast and Maureen bought a lovely crystal shamrock for her mum and some fridge magnets for herself. Hector bought a set of coasters with local pubs on them and managed to slip away from Maureen long enough to buy her a silver Celtic cross, which he gave to her when they nipped into a coffee shop for a mid-morning cup of coffee. She was thrilled and put it on immediately. They had to be back at the hotel to catch the bus down to Ballygobackwards at about two o'clock and made it back with plenty of time to spare. Several of the group looked worse than they had done yesterday and two or three of the players looked as though they would not be fit enough to play football by Christmas, let alone that night. Quite a few had to be almost dragged out of the bar and on to the coach, but they set off about half an hour late in good spirits (some of them literally). The coach trip itself took just over an hour and a half and they were all quite glad that a proper coach had been arranged for them and not the old minibuses that they had used on Saturday. An hour and a half of travelling in them and no one would have been fit enough to play football for a fortnight. The roads were not like in England and although it took closer to two hours than one, they probably only went about forty miles. At one stage they were in a lane so narrow that trees were brushing along both sides of the coach at once. They also had to stop twice so that those who had already been in the pub could go to the loo.

The town of Ballygobackwards was postcard pretty. It was the type of village that Hector had seen in pictures advertising holidays in Ireland and Maureen fell in love with it straight away. It was only really one road with little cottages all along it and a post office with huge hanging baskets full of flowers hanging outside. There was one pub with the football ground next to it and a small convenience store and that was it. The football ground was tiny. There were no seats and very little cover, just a few rusting sheets of corrugated iron held up by equally rusting framework on top of a large grass bank opposite the players' benches. This grass bank went round the whole of the four sides of the ground and was particularly steep behind both goals. There was nothing else in the ground except a rusting old floodlight pylon in each corner and the players had to change in the pub across the road, which doubled as the football club's social club. The people in the pub, however, were very welcoming and had put on a big spread for the fans and officials before the game with the players apparently getting another massive spread afterwards. The food was excellent, as was the beer, and everyone was in an exceptionally good mood until someone came back in from outside and announced it was raining.

'Never mind,' said one of the locals, 'it will only be a shower.'

By ten minutes to kick-off the shower had turned into a storm and most of the fans stayed huddled in the pub. There were nearly as many Boro fans as home fans and a couple of the locals explained to Hector and Maureen that they were only a little local village club and were only used to playing other similar sides. They were tickled pink to be playing such a big famous club and that was why there was such a big turnout. Hector wondered whom exactly they thought they were playing but didn't like to say anything. As to there being a large turnout, if there were thirty people in the pub then Hector would have been surprised. Maureen quietly asked him how many he thought they got for a regular match and Hector guessed at about ten. He was almost spot on. Still, at least they had bothered to do a programme, and what a good one it was: loads of information about the club, the league they were in and even four pages about Boro.

The rain eased just as the players were leaving the pub and players, supporters and officials alike made the dash across the road and into the ground. Maureen, quite wisely, said she was staying in the pub until the weather got better but Hector headed, along with everyone else who was not playing, to the small covered area on the far side.

The local side was no match for Boro, even allowing for hangovers, and the visitors went in at half-time four–nil up. Everyone else galloped back to the pub for refreshments and to dry off. The rain stopped completely during the break and everyone, Maureen included this time, went outside for the second half. One of the local officials came round with a box asking for donations (they didn't charge admission) and, especially as Boro were by now six–nil up, everyone gave generously.

Midway through the second half, Hector had to go to the toilet after yet another couple of pints of the local brew at half-time, and Kevin accompanied him. This was to lead to total disaster.

The rain had made the grass banks very slippery and as the toilets were below pitch level behind one goal, great care was needed to get down the bank to reach them. Kevin led the way and had got halfway down when he went base over apex and slid down the rest of the bank, landing in a heap in a big puddle at the bottom. Hector laughed so hard he almost slid down after him, but he grabbed an old piece of fence stuck in the ground that just about held. Hector continued to laugh himself silly, as did Kevin, by now floundering in the water like a drowning hippo.

Suddenly the fence gave way and Hector bowled down the bank straight at Kevin. They collided with a loud squelch at the bottom, and on clambering to their knees both burst out laughing again. They carried on laughing as they got to their feet, or rather didn't in Hector's case. As he put his weight on his right leg it collapsed underneath him. He stopped laughing as he felt a searing pain go up his leg from his ankle and knew that all was not well. He managed to crawl up the bank until he was sitting on the top of it, while Kevin, still nearly wetting himself, ran and got Maureen. Hector managed to ignore the pain long enough to ensure that his programmes were still in his pocket and dry, before slumping back on the damp grass and cursing to himself.

Maureen, assuming Hector was drunk, did not exactly hurry. By the time she did arrive, the initial scorching pain had gone from his leg; but when he tried to stand, the same thing happened, this time causing Hector to swear at the top of his voice. Maureen knew by now that it was pretty serious and helped him over to the pub where she sat him down with a large Jameson's and asked if anyone had any first-aid experience. Fortunately the landlady used to be a nurse and, after examining his ankle, she said that he might have broken it and ought to get an X-ray. She strapped it up as tight as she could and told Maureen what to do later when it needed re-bandaging. The nearest hospital was back in the city, so they decided to see how it went and try to wait until the morning, or possibly even try to get home and get to their local hospital where Maureen's mum had once been the senior nursing officer.

Hector, having been given another large Jameson's, was quite happy being the centre of attention for once and merrily sat in the corner showing the rest of the party his heavily strapped leg. They had come back in as soon as the game had finished; Boro had gone easy for the last twenty minutes and the final result was six–nil. The players came in about ten minutes later and the whole event turned into a party.

When they finally left, nearly two hours later, Hector had absolutely no idea who, let alone where, he was. People had been topping up his glass for the last two hours and the landlord had given him a bottle of Jameson's to take with him as compensation for his injury. They managed to carry him onto the coach and sat him in the front seat. By the time they pulled away, he was fast asleep. It only took about an hour to get back to the hotel with a lot less traffic about and Hector was carried upstairs, still more or less unconscious, and laid on the bed by his mates at about one o'clock in the morning. Maureen just pulled the duvet over him and let him sleep.

When Hector awoke he was still considerably under the influence of the previous night's alcoholic intake and stank like an old brewer's dray. Maureen managed to get him into some clean clothes and re-bandaged his ankle as tight as she could, having taken the strapping off for the night. It did not feel too bad to Hector, but as soon as he put any weight on his foot it hurt like hell. Between them they decided that it would be best to try to get back to England if they could before going to hospital just in case they kept Hector in. Maureen said it was unlikely as the health service in Ireland was probably no better than in England and would only keep him in if he had contracted rabies or something similar. Hector was not so sure and did not want to be left in Ireland on his own.

With the help of Billy, Neville and Kevin (who, despite trying to look serious, still occasionally burst out laughing despite getting some very serious looks from Maureen), they got Hector into a taxi and to the airport. He announced that he would like to wait in the bar – surprise, surprise – and was duly sat in the corner with another large Jameson's (for medicinal purposes, you understand), while the rest booked in. On their return Maureen figured that as long as he was sober enough to get on the plane, then the more alcohol he had in him the better, so he had got another couple of large ones before they left.

Hector knew very little of the flight back to England, which was probably just as well as the storms of the previous night were still hanging around and the small plane ducked and dived alarmingly. Even the redoubtable Maureen felt a little queasy at times, and the only one to enjoy it, unbelievably, was Hector. Every time the plane hit a pocket of turbulence and fell a few hundred feet he would yell, 'Wheeeee!' like a kid on a fairground ride. This, he had decided, was the only way to fly, and in the unlikely event that anyone managed to get him on to one of these things again, he would make sure he was at least nine sheets to the wind beforehand.

They landed safely and Maureen brought the car round to the terminal to pick Hector up. The drive back went well, although he fell asleep as soon as they pulled away and woke up halfway home feeling awful. Maureen dropped Billy off home and went straight round to the hospital where her mum had once worked. Maureen had rung an old friend of her mum who still worked at the hospital from the airport and Hector received special treatment. He was met by a porter with a wheelchair and rushed straight in to see a casualty doctor. From there he was taken straight to X-ray, past a line of people looking as if they had been waiting all day and then back into Maureen's mum's old office. Half an hour later he was having his leg plastered and was told to keep his weight off it for four weeks. Within an hour and a half of arriving at the hospital, Hector was back in Maureen's car and on his way home, equipped with a gleaming new pair of crutches.

The next four weeks went very slowly for Hector. Maureen, bless her, came in to see him every morning before setting off for the station and spent every evening round at the flat with him, cooking and cleaning up. Typically Harry was expected to be off for the whole of the four weeks and Maureen could not turn the work down. Hector spent the time watching indescribably boring daytime programmes on Sky, or endless football videos. He learnt, amongst other things, how to install a patio at a bungalow in Florida, how to cook kangaroo meat twelve different ways and how to track, kill, skin and cook a lesser-spotted greebo in the Amazon jungle. All things that were obviously going to be so very useful to him, especially as he had vowed never to set foot in an aeroplane again. He could also recite every Premiership goal scorer, in order, for the last four seasons; name almost every player in an FA Cup final since 1963; and recite all England's international opponents since the war.

Hector was bored. Bored, bored, bored, bored, bored. To try to relieve the boredom he re-categorised his programme collection twice, although he had to wait for Maureen to come round and move his boxes of programmes one at a time for him, as he could not manage on one leg. He reread all his old football magazines; he had just known they would come in handy one day.

On the fourth Friday, Kevin came round and asked him if he was fit enough to go with him, Neville and Billy to see Boro's first league game of the season at Port Chester the next day. Hector leapt at the chance. He was so bored by now that, given half the chance, he would have walked to the game. When she got in that evening, Maureen was not too sure how wise it was to let him go. But understanding how bored he was and having spoken to Kevin on the phone to make sure he would look after him, she relented and agreed he could go, as long as he was careful.

The three lads arrived for Hector half an hour late the next morning. Kevin had apparently been held up on the golf course, to no one's surprise. Hector was loaded in the car and off they went. The trip only took about an hour and they were sat in a pub in the middle of the town an hour and a half before the game started (Port Chester did not let away fans into their club bar). Hector was surprisingly sensible, figuring that getting half-cut in a pub and falling down in the toilet would probably not impress Maureen, and only had a couple of pints of Prince and Jenkins Triple Crown. After a few rounds, they dropped Hector right outside the main entrance to the ground, but as the car park was full Kevin had to drive off down the road to park the car. It took him ages to get back to the ground and he nearly missed the kick-off, saying that he had to park over half a mile away.

The game went quite well for Boro after the shock of conceding an early goal and they bounced back to get a two–all draw. Debutant Kumah Nielsen scored just before half-time and they snatched an equaliser five minutes from the end through Easterby. Having dominated the second half almost entirely, they probably should have taken all three points, but a draw away in the first game of the season went down pretty well all round. Hector, who had spent the entire game sitting in the main stand for a change, hopped down to the main entrance where Billy and Neville were waiting for him. Kevin had apparently gone to get the car and would not be long.

Fifteen minutes passed with no sign of Kevin. Another ten minutes went by. They were all getting worried in case something had happened to him, when, five minutes later, the car swung round the corner and the three of them pulled the doors open to be greeted by the unmistakable smell of fish and chips. Kevin explained that he was hungry, just for a change, and as he had parked outside a fish and chip shop, he had decided to get himself some before returning for his friends. He totally failed to understand his fellow travellers' anger and the trip home was done in almost total silence. Maureen was waiting when they arrived back and when Hector told her what had happened, after she had half carried and half dragged him up the stairs, she just laughed. She had not known Kevin for that long but was not surprised in the slightest. You had to still love him though, she said; he just needed a good woman to sort him out.

The weeks went by and the ankle slowly mended. Hector was put into a walking plaster when he next visited the hospital, which eased his mobility problems immensely. While in the clubhouse at Boro one Friday night, talking to Billy and Neville, Hector decided that the time was rapidly approaching for revenge. Revenge for breaking his ankle and then for leaving everyone stranded at Port Chester. Kevin would definitely have to pay. Everyone, including Maureen, agreed. The question was, how?

The decision was made to try to teach Kevin a lesson at the upcoming Riddler and Gresham's Cough Linctus ('It's sticky; it's sweet; it goes down a treat') FA Trophy game away at Ackleton Hardy in Shropshire. Hector was all in favour of leaving Kevin up there with no money to see if he could get home, like the plot of a film he had seen, but the rest of them decided just to try to teach him a lesson. They were all due to go on the club coach, minus Maureen, who had to work again, for the long trek north and they met in the club car park at nine o'clock on the day of the game. Kevin, of course, was ten minutes late and Sid Melbourne, the first team manager, was just telling the coach driver to pull away when round the corner running at full pelt came Kevin, bacon sandwich in hand, waving at the driver to wait. He had stopped at the café round the corner for breakfast, even though he was late, and he was manhandled on to the coach as it sped away on its long journey.

The journey itself was pretty uneventful, except for Kevin being late back from a loo stop as he just had to have another burger, and the time passed fairly quickly. At one o'clock exactly they pulled into the club car park in Ackleton and with the players making their way to the dressing rooms, the rest of the party piled into the club bar. Neville stayed behind for a few minutes to talk to the coach driver and tell him their diabolical scheme. The driver, Paul, was all in favour of doing something about Kevin as he had caused two delays already and eagerly agreed to the plan.

The game went well for Boro, with Easterby grabbing a late winner after goalkeeper Damien Line had saved a penalty ten minutes from the end. Although Ackleton had taken an early lead, this had been cancelled out by a spectacular own goal by their centre half, who had inexplicably lobbed the ball over the head of his own goalkeeper from fully thirty-five yards. It was, therefore, in high spirits that everyone crowded back into the cosy little bar after the game, and the beer flowed generously for over an hour before they got back on the coach for the long drive home.

The plan was simple. At the first stop on the way home, Neville would get Kevin to go and buy something from the shop for him and the coach would pull round the back of the services and hide, making it look to Kevin like it had gone without him. It worked like a dream and Kevin wandered around the services for a quarter of an hour in a near state of panic before Neville appeared from behind a line of HGVs and pulled him, very relieved, on to the coach. Everyone thought it very funny, except Kevin, of course, who vowed there and then that he would never be late again. Nobody believed him, but at least they had got some sort of revenge.

The coach pulled back on to the motorway and the laughter lasted for nearly half an hour before Billy noticed something was wrong. They had got Kevin back on the coach, but Hector had disappeared. Someone remembered that he had got off to go to the toilet again quickly when Neville had gone off to find their victim, but no one could remember him coming back, what with all the hilarity about Kevin.

Hector was, at that moment standing by the petrol pumps back at the services trying desperately to get a lift from a lorry going his way. He had figured out what had happened pretty quickly and, not knowing if the coach would return or not, had decided that his fate lay in his own hands. He was very grateful that he had put his jacket on to get off the coach, but as he only had a couple of quid left, he knew that hitch-hiking was his only option. He had tried to phone Maureen and let her know what had happened but she had told him that she was going to Uncle Harry's for tea after work. Hector had no idea of how to spell Harry's surname, only that it was something strange and foreign sounding, let alone his phone number.

In the way that these things usually seem to happen, Hector had finally got a lift and was climbing into the cab of a giant petrol tanker just as the returning coach screeched into the other end of the services. As Neville, Billy and Kevin ran inside the main building looking for him, Hector's tanker pulled out on to the motorway, with Hector completely oblivious to the chaotic searching that was going on behind him.

He thought that he had got quite a good result with the tanker driver, as he would be passing about five miles from where Hector lived and he thought he could always walk from there if he could not get a bus. Anyway, Maureen would be home by then and she would come and get him, he felt sure. However, sometimes things do not work out quite as planned. This was to be one of those times. The driver, a big burly man with long greasy hair and tattoos up both arms, had seemed to take a shine to Hector as soon as he had asked him for a lift. Under normal circumstances Hector would have been quite wary of accepting a lift from such a character. But as he did not have a lot of choice – he had stood in the petrol garage for over half an hour unsuccessfully trying for a ride home – he had accepted the man's offer gratefully.

All went well for an hour or so. The cassette recorder blasted out heavy metal music and the driver would occasionally burst out laughing and mumble something unintelligible into his CB radio. It was only when the tanker pulled off the motorway and on to a minor road that Hector first became suspicious. He knew that to get where the driver had said he was going it was best to stay on the motorway and Hector grinned a nervous grin and asked him why he had pulled off.

'Need the toilet,' said his host. 'Transport café up ahead; we'll stop there for five minutes.'

As they pulled into the café's car park, Hector could see over a dozen motorbikes lined up outside with the sort of people he did not want to meet any time, let alone at night in the middle of nowhere, lolling about all over them. When the lorry driver let out a long low blast on his hooter and all the bikers waved back at him, Hector started to panic. As the lorry pulled up opposite the bikes, Hector flung the door open and slid down to the ground. He hit the ground running and made straight for the café. He ran inside, not stopping to speak to anyone, pulled open the door he supposed correctly to be the one to the kitchen and sped on through and out the back door. Outside, the leader of the bikers ambled up to the driver of the tanker, who was by now standing beside his cab.

'Hi, Hank, long time no see,' he said.

'Yeah, just had to pull in for a pee, had three cups of coffee back at Thrumpton,' replied the driver.

'Who was that who dashed out of your cab?' the biker asked.

'Some little bloke got stranded at the services; I was giving him a lift home. Must have something really wrong with his guts the way he shot in there,' said Hank, pointing at the café. 'Funny, really; he never mentioned anything.'

Hector would have loved to hear this conversation. Instead, convinced that he had been about to be kidnapped at the very least, he fled outside, clambered over the back fence and ran into some open farmland, where he crouched low in a field of something. He had no idea what it was, but it was over two feet high and hid him from view. It would do. For fifteen minutes he crouched, barely daring to breathe. Eventually he heard the sound of the tanker engine start up. Hank had got fed up waiting for him and a minute or so later he heard it pull back on to the road and drive away. Five minutes later he heard all the bikes start up and stream away towards the motorway, and with a huge sigh of relief Hector sad down on the ground.

For half an hour he waited to make sure he was alone. When eventually he found enough courage to go back to the café, he was horrified to find it completely in darkness and all locked up. He rattled the door and knocked as hard as he could but all to no avail. There was no one there. There was no one anywhere.

He looked around. Apart from the glow from a couple of roadside lights there were no other lights for miles around. Hector was distraught. The only open building he could find was what appeared to be an old outside toilet and it stank. Mind you the weather had turned cold by now and it had just started to rain. He had no choice. He clambered into what was left of the old tiny building and, heaving the broken old wooden door into roughly the space that had been designed for it, he crouched in the only corner he could find out of the wind and settled down for a cold and miserable night.

He did not sleep. He dozed off a couple of times but awoke almost immediately when the wind, which had got up considerably, banged some loose planks in the roof of the decrepit building together.

Eventually dawn broke, a grey cold dawn with no hint of sunshine or warmth. Hector dragged his body out of the gloom and into the daylight. He was cold and damp and shivering almost uncontrollably. He looked at his watch. Ten past seven. He wondered what time the café would open. He still had his two quid so he could at least get a cup of coffee and wait for someone to come in and give him a lift home. He hoped the owners would not be long; he hoped Maureen would not be working today. Maybe if the café had a phone he could ring her and she would come and get him.

He waited and waited. And then it suddenly struck him. Today was Sunday; the bloody café probably would not open on a Sunday. He slumped to his knees and slowly started to sob. Why him? It was Kevin who was supposed to learn the lesson, not him. He was never late in his life; why was he stuck out here in the middle of nowhere in the freezing cold? He was almost in a state of total despair, when a miracle happened. A car pulled into the car park. And not just any old car either. It was Maureen's. She pulled to a halt in front of him and rushed from the car with a blanket, which she threw over his shoulders. Kevin was there too and he gave Hector a bottle of something. Hector did not know what it was, but it was very warming and sweet and made him feel much better almost immediately. Between the pair of them they got Hector into the car and they sped off towards the motorway and home.

At some point before he fell asleep in the car, Hector found out what had happened. The tanker driver, worried at his disappearance, had stopped at Boro to let them know what had happened. Hector had told him that he was coming home from their game when he had got left behind and the driver knew where the club was from years ago when he lived in that area. Maureen had stopped in at the club on her way home from Harry's, expecting Hector and all his pals to be drinking heartily at the bar. When the steward told her that the coach was very late as they had left someone behind, Maureen, who knew about the joke, assumed it was Kevin they had had to wait for and settled down with half of lager to wait for them all to return. The coach and tanker driver arrived at almost the same time, and when Maureen realised it was Hector who was missing, she wanted to set off there and then to find him. Hank, who had realised on the way back what had probably happened, assured her that Hector would be all right and was probably going to stay the night at the café. He obviously did not know that it shut down late at night, and between them all they convinced Maureen to wait until the morning.

At five thirty in the morning Maureen, who had not slept much, picked up Kevin, who for the first and probably only time in his life was ready on time. He had volunteered to go with her, as he felt strangely responsible. It had taken them over an hour and a half to get to the turn-off, but they found the café easily and they could not miss Hector, slumped in a heap outside the door.

Hector dozed fitfully most of the way home and Maureen helped him up the stairs of his flat and put him to bed with a hot water bottle. The last thought he had before slipping into a deep and restful sleep was that the next time he thought about getting revenge on anyone, especially Kevin, he would think again. All in all, it had been a long, long weekend.

Hector Strikes Out

Hector had to make a decision. He was not good at making decisions, but this was important. Maureen, his girlfriend, for want of a better word, had asked him to go to Los Angeles with her on holiday. He could not think of anything he would rather do, so what was the problem? The problem was that the only way of getting to LA was by flying. Hector had only had one previous encounter with aeroplanes and he had not enjoyed it at all. He had gone on a preseason football tour to Ireland and had ended up on crutches. He did not blame the plane journey for that, but apart from actually breaking his ankle it had probably been the most horrendous experience of his life so far. He had sworn after that trip that he would never leave the country again by any means of transport at all, let alone flying. Now Maureen had put him on the spot.

She had been to America many times, including various trips to LA. She was a big baseball fan and wanted to take Hector to see some games in California. Flying was not Hector's only problem with going to California. He had been talking to his friends at Harwood Borough Football Club about going. Billy, Neville and Kevin had been to the States on innumerable occasions to watch sport. Talking to them was a bit like talking to the three wise men. Neville, in fact, had been to just about every sporting stadium in the world, it seemed to Hector. Billy had been to the fabled Dodger Stadium in LA – where Maureen especially wanted to go with Hector – about twenty times and he told Hector that it was probably the most spectacular sporting venue on the face of the planet. Kevin had been there several times too, but had spent most of his time there either eating or sunbathing so was not much help in describing its grandeur to Hector. Mind you, he waxed lyrical about something called a Dodger Dog, a fabled comestible that was only available in this particular sporting temple.

The problem was the way they all laughed and joked about Los Angeles itself. How there were more murders there in an average week than in Britain in about ten years. How the congestion on the freeways there was legendary, with road rage apparently leading to scenes resembling the shoot-out at the OK Corral on a regular basis. The fact that just about everyone in the entire state of California seemed to be on drugs or drunk or both most of the time. These things worried Hector immensely. The most violent place he had ever been to was probably the Den at Millwall and he could not imagine anything much worse than that. Billy had joked that the streets of LA were a bit like spending a week in the Den with everyone else there carrying a gun. Neville had joked that while there was no violence at sport in America, it could take some doing getting back to your car without getting mugged or shot. They had given him the impression that there was a police shoot-out every twenty minutes and innocent bystanders were shot as a matter of course.

But Hector still thought that he wanted to go. It would be the most exotic place he had ever been to in his life by a mile. More exotic than the weekend in Torquay he had spent when Harwood Borough had reached the fifth round of the Peabody's Balsam FA Trophy a few years ago and had been drawn away to Babbacombe Athletic. He had been amazed by the palm trees in Torquay and had spent the whole of the Sunday strolling around them secretly pretending that he was somewhere in the Caribbean. The fact that it was mid-February at the time and he nearly caught frostbite had not fazed him one bit. He was sure that he would be safe with Maureen there with him in LA and that was all that really mattered. She had told him that these stories were exaggerated and that no harm would befall him as long as he was sensible. This could be yet another problem for Hector; he was not famous for being sensible. If he was famous for anything it was for inevitably being in the wrong place at the wrong time. This was another thing that worried him. If anything was going to happen in LA, you could bet your life that he would be involved somehow.

He had more or less made up his mind to go but he was still very nervous about it. He had told Maureen that he would give her his decision that night at the pub and he was still not one hundred per cent sure what he would tell her.

That was about twelve weeks ago. Hector had said yes and here he was standing in the queue for the check-in desk at Terminal Four at Heathrow. He had never been in a building this large in his life; it was absolutely massive and was packed full of people. There were mobs of people everywhere weaving this way and that like schools of fish on a coral reef. And what weird-looking collections of humanity most of them were. Quite a few of them were in the national costume of their intended destination and it struck Hector that it looked a bit like a dress rehearsal for the opening ceremony of the Commonwealth Games. Most people seemed to have at least a couple of small children in tow, usually yelling something incoherent at the top of their little lungs, and the whole scene seemed to be one of total confusion. Some people were in the huge queues at the check-in desks, along with Hector and Maureen, while others were milling around apparently lost. People were waving tickets, hankies and just about anything it was possible to wave at other people, and various groups of Japanese people were wandering around in long snake-like lines behind guides carrying umbrellas held above their heads. A particularly small man who was waving what appeared to be an extended car radio aerial with a little red flag at the end led one group that appeared to contain nothing but a massive collection of suitcases. This resembled a Roman shield wall attacking a small fortress, in what looked to be a never-ending dance around the entire terminal.

Hector's concentration on this bizarre ceremony was interrupted about halfway down the queue, when he was asked by an official-looking man all sorts of questions about his luggage. Luckily Maureen took over and answered everything to the man's satisfaction and he soon moved on to the person behind. Hector was very grateful that Maureen had intervened as he suddenly realised that he had absolutely no idea of the contents of his suitcase. Maureen had told him to pack all he needed for the trip the previous Sunday and had come round late in the day to 'help him' as she put it. On examining the contents of the sparsely packed case she had begun tutting loudly to herself and tipped everything out on to the bed. Most of what Hector had packed was rejected in favour of the things Maureen thought were more suitable. Although Hector realised that Maureen had much more of an idea about the weather in California, he had particularly wanted to take things like his favourite football anorak as it had lots of pockets that could be invaluable on holiday. The fact that it was designed to keep out the extremes of an Arctic winter and not a cool Californian summer evening had not occurred to Hector and it now lay in a rejected pile on the floor. As she packed things, Hector was surprised to see various brightly coloured items of clothing that he did not recognise. When he asked her what they were, he got one of Maureen's cold stares as she explained that they were her things that she did not have room for in her case and was sure he would not mind taking for her. With this, Hector left her to it, flopping down in his favourite chair in the living room to watch the cricket on TV. Thus it was that he had no real idea of what he had inside his case and had he answered the official in the queue himself, he would undoubtedly have held up their progression to the check-in desk considerably.

This was all getting too much for poor old Hector. His previous experience of airports was one trip to Ireland from Bognor Regis (they had one flight a week to Amsterdam on Dike Airlines, an airline Hector had promised himself not to travel with, ever). This had not prepared him for the unnerving experience of Terminal Four at Heathrow. He was just starting to wish he had stayed at home for the fifth time that morning when they arrived at the check-in desk to be greeted with a warm smile from the young lady behind the desk. Closer inspection of the woman in question proved that appearances can indeed be very deceptive. Far from being young and eager to please, she was in fact on the wrong side of middle-aged but with so much make-up plastered on her face that her false smile remained fixedly in place whatever she actually did with her facial muscles. Maureen as always took charge and they were soon on their way through passport control and into the airport's inner sanctum.

This really did take Hector's breath away. There were more shops here than in his local high street and he just could not believe what he was seeing. Apart from the mass of people sitting anywhere there was a space big enough, and a number who were sitting in spaces that were not big enough, he just could not believe all the shops. It was like a massive indoor shopping mall built specifically for the upper classes. There were silk scarves and expensive scent. Genuine Belgian chocolate (Hector had always wondered why genuine Belgian chocolate was so expensive; he had had some once and thought it couldn't hold a candle to a bar of Galaxy) was seemingly on sale everywhere, as were extremely tacky souvenirs of London and mountains of booze and cigarettes. The restaurants and cafés dotted about the terminal were full to the brim with people all staring up at the little monitors that seemed to have sprung up on every square foot of ceiling. Hector noticed that most of the people in the entire building were craning their necks to look at these monitors, giving the appearance of ducks in the park at feeding time. He wondered if the roof opened occasionally and a kindly old woman threw in a loaf or two of bread.

Maureen, sensing that all this was becoming a bit too much for Hector, sat him down in the window seat of a bar tucked away in the corner of the terminal and provided him with a pint of Timothy Tinkers Trident. This was a particularly favoured brew, although she hoped he would not find out how much she had had to pay for it. Maureen never could understand, when everything else was duty-free, how airports got away with charging so much for drinks. She had already bought him a copy of *USA Today* so he could check what was happening in the sporting world of their destination, and, on hearing him muttering his contentment, left him to do some shopping.

Hector had been on an intensive course of 'learning' about American sport. Not only Maureen but also Neville, Billy and Kevin had all helped in introducing him to the statistics explosion that constitutes an American sports supplement. He could already name all the teams in the NFL, NBA, NHL and MLB and could even study a baseball box score (a fiendishly complicated jumble of numbers undoubtedly devised by the Americans to pay the English back for cricket scorecards) with some degree of competence. After finishing his pint, he was just contemplating whether or not he could get to the bar to order another one without losing his seat when he was amazed to see the small man with the extended aerial sweep slowly past the bar. Divested of their cases, his accompanying party seemed a truly comical sight to Hector. They all appeared to be dressed similarly in flowing orange and pink robes exactly like the followers of the Hare Krishna cult a few years back who used to roam the streets of his local town. They swayed gently back and forward mumbling softly to themselves as they went past where Hector was sitting, leaving him feeling sorry for the people of wherever it was they were going. He desperately hoped they were not going to LA but somehow he knew that they were, and on his flight too. He was right, of course. Where they were now was a mystery to Hector (they were actually in the British Airways Executive Lounge sipping gin and tonics).

He had just dashed up to the bar for a refill and beaten two large Germans dressed in lederhosen back to his seat, when Maureen arrived back from her shopping expedition.

'Had a good time?' she asked.

'Not bad,' he replied. 'How the hell do they get away with charging what they do for a pint in here? I thought it was all duty-free.'

'Funny you should ask that,' said Maureen.

Two pints later, with Hector complaining bitterly about the price of the beer every time he went to the bar, it was time to board the plane. He had told Maureen about the weird people in the robes and as soon as he told her she just knew that they would be on their flight.

Hector was expecting to get straight on the plane and was not best pleased that they had to wait another twenty minutes in a small lounge at the gate while various announcements like 'Will Mr and Mrs Harvey T Wallflower please report to gate 39C' or 'Would Henrietta Curry please make herself known to a member of staff' were broadcast.

When the announcement was made for the group travelling with the Reverend Running Orange Water to please go to gate 39C, they both knew what was coming. Sure enough, a couple of minutes later, accompanied by a tinkling of small bells, the orange and pink procession of the Divine Followers of the Church of Hallowed Fulfilment (San Luis Obispo Chapter) gently swayed its way from the delights of the Executive Lounge up the corridor towards them.

'Pity any poor sod who gets stuck with one of them,' Hector whispered out of the corner of his mouth as the disciples bobbed past.

Maureen said nothing. She looked at Hector and wondered if eleven hours sitting next to one of them would be any worse than eleven hours sitting next to Hector. She was soon to find out. And it was.

They boarded the plane and Hector stood aghast at the size of it. It was to him like a massive tube train and he flatly refused to believe that it could possibly heave itself up into the air. As his only previous flying experience had been on a tiny twenty-seater from Bognor to Dublin, it was perhaps not surprising that he was stunned by the size of the vehicle that was to transport them nearly halfway round the world.

'Considering this plane is so big, you don't get a lot of legroom,' he remarked to Maureen as he slid into his seat.

Maureen had booked the window and aisle seats of a section of three, as she had been assured by the woman at check-in that the flight was not full. Maureen knew that the last seats to go were the middle ones of a set of three and thought that this would give them lots of extra room. Of course, the woman at check-in had not known at the time about the Divine Followers of the Church of Hallowed Fulfilment (San Luis Obispo Chapter). They were roaring round the M25 at a most ungodly speed at the time, having previously stopped to change a wheel of their minibus on the hard shoulder.

Maureen nervously looked up as the true believers made their way up the aisle. Sure enough, one stopped next to Hector, who had taken the aisle seat and introduced himself as Lonely Butterfly Wing. He smiled warmly and said it would be his pleasure to accompany them today. He was quite young and seriously good-looking, thought Maureen as he climbed into the window seat that she had rapidly vacated. She thought it was wise to sit next to Hector. He had spent his last flight clinging grimly to her knee for most of it and she did not know what Mr Lonely Butterfly Wing would make of having a strange man gripping his leg as they sailed along thirty-five thousand feet above the North Pole. She wondered for a moment if Lonely was his first name or whether it was something like Norman. Norman Lonely Butterfly Wing. She liked that; it made her laugh out loud.

'Laughing is good for the soul,' announced Mr Norman (possibly) Lonely Butterfly Wing. 'Tell me, what do you find so funny?'

'Nothing,' stammered Maureen. 'Just a joke I heard inside the terminal.'

This seemed to satisfy Mr Wing, who then told her to call him Simon (she never did find out why).

Because life is full of surprises, the flight was not what either Hector or Maureen had anticipated. Hector, who had supposed it would be eleven hours of living hell, had a wonderful time. Apart from the anxiety of take-off, when he was convinced that the plane would never leave the ground as it lumbered up the runway, and the state of the 'food' served to him, he really started to enjoy himself. He had never heard of 'plastic chicken' and his introduction to it did not go down too well. He could not understand how every different piece of an apparent four-course meal could taste exactly the same. Starter, main course, dessert, and cheese and biscuits all tasted the same. In fact they tasted of nothing much at all. This amused Hector enormously. What on earth was the point of serving up stuff that was so obviously unpalatable? Surely the airlines would be better knocking ten quid off the price and getting everyone to bring sandwiches. The thought of hundreds of people picnicking on a jumbo jet amused him so much that he burst out laughing. He had been enjoying the free wine that accompanied the meal – he even had Maureen's bottle – and this obviously added to his good humour.

Maureen was not laughing. Other than looking after Hector, she had been looking forward to a good flight. Maureen loved flying. She was all prepared with a new book she had bought specially for the journey about two months ago and was absolutely dying to read. She also had various magazines and crossword puzzle books to help pass the time and had been looking forward to it for weeks.

Then along came Simon. Although he was a pleasant young man, and she had to admit that he really was extraordinarily good-looking, he just would not shut up. It turned into the flight from hell for Maureen, and long before they landed in LA she had various thoughts of sending the aforementioned Mr Lonely Butterfly Wing to personally meet the God to whom he had become so attached.

Over the course of the forty-eight hours Maureen thought the flight had taken, Simon told her his life story about twelve times over. Even though he repeated about every three minutes that he would under no circumstances try to convert Maureen to his religious beliefs, that was exactly what he had been doing for the entire flight.

He told her that he had been brought up in Indiana, where he had become a professional driving instructor. He had 'seen the light' one day while parked on the side of the road awaiting a crash repair truck. God had apparently appeared to him beside the road disguised as a fire hydrant and told him to go to Los Angeles and join His children at the Church of Hallowed Fulfilment. He had quit his job – remarkably the day before he was to be fired for incompetence – sold his apartment and moved immediately to California. He had been welcomed with open arms by the Church in question, especially after he offered to donate the profits from selling his apartment to Church funds. He had been indoctrinated into the San Luis Obispo Chapter by the fearsome Reverend Trenton P Thunder and his name was changed from Hank Greensboro to Lonely Butterfly Wing (no mention of Simon).

After three years in the San Luis Obispo area he had been chosen with twenty others from the region to spread the word of their beliefs to Europe. He and three 'brothers', Weary Riverdog, Brightfin Mudcat and Tearful Swampdragon, had spent the last three months trying to convert the ex-mining communities of Tyne and Wear to the teachings of Prophet Kazza. This somewhat unsurprisingly proved to be of limited success. In the three months in question, Simon had apparently been hospitalised four times, robbed a further six times and sexually molested by a gang of teenage girls on two separate occasions, which had particularly shocked him. They had not managed to convert so much as a farmer's dog in all that time and were now being recalled to the States to explain their lack of success.

This setback, however, had not discouraged Simon; far from it. He explained, at considerable length that the English were just not ready for the teachings of Kazza. It was very difficult for Maureen to work out exactly what the teachings of Kazza entailed, other than giving all your worldly goods to some dodgy organisation and then living a life of poverty and almost total abstinence from anything worthwhile on a commune several miles from nowhere. At least, abstinence was strictly observed when any senior person from the organisation was present, as the unsupervised forty-five minutes in the Executive Club at Heathrow had proved. Simon even admitted to have been tempted by the delights of Old Camthwaites Pit Shaft Bitter while in the north-east and Maureen was not surprised he had been mugged so many times if he had been imbibing large quantities of that stuff. Even Hector was wary of Pit Shaft; it was said that three pints could put you in hospital, so what it could do to a young lad from the back of beyond in Indiana was anybody's guess. Still, he did not look any the worse for the experience and Maureen secretly wondered what else he had or had not been abstaining from in England. She also wondered what he had been drinking on the day that God appeared to him as a fire hydrant.

Maureen did get some welcome relief from dear Simon on occasion. Firstly she had ten exciting minutes trying to get Hector to stop singing. He was fresh from drinking both his and Maureen's wine from lunch and also consuming two other bottles he had surreptitiously swiped from the trolley as the stewardess had come back with coffee. He then donned his headphones and was happily singing along to the Phil Collins cassette in his tape player and had to be asked to stop by the stewardess. That he didn't stop but, if anything, got louder was a source of annoyance to everyone around him and Maureen had to be quite firm with him to get him to turn it off. He soon afterwards drifted off to sleep, leaving Maureen with the excitable Mr Wing, who had not appeared to stop talking throughout the entire incident.

Another break came when they had to fill in their immigration form for the States. Hector managed to ruin three separate copies before he filled one in to Maureen's satisfaction, and even then she was not sure what would happen on their arrival in California. To Maureen's surprise he appeared to have filled in his customs form okay, but knowing the vagaries of the US immigration system, you could never be sure. She had once been stopped entering the good old US of A when the customs officers in Nashville thought she was smuggling in steak and kidney pies. Her bursting out laughing at the solemn-looking officials had not helped as they attempted to convince her that the smuggling in of said pies to expats was rife in Tennessee. She managed to escape without a strip search, although where exactly they thought she would be carrying the illicit produce still puzzled her to this day. This episode had naturally made her very wary of the US immigration system, so she collected their forms and tucked them safely into her bag in preparation for their arrival.

Simon, of course, had not shut up once during this interlude, although she was now managing to block him out of her thoughts. He made one last desperate attempt to convince her of the benefits of owning nothing and living thirty to a hut eating nuts, berries and cabbage for the rest of your natural life as the plane began its descent into Los Angeles International Airport, lovingly known to millions of travellers as LAX. He had to admit defeat, however, when Maureen stuffed a large lump of cotton wool in each ear, explaining how the change in air pressure hurt her ears.

Hector, by now wide awake and stone cold sober, enjoyed the landing immensely. He had decided that the landing was perfectly natural, as you had to come down eventually. It was the taking off that worried him; that wasn't natural at all. Still, he had seventeen days before he had to worry about that again.

Immigration was a surprisingly easy process. Mind you, after they had processed the members of the Church of Hallowed Fulfilment, who although claiming to all be American citizens were actually flying on a variety of passports, the officials seemed to have lost their natural will to harass as many of the incoming public as possible.

Hector had been convinced that the customs official who let them through would arrest him for possessing a bag of cheese and onion crisps he had forgotten to eat on the plane, after hearing Maureen's horror story of the steak and kidney pies. He had no idea what they would do to him for this heinous crime, but the fact that all the officials seemed to be carrying enough weaponry to invade a small country made him very nervous indeed. He had nothing to worry about, however, and they both passed on into the delights of baggage reclaim. Now Hector knew there were a lot of people on a jumbo jet. What he did not know was how much luggage they had between them and exactly how long it would take to meander its way the half mile or so from the plane to the baggage reclaim hall. When he had travelled to Ireland there had been so few people on the plane that he had watched his own bag come off and had carried it himself inside the terminal. This was different. The baggage hall was packed with people, most of them trying to control trolleys that had obviously been designed by the same people who had produced the ones in Hector's local supermarket. No matter which direction the people wanted their trolleys to go, the trolleys wanted to go the other way.

He suddenly became aware that he was alone. Before he could panic he saw Maureen skating towards him behind one of these wildly careering trolleys, which she quickly passed to Hector. This was a mistake. As they made their way to their particular carousel, Hector, who was rather proud of the fact that he had what he assumed to be total control of his trolley following several years of doing his own shopping, wondered what the black lever below the handle was. He pulled it to find out. It was the brake. The trolley stopped dead in its tracks; Hector did not. He crashed forward into the now immobile object, giving himself a sharp knock on the shin, which caused him to fall sideways.

Now, falling sideways in a crowded baggage hall is not the best way to keep the flow of people moving. As he fell, he grabbed the first thing that came to hand. This was not a good move, as the first thing that came to hand was the billowing skirt covering the nether regions of a monstrously large woman from North Carolina. The woman yelled out, causing her husband to thump his trolley into the backs of two security guards, who in the desperate search for perpetrators of some mythical felony were scanning the incoming crowds like Darth Vader looking for Luke Skywalker. She flailed at the air for a second or two and fell herself, knocking over several members of the Church of Hallowed Fulfilment, who hit the floor like skittles in a bowling alley. Both of the security guards, reacting to being struck from behind and seeing the ensuing chaos of several people in what at a glance appeared to be Arab costumes diving to the floor, immediately drew their revolvers and screamed at everyone within earshot – which happened to be a lot of people – to 'Hit the floor and don't move!'

Now the fun really started. As the mass of people in the adjacent area all tried to hurl themselves to the floor at once, leaving empty luggage carts smashing into one another like headless chickens, the first security guard was screaming into his walkie-talkie about a security alert. This brought armed guards swarming into the area like the Seventh Cavalry charging in to attack a Red Indian village. The noise of semi-automatic weapons and pistols being cocked was almost deafening for a few seconds and then, very suddenly, the noise of the chaos subsided, leaving almost total silence.

In the baggage hall all was still. Everyone was lying face down on the floor exactly as they had seen it done in thousands of American cop shows. Everyone, that is, except Hector.

Hector was standing, bent over rubbing his wounded shin. As he slowly straightened up, he was stunned to find he was staring straight down the barrels of more guns than he had ever seen in his life. This was not too difficult as the only guns he had seen in real life were when he had gone to see trooping the colour with his mum. Then and a minute or two previously in the customs area. This was, however, an impressive array of firearms by any standards; it was just a pity that Hector did not have the senses available to him to notice.

Hector did what most true Brits would do in such circumstances. He fainted.

When he awoke, he was relieved to see that the first person he saw was Maureen. The rest of the people he did not recognise, but when he realised that they all had uniforms on he leapt up. This was not a good move. He had hit his head when he fell and the pain hit him like a brick.

As his head started to clear, he realised that he was in some sort of first-aid room and that the people in the uniforms were paramedics. Had he been to America before, he would have realised that the paramedics were probably more dangerous than the armed security guards who had now almost finished clearing up the chaotic scenes outside in the baggage hall. However, as he had no knowledge of this strange anomaly of American life, he was calmed immediately at the sight of medical personnel.

Maureen explained to him that it had all been straightened out and that it was extremely unlikely that the woman from North Carolina would press charges for assault, although they both had to report to the police station near their hotel the following day to find out.

Half an hour later they were allowed to leave. Their cases had been collected for them and piled onto a trolley. Maureen quickly took charge of this and they headed across the now almost empty baggage hall – passing several bent and mangled luggage trolleys in peculiar deathlike poses on the way and out into the fresh air.

Fresh air? Hector had never smelt, or seen, anything like it. Seen was the right word. He could actually see the air moving in front of his eyes. And it was foul. It tasted almost like drinking neat petrol, which was not too far from the truth. Stuck as they were between the massive car parks and the airport terminal, the car fumes were almost overpowering. And it was hot. Very hot.

He assumed that all this was a reaction to the blow on the head. It wasn't. Maureen explained as they waited for the car hire bus that it was smog. Hector knew LA was famous for smog, but did not realise that it was quite as solid as this. You could literally see small particles floating along in the air. It was exactly like watching an old Jacques Cousteau film on TV, with trillions of plankton swimming past. It was really quite fascinating to watch, but Hector soon had to stop as it was making his eyes go funny squinting at it and this was definitely not helping his headache.

The bus soon came and they were whisked off in air-conditioned luxury to the car hire compound on the edge of the airport. Hector was glued to the window. Not only was the surrounding area strange to him as it was an airport and he was not used to airports, but it was a large airport – enormous, in fact – and it was foreign. Very foreign.

They arrived at the car hire compound in a few minutes and Maureen very wisely left Hector sitting outside on the cases appearing to stare at fresh air, which was exactly what he was doing, while she sorted out the car.

After what seemed to be an age, Maureen emerged clutching a wad of documents and a set of car keys. It didn't take long to find bay number T67, although it was a long hot walk with all the luggage. Sitting in the bay was their transport for the next two weeks or so. A gleaming bright red Pontiac. Hector was secretly very disappointed. He had seen his share of American films and thought that all American cars were huge big things about the size of a small bungalow. This was almost identical in size to Maureen's Nova back home.

Maureen climbed in and a couple of seconds later the boot flew up, nearly knocking Hector over again. He heaved the two heavy suitcases inside and, after giving the boot a good slam, moved round to get in the car. He pulled the door open to find Maureen staring at him. Not surprisingly it was a great shock to Hector to find that the driver sat on the other side of American cars. During all those American films and cop shows he had seen on TV, it had never occurred to him that the driver was sitting on the other side of the car. He went round and got in the passenger side and the simple fact of sitting on the wrong side of the car was a real novelty for him for quite a few minutes.

Then it was time to go. Maureen seemed to have made more checks and adjustments than the average space shuttle pilot appeared to make before take-off, but Hector knew it was better to be safe than sorry. He realised that if it was strange for him to be sitting on the wrong side of the car as a passenger, then it must be very peculiar for Maureen having to drive it. Slowly they inched their way towards the barrier that would let them out into downtown LA. Maureen stopped at the hut by the barrier and after a quick exchange of papers they were through. The barrier lifted and they were off on their great American adventure. Hector had a knot in his stomach to rival the size of the lump on his head, but the pain did not matter any more.

Hector held his breath. Could he cope with America?

Outside the car compound, America too held its collective breath. The real question was, could America cope with Hector?

They would both soon find out.

From another car compound on the other side of the airport a large white minibus pulled out on to the freeway. Inside, the newly arrived and somewhat shaken-up members of the Church of Hallowed Fulfilment settled down into their seats for the journey home to San Luis Obispo. One member of the faithful wondered if he would ever see the girl whom he had travelled with again. He hoped so. He had secretly decided that he really liked her. Fate was to ensure that meet again they indeed would. And sooner than either of them could have ever imagined. In fact, if Maureen had even given a thought to meeting Simon and the rest of his entourage again, she would no doubt have turned the car round, driven straight back into the car hire compound and caught the first flight back to England. With hindsight, it might have been better if she had.

The journey to their hotel was one of total awe for Hector. He had seen this in the movies for donkey's years, but this was for real. The sun was shining, the sky was a clear bright blue and a gentle breeze ruffled the huge leaves of more palm trees per mile than Torquay could offer in its entirety. And the traffic was all he believed it would be. *It may be okay having eight-lane freeways,* he thought to himself, *but it's not quite so handy when the equivalent of fourteen lanes of traffic is attempting to use them.* It took them about an hour and a half to crawl the twenty miles or so to the suburb of Glendale, which would be their base for the first half of the trip.

The hotel was quite smart and clean and the room, to Hector's eyes, was enormous. Two huge double beds sat in the middle of it and while Maureen started to unpack on one of them, Hector switched on the TV. He could not believe how many channels there were. He also could not believe how much rubbish was on them and how poor the picture quality was. About four channels were showing different episodes of *M*A*S*H*, another three had reruns of *Taxi* and three more had *The Cosby Show* on. There were about six news channels, two showing nothing but weather and the three sports programmes available had tractor-pulling, surfing and live rodeo to delight their viewers. Hector could not help drawing comparisons to Sky back home. The only real difference was that whereas one third of the Sky programmes in England were completely incomprehensible to Hector as they were in German, over here two thirds of them were completely incomprehensible to him as they were in Spanish, apparently catering for the large Mexican audience.

He eventually settled for the tractor-pulling and, having flipped open the top of his case, was quite happy to accept himself as unpacked. Maureen had other ideas. Every single item was taken out of both cases and carefully filed away in either the chest of drawers under the TV or the open-style wardrobe in the corner of the room.

After an hour or so's nap Maureen announced that she was hungry and they set off in the cool evening air to find somewhere suitable. They settled on what looked to be a diner straight out of *Happy Days* called Fenderbenders, and sat down in a large booth by the window to await proceedings. What happened next would remain in Hector's memory for ever. Now Hector had always liked his food, but what was set before him made his jaw drop almost into his lap. He had ordered a cheeseburger, curly fries and extra onion rings (he thought this sounded very American) and a bottle of Budweiser. Maureen had gone for a Philadelphia Cheesesteak with all the trimmings. How the waitress carried the huge mound of food on the two trays to their table he would never know. Come to that, he could not understand how the table took the strain of all that food without breaking. He had never seen anything quite like it. The cheeseburger was so huge it must, to Hector's eyes, have contained about one and a half cows. And the fries (he had been repeatedly warned by Maureen to call them fries; chips, she had explained, were what Hector would know as crisps)! If his local chippy had given out portions like that then they would have gone bust years ago, he thought. The real pièce de résistance was the onion rings. They both loved onion rings and had shared a bowl of them on many occasions. Neither of them had ever eaten anything like this though. It was huge. And it rather resembled a small loaf of bread. As it was placed on the table between them, they looked at each other with a sort of 'what do we do now' look. It was Maureen who came up with the answer. Fortunately, two booths down, behind Hector, the occupants had ordered the selfsame thing, which they were happily dismantling in great chunks with their steak knives. Once they had got the hang of this there was no stopping Hector or Maureen and they demolished this mass of food with relish (or was it tomato sauce).

An hour and a quarter and a hundredweight or two of ice cream later, the pair of them managed to propel their bloated bodies out of the door and up the street back to their hotel. After a couple of bottles of beer in the hotel bar they were soon both out for the count back in their room.

The next morning dawned bright and clear and they were both up early with Hector eagerly awaiting his first proper look around Southern

California. Disaster struck early as they both noticed at once that the car had a flat tyre. It took a very long forty-five minutes to change the tyre for what was laughably called the spare wheel in the boot. Fortunately the car manual was still in place in the dashboard or the process would have taken far longer, due to the fact that neither of them had ever had cause to change a spare wheel before. Hector had a sudden panic attack as he thought they might not make it to the police station. He had visions of masses of squad cars flying down the road, all lights and noise, hunting him down. But as they finally heaved the spare wheel into place, he calmed down noticeably. A quick phone call to the car hire company and they drove off to their local branch.

Half an hour later they were off again, this time in a green Buick, and not before time. While inside the office awaiting the new car, they were accosted by a sales rep who proclaimed himself as being from Boca Raton in Florida. After accusing Hector of being Australian, his face positively beamed when Hector told him that he was English. The man apparently had an aunt living in Eastbourne and when Hector rather inadvisably admitted to having been to the town a few times, the man started to describe his aunt, positive in the knowledge that Hector must have met her. The man appeared to be under the misapprehension that the town of Eastbourne had a population of somewhat under two dozen. It was a very relieved Hector who drove off with Maureen, holding one of the man's business cards with rough details of the old lady's address scribbled on the back.

Their enforced visit to the local police station turned out to be a big disappointment to Hector, apart from the fact that the woman with the huge buttocks from North Carolina (and probably the rest of her as well) had decided not to press charges. Hector had imagined something like an episode of *Hill Street Blues* inside with fights going on and drunks and local ladies of pleasure being herded into cages yelling blue murder at their captors. Instead, all was quiet. A desk sergeant without even a gun dealt with their problem and inside half an hour they were free to go. That was it. No fights, no screaming suspects, no squealing tyres and blaring sirens outside from police cars screeching to a halt. All rather boring really.

An afternoon trip to Santa Monica soon cheered Hector up. He could not believe all the activity. Three times he was nearly knocked down by bronzed young girls wearing almost nothing whizzing along the seafront on roller skates. He did not know where to look. Well, he did, but Maureen gave him a stern glance every time!

The next three days sped by as Maureen dutifully took Hector around all the tourist sights of the district. They had a day down in Anaheim at Disneyland, where no amount of encouragement whatsoever from Maureen could convince Hector to take a ride on Space Mountain. They had a day at Universal Studios where Hector got his eyebrows singed at one of the spectacular shows, and they had a day at Knott's Berry Farm where Hector nearly got run over by a large float containing a twenty foot high boysenberry. After narrowly escaping this particular jam, they spent a miserable half an hour trying to escape from a particularly loathsome English couple who had proudly announced themselves, on hearing Hector's English accent, as being from Preston in Lancashire.

It was the fourth day that Hector had really been looking forward to, however. They got up late, took in a leisurely late breakfast and early lunch at Fenderbenders, by now their favourite eating establishment, and had a leisurely stroll around the shops in Glendale for an hour or two. This was Friday and that evening was to be the first of Hector's trips to the baseball.

He was seriously excited as they drove around and up the massive extinct volcano that lay no more than a couple of miles from their hotel, on top of which stood Dodger Stadium. Although Hector was not too impressed with having to pay six dollars to enter the stadium car park, he calmed down when Maureen told him that if they parked anywhere else it would take half an hour's walk up the mountainside to get there.

His first view of the stadium simply took his breath away. To a sports fan like Hector it was beautiful. Huge tiers of different coloured seats rose sharply up in front of him, built into the mountainside around about half of the stadium. The end away from the massive stands seemed curiously open and the whole thing was surrounded by palm trees. Hundreds of them. Small ones, big ones, some of them so tall as to be almost touching the roof that covered the steeply rising tiers of seats. Hector decided that he liked palm trees. The ones in Torquay just weren't the same; these were the real thing. A curious thought struck him as he stood staring at the sight. He wondered if it was possible to get palm trees so small that he could grow one in the window box of his flat. He would endeavour to find out as soon as he returned home.

Maureen had got tickets for the game on the very top level, explaining to Hector that this was where you could get the best view of the whole stadium. The novelty of travelling up escalators inside a sports stadium made him chuckle as they made their way up to level six. Level six. Hector had rarely been in a stadium that went past level two before and, even then, not very often. Maureen had been right about the view from up there. It was, quite simply, stunning.

The whole stadium opened up before them as they made their way down the extraordinarily steep gangway to their seats. What Hector had thought was an open end opposite them actually contained two large single tier stands with gently undulating roofs. The grass field was of the brightest emerald green and the mix of colours with the blue paintwork of the stadium and the red and yellow of the seats was sensational. They had arrived quite early and Hector watched in awe as the crowd of about thirty-five thousand people made their way slowly to their seats. Everywhere was noise and colour. Most people seemed to be wearing bright blue baseball caps with 'LA' picked out in white on the front. Hector felt quite strange without one, until Maureen pushed one she had bought at a souvenir stand for him on to his head.

People milled about everywhere, most of them not apparently sure where they were supposed to be sitting. Up and down the aisle a profusion of vendors plied their various trades. They sold everything from ice cream to red liquorice bootlaces, to small furry koalas with Dodgers hats and pennants, to peanuts and beer. Beer, now this was *it.* Hector thought that someone bringing beer to you while you were watching the game was just about the most civilised thing he had ever seen. Mind you, he thought that the price of said refreshment was most uncivilised. He ordered one though, just for the novelty value he told himself, as he settled down to watch possibly the greatest free show in the Western world: the baseball peanut vendor. These men could hurl bags of peanuts with unerring accuracy over dozens of rows of people and hit their intended target every time. They were invariably let down by their client dropping the bag, unless, seemingly, they had a huge baseball glove on their hand into which the bag would thud, invariably spilling its contents all over the floor. It was really something to behold.

Hector was just on the point of being completely mesmerised by the magical sight of the sun slowly dipping down below the skyline and the powerful floodlights of the stadium taking over, when the man on his right suddenly thrust five one-dollar bills into his hand. Hector was bemused. Why should someone he had never seen before give him money? He had absolutely no idea and offered them back in the direction from which they had come. Maureen suddenly leant across him, snatched the money from his grasp and handed it to the frustrated-looking beer man kneeling on the step by her elbow. A cold plastic cup full of beer and fifty cents change went the other way, Maureen sensibly bypassing Hector completely with this, as Hector realised that passing the money from one to the other was the only way of paying for the beer in question.

Suddenly there was a huge roar as the combatants for the evening took the field way below them for the contest. They weren't exactly like ants, but they were so far away that they looked like little Sindy dolls. All were dressed in pure white with little blue hats on. Everyone stood and took off their hats. Everyone, that is, except Hector, whose new favourite cap was wrenched from his head by Maureen. Three smartly uniformed marines marched out on to the field carrying flags and the monstrous stadium organ played the national anthem to the accompaniment of over thirty thousand tone-deaf voices. With another huge roar the music ended and everyone sat back down.

This was it then. The ball game was on. It was to be between the hometown Los Angeles Dodgers and their visitors from Canada, the Montreal Expos. Now Hector did not know too much about baseball, but he did know that whereas the Dodgers were roughly the equivalent of an American Manchester United, the Expos were about the Canadian equivalent of Doncaster Rovers. It would seem strange then to others that Maureen should be sitting at his side proudly wearing an Expos hat and her best Montreal T-shirt. Hector had a good look around him. Away fans were in a definite minority. A minority of one by his observation.

This did not surprise Hector. Maureen had told him of her love of the Montreal Expos long ago. She had apparently been to Montreal many years before (with a previous partner who was never mentioned) and it was here that she had first experienced baseball. On enquiring why there were so few people at the game, she was told quite unceremoniously that no one supported the Montreal Expos, not even the people of Montreal. That was it as far as Maureen was concerned. There was only going to be one team for her from then on. Unfortunately for Maureen, that team was the Expos. A team that she had suffered with over the years as they were continually on the verge of upping sticks to somewhere in America; a team that played in one of the most antiquated and, some would say, thoroughly awful stadiums on the North American continent. Although Maureen would strongly deny this, saying it was not as bad as people made out. One day they would have a new stadium, she would tell Hector. Hector had his doubts as the people of Montreal seemed to have more interest in tobogganing than baseball, but he never let on. Anyway, she was proud of her team and she had come halfway round the world to see them. Hector was secretly very proud of her sticking to her principles like that, even though he secretly wished she supported these Dodgers, then he could come here regularly with her. He would enjoy that, he thought. Sitting back in his seat in the last rays of sunshine as the game got under way, he thought he would enjoy that very much indeed. If heaven was any better than this, then he thought dying might not be so bad after all.

The game went mainly as Hector had imagined it would. Montreal tried ever so hard and even led the game on a couple of occasions. The Dodgers eventually prevailed, although it took a monster home run from their star player right at the death to do it for them. Hector had not understood all the nuances of the game, but found that he had been able to follow the general gist of it quite easily. Maureen's course of home baseball instruction had really done the trick. Hector thought Maureen looked a little sad on the way back to the car park, but she insisted that she had enjoyed herself and that it was nice to see her team again, even if they had come second. Hector hoped that the Expos would win tomorrow night when they were playing again, although he knew that the Dodgers' best pitcher, Japanese star Hideous Nomore, was pitching for them so it would not be easy. Maureen had already bought tickets for tomorrow's game and Hector could hardly wait.

They listened to the radio on the way home as endless streams of Dodgers fans phoned in to moan about their team in general and certain players in particular. If they could moan like that when they won, neither Hector nor Maureen could imagine what they would be like if they lost. Maureen said she hoped they would find out tomorrow and gave a little laugh.

They parked at the hotel and walked back a fair way to a small bar that they had noticed the day before and went in for a few beers. As they walked in they were both hit by the stunning coldness of the place and the fact that it appeared to be completely dark. As their eyes slowly got used to the light, they noticed other people inside and several TVs flickering in the gloom.

Hector ordered a pitcher of draught beer and they settled down in the corner to unwind and watch what turned out to be almost endless highlights of the day's baseball games. Maureen had cheered up tremendously, although her general demeanour did not improve with the continual showing of the Dodgers' winning home run every few minutes. They ate in the bar, yet another monstrous cheeseburger for Hector and chicken fajitas for Maureen, and worked their way through two more pitchers of beer, before wending their way back to the hotel exhausted.

It had been a wonderful day, thought Hector as they made their way back. Probably the most memorable day of his life so far. Until tomorrow at least!

Saturday, as ever, dawned bright and sunny, and after a bit of a lie-in Maureen told Hector that she was taking him to see the famous spot outside Mann's Chinese Theatre where all the stars had left their handprints in the cement. Hector was seriously excited and enjoyed every moment of Maureen's drive around Beverley Hills and Hollywood on their way to the theatre. This was where the excitement stopped. The area that the theatre was in, far from being exclusive and upmarket as Hector had always thought could only be described as seedy. The shops were all rather dingy and a group of most unsavoury characters were hanging around outside the McDonald's across the street.

Maureen and Hector were just on their way back to the car after inspecting the concrete when a curious sight grabbed their attention. Coming up the street towards them was a chanting, swaying mass of none other than the brothers of the Church of Hallowed Fulfilment. As well as their jingling little bells, several of them were carrying placards proclaiming statements such as 'Freedom for Kazza' and 'Goddesses must be free'; there was even one that rather mysteriously said 'Yankees go home!' Quite a crowd was following them up the street, including two or three uniformed police officers. As they got adjacent to the theatre, the entire brotherhood suddenly sat down. One or two of them quickly chained themselves to the railings of the theatre and they all started to chant 'Free Kazza now!'

This was turning out to be rather fun. All the shops along the street started to empty as people rushed out trying to find out what was going on. Someone coming out of McDonald's told Hector and Maureen, through a half-eaten mouthful of Big Mac, that the police had arrested the Church's leader, someone going by the name of Kazza, the day before for non-payment of taxes and fraud. This was her followers' protest to try to get her back.

Suddenly the air was full of sirens as almost a dozen police cars, lights flashing, wailers wailing, entered the scene. *This was more like it,* thought Hector, taking photos as fast as his camera would work. Police officers piled out of the cars, drawing their riot sticks as they did so, which seemed to intensify the feelings of the protesters. Someone threw what looked from across the street like a small dog at the onrushing police and suddenly all hell broke loose. Those protesters who were not chained down quickly stood and charged at the police. Most stopped short, but some odd ones got past the line of police and turned to rush back at them.

Maureen's jaw dropped as she saw that one of the brothers turning back for another go was Simon. She suddenly took off running towards him, with a totally mystified Hector about two paces behind her. A policeman turned to face Simon and raised his riot stick to strike him. As he was about to bring the stick down, however, Maureen barrelled into him, knocking him over. Before the officer could recover, Maureen grabbed Simon by the neck of his robes and started half dragging, half carrying him towards the onlooking crowd. Hector was completely bemused by all of this but carried on running and grabbed the other side of Simon's robes to help Maureen. As he stumbled past the police officer, he thought he heard him try to yell something after the fleeing threesome, but his cries were soon extinguished by another member of the brotherhood. This one's beard and stovepipe hat gave him the appearance of Abraham Lincoln as he whacked him around the side of the head with a placard proclaiming 'Free the Goddess of peace now!'

They managed to drag the by now protesting Simon through the ring of interested spectators and round the corner to where Maureen's hire car was parked. The struggling protestor was bundled into the back by Hector, while Maureen wrenched open the driver's door and threw herself into her seat. Hector only just had time to leap into the passenger seat before Maureen performed a three-point turn straight out of *Miami Vice* and headed off back towards Glendale.

The journey back to the hotel took about twenty-five minutes, by which time Simon had calmed down enough to thank them for getting him away from the mêlée. He explained that the police had come under cover of darkness the morning before, knocked down the doors of the large mansion that was their headquarters and taken the divine Kazza away in a van. Three minutes later you would never have noticed that anyone had been there apparently. Except for the two large wooden doors lying on the steps, of course. The Very Reverend Trenton P Thunder had initially demanded that the brotherhood storm the local police headquarters to get her released. However, after careful thought and a three-hour prayer and meditation session, they had decided to mount their protests in Hollywood where they were sure they would get the maximum publicity. Some people had warned that it might get a little nasty, as the local police were well known for breaking up demonstrations by religious groups rather forcibly.

The escapees arrived back at their hotel without further incident and bundled Simon into their room before pulling the curtains and switching on the TV. One of the news stations was carrying live reports of the protest and was showing the man with the beard and stovepipe hat being pushed forcefully into the back of a Black Maria.

'That's him!' shouted Simon. 'That's the Reverend Trenton P Thunder.'

Maureen told him to shush. There could be trouble if anyone knew he was here. On TV the police were rounding up the rest of the transgressors and had them sitting in the middle of the street with their hands on their heads like prisoners of war. Behind them other officers were desperately trying to saw through the chains securing the more obdurate members of the demonstration to the theatre railings.

The report on TV went on to explain that Kazza, real name Dorothy Delores Thunder, wife of the aforementioned Reverend Trenton P, would appear in court later that day charged with embezzling over a quarter of a million dollars from several of her followers. Also, and far more seriously, for not paying tax on it to the IRS.

It was alleged that Mrs Thunder (née Pickens) had spent three years in jail in Arkansas on similar charges eight years ago when she was running an organisation called the Fellowship of Divine Accomplishment and was caught selling bootleg whiskey from the back of a pickup truck. She was also linked to another so-called Church, the Brotherhood of Man, but had fled charges of prostitution and gunrunning in Louisiana in the late 1970s.

Simon sat on the bed with his mouth open. 'I just don't believe it,' he gasped. 'The reverend told us all that she had been chosen by God to lead us to a better place. She had had visions and everything.'

'Probably the bootleg whiskey,' said Hector sarcastically. 'The better place was probably her bank account.'

It became pretty apparent as they watched that the police were not looking for anyone else in relation to the incident in Hollywood, so at least they were all in the clear. But Simon was sitting on the bed looking like the leading man in a paper hanky commercial, all flowing robes and plastic gold-coloured chains.

'What are you going to do now?' asked Maureen.

'I don't know,' muttered Simon. 'I suppose I will have to make my way back to Walleyville Indiana and my folks.'

Maureen dug out a pair of Hector's shorts and an old T-shirt for Simon and he went into the bathroom to change out of his ceremonial attire.

'Call me Hank,' he called out as he was changing. 'I've had enough of this Simon rubbish.'

Hector nearly fell off the bed laughing. Hank the plank from Walleyville, Indiana; it just could not be true.

'Tell me,' said Maureen, 'why all the different names?'

'God knows,' replied Simon. '*She* called me Simon after one of her bloody Pekinese, I think. This Lonely Butterfly Wing must have been some kind of piss-take, I suppose.'

Hector had left the room and was standing outside holding his ribs. He was laughing so hard they hurt. Maureen briefly – very briefly – wondered what a brother of the Fellowship of Divine Accomplishment wore underneath his robes, but the sound of Hector nearly wetting himself in the corridor outside brought her quickly back to reality.

When Hank reappeared from the bathroom, Maureen went just a little weak at the knees. The shorts and T-shirt were about two sizes too small and clung to his body like Lycra. *He was good-looking. Very good-looking*, she thought. *But thick, oh so thick. And gullible.* She used to think that Hector was a ham sandwich short of a picnic, but this bloke knocked him into a cocked hat. How could anybody be so dumb as to give up all his worldly goods and go off to a place he had never heard of and worship some old tart just because she said she had had a vision? *And a vision of what?* she wondered.

The newly renamed Hank sat down on the edge of the bed and looked glum. Hector came back in, still smiling mightily, and pronounced that he was hungry. They took Hank for a slap-up lunch at Fenderbenders, the whole thing costing less than fifteen quid, and while Hank went off to phone his folks they tried to decide what to do.

'What are we going to do with him?' Hector asked.

Maureen had to admit that for once in her life she did not know.

The problem was solved by Hank himself, who said that his folks would wire him the bus fare home and that if Maureen would very kindly take him to the local Greyhound bus station, he could sort out his ticket home from there.

Over the course of the meal it started to dawn on Hank what had really happened to him on the day he had become 'converted'. He had been on a driving lesson at the time with a good-looking, slim young lady calling herself Innocence, who, he now realised, bore a striking resemblance to a younger version of the former Goddess Kazza (whom he now referred to as 'that fat bitch with all the damn dogs'). The girl had inexplicably driven into a telegraph pole in the middle of nowhere and he had spent a 'very entertaining' half-hour in the back of the car with her while they awaited rescue.

It was after this, as they sat by the deserted roadside, that the girl had suggested they have a drink together. She produced a bottle from her bag and, after the initial shock of the rough liquid grabbing his tonsils like a half-starved coyote; he had started to enjoy himself immensely. He could not for the life of him remember if she had had a drink with him, but as it was very probably some of her undoubted mother's specially distilled moonshine he was pouring down his throat, he would be very surprised if she had.

Soon after this he had had his vision, surprise, surprise, and, if he remembered correctly, it had been the girl who had translated its meaning to him. Now he came to think about it, what the hell was a fire hydrant doing five miles outside town in the middle of nowhere anyway? The next couple of days went by in a bit of a haze – lots more moonshine, he remembered, thinking back – and the girl had in fact accompanied him to San Luis Obispo for his indoctrination into the brotherhood. And it was no doubt *her* idea that he invested all his money in the Church. No wonder they were so pleased to welcome him.

He remembered now that he had not seen dear Innocence from the time of his arrival to this day and wondered how many other lost souls she had 'worked on' since then. Since his arrival the everyday running of the Church had just taken him over and he had become as fervent a follower of Kazza as anyone. The free love had helped, he had to admit, and Maureen had to give Hector a kick under the table as he started to ask a few too many pertinent questions about this particular aspect of their religious lifestyle.

After leaving the diner they hunted around for a charity shop and bought Hank a cheap jacket and shoes for his long journey home and then took him off to the bus terminal. Hank hugged them both passionately before he boarded his bus, Maureen a little too passionately for Hector's liking. And as Maureen pushed a twenty-dollar bill into his hand, 'to cover anything you might need on the journey', he made his way up the steps and on to the bus, promising to repay them one day.

They both waved farewell and returned to their car convinced that they had seen the last of him. They went back to their hotel and simply lay in the dark for an hour not saying a word. Suddenly Maureen started to giggle, which started Hector off, and they were soon almost rolling on the floor in fits of hysterical laughter.

'Just how dumb can Americans get?' asked Hector through his tears of laughter.

'I don't think I want to find out,' said Maureen thoughtfully.

She had to admit to herself: he might be terminally thick as a barrel of treacle, but he *was* good-looking.

The rest of the day passed without incident and they were soon on their way back up the mountain to the ball game. It had exactly the same effect on Hector as the day before and he just sat in his seat almost on the roof of the world in total awe of his surroundings. Everything was much the same as the night before. The colours, the sounds, the smells of the food cooking on the concession stands. It was from one of these concession stands that Hector had one of his biggest disappointments of the entire trip. About half an hour before the game, he treated himself to a Dodger Dog. Kevin had waxed lyrical about this almost mythical type of hot dog and Hector had been really looking forward to having one. All over LA great big posters positively screamed the advantages of eating this supposedly superior foodstuff at passers-by. On billboards alongside the freeways, on the sides of buildings, in the newspapers and on seemingly every TV and radio show, adverts implored the masses of Southern Californians to eat this apparently heavenly tasting comestible. Hector was not at all surprised to find that, unlike its pictures in the programme, the famed Dodger Dog was not about a foot long – less than half that, in fact. Hector had long since given up complaining about the size nowadays of different foodstuffs. Indeed, ever since Maureen had bought him a Curly Wurly some months before. Hector could remember the days of his childhood when it took three different people just to carry a Curly Wurly out of the shop and the rest of the day to eat it. The pathetically small offering Maureen had bought him just about summed up life, Hector had thought at the time: nowhere near as good as it used to be.

Size was, of course, irrelevant, as Maureen often told him. What counted was the quality. And this was a fabled Dodger Dog. It did not matter how big it was; it was going to be a real treat for Hector. Having smothered it in relish and raw onions from the huge containers at the cutely American-named 'fixings station', he very reverently took his first bite.

It tasted, well, sort of plain. It tasted of nothing much at all, actually. When he came to think about it, it tasted of relish and raw onion. It wasn't that it was at all unpleasant; it just did not taste like the real taste treat he had expected or that the adverts had promised. It might have contained one hundred per cent pure beef, but it was totally bland. A good quality English sausage made with sawdust and breadcrumbs had at least three times the taste of this sad offering. His opinion was obviously not shared by the surrounding throng of Americans. They were buying Dodger Dogs as fast as the people in the concession stand could wrap them up.

Poor buggers, thought Hector as he bought a bucket of popcorn about the same size as his kitchen sink back home and about a gallon of Coke with enough ice in it to sink the Icelandic navy. He sat for a few minutes gazing over the back wall of the stadium at the majestic sight of the city of LA in the distance. It was another clear day and the city stood out superbly against the blue sky. It's a pity about the smog, he mused, stuffing another handful of popcorn into his mouth; without it you could probably see the Pacific Ocean from here. He thought Maureen might be wondering where he was, so he picked up his mug of Coke and made his way back to his seat.

This was to be the day that Maureen was to get her revenge on the Dodgers. Montreal exploded for five runs in the first inning and the Dodgers' Japanese star home pitcher, Hideous Nomore, was on his way out of the game almost before it had begun. This caused the half a dozen or so sushi salesmen to return to the bowels of the stadium with their baskets of raw fish unsold. Three of these runs came on homers from the bats of Rupert Black and the 'flying Garrulous Brothers', Wilber and, Maureen's particular favourite, Igor. Montreal went on to win by the score of nine–two, the final couple of innings being watched by about thirty-two thousand fewer people than the thirty-eight thousand or so present at the start. By the time that Expos pitcher Ugli Ribena closed out the game, Hector and Maureen were the only people left on the entire top deck. By the time they got back to the car, the car park was practically deserted and the drive out of the stadium confines was a very pleasant and happy one indeed.

On with the radio and the post-game phone-in show was in full swing. The fans wanted all the players, the manager, the coaches, the ground staff, the kit men, the programme sellers and even the tea boy sacked immediately. The man hosting the show tried to calm the people down, saying that it had just been a bad night and that all would probably be okay when the teams met for the third and final time on Sunday afternoon.

A few celebratory drinks were called for and Maureen attacked a few with relish (but not the same relish that was on the hot dogs) back in the same bar they had been in the previous night. Maureen was rather disappointed to find that the TV did not show her team's four home runs with the same regularity as they had the Dodgers' winning one the night before. By the time they showed them for the second time though, she had consumed rather more beer than she was used to and cheered loudly as the fourth one disappeared into the cheap seats. Realising what she had done, she burst out in a fit of giggles that lasted all the way back to the hotel.

The next morning dawned cloudy. It was drizzling when Hector pushed his nose between the curtains; he didn't feel too good. Maureen apparently felt even worse; she did not stick more than the top three inches of her head out from under the duvet until Hector returned from the coffee shop with a cup of coffee and a doughnut for her. He had been out to get the papers as he had done every morning since their arrival. This morning had been different. It had involved Hector pouring nearly all his loose change into the newspaper-vending machine in the street outside the hotel and then carrying back what appeared to be a large-sized telephone directory. It took Hector a full five minutes to find the sports section inside the massive amount of papers and magazines. *No wonder the rainforests are disappearing*, he thought to himself, *most of them are going into the production of the Sunday papers over here*. Maureen's tousled head appeared over the top of the duvet as he found the correct section and she asked him what the news was. Hector told her that the man writing the front page of the sports section appeared to want the sacking of the players, the manager, the coaches, the ground staff, the kit men, the programme sellers and even the tea boy after last night's abysmal performance by the Dodgers. Maureen gave a little laugh, took a small bite of doughnut, a large swig of coffee and disappeared back into her pit.

An hour and a half later and they were on their way back up the mountain for the last time. Hector was getting the hang of the routine now, but today there was a difference. Maureen had got seats downstairs on the second level. It was a totally different view and Hector did not like it anywhere near as much. He had to show his ticket to an usher in a straw hat every time he went back to his seat from having a wander round. People were everywhere; there did not seem to be a spare seat anywhere, although about half of them were permanently empty as a non-stop collection of people went backwards and forwards to the concession stands. The crowds of people arriving late were met head-on by the crowds of people leaving early and

Hector wondered how many of them actually saw the whole game. In fact, he wondered how many of them saw any of the game, what with the way they all seemed to be permanently on the move. No, all in all he preferred his seat up on level six, which seemed to be almost empty compared to this constant movement downstairs. The game itself was a poor one, with the Dodgers winning three–two. Maureen was quite happy on the way back to the hotel. She was amused to hear that although the people on the phone-in show still wanted the sacking of the players, the manager, the coaches, the ground staff, the kit men and the programme sellers, the tea boy's job was safe for another week.

They spent their last evening in Glendale in Fenderbenders. Hector was getting much more used to the portions in America and Maureen thought he was already looking a bit chubby. This time Hector tucked into a Fenderburger, their top of the range half-pound burger containing just about everything it was humanly possible to pile in a bun. He topped this off with spicy curly fries, another onion ring log, coleslaw and about six bottles of Coors Extra Gold. He followed all this with an enormous hot fudge sundae and another couple of bottles of beer before pronouncing himself satisfied. Maureen, who had watched him plough through this pile of food in amazement, had finished her home-made meatloaf and mashed potatoes some time previously and was on her fourth cup of coffee before Hector was ready to go. They walked back to their hotel, Hector with some difficulty, and watched an hour or so's TV before crashing out for the night. Tomorrow was a big day; they were off on the second part of Hector's Californian adventure. They were going a hundred-odd miles due south to San Diego. Beaches as far as the eye could see, Sea World with its killer whales and of course, more beer, more massive burgers and more baseball.

Hector loved San Diego. Maureen had told him what a lovely place it was and she was right. The sun never stopped shining while they were there and the beaches were simply superb. The three days they spent down there were probably the happiest of Hector's life.

They spent one day doing nothing but lounging around on the beach. Hector had been intrigued at the baseball by the fact that Americans seemed incapable of catching anything without wearing a huge glove on one hand. On the odd occasion that someone caught a ball in the crowd without a glove on, they seemed to get more applause than the players did when they hit a home run. This fascinated Hector to the extent that he had gone out and bought a cheap baseball bat, glove and ball and he had Maureen throwing the ball to him for hour after hour on the beach, until her arm got too tired to throw any more.

He found that he could catch the ball quite easily with his bare hands, but all attempts to catch it in the glove failed miserably, to the great amusement of the watching American public. When he tried hitting the ball it was no different. He probably missed seventy per cent, but the thirty per cent that he did hit caused chaos. One hit a dog that was catching frisbees thrown by his master. Four disappeared out to sea and necessitated long underwater searches by Hector to retrieve them (Maureen was all in favour of these as she got some peace and quiet while Hector searched). One thudded into the sand about four inches away from two old ladies having a quiet afternoon snooze on the beach and one almost decapitated a roller-skating bimbo (or 'Hardbod' as Hector had found out that they were called) belting along the cycle track that ran alongside the seafront. Maureen decided enough was enough and confiscated the entire collection of weaponry leaving Hector to lie in the sun and sneak glimpses of the women's volleyball game that was carrying on not far away.

Another day they spent at the zoo. The giant tortoises that were apparently over a hundred years old intrigued Maureen. *She seemed a bit too keen*, thought Hector to himself, on the fact that even at that advanced age the tortoises apparently thought that almost constant sex was the ideal way to spend a sunny afternoon, but he did not like to mention it to her. The zoo was marvellous, even Hector had to admit that. He had not been to too many zoos in his life (probably only London Zoo when he was a kid) but he really enjoyed this. It was huge and it took them about six hours to wander round it all. They spent three-quarters of an hour of that swaying about in a gondola high above the trees looking down on all the wildlife on a jungle ride, which was fun, although Maureen didn't seem to think so. Hector could not understand her logic. She felt unsafe less than a hundred feet from the ground in the gondola, yet she enjoyed being in an aeroplane at thirty-five thousand feet; but he let it pass. They watched the gorillas playing about for ages and Hector really liked the reptile house, not the least because of how cool it was inside compared to the hot sun outside. It was certainly a very good day.

The third day they went to Sea World, which was quite a revelation to Hector, although Maureen was a bit sceptical about Baby Shamu the killer whale as she had seen another so-called Baby Shamu in Florida a couple of years before. She failed to believe that it was the same one, especially as this one was smaller than the one two years earlier, and wondered how many more there were dotted around the USA. It was another excellent day, however, made particularly memorable by Maureen's diving save to stop Hector falling into the manatees' tank. Hector, of course, had leant far too far forward trying to take a photograph and it was only Maureen's quick thinking and even quicker reactions that saved him from a drenching and the manatees from a most unwelcome intrusion into their daily routine. They didn't look dangerous but who knows what they would have done if Hector had dropped unceremoniously on top of one. They watched the sea lion show and wandered through the giant shark tank very cautiously having both seen *Jaws 3D* at home when a tank exploded causing mayhem amongst the poor unfortunates in it at the time. They both knew that it had been a film and not real life, but it still made them a bit wary.

They unwound by spending almost an hour watching the penguins in their own huge exhibit and laughed at the frogman-like figure who came in to feed them their lunch. It was only the cold of this refrigerated area that drove them back outside into the sunshine and a lovely day was completed when they went up the huge viewing tower to look over not only all of Sea World but most of the San Diego area as well. With the sun glinting off the azure blue of the Pacific Ocean it was breathtaking.

The evenings in San Diego were, naturally enough, taken up with baseball, which they both enjoyed. The games were played at the rather inelegantly named Qualcomm Stadium, home of the San Diego Padres. Again it was a spectacular stadium, rising out of a monstrous car park almost like a Roman amphitheatre. Indeed, with its huge arches round the very top, it looked a little bit to Hector like pictures he had seen of the Colosseum in Rome. It may have been spectacular, but it just wasn't the same as Dodger Stadium and Hector did not like it anywhere near as much. Maureen said it had seemed a little bit friendlier the last time she had been there when it was called Jack Murphy Stadium. She hated the way that the Americans tended to change the names of their stadiums whenever some large corporate body offered them money to do so, but they still enjoyed themselves. Maureen's Montreal Expos had moved the hundred miles or so down the coast from LA and played the Padres on all three nights they were there, winning the last two of them to make Maureen very happy indeed.

There was one extraordinary moment at the baseball to go along with the comical sight of what Hector took to be college students staggering around inside the stadium seemingly permanently drunk. Hector wondered where on earth students got the money from to drink at baseball games, since the beer was not cheap by any means, but drink it they did and in vast quantities. The extraordinary moment came when a reasonably elderly gent fell down the steep steps of the top tier. He fell down about six rows and, despite blood coming from a wound in his head, positively refused to go with the attending paramedics as apparently he had a problem with his medical insurance and could not afford the first aid that was being offered. No matter how hard the paramedics pleaded with him to go with them, he just stubbornly sat on the steps, covering his wound with an old handkerchief, and refused to budge. *What a wonderful country*, thought Hector rather ruefully. They could afford to put men on the moon and have a profusion of warships cruising around the world looking to 'protect' people who would probably rather be left alone, and yet they could not treat one of their own OAPs because he did not have the right type of medical insurance.

All too soon it was time to start to prepare to make the long journey homewards. On the last morning of their trip they left San Diego for the drive back to LA and the flight home. They had no hold-ups on the way and pulled into a Sizzler restaurant for a final meal before going back to the airport. Hector was going to miss these American meals. This particular restaurant did an all-day 'all you can eat' buffet for $7.99 and Hector just could not resist it. He saw it as some sort of final challenge and he tucked into his mixture of American and Mexican food with gusto (they had no relish). No fewer than four platefuls disappeared inside Hector and that was before he saw the ice cream machine in the corner. Maureen could only look on in wonder as he piled two enormous bowls of ice cream into himself before announcing he was ready for home.

They had one small task to do on the way to the airport and that was to fill the car up with petrol, as it had to have a full tank when handed back. This had turned out to be a bit of a painful operation on the three previous times they had tried it, American petrol pumps proving very different from English ones, and it took quite a bit of muscle to hold the pump handle inside the filling hole in the car.

They stopped at a petrol station about two miles from the airport at a seedy-looking crossroads, and Hector, now almost unable to move after his enormous lunch, rather unfairly let Maureen struggle with the pump herself rather than help her as he had done on the previous occasions. Maureen huffed and puffed her way to a full tank and then rather sarcastically asked him if he wanted to go inside the shop for anything or if he was too busy. Hector refused the kind offer, saying he just couldn't move, and Maureen wandered off to pay for the petrol.

It was as she was coming out of the shop that things started to happen rather quickly.

She took three steps before two young-looking hoodlums bumped straight into her. One attempted to snatch the handbag off her shoulder, while the other pulled a handgun out of his jacket and told her to drop the bag.

Maureen was completely confused and let rip with a scream at the top of her voice that not only woke Hector from his slumber in the car, but was probably audible for about half a mile. Hector, hearing his Maureen scream, was on the move immediately. He threw the door open and heaved himself out on to the forecourt. He saw Maureen still clutching her bag and the two ruffians trying to get it off her. He did not see the gun. He rushed towards her and the two robbers turned to face him.

It was then that Hector saw the gun for the first time. The gunman started to panic as he saw Hector rushing towards him but still waved the gun in his direction. Hector, unable to stop now he had got his recently expanded girth mobile, carried on involuntarily towards them. The two robbers started towards Hector, but Maureen now thinking they were trying to attack Hector, managed to trip one of them up as they ran away from her. The tripped assailant fell sideways, crashing into his accomplice who still brandished the handgun. Hector, completely unable to stop, fell headlong into the pair of them and all three smashed into the side of a nearby petrol pump and collapsed in a heap.

It was while the three of them were falling that the gun went off. Hector felt the bullet enter his leg but could strangely feel no pain. He fell on top of the two hapless assailants and there he stayed, totally incapable of moving. It was no doubt to do with his enormous intake of food during his stay in the United States that his falling on the two robbers knocked one completely unconscious and left the other trapped at the bottom of the pile of bodies. Maureen bravely ran forward and picked up the gun which had been knocked to the ground in the mêlée. She pointed it at the immobile heap on the ground rather shakily as at that time she had no idea who, if anyone, had been shot. Before she could do anything at all, she heard the approaching whine of a police squad car. She had never been so relieved in her life as the car screeched to a halt on the garage forecourt. She dropped the gun instinctively and just pointed at the jumble of men now starting to writhe on the ground.

'Freeze!' yelled the first officer piling out of the car.

Maureen was horrified to notice that he was pointing his gun at her. She froze. 'It was them!' she screamed. 'They tried to rob me.'

The officer, now joined by his gun-pointing colleague, turned his attention to the three men on the ground. 'Get up slowly,' the officer growled at them.

'I cant!' shouted Hector. 'I think I've been shot.'

Maureen screamed, the owner of the petrol station ran out yelling something in Mexican at the top of his voice and the two officers started squawking into their walkie-talkies. All was chaos for a few minutes.

Hector did what was expected of him. He fainted.

He came round in an emergency room with Maureen holding his hand. There was nobody else around. He looked at Maureen. She had obviously been crying. Her make-up had run down her face and had dried where it had run. She saw Hector looking at her and burst into tears again. He attempted to raise himself up to comfort her. The sudden pain of the bullet wound in his leg knocked all the breath out of him and he fell back on to the bed.

'Shit,' he muttered breathlessly.

'Oh, Hector,' blubbed Maureen. 'How do you feel?'

'Terrible,' he replied. 'What happened?'

'The gun went off when you fell with the two robbers; you got shot in the leg.'

'Bloody hell!' Hector exclaimed.

'The police carted the two robbers away and an ambulance brought me and you here,' Maureen went on. 'I've given a statement to the police and they want to see you later. Oh, and there's a man here from the *Los Angeles Times* who would like to interview you. They think you are a hero taking on two gunmen unarmed and capturing them.'

'But I didn't take them on,' protested Hector. 'I... I... I just...'

'I know what you did; I told the man from the papers what you did, but they just don't believe me. They think you're a hero.'

'Bloody hell!' he exclaimed again.

The next few days went by like a dream for Hector. He was given his own private room at the hospital, with TV and everything. He was interviewed twice by the police, who said that the perpetrators had been in court and would be sentenced very soon. They would go down for a good few years thanks to Hector's prompt action in capturing them. He had even seen his story on the news the first night, although the hospital would not let the cameras in to interview him.

Three times the man from the *LA Times* came to see Hector and he was amazed to see that the story had been in the paper three days running. There was even a photo of Hector in his hospital bed with Maureen sitting beside him. UNARMED BRITISH HERO TACKLES GUNMEN, the headline had said the first day. Not on the front page, but pretty near the front nonetheless. The next day the story had slipped back about four pages and the day after that was only three pages from the back, but it was still there.

The hospital had told him that the bullet had gone straight through the side of his calf muscle and although he would be very stiff and sore for a couple of weeks, there would be no after-effects. He would be discharged tomorrow.

Maureen had changed the flight tickets. British Airways had been extremely helpful after she had explained what had happened. They were flying home tomorrow night. Not only that, but through the kind arrangements of both BA and the LAPD they were flying home first class.

Hector lay back in his bed. He was a hero. He really was. He had forgotten what had really happened and had now convinced himself that he had leapt on the armed gunmen in an unselfish attempt to save his girlfriend. He slept with a huge smile on his face all three nights he spent in the hospital. Even the leg did not give him much pain; mind you, that could have been on account of the numerous different coloured pills they gave him three times a day.

They were taken to the airport in style in a limo sent by the *LA Times* and Hector gave another interview to the waiting pressmen inside the first-class lounge at the airport. He was getting used to the interviewers now, and the cameramen. It was just a pity that the hospital had not let him be interviewed for the TV, he thought. He was sure that he would have looked good on TV.

It was soon time to board the aircraft and Hector, with a last wave to the press, hopped his way on board with the help of the brand new crutches the hospital had given him as he left. He was going home a hero, he thought as he settled down into his sumptuous first-class seat and drained his first glass of complimentary champagne. As he drank more champagne, the stories he decided he would tell his friends became more and more removed from the truth. *Still,* he thought, *they would already know all the details, as all the papers in England would be flooded with the news.* He decided he had better not drink too much champagne, as he would need a clear head to deal with the waiting press at Heathrow.

He enjoyed the flight home, his anticipation of what was to come growing steadily by the hour. Maureen continually tried to calm him down, but he was having none of it. He was a hero. He wondered what pictures of him they had used on the front pages in England. He supposed they would have wired them over from the States. He would look good, he thought, lying in bed in an LA hospital – very classy for the tabloids. Eventually he dozed off and dreamt of popping flashbulbs and people with fedoras on with little cards in the brim with 'Press' written on them asking him questions and making him pose with a bevy of supermodels. Again he slept with a grin on his face. Maureen dozed alongside him and hoped he would not be too disappointed.

The plane landed in heavy drizzle. Hector was met at the aircraft's entrance by a BA official with a wheelchair and both he and Maureen were whizzed straight through passport control in a flash. *Now this is more like it,* thought Hector. *I could get used to this VIP treatment.* Maureen collected a trolley, and their cases, as if by magic, were two of the very first into the baggage hall. The customs department was completely deserted and Hector and his wheelchair, with Maureen alongside pushing a trolley full of luggage, slid triumphantly through the doors and into the arrivals hall.

The BA man helped Hector on to his crutches and wheeled away the chair. Hector stood expectantly. He was not sure if the photographers would have preferred him in the chair or on crutches, but the BA man had gone now. Crutches it was. He stood waiting.

Nothing happened. No one approached him. No cries of 'There he is!' and an excited stampede by the oncoming paparazzi. Nothing. No one. Not one lousy reporter. Only Maureen telling him get a move on; they had to get to the bus stop.

Hector could not believe it. He was a hero. Where were they all? Surely someone would want to interview him. He was a hero. He had tackled armed gunmen.

With a huge sigh he hobbled along behind Maureen and out of the terminal into the rain towards the bus stop. *Oh, the injustice of it all,* he thought. Twice he had gone abroad by plane and both times he had come home on crutches.

'It's just not fair,' he muttered under his breath, turned his jacket collar up against the drizzle and hobbled off after her.

Hector's Travels

It was Friday morning and it was raining. Hector peered miserably out of the window of his flat and wondered why God hated him so much. He had been waiting months for this day; he was travelling up north to meet some friends and go to three non-league football grounds he had never seen before. It was a long way to go and it would take him all day. And it was raining. Hard. He would get drenched walking to the station, but what really worried him the most was that if it was raining this hard down here, what would the conditions be like up in the north?

Hector had not travelled much in his life, but he had been up north many times in his passion to visit new grounds and he knew that the weather was always worse there than it was down in the south. A sudden unwelcome vision flashed across his mind as he thought that the games they were going to see might be rained off. What a tragedy – all that way and no football. Surely nothing could be worse.

He had been preparing for the trip for months, ever since he had met his two new friends, Harry and Brian, in the station bar at Huddersfield. Harry and Brian were, like Hector, groundhoppers. In other words, they were two of a peculiar breed of middle-aged men who consider that the only thing in life that matters is to visit a different football ground every Saturday afternoon.

Very strange creatures, groundhoppers. They all tend to fall into the same category of person. Male, middle-aged and single. Definitely single. None of them can drive or would have a car even if they could. They all possess a strange dress sense that separates them from other people and makes them extremely easy to spot on a Saturday morning as they hurry to catch a train or a bus. They all have a passion for anoraks and/or plastic raincoats, often in glaringly bright colours. All carry some form of carrier bag, usually from either their local supermarket or very occasionally some faraway duty-free shop they visited on a brief holiday several years before. These bags are invariably very tatty, with at least one of the handles broken, sometimes both. Groundhoppers are creatures of habit and would no sooner change their carrier bag than, say, their 'lucky' clothes. Again, these always follow the same pattern. From the ground up they invariably consist of the following. Sensible walking shoes (preferably brown). Very important these. Must be comfortable as the hopper in question will frequently miss the last bus home and have to walk several miles to complete his journey. Trousers will be of a sturdy nature. Usually dark in colour, they will be of material thick enough to stop the fiercest bramble penetrating through – very necessary at some of the more rural grounds. Jeans are shunned by the hopping fraternity. No one knows why, since they would be very sensible, but no true hopper would be seen dead in a pair of 501s!

An old work shirt is usually worn under a woolly jumper bearing a legend such as 'CAMRA Beer Festival, Margate 1979'. Again, very important this. All groundhoppers are members of CAMRA and as such are experts on all things drinkable. Well, all things drinkable that are brown, flat and extremely pungent. The complete ensemble is topped off by the obligatory anorak. It is important that it is of some appallingly glary colour. Day-Glo green, sunshine yellow and highlighter orange are popular, although Hector's personal favourite was bright red (he had three). A contrasting lining is vital to the ensemble with a furry one being preferable (Hector's favourite red anorak sported what was once a ghastly yellow fur lining, but had over the years grown to resemble a very jaundiced rabbit with severe alopecia).

Hats are not compulsory and are indeed frowned on in many hopping communities. On the odd occasion they are worn they are nearly always of the old northern 'flat cap' variety, or even an old school balaclava. Gloves are again very rare but the woolly type with cut-out fingers remains very popular in the far north. Scarves have to be very old, very dirty and from the hopper's favourite league club. Hats, scarves and gloves are only ever seen in the depths of winter, as they usually necessitate the carrying of a second bag or are crammed into the pockets of the anorak leaving less room for the essential supplies all groundhoppers carry. These include several pens, several spare pens, bus map, train timetable, notepad, plastic wallet to keep match programme in pristine condition, spare plastic wallet, stopwatch, spare stopwatch, more spare pens, leather purse for small change and some extra spare pens *just in case*!

Hector trudged through the rain on his way to the station wondering if this bank holiday weekend trip was going to be quite what he expected. Maureen, his girlfriend, had turned down the opportunity of going with him on the grounds that she would 'rather gnaw my own arm off than spend three days with you and some grimy hippies drinking flat smelly beer in a no-star hotel halfway up a backstreet of nowhere'. *No sense of adventure*, Hector had thought at the time. Now he wasn't so sure. She might have a point; he ruminated quietly as the rain dripped down the back of his neck.

He walked on and reached the station in plenty of time for his train. It was in fact Maureen who sold him his train ticket at the station and he was very close to abandoning the trip as soon as he saw her standing behind the ticket counter.

'Still going then?' she enquired.

'I suppose so,' replied a very soggy and now quite gloomy Hector.

'You could always change your mind and come with me to see Auntie Maude this weekend,' said Maureen, smiling slightly.

That was it then, decision made. Ticket in pocket, Hector boarded the train and settled back to reread his non-league magazine. He had already read it twice since he had bought it almost a week ago, but it did not seem appropriate to be reading anything else.

He would have to change trains twice to reach his intended destination of Newton Aycliffe where he would meet Brian and Harry in the pub across the road from the station, the Rampant Griffin. A room had been booked for him in a local bed and breakfast establishment, although he had no idea where exactly it was. The trip proper would start the next morning when the three would take a short bus ride to Trimdon, home of Trimdon Town FC, for their local derby in the Basewinger & Huckstable Stainless Steel Rivets Northern Premier Alliance League Division Two with Wingate Wanderers. Trimdon was Brian's local team and he had been waxing lyrically the last time the three had met up about the importance of this fixture for bragging rights in the local district.

Sunday they were to make their way by train a bit further north for a game in the magnificently named Grimshaw Foundries Northern Collieries and Welfare League between the little known Cramlington Dynamo and the even lesser known Higham Dykes FC. Hector had been assured that Higham Dykes was the name of the team and not the nickname for a fierce local lesbian tribe. He had awful visions of the away team being followed by a gaggle of huge crop-haired tattooed biker girls that carried off their victims on the back of grotesquely engineered motorbikes. There was a brief moment when the dreams had turned into a bizarre fantasy, but Hector had decided not to dwell on that.

The trip would finish (hopefully) with an eleven o'clock game in the Heppleton's Anglo-Saxon Lager North-Eastern Conference Division Two (South) game between table-topping Middleton St George and their dire enemies and near neighbours Middleton One Row. These were the type of games that separated the boys from the girls, or in Hector's case the groundhoppers from the sane, he thought as his train lumbered into Newton Aycliffe station.

To his great relief, not only was it not snowing, but it wasn't even raining. It was a very pleasant early evening that greeted Hector as he stepped from the gloominess of the old station out into the sunshine. There was the pub over the road as he had been told, but were his friends there? No, they were not. Still, Hector thought to himself as he supped a very reasonable pint of Lumsdens Old Swordfish, his train had been on time. A great rarity, this had probably surprised Brian and Harry.

A little while later, as he gulped the froth from his third pint, he was starting to get a little worried. Seven o'clock, they had said; it was now almost half past eight and there was no sign of them. What was worse was that he had absolutely no idea where he was supposed to be staying. Why hadn't he thought to get the name and address of the place from Brian, who had arranged it? Because he was dumb, that's why, and now he would probably have to spend the night curled up in the station's waiting room – if it had one – to pay for his stupidity.

The wait went on and on. After six pints Hector decided that he had to do something about his dire situation. This in itself was pretty impressive, as after six pints of Lumsdens Old Swordfish most people normally can't remember their name, let alone their situation. Suddenly the door to the pub flew open and through it came Harry.

''Ere you are then,' gulped Harry, trying to catch his breath. 'Sorry we're so late, but Brian's memory ain't what it was and he forgot what pub we told you to come to. We've been into every pub in the town looking for you,' he went on, 'and you know what it's like: you can't just nip into a pub without having a swift half!'

'It's just a shame that someone had forgotten his wallet,' came a voice from behind him. Brian's bald head pushed its way under Harry's arm. 'Well, we're here now.' Brian grinned. 'Get here all right?'

Hector grinned back at the pair of them. He was suffering from the effects of the six pints of beer now, but he couldn't understand their confusion. After all, they knew he had come up by train and this was the only pub he could see anywhere near the station. Never mind, they were all there now, and Hector walked rather carefully up to the bar to get them all a drink.

With the room swaying slightly before him, Hector tried to focus on his companions as he supped his latest pint. Harry sat opposite him. Quite thin with a receding hairline, Harry was in his late forties with a nose that any ancient Roman warrior would have been proud of. He was dressed in what looked to Hector to be late 1970s style clothes and although he couldn't quite see under the table, he would have bet money that Harry was wearing a pair of flares.

Brian was considerably older. Almost completely bald, he was dressed much more smartly and, Hector thought, looked like he might have a bit of money. He had a very smart, if slightly old-looking shirt and tie on, while Harry sported what was obviously a fake Gucci polo shirt. Neither of them wore anoraks, which slightly surprised Hector as he had never seen either of them without such a garment before.

This made him think about their previous meetings. He had first seen them in the station bar at Huddersfield about a year ago. He himself was on the way home from an FA cup-tie at Kirkburton Welfare (best cheese and leek pasties outside Wales). He saw these two figures huddled over pints and studiously reading programmes he recognised as being from local team Fartown Friday, one of all groundhoppers' 'must go to' grounds. As one of them looked up, he could not remember which; Hector smiled and displayed his programme from that afternoon's game.

'What did you think of the ground?' asked the one who turned out to be Harry.

'Not bad,' replied Hector. 'Bloody good cheese and leek pasties.'

'Best outside Wales,' added Brian.

Hector nodded his agreement.

That was it then. The ice was broken. Hector moved over to their table and they talked and talked about their hobby until it was time for Hector's train. A quick exchange of phone numbers and he was off.

Two weeks later he got a phone call from Brian. They were both coming down south to see Hector's favourite team, Harwood Borough. Hector was delighted and the three of them spent an entertaining afternoon together reminiscing about the various grounds they had been to. Harry and Brian were quite impressed with Harwood Borough and it was in the club's main lounge after the game that the plot was hatched for Hector to visit the pair of them in the north-east one weekend. It had certainly seemed a good idea at the time and still seemed a good idea later that season when they all met up in the Midlands at Tutbury Town in the Ravenshore and Goodbuddy's Linctus Midlands Counties League. It had even seemed a good idea yesterday when Hector was packing for his trip. Now, however, sitting in a dank and gloomy northern hostelry with a couple of drunks who appeared to have no intention of either showing him where he was going to be staying the night or indeed paying for another round, he was not so sure.

He was still not sure when, about an hour later, they stood outside a large and very imposing old Victorian house with a small sign swaying in the breeze which read: MRS MIGGINS'S B&B. *Its gloomy spires rose up into the pitch-black sky and,* Hector thought through his boozy haze, *all it needed was a clap of thunder and a couple of lightning flashes and it could have been straight out of* The Munsters.

'This is it then,' announced Harry.

'It's quite nice for around here,' added Brian.

God only knows what isn't quite nice around here, thought Hector, hoping against hope that he would never find out.

They went up the steps. This took some considerable time as they seemed to go back two for every one they went forward. Reaching the top, Hector pushed the huge ceramic doorbell.

He wasn't sure what he had expected, maybe a distant booming of bells, or even a clanking of chains. What he definitely didn't expect was a tinkling version of 'Rudolf the Red-nosed Reindeer'. In fact, he was not at all sure that it was what he had heard, so he pushed it again. Sure enough, that was what it was. And it was May, for God's sake. What sort of person had a door chime that played 'Rudolf the Red-nosed Reindeer' in May?

He was very soon to find out, as the door suddenly swung open and there before him stood what could only be described as, well, Mrs Miggins.

She was huge – well, at least sideways she was huge. She was fatter than any woman Hector had ever seen. As she was no more than five feet tall, she looked a bit like a huge ball. Given that she was wearing some form of old green jogging suit (although it was a good bet that she had never been out walking, let alone jogging, in her life), Hector decided that she looked like a bowling ball. Probably in her early fifties, she had very obviously dyed blonde hair and a face like an onion bhaji. And she was angry.

'What time of night do you call this then?' she barked in a gruff northern accent.

As she clapped eyes on Hector standing on the top step, her mood changed visibly. The dark scowl on her face cracked into a warm and cavernous smile. Hector suddenly became very nervous.

'Ooh, hello, love,' she beamed. 'You must be Mr Blenkinsop. I've been expecting you.'

She grabbed Hector by the sleeve of his anorak and dragged him through the open doorway. She slammed the door shut behind her with her foot and Hector could not help thinking of himself as a fly being drawn into a spider's web.

A muffled shout came through the solidly closed door. It was Brian. 'We'll pick you up here about ten in the morning,' he yelled.

Hector wanted to cry out and beg them not to leave him alone with this woman, but no words would come into his throat and he started to sweat quite profusely as he heard his friends going back down the steps.

'This way, love,' said Mrs Miggins, shoving Hector up a flight of stairs in the hallway. 'Your room is on the first floor, right next to mine.'

Hector shuddered. It was a nightmare. Where was Maureen when he needed her? Come to that, where was anyone? Mrs Miggins kept pushing him upwards with Hector getting more and more tense with every step.

At the top of the stairs they went round to the left and straight through an open doorway into a room so hideous Hector could hardly believe his eyes. Everything was pink. Bright pink. Carpet, bedspread, curtains, wallpaper, everything. There was a pink lamp on a pink tablecloth on a small bedside table and even a pink toy poodle in the middle of the bed.

'No, love, not in there, you naughty man; that's my room,' came a voice from behind him.

A yank on his arm propelled him back on to the landing and along to another door. A hand appeared under his arm and turned the doorknob. One last shove and he was through the door and standing inside a room roughly the same size as before but so different that it was hard to believe it was in the same building. Rather than everything being bright pink, everything was, well, sort of missing.

Hector saw a dilapidated and obviously well-used single bed in one corner covered by a tatty blanket, and a small wooden chair in another. An old wooden double wardrobe with only one door leant against the far wall. What passed for a carpet was a threadbare rug in the centre of the floor that may or may not have once had a pattern on it, and that was about it. No curtains, no bedspread, no bedside table, no lampshade, nothing.

'I'm sure you will be comfortable in here,' came a voice from the doorway. 'Anyway, if there is anything you want, you know where to find me.'

Another huge shudder racked Hector's body.

'I will leave you to get settled in,' said the bowling ball and left, slamming the door behind her.

Hector sat on the edge of the bed for ages. What was he to do? He was caught up in the middle of what felt like a cross between a 1960s Ealing comedy and a remake of *The Exorcist*.

After what seemed like two hours, but was probably only ten minutes, he decided that maybe things were not as bad as they seemed and he took a good look around. The single light bulb hung from a piece of old brown flex that would have been illegal down south and cast an eerie glow around the whole room. He noticed that the ancient sash window was propped open about three inches, but despite his best efforts he could not get it closed. He looked at the threadbare blanket on the bed and thought gloomily that the night ahead might be a chilly one. A sudden awful vision of pink flashed before his eyes and as his body shook with another huge shiver completely unrelated to the temperature in the room, he leapt to his feet with a sudden resolve. He might be cold in here, but the only other alternative that he could think of was the most terrifying prospect he had encountered since his waste-paper basket caught fire and nearly consumed his collection of Charlie Buchan's *Football Annuals*.

There was no time to waste. He had to stop that woman from coming back.

Too late.

There was a tap on the door. Before Hector could move, the door burst open and in swept the most ghastly apparition he had ever seen. To no surprise at all it was pink. And large. And fluffy, very fluffy. What exactly it was, Hector was not sure, but in a surprisingly delicate little voice it said, 'I hope you are decent, Mr Blenkinsop,' and promptly sat down on the bed.

Hector pushed himself back against the far wall and stared. All he could make out was a pair of huge legs dangling from a sea of pink frills. Masses and masses and masses of pink frills. These legs terminated at the fattest pair of ankles Hector had ever seen and he had once been out with a man mountain of a woman called Mary. The gnarled feet attached to these ankles were so ugly that they drove Hector's eyes upwards. This was a mistake. A big mistake. A huge mistake.

What he saw above the swollen dangling legs was so unbelievably comical that he had to stifle a laugh. It was hard to describe in mere words, but resembled the biggest, fattest birthday cake the world had ever seen. Yards and yards of brushed pink nylon were wound round Mrs Miggins's body, or at least Hector assumed it was Mrs Miggins, he couldn't be absolutely sure. Keeping it all in place appeared to be about twelve miles of pink ribbon. This ribbon was stretching itself so tightly that the colour of her legs was starting to resemble the colour of the material more and more as the seconds ticked by. This was obviously becoming uncomfortable for the wearer and suddenly the room seemed to move as she shifted position. The bed gave a huge groan at approximately the same time as Hector did, as the top half of Mrs Miggins appeared like a gigantic pink whale surfacing for air.

If anything the top half was worse than the bottom half. Now he could clearly see that it was indeed Mrs Miggins inside this concoction. Her hair was tied in a big pink bow of the same material that held the main garment together (Hector was not sure what exactly the main garment was meant to be, a nightdress, a dressing gown, a tent or what). Her face resembled an explosion in a paint shop. She had put on fake eyelashes that were so long they waved around like fly swatters as she blinked. About half a pound of bright crimson lipstick had been applied to her bloated lips and so much blusher and other powder had been slapped on her face that it fell in little pink clouds as she spoke.

'I hope you will like it here.' She smiled. 'It will be nice to have a man about the place for a few days. I haven't had a lot of guests since my husband died last year.'

Hector recoiled in horror. The beer he had drunk was a forgotten memory. He had never been so sober in all his life. His back was so firmly pressed against the wall that the sweat was beginning to darken the ancient wallpaper. He thought he had a good idea why she had not had many guests lately and he also had a good idea why Mr Miggins had died. *Suicide*, he thought to himself. *Undoubtedly suicide.*

'I can't go on calling you Mr Blenkinsop,' the pink monstrosity whispered. 'What's your first name?'

'H–H–Hector,' he stammered, lowering his eyes as he did so.

This was his biggest mistake so far, for below the huge flabby neckline swelled the most enormous pair of breasts Hector had ever seen in his life. Granted he was no expert on the subject, but these were enormous. They made Mary look like a stick insect. Fortunately only the top half of these gargantuan appendages were visible, rising like two enormous mountains through clouds of pink nylon.

I only hope they are safe in there, he thought desperately. *God knows what damage they could do if they escaped.*

'You must call me Ethel,' came a soft voice from somewhere above the mountains.

Hector could not take his eyes off those breasts. They were possibly the most terrifying things he had ever seen and the cleavage between them appeared to be endless from his angle. Hector was sure that a grown man could slide down there and never be seen again. He wondered if any man ever had. He suddenly wondered if that had been the terrible fate of Mr Miggins. He gulped.

'You might be a smidgen more comfortable next door in my room,' came the voice.

Hector could think of nothing worse. 'I… I… um…' he mumbled.

'That's settled then,' she replied and an arm the size of a side of beef reached out and grabbed at Hector's sleeve.

He was trapped. He couldn't go back any more and the pink monstrosity was now sliding across the bed towards him. There was only one temporary escape route. He would never make the door; anyway, that was what she wanted. Hector made a dive under the outstretched arm and flung himself towards the open doorway of the wardrobe. He landed in a heap on the floor, the clothes he had started to put away spread all over him.

'I… I… I,' he continued to stammer.

'That's all right, love, I didn't realise you hadn't finished sorting yourself out yet. I will go and make myself more comfortable. Don't bother to knock when you come in,' she said. 'I will not be decent, I promise.'

She gave a giggle that made her chest wobble like the sum total of every jelly at every birthday party there had ever been. Hector was sure that if she didn't stop soon it would cause an earthquake. He felt the bile rising in his throat as he slowly rose to his feet.

And then she was gone. A huge swirl of pink nylon caused a near gale to explode around the room and the door slammed shut behind her. Hector slumped to the floor. He was still sweating profusely and he could hear his heart banging inside his chest as if it was trying to escape.

What could he do? He knew that unless he did something quickly, he would suffer the same fate that poor Mr Miggins undoubtedly had.

For once in his life Hector reacted swiftly. This was not a natural reaction for him, but this was an emergency and his body reacted magnificently. He leapt to his feet, grabbed the chair in the corner of the room and jammed it under the door handle. He gave it a couple of tugs and it held. *That should hold her*, he thought. He wasn't at all convinced, but he could think of no other option. It was almost midnight. Even if he could get out of the building, where would he go? He had an awful vision of Mrs Miggins chasing him down the road in all her glory and nearly fainted at the thought.

He sat on the chair. It was not easy, as it was propped up at an angle, but fear had overtaken him now and if that was how he had to spend the night, then so be it. His fingernails dug into the old wood of the chair and he waited. He could not stop sweating and his heart was still beating far too fast, although at least it appeared to be staying where it was.

He waited.

About fifteen minutes later he heard a small tapping at the door.

'Cooee, Hector.'

His fingers tightened even more and his heart moved up several beats again.

'I'm ready for you now, you naughty little man,' she whispered.

Hector was paralysed. He could no longer feel his fingers and he thought his chest would explode at any moment.

'Come on,' went the voice. 'Don't be shy.'

Suddenly the mood outside the door changed and the handle started to rattle alarmingly.

'Come on,' she snapped. 'I know you are in there. Don't be frightened,' she continued. 'I wont eat you. Well, not unless you ask me nicely.' She giggled again.

Hector could feel the door shake. He thought that if she didn't stop soon he would fall off his chair.

Abruptly the shaking stopped. So did the voice. A few seconds later he heard the door to the next room slam. He was safe. For now at least. What he would do in the morning he had no idea, but for now he was safe.

He contemplated going to bed, but wondered what would happen if she came back. He decided to stay where he was on the chair and relaxed slightly. His fingers started to throb as the blood flowed through them again. He smiled slightly to himself. He sat and waited for the dawn.

After a long time he dozed off.

The morning came eventually. It had been a long night. Twice during that time the indomitable Mrs Miggins had tried to gain access to Hector's room, once collapsing outside the door in tears as she softly begged him to let her in. Hector was having none of it.

After watching dawn break through the window, he slowly rose to his feet and quietly moved over to the wardrobe. He flung his belongings back in the holdall he had brought with him and eased himself towards the door. He very carefully slid back the chair, turned the handle and pulled the door open gently. To his great relief it did not squeak.

He inched himself outside and crept past the wide open door of Mrs Miggins's room. He could see her lying on top of the bed looking like a pink scale model of the Atlas Mountains and he could hear her gently snoring away to herself. He edged down the stairs and up the hall towards the front door.

As he reached the door he paused. He thought he heard something behind him. He turned round. Coming down the stairs at a rate of about ten yards per second was dear old Mrs Miggins, her chest bouncing up and down like two massive pink barrage balloons trying to break free of their moorings.

Hector panicked. His hands started to sweat. He couldn't turn the doorknob. She was getting nearer. He tried again. At last the handle started to turn and he yanked the door open with all his might. He could hear her behind him. She appeared to be whimpering. He threw himself through the doorway and pulled it shut behind him.

He heard, or at least he thought he heard, a crash as Mrs Miggins got to the door a second or two late.

That could be messy, he thought to himself as he sprinted up the road.

A short while later as he sat in the station café having a nice fried breakfast – Maureen would definitely not have approved – he wondered what he was going to do. He wanted to go straight home on the first train south, but that would be rude to his friends. It wasn't their fault what had happened. Or was it? It was they who had booked him into that pink bordello after all. After a second helping of toast, he decided to see what the day would bring. He was sure he could find somewhere else to stay the night. He would ask Brian and Harry when they arrived. He could see the doorway of the house from hell from his seat in the café and so he could intercept them when they turned up to collect him.

He must have fallen asleep, because the next thing he knew Brian was shaking him awake. And he didn't look too happy.

'What have you done to Auntie Ethel?' he shouted.

'Sorry, who?' replied a sleepy Hector, not yet realising what had happened.

'My auntie, who had the decency to put you up last night, is in a hell of a state,' went on his friend. 'What on earth did you do to her? We found her sitting in the hallway crying her eyes out.'

'It's not what I did to her that's the problem,' exclaimed Hector, 'it's what she wanted to do with me!'

Hector went on to relay the tale and slowly Brian's anger receded.

Harry thought it would make a bloody good film. Hector rather hoped he was right.

'I'm sorry,' Brian said after a while. 'She can get a bit frisky sometimes since Uncle Mordecai passed away.'

Uncle Mordecai, thought Hector, *what sort of name is that*?

'What exactly did he die of?' he enquired.

'Fright, apparently; his heart just stopped.'

Hector gave a knowing nod and the three friends left the café and ambled towards the bus stop. Whilst they waited for the bus, Brian told Hector that he could probably stay at his house that night in his brother's room. Quentin was away for the weekend, so there was plenty of space.

Mordecai, Quentin, pondered Hector. *What sort of family was this*? Still, it had to be an improvement on last night.

They sat on the top deck of the bus as it sailed past the front door of the house, visions from which Hector was sure would dominate most of his nightmares for the next few years at least, if not the rest of his life. 'At least things can't get any worse,' he said softly to himself.

He was wrong!

The journey to Trimdon was completely uneventful – at least it was for Hector, who slept soundly the entire way. By half past ten they were standing outside the ramshackle-looking ground listening to Brian proudly relating the club's history. *Founded as recently as 1965, they had not really achieved anything much at all*, thought Hector as he tried to listen attentively. Their greatest achievement seemed to be winning the Basewinger & Huckstable Stainless Steel Rivets Northern Premier Alliance League Division Three title two years ago (although technically at the time it was called the Crambletons Crumpets Northern Premier Alliance League Division Three). Hector tried to show his enthusiasm for this obviously memorable local achievement, but he was so tired it was taking all his concentration just to stay awake.

Brian decided to take Hector to his house before the game so he could leave his bag there. It seemed like a good idea at the time, but after fifteen minutes' walk Hector wished he had just stayed at the ground and waited for it to open.

Eventually they arrived at Brian's abode and very comfortable it looked to Hector. Inside it was clean and tidy and he wondered who did all the cleaning; Brian didn't seem the type to do it himself and he knew for a fact that he didn't have a partner. *Never mind*, he thought, *it looks better than last night's accommodation*. And he shivered violently at the nightmarish thoughts that flew into his mind.

Realising Hector was very tired, Brian and Harry suggested that he had an hour or two's nap before they left for the ground and Hector was soon blissfully asleep upstairs lying on what was apparently Quentin's bed.

He was woken at about one o'clock by Brian with a cup of tea and they were soon on their way back to the ground, Hector feeling much more refreshed than he had the first time they had arrived there.

It was not as poor a ground as Hector had first imagined, now he was more rested. It had quite a nice little stand and the clubhouse was excellent. There were, of course, the essential ingredients of all non-league club bars. The non-matching furniture, the table legs supported by beer mats and the array of other clubs' pennants behind and above the bar (including, naturally, one from Leyton Orient FC).

The three sat in the corner of the main bar drinking pints of Musselthwaites Amber Throat Warmer and happily read the excellent programme. Programmes were Hector's main passion in life. There were times when he honestly thought more of his programmes than he did of Maureen, but he hoped he had never let on to her about this. In reality Maureen had known this all along, but she forgave him and knew secretly what Hector did not, and that was that it would not always be so.

This particular programme was splendid, thought Hector. A good quality colour cover, lots of reading inside and page after page of statistics. All groundhoppers love their statistics. Most can quote them off the top of their heads just as well as they can recite the national anthem. Who won the 1956 Amateur Cup, who played left back, who scored the first goal and probably the Christian names of the two linesmen? Hector was particularly good at this having spent many, many years before he had met Maureen reading and rereading all manner of football books.

No groundhopper is worth his salt unless he can alphabetically list the teams in the Follingdale and Normans Agricultural Implements East Anglian Combination (all three divisions). Or even the last seventeen winners (in order, of course) of the Edna Grimble Memorial Shield (given to the player scoring the most own goals in the Thrapshaw and Fosset Flanges Lancastrian Intermediate League). Hector would pass these tests with flying colours and any others thrown at him. Brian and Harry were secretly amazed at his vast store of useless knowledge. They had met many, many groundhoppers on their journeys, but Hector was the king of them all. They listened in fascinated awe as he recalled the entire Shepton Mallet team that had played in the 1965 FA Amateur Cup semi-final second leg. There were, of course, very special reasons why Hector could do this, but Brian and Harry weren't to know that.

At exactly ten minutes to kick-off they left the confines of the bar and ventured out into the ground. As the announcer cleared his throat, the three friends all pulled out identical notebooks from the inner sanctums of their anoraks and waited, pens poised for the team changes. This ritual is the single most important event of the afternoon for a groundhopper. While most casual fans will scribble any changes on the team sheet inside the programme, all groundhoppers will have already secreted said journal into a secure plastic wallet and placed it in their inside pocket. (Note: all groundhoppers' anoraks have to have inside pockets. Without them they are as much use to a true hopper as a copy of *Thandor's Guide to the World's Best Lagers.*)

Programmes are to be treated with true reverence. As sacred an article as a Bible is to any clergyman and probably kept in better condition than most. They are read through once and once only (presumably in case the printing fades) and filed securely away on reaching home. The fact that these programmes probably never see the light of day again once they have been filed is of absolutely no consequence to a hopper; it is enough just to know that they are *there*!

Team changes duly noted; they settled down to watch the game. To be truthful it was not much of a match, but Trimdon Town ran out two–nil winners, which made Brian very happy. The small band of Wingate Wanderers fans had lived up to their name and wandered off back to their own club about three miles away before the whistle had blown for full time.

Brian was in such a good mood in the bar afterwards that not only did he buy the first round, but he managed to get Harry to buy the second. This seemed to be a great rarity and Hector made a mental note of it. When he thought about it later, he did seem to have spent quite a large amount of his time since his arrival ordering drinks at the bar, but as he had not paid anything for his previous night's 'accommodation' he was not too worried. Again the thought of last night brought a shiver to his body, despite the warm May temperatures. Once more he could picture swathes of pink nylon and flesh bearing down upon him and he drained his glass in one gulp.

'You all right?' asked Brian.

'Yes, I guess so,' replied Hector. 'I just had a rather nasty thought.'

'You look like you have seen a ghost,' Brian remarked. 'Maybe it's the beer,' he went on. 'Too much of that stuff will have you seeing pink elephants.'

This was all too much for poor Hector to take and he lurched off to the toilet where he was promptly sick.

They left the bar about eight, by which time they had all drunk far too much and Hector was staggering up the road trying to work out how many times Harry had gone to the bar. He was sure it was only the once, but he was having so much trouble putting one foot in front of the other that he thought it would be dangerous to try to think of anything else too deeply.

They arrived back at Brian's soon after and Hector could vaguely remember watching TV for a while and drinking a mug of coffee, before total tiredness overcame him and he made his excuses and retired to bed.

The next conscious thought he had was many hours later in the middle of the night. He stirred in the blackness and was absolutely sure he could sense someone else in the room. He thought he must be dreaming and promptly nodded off again.

Suddenly he felt a cold hand on his bum.

'Ooh, what's this then?' said a high-pitched but undoubtedly male voice.

Hector was immediately awake and sat up sharply as the bedside light came on. Lying next to him in pale yellow silk pyjamas was a funny-looking round-faced man with a beaming smile.

'You must be one of Brian's little friends,' he announced. 'Now what are you doing in my bed?'

Hector realised in a flash who it was. It was Quentin, Brian's brother. And he had come home in the middle of the night. He leapt straight out of bed and made for the door. He was naked, having been too tired (and drunk) to put his pyjamas on when he came up to bed. A silky yellow arm tried to grab him as he passed, but Hector swerved round it as he ran from the room.

'There's no need to run, big boy,' said the other voice admiringly. 'There's plenty of room for two.'

I can't take much more of this, thought Hector as he charged down the stairs three at a time.

He reached the front door, wrenched it open and bounded outside. It was only as the cool night-time air hit him that he realised he was still naked. As he turned round he saw the front door swing shut behind him with a click.

Oh great, he thought, *at least last time I had my clothes.* He didn't know what to do and really started to panic when the door opened revealing Quentin in his yellow jim-jams framed in the doorway.

Hector leapt over the garden wall. It was only three feet high and he cleared it in one bound. Unfortunately the other side had an eight-foot drop and he crashed down into the undergrowth with a yelp.

What happened next Hector was not too sure. He knew his ankle hurt and he felt someone put a blanket around him. Hands helped him up and back into the house where he slumped into a large armchair. He looked up.

'Ooh, I am sorry,' said Quentin, standing in front of him. 'You gave me such a start.'

What the bloody hell do you think you gave me? thought Hector, trying to lift himself out of the chair. His ankle hurt like hell and he didn't think he would be able to make a run for it.

Just then Brian walked in from the kitchen in a voluminous paisley dressing gown. 'Are you all right?' he asked Hector.

'I'm not sure,' Hector gasped, 'my ankle is very sore.'

'I'm not surprised,' squeaked Quentin. 'Why did you run away like that?'

Hector was just about to answer when Brian thrust a mug of coffee into his hands. 'Here, drink this,' he said, 'and let's have a look at that ankle.'

Some time later Hector sat alone in the chair. His ankle was bandaged and Quentin and Brian had gone back to bed. Quentin had apologised profusely for barging in on him; he had driven home early from a friend's house after they had apparently had some sort of tiff.

Despite various offers, Hector had insisted on remaining in the chair for the night, although he knew sleep was out of the question. He stayed in exactly the same position the entire night. Eyes fixed on the closed door, with the empty coffee mug clenched in his fist like a weapon. This time he was dreading the dawn. He knew not what it would bring, but he also knew that the way things were going it would not be pleasant. For once in his life he was right!

The morning finally arrived, and as the first rays of sunlight appeared through the front room windows, Hector finally closed his eyes and slept.

Brian bounded into the room about four hours later with yet more coffee and an explosion of apologies. Hector was too tired to listen attentively, but it appeared that Quentin was quite often away on Saturday nights and had never arrived back in the early hours before.

Life slowly returned to Hector's tired body and after a good wash and shave he felt considerably better. Quentin had gone out around eight o'clock, obviously embarrassed by the whole affair, and was not expected back until late the following evening. Brian offered Hector his own room for that night, in case he was worried that Quentin might reappear, and as Hector knew that it would be damn nigh impossible to get home on a Sunday, he accepted the offer.

Harry arrived about two hours later and nearly fell over laughing when Hector told him what had happened.

'It's just not your weekend,' said Harry beamingly.

'It's just not my bloody life!' said Hector.

The train journey to the tiny hamlet of Cramlington took ages and again Hector caught up on a bit of sleep on the way. His ankle was not too bad, but it was still quite sore as he hobbled his way down a long leafy lane to the compact and rather delightfully positioned ground of Cramlington Dynamo FC. There were not a lot of facilities at the ground and no floodlights, but the bar was comfy if rather small. Unsurprisingly it was Hector who went to the bar first to get the drinks in and he noticed to his surprise that there was no Leyton Orient pennant to be seen. *How odd*, he thought to himself. *I thought it was compulsory*.

He was determined to keep his drinking to a minimum today, as he did not feel at all good and he thought only part of that was down to a lack of sleep, but halfway through his first pint of Plimwicks Golden Obsession he perked up considerably.

The programme was not at all like the one for the game the day before, but it was a programme nonetheless and protocol insisted that it be treated with the same reverence. It was basic, but did list the teams and the league tables although they were about three weeks out of date. The half-time quiz had obviously been photocopied out of a Liverpool programme of about twenty years ago and even Hector struggled to answer some of the questions. There was only time for three pints each before the game, although Hector still somehow bought two of the rounds, with Brian getting the other, and then it was off out into the spring sunshine to watch the game.

Quite a crowd had built up outside and a section of them made Hector start to feel nervous. It would appear that his almost joking worry about the away team's nickname was coming true. They were called Higham Dykes FC after the village they came from, but standing behind the goal they were warming up into was the dodgiest group of women Hector had ever seen in his life. There were about fifteen of them, all with cropped hair, nose rings and various tattoos. Several of them were wearing badges sporting the unforgettable legend 'North Yorkshire Lesbian Alliance'. Hector had absolutely no idea in the world who – or what – would form an alliance with this bunch, but he didn't like the look of them one bit and resolved to keep well out of their way.

Harry returned from the toilet to tell the others that he had been told by some of the locals that these women had adopted this team the season before because of its name and that they had been an embarrassment to the club ever since. Club officials had even thought about changing the club's name during the summer, but they had all thought that the novelty would wear off and these people would lose interest in the close season. They had been wrong and the numbers of this collection of unfemininity had actually risen during the current season.

The match kicked off, and what a good game it turned out to be. The away team, cheered on by much yelping and screaming by their relatively newly acquired gang of fans, roared into an early two-goal lead. Each goal was accompanied by loud whooping noises from behind the goal, although it was noticeable that the goal scorers were none too keen to rush towards their apparently adoring supporters.

Dynamo though were not beaten yet and pulled a goal back on the half-hour mark. Then, with almost the last kick of the half, they forced an equaliser. This did not go down well with the travelling fans and surreal chants of 'Come on you Dykes' lapsed into much obscene catcalling at the home players as they left the pitch.

During the half-time interval, Hector decided to queue up at the tea hut for a pie. This was yet another of his mistakes. In front of him in the queue were two of the larger members of the band of Higham 'fans' and they were obviously not best pleased with life.

'What the fook is going on at the front of this queue?' demanded one.

'Fnunk nus,' muttered the other.

'Whf dnt yo pff thm art de wy?' she went on, accompanied by a curious clicking sound.

Hector couldn't help it; he laughed.

The larger one of the two, the one with the speech impediment, turned round and glared at Hector. 'Wht th fk ur yo lffing ut?' she mumbled. Click, click.

Hector was immediately aware of the girl's problem. She had what looked like an iron bar through her tongue and the clicking sound was the noise it made as it hit the back of her teeth every time she spoke. Hector was aghast at the sight that confronted him. This creature not only had the metal bar in her tongue, but she had a ring through her nose that was connected to her top lip by a chain. Most of both eyebrows were hidden by small metal rings and she had at least half a dozen earrings in each ear of various sizes and colours.

'Wll, I sked yo a keftiun.' She glared at him.

'I'm sorry,' Hector gasped, but he was still unable to stop smiling.

'Yud bttr be,' the horrific apparition spat out. As she did so she dribbled down her 'North Yorkshire Lesbian Alliance' badge that she was wearing on the front of her huge plain black T-shirt.

The two turned round and continued mumbling unintelligibly until they were served. How the bloke serving knew what the big one wanted Hector could not guess, but he sure as hell wasn't going to ask.

Hector got his pie, but disaster struck as he attempted to squirt some brown sauce on to it. He squeezed the dispenser too hard and a stream of thick gooey sauce squirted right across the back of his newly found friend with the metal face. She spun round with true hatred in her bloodshot eyes and a fist the size of a large packet of sausages shot out towards Hector's face. He managed to duck under it, although he dropped his pie in doing so, then he turned and ran. His ankle hurt like hell, but he was stopping for nothing. To his surprise the creatures from the black lagoon didn't chase him, but Metal Mouth raised her fist at him and yelled something like 'Ll se yo ltr!'

Hector quickly found his friends and Harry looked fit to burst. He had seen the whole incident from where he stood. 'You should be on the stage,' he chuckled. 'The things that happen to you are funnier than *Monty* bloody *Python*. You should change your name to Norman Wisdom.'

'I think I will change my name to "Gone Home Early",' Hector panted. 'If it's all the same with you, I think I might get an earlier train back.'

'There's one in about fifteen minutes,' said the now smiling Brian. 'Are you sure you want to go?'

'Too damn right,' said Hector. 'There's no need for you two to leave. I'll get the train back to Trimdon and meet you in the pub at the end of your road.'

'Okay,' said Brian, 'if you're sure. It's a bloody good game this; be a shame to miss the second half.'

With that Hector limped away from the ground. He looked this way and that as he walked back up the lane to the station, but was relieved to see that no one was following him. As he turned back to face the way he was going, he noticed a large black van reversing at some speed towards him. Suddenly he felt a huge blow on the back of his head.

Oops, he thought as he slipped into unconsciousness. It was to be his last thought for some time.

Hector awoke abruptly. He had no idea where he was, but it was very dark. His head hurt like crazy and his ankle throbbed relentlessly. It took a few seconds for his eyes to adjust to the conditions and he used the time to try to think what on earth had happened.

He remembered the van and he remembered the pain in his head, then nothing. He groaned. He was not sure, but he would have put money on the fact that he was in the back of the very same van. He was also sure it was something to do with those awful women at the football. Unusually for Hector, he was right on both counts.

He looked at his watch (it had a luminous dial – another essential item for groundhoppers). It was a quarter past eight. He must have been here for over four hours. He was not tied up or gagged, which was a relief, but with the state of his head and his ankle, he wasn't going anywhere fast anyway.

He edged towards the doors at the rear of the van and tried to see out. It was hopeless. It was pitch black outside and although he could see a slight glow he was unable to see what it was through the crack in the van doors. He could hear voices. Only very faintly and he couldn't make out exactly what they were saying, but there were definitely people out there. He imagined whose voices they were likely to belong to and he shuddered. He had been doing a lot of shuddering these past few days and once again his mind was filled with terrible images of the past forty-eight hours or so. He suddenly didn't feel very well.

He had two choices as far as he could work out. He could either kick the doors open and run for all he was worth, or he could just lie back down and await his fate, whatever it might turn out to be. Plan one seemed good, although his ankle was throbbing badly and he wasn't sure how far he would get before he was run down and he also didn't know how many of them were out there. Plan two was worse. He could not imagine what these women would want with him, but he was pretty sure that whatever it was, it would make the last two nights look like some kind of picnic.

He groaned again. Not very loudly, but sound carries at night and it was the latest in a long line of mistakes he had made that fateful weekend.

The voices outside got louder.

'Sounds like Sleeping Beauty is awake,' said one.

'Mff ny tkng sndg,' came a muffled reply.

Oh my God, thought Hector. *I know whom that voice belongs to.*

The doors burst open and there, framed in the opening, was Metal Mouth herself. With the glow of a nearby bonfire gleaming off her facial ornaments, she looked even more horrific than she had done in daylight. It was all Hector's nightmares come true at once.

'Wht hv ve gt er ven,' it mumbled.

'At least you didn't kill him,' said her companion.

'Pty,' Princess Metallica replied.

'Let's get him out in the light and have a look at him,' said the coherent member of the kidnap committee.

Two huge but noticeably smooth arms grabbed Hector and he was yanked out of the van in one swift movement. He hit the ground with a bang.

'Ouch!' he yelled.

'Sht op,' muttered the metal-mouthed one.

Hector sat up and looked around him. They were in a clearing in the woods. There was a campfire burning happily in the middle of the clearing and the van that he had just parted company with was parked to one side under some very large and very dark-looking trees. There did not appear to be anyone else around.

That's good, thought Hector. *At least there doesn't appear to be a whole tribe of them.* Mind you, these two on their own were more than enough for Hector. Not the bravest or toughest of souls at the best of times, with his head and ankle in the state they currently were, it was probable that a couple of junior school girls could have given him a good kicking, never mind these two big crop-haired thugs.

Metal Mouth lifted a large black boot as if to kick him and he tensed, waiting for the impact.

'Careful,' said the other one. 'Don't damage the goods, we don't want to lower its value.'

Value, thought Hector. *What the hell is she talking about?* 'Er, w–w–what are you going to do with me?' he stammered.

'We're not too sure yet,' replied the less dangerous one.

'Kll hm,' the other one mumbled.

Hector tried to scramble back to the van, but a massive boot slammed down an inch from his hand and he decided to stay exactly where he was.

'Wh dd w kll hm n fd hm t th dgs?' Metal Mouth asked her colleague.

The other one gave a little laugh and turned towards Hector. 'My friend Jessica here would like to dispose of you, as you can probably gather,' she said. 'But I have other ideas.'

She leered at Hector and he felt seriously sick to his stomach.

Although not as awful as her chum, this creature was certainly no oil painting. She had at least as many earrings as her friend but, apart from a stud in one nostril, she had no facial metalwork at all. She must have been twelve stone at least and she had two ghastly tattoos on her arms. And her breath stank like hell. She had pushed her face very close to his as she spoke and the stench from her mouth nearly made Hector retch.

Suddenly she clamped her mouth on to Hector's and kissed him. Hector was so stunned, his mouth fell open and her tongue shot inside like a rat up a drainpipe.

After what seemed like an age, she pulled away and Hector grimaced in disgust. Both of the hideous creatures were laughing loudly as he tried to spit away her drool.

'You'll do for me,' said the one that had violated him. 'Just look after me and I'll keep you in one piece.'

Hector was terrified. He had never been so scared in his life. For the first time he got some flashbacks from the last two nights and he didn't shudder. Compared to this they were practically enjoyable.

He looked up at his captors and could no longer keep the contents of his stomach inside him. The two of them were locked in an embrace that looked like two grizzly bears trying to eat each other. They broke away as they saw him retch and burst out laughing again.

'Get him to wash his mouth out,' said bear number two, 'and then bring him into the van.' With this she pulled off her 'Yorkshire Pride' T-shirt and started to undo her jeans.

Hector couldn't move. Her body was repulsive; her two pendulous breasts were tattooed with something or other and had a chain linking them together via nipple rings. Her stomach flopped over the ridiculously tiny pair of knickers she was wearing under her jeans and her tree trunk legs were covered in tattoos.

Hector turned away. Now he really was in a jam. Big Jessica was lumbering towards him with a grin that threatened to turn her face inside out. Hector recoiled in horror at the thought of what was going to happen to him. If the other one's body was repulsive, he couldn't bear to think about this one's. She was nearly half as big again and as she moved towards him Hector could distinctly hear metal clanking together.

God only knows where else she has metalwork, he thought as he contemplated hurling himself at her. He wasn't sure exactly what effect it would have on the creature from the black lagoon, but he couldn't just stand there and do nothing. He put his head down and charged.

At that exact moment two figures burst out of the woods and into the clearing. It was Brian and Harry and they had come to the rescue.

Hector could see none of this as he was now on a collision course with big Jessica's huge stomach. The two figures emerging from the woods at some speed had distracted both of the kidnappers and they turned to see what was going on. Hector tensed his neck muscles to collide with the soft quivering mass of Jessica's belly, but as she turned to look at the intruders he caught her fair and square on one of her gargantuan and solid hips.

Once again Hector's life dissolved into blackness.

This time when he awoke, he kept his eyes closed. He listened carefully. All he could hear was the crackling of the fire. Very slowly he opened one eye. He could see no one, just the fire burning as it had before. The van was still where it was, but there was a movement in it and it gently rocked backwards and forwards.

Now's my chance, thought Hector and he jumped to his feet. 'Oooowwwww!' he screamed as the foot attached to his bad ankle hit the ground.

The doors at the back of the van flew open and Hector's eyes widened in terror. Out of the back of the van jumped a smiling Brian and Harry and they ran over to him. He couldn't see the horror sisters and suddenly an awful thought crept into his mind.

'Don't worry,' said Harry, 'we've tied the two bitches up in the van. They won't be going anywhere too soon.'

Hector let out a huge sigh of relief.

'The big one knocked herself out on a tree stump when you hit her,' said Harry, 'and the other one didn't give us too much trouble without her mate, so we tied them up together.'

'Trouble is,' chipped in Brian, 'the two old cows are probably enjoying it!'

They told Hector that they had seen him being bundled into the van and had tried to follow it. It had taken them over four hours to track it down and they had been watching the scene from back in the woods since they had arrived at about the same time that Hector had emerged from the van. They were going to wait and see what happened, but when they saw the smaller one taking her kit off, they thought they had better make a move.

'Christ,' said Harry. 'I haven't seen tits like that since Brian's Auntie Ethel got pissed up in the Stoat and Lizard last New Year's Eve and did a striptease, although those ones never had their own bog chain, of course.'

Hector's body gave its customary shiver at the thought.

Twenty minutes later the three were walking – or, in Hector's case, limping – back towards the station.

'What about those animals back there?' Hector asked.

'They'll be all right for now,' said Brian. 'I will phone the police anonymously when we get back to Trimdon and tell them where they are.'

Hector gave a little smile. That would do nicely.

It was gone eleven when they got back to Brian's house. Too late for Harry to go home, so various sleeping arrangements had to be made, although fortunately Quentin wasn't around to complicate matters.

Brian had rung the police from Trimdon station and told them of the miscreants' location and exactly what they had done. Hector had made it quite plain that the last thing in the world he wanted was to set eyes on them ever again, so Brian was most insistent that he would not give any names. The police said that obviously they would not be able to press any charges, but that they would go and release them when they could. Brian warned them to make sure they sent more than one carload just in case they had got loose and were looking for revenge on the male gender.

Sleeping arrangements sorted back at the house – Brian was indeed going to use Quentin's bedroom – Hector nervously snuggled under Brian's duvet and thought about what a weekend it had been. Harry, who was spending the night downstairs on the couch, had suggested on the way home that Hector should write a book about it all, but Hector had said that no one would believe it if he did. Her pulled the duvet tightly up to his chin and prepared for yet another sleepless night. His tiredness soon overcame him, however, and in minutes he had drifted off into a deep and mercifully dreamless sleep.

They were all up early the next morning and after Hector had decided that he might as well go to the game at Middleton with the other two as it was on his way home, they set off to the station whistling the tune from *The Great Escape*.

They arrived at the ground with plenty of time to spare for the eleven o'clock kick-off, but Hector refused a quick pint in the bar in favour of a good strong cup of coffee. His ankle felt a good deal better after a decent night's sleep and Brian had bandaged it up tight for him. He even had a little smile on his face as he queued up for his drink.

Sudden fear overtook him as he heard a voice behind him yell 'Oi!' loudly and he broke into a cold sweat as he tentatively turned round expecting to see the Ugly Sisters looming up behind him. The relief that coursed through his whole body as he realised that the noise had been made by a father whose small son had wandered on to the pitch and that there were no crop-haired monster women to be seen was truly memorable.

The game was a good one and Hector temporarily forgot his troubles and really enjoyed himself. The away team, Middleton One Row came from two goals down to draw three–all with their hosts, Middleton St George, and the comparatively large crowd seemed in general good humour as the threesome wandered back towards the station.

Hector had one last scare as someone with cropped hair and boots pulled up sharply on a bike outside the station as they arrived, but as soon as he realised it was a boy he nervously shook hands with Brian and Harry and scurried away to catch his train.

As he sat on the train he wondered exactly how much he should tell Maureen of his adventures. It wasn't that she wouldn't believe him – after all, he did have Harry and Brian to back him up if he needed it – it was just that he didn't want to worry her. You never know, she might not let him go on another one of these trips if she knew the troubles he got himself into.

With a laugh Hector realised that he wouldn't go on another trip like this even if Maureen insisted that he did. He patted his inside pocket to check that his programmes were still there. What he had gone through was bad enough, but if he had lost his programmes it would have been a true disaster.

As the rolling countryside of Yorkshire sped past the train window, Hector once more fell into a deep sleep. This time he dreamt of pink elephants and grizzly bears with boots on and big fat yellow fairies, and as he slept a slight smile crept over his lips. The train sped on and so did Hector's unconscious imagination.

Hector's Final

The ball lay in the back of the net. Hector stood on the terracing behind the goal and time seemingly stood still. All around him was chaos. People were leaping into the air and screaming with delight. Even Maureen was leaping up and down while still clinging to Hector's arm. But Hector was calm. Inside he thought he was probably reaching boiling point, but outside he just smiled.

It had really happened. The greatest moment of his sporting life. Right there in front of him. Harwood Borough had made it to the final of the FA Trophy. At last. They were two–nil up after the first leg at home and now, with just two minutes left in the second leg, they had scored. It was now one–nil on the day and three–nil on aggregate. There was no stopping them now. And everyone could see it. Joy was unconfined all around him.

Suddenly it all became too much for Hector and he leapt into the air. As he leapt he screamed. At the top of his voice. Coming as it did about six seconds after everyone else's celebrations it all looked rather silly. As everybody else was coming back to earth, Hector was just taking off.

But nobody cared. It is doubtful if anyone even noticed. Harwood Borough were going to Highbury, the venue for this season's Trophy final.

Everyone had agreed before the second leg in the club bar at Cannock Rovers that it just wasn't going to be the same, what with Wembley being a pile of rubble now. But the new Highbury was a pretty good consolation prize. Only a year old, the new stadium was just about as close to being the eighth wonder of the world as Hector had ever seen in his life. He had been there about four times with Maureen, who was an Arsenal fan, and he couldn't believe that his Harwood Borough were going to be playing there.

All this had been speculation though. They all knew that Boro should be capable of holding a two-goal lead against Cannock, but football was, as they say, a funny old game.

It only needed Cannock to nick an early goal and Hector just knew that Boro would be in trouble. Panic would set in and then anything could happen. And Hector didn't know if he could cope with the disappointment of defeat.

It wouldn't be the first time. It wasn't that many years ago that Harwood Borough had thrown away a three-goal lead in the second leg of the FA

Trophy semi-final to Tellisford Town. Hector had cried that night and did not want to repeat it. Mind you, he didn't want to repeat his last Trophy semi-final experience either, when he had had a very strange encounter at Shepton Mallet Rangers.

He hadn't needed to worry. Boro had held on easily for the first half of the game and might even have gone in at half-time with the lead if a rasping drive from the edge of the box by Matt Zanardi hadn't rebounded off the post.

As the second half wore on and Cannock failed to peg back the two-goal advantage, the confidence in Boro's play increased visibly. Hector was convinced that his side should have had a penalty in the seventy-fifth minute when star winger Lenny Easterby was hacked down from behind as he was going to shoot, but the referee had just waved Boro's fervent appeals away.

But in the end it didn't matter. With two minutes left on the clock and Cannock desperately throwing men forward, Boro struck the decisive blow.

Easterby collected a long clearance from the defence and scampered up the wing past his marker. As he looked across the field, all he could see was one single defender and his own partner Ned McFraser streaking towards the home team's goal. Judging his pass to perfection to avoid McFraser getting caught offside, Easterby threaded the ball past the stranded defender and into the path of the onrushing striker. With the goalkeeper bearing down on him McFraser simply let the ball run on, which confused the goalie so much he ran clear past the ball, leaving McFraser with a totally open net to fire the ball into.

To the absolute delight of the four thousand or so Boro fans watching, this was exactly what the striker did. And it was this that set off the scenes behind the goal.

Four thousand celebrating fans – that in itself was not too far short of a miracle. Harwood Borough only averaged about two hundred and fifty people for a normal home league game and sometimes, if the away teams didn't bring many fans, they even got gates as low as one hundred and fifty. But seemingly the whole town of Harwood had come to this one. Instead of just the usual team bus, the club had had to order almost fifty coaches to ferry everybody the hundred miles or so to Cannock's ground in the Midlands. And the carloads of Boro fans that had passed Hector's coach on the motorway with their red and white scarves and banners streaming proudly out of the windows had been too many to count.

Hector had watched them go past from his seat in the front. He wasn't sitting next to Maureen for once. He wasn't even on the same coach as Maureen. It was *his* coach. He was in charge of it. Maureen had her own coach somewhere back behind him on the motorway. In fact, almost everyone he knew at Harwood Borough had their own coach. Billy Smallwood, Kevin Loony and Neville Prince, they all had coaches to look after. They had all been made stewards for the day and had been given a coachload of fifty-odd people each to look after and make sure they got to the game and home again safely. But Hector's coach was different. Hector's coach was number one. The very first one out of the club car park. Maureen was in charge of number six and the others were all well down the list. But Hector's coach was number one and that meant something special to Hector. And he smiled the whole length of the motorway thinking about it.

All the stewards had been offered complimentary seats in the main stand for the game as a thank you for looking after a coach each, but Hector, Maureen and the other three had turned them down in favour of ground passes. They didn't want to sit all squashed up in the main stand behaving themselves. They wanted to be behind the goal where they always stood, yelling abuse at the linesmen and the other team. People tended to look at you rather strangely like if you let rip at a linesman while you were sitting in the stand. But out on the terraces behind the goal it was almost compulsory. They wouldn't be able to stand for the final though. The new Highbury stadium was all seats. Almost seventy thousand of them. This simple fact made Hector's head spin whenever he thought about it. But all that had been for the future. But the future was getting closer.

And then it was all over. The referee blew the final whistle and the Boro fans and players went bananas. Hector even got his timing right this time and he and Maureen both launched themselves into the air in celebration at the same time.

The scenes in the clubhouse bar after the game were absolutely stunning as fans and players alike hugged and shouted and drank and hugged and shouted and drank. And some of them drank and shouted and hugged, but nobody minded.

And then it was time to go. Back into the coaches everybody piled, some of them even into the proper ones. Nobody cared. All that mattered was getting back down the motorway to Harwood Borough's ground where a party was going to be had that people would talk about for years and years to come.

That had been the plan. As Hector lay in bed late the next morning he couldn't remember a thing about it. And somebody was hitting his head with a hammer. At least it felt like a hammer; it could have been any number of things. As he forced his eyes open he realised that there was nobody hitting him with anything; the pain was coming from inside.

The room slowly came into focus. It didn't stay still, but it did come into focus. So he was home. That was good. And he was in bed. That was good too. And Maureen was with him. That was… No, she wasn't. His arm reached out to where Maureen should have been but there was nothing but duvet.

He was just about to hit the panic button when the door opened and a beaming Maureen walked into the room with the biggest mug of tea Hector had seen in his life.

Hector was confused. His last recollection of the night before had been of Maureen swaying about at the bar of the clubhouse trying to dummy her way past a stool in imitation of McFraser's magnificent swerve round the hapless Cannock goalie a few hours before. And she had been pickled. Totally and utterly plastered. How could she be smiling like this then? Why wasn't she feeling like death like he was? It just didn't make sense. Mind you, she hadn't been drinking gallons of Kilgarvan Cream like Hector had. When would he learn that it was much stronger than it tasted? *Probably never*, he thought as the object in his head increased its hammering. It still wasn't fair though. Maureen had been downing glasses of white wine like they were going out of fashion. She must feel awful, surely?

'Morning,' she said. She didn't seem hung-over. *It must be a front*, thought Hector to himself as he tried in vain to lift his throbbing head from the pillow.

'Had a few too many then, did we?' she chided him.

'I… er… probably,' he admitted. 'But what about you? You were absolutely—'

'No, I wasn't,' she interrupted brightly. 'I know how to look after myself. I don't go around getting smashed out of my tiny mind and making a fool of myself like *some* people.' She looked at him in that funny sort of way as she said it that left Hector in no doubt that the 'some people' she mentioned definitely included him.

'You don't remember, do you?' she asked him.

'I… er…' he stammered.

'Thought not,' she said smugly and, putting his tea on the bedside table, quickly turned and left the room.

Bloody hell, thought Hector to himself. *What the heck did I do*?

He looked around him. Nothing looked too bad. His red and white scarf lay over the chair but everything else looked fine. Then he started to get this strange feeling. Something buried in the murky depths of his mind was waking up and Hector wasn't sure he wanted it to.

He peered under the duvet. All he had on was one red Harwood Borough football sock. That and a lot of lipstick. This was very strange. He didn't own a Harwood Borough sock.

Then it hit him. He remembered the stage. He remembered the lights. He remembered the music. And he remembered standing there in a Harwood Borough football kit. And then he remembered nothing.

At that moment Maureen came back into the room and opened the curtains. The bright sunlight hit Hector's eyes like a shovel. He yanked the duvet over his head and groaned.

'I hope all the pictures come out,' said Maureen. 'Although I'm not sure that Boots will be allowed to print *all* of them.'

Hector groaned again. Surely he didn't... He couldn't possibly have... But he had and he was starting to remember it.

Somehow a couple of strippers had turned up at the club and Hector could very vaguely remember heckling them from the safety of the bar. Then he remembered getting changed into a football kit in the changing rooms. He had no idea whose idea it had been or why he was doing it, or even whose kit it was, but he could now quite clearly remember doing it.

Then he remembered being on the stage *with the strippers*!

He groaned again. This time louder. 'Oh, my God,' he mumbled from beneath the duvet.

'He won't help you,' came a terse reply. 'After last night, I'd be very surprised if you haven't been excommunicated!'

Hector just groaned. Now he could suddenly remember where the lipstick had come from. And how it had got where it had. He groaned again.

'At least you had a good time,' said Maureen over her shoulder. 'That much was obvious,' she added as she left the room closing the door behind her with a slam.

This would never have happened to me a few years ago, Hector thought ruefully to himself. As he slumped back under the duvet, he had just the faintest of smiles on his lips. He would never be able to go back there. He was staying exactly where he was. For ever!

All this had been over a month ago now. It had taken Hector two days to pluck up the courage to go outside at all. It had taken him almost a week to pluck up the courage to venture back into the club. And when he had, he had been greeted by a standing ovation. The word embarrassment didn't quite cover it. In fact, it didn't even begin to cover it. The only saving grace was that very few of the photos of that fateful evening had come out, and those that had were very blurry. *So there is a God up there*, thought Hector as he looked through them sitting at a dark table in the far corner of the bar on that first evening back.

Maureen had never gone as ballistic as Hector had feared. He guessed that in truth she had no idea what really happened as she had been drunk herself and couldn't remember too much of the details at all. It soon became evident that fortunately no one else could either. Hector could by now though. It had all come back to him slowly but surely over the following days and every time he thought about it he broke out in a cold sweat. When he suddenly remembered the snake, he almost collapsed.

As they all sat in the bar laughing about it, the club chairman suddenly grabbed Hector by the arm and asked if he would follow him to the secretary's office for a little chat. Hector stopped laughing so quickly that he gave himself a severe bout of hiccups.

This is it, he thought. *I'm going to be thrown out of the club in shame*. His head was drooping as he walked into the secretary's gloomy little office.

To his staggering surprise, the chairman suddenly burst out laughing, slapped him on the back and poured him a brandy from a bottle on the desk.

'Bloody good show last week,' he roared. 'Don't know how the bloody hell you had the bottle to do it, but it made us all laugh so hard my wife was nearly sick!'

Hector just stared at the carpet.

'Bloody good, bloody good,' the chairman went on. Suddenly he stopped and looked Hector straight in the eye. 'Now, I've got a little job for you, young man, that's very important for this club. And you can keep your clothes on while you do it.' And with that, off he went roaring with laughter again.

Hector started to tremble. What on earth was it that the chairman wanted? He hoped to God it wasn't a request to repeat his act of the previous Saturday night. *But it can't be*, he thought. *He's just said I can keep my clothes on.*

He need not have feared. What the chairman actually wanted, he told him, was for Hector to write a match report. A very important match report. The match report of the final itself at Highbury in three weeks' time. For the club.

Hector was gobsmacked. He couldn't have been more gobsmacked if the chairman had physically thrown him out of the club for his indiscretions with the strippers.

The match report of the final.

Christ, though Hector. He had written match reports of the club's matches before for the two local newspapers and had had various articles printed in the programme, but for the chairman to ask him to write the official report of the final itself – this was nothing short of an honour.

It was also not quite right. Why wasn't Terry O'Booth doing it? He was the club's normal reporter. Or Harry – he always did it when Terry was away. Hector only did it when both were unavailable, which wasn't very often. He was going to ask the chairman, but his mouth wouldn't work.

And then the little chat was over. Hector was hustled back into the corridor by the chairman. 'Don't worry about a ticket; you'll be in the press box,' he said as he marched a still speechless Hector back to the bar. 'Just be here at the club about eleven on the day. You can come with us on the team bus,' he added. 'Oh, and you'd better bring Maureen with you; she could come in handy.'

And that day was today. The day of days. For a club the size of Harwood Borough occasions like these really were once in a lifetime. Hector, with due reverence for the occasion, had decked himself out in club tie, red and white striped shirt, grey flannel trousers and his best blazer. Maureen had supervised the buying of these new clothes, as she was a little embarrassed at what he owned in the way of clothing. The blazer he wore on their first date would have been better off on a scarecrow, she had decided, although on later reflection she didn't think it was good enough even for that. Maureen had also bought herself a new red and white dress especially for the occasion. Hector thought secretly that she looked a bit like a stick of rock, but he didn't have the bottle to tell her!

They were at the clubhouse over an hour early, so paranoid was Hector that he would miss the bus. The players all started arriving soon after and Hector hardly recognised them. Instead of the usual ragtag band of scruffs who arrived five minutes before they had to, this smart, well-groomed collection of young men all in matching brand new grey suits started to assemble in the car park along with their wives and loved ones. And these were all done up like a dog's dinner themselves. The girls were all in new dresses and hats and the kids had all been scrubbed, their little faces glowing red in the sunshine. *It was all a little surreal*, thought Hector. There was even an official photographer, who lined everyone up as soon as they all arrived and snapped away happily. It was just like being at a giant wedding. One of these cult ones in America where about twenty couples all got married at once. It was already turning out to be the best day of Hector's life when he was asked to be in the official photograph with the players and directors.

I'll teach all those others to laugh at me about the other week, he thought as he grinned happily at the back. All his friends had arranged to meet in a pub near Highbury and were not at the ground for the big send-off. They would all be dead jealous when the photos came out. Hector hoped that it was this picture of the whole party that was picked to be blown up and stuck over the bar in the clubhouse. Now wouldn't that be something? Hector and Maureen immortalised forever behind the bar of the club. Wow!

And then they were off. The journey only took around an hour after they eventually got going just before twelve and it was dead on one o'clock as the coach pulled up to a halt outside the main gates of the massive ground.

There were fans everywhere, yelling and cheering and clapping the players off the coach; they swarmed all over them. To prove that most of them didn't really know much about the club at all, Hector got nearly as many thumps on the back and good wishes heaped on him as the players did as they filed off and walked the short distance to the main entrance. Hector had never seen so many red and white scarves in his life – not at such close proximity anyway.

Various officials and security guards swept them all through the main entrance and into the hugely impressive foyer. And then suddenly Hector was all alone. The players had been led off one way to the changing rooms and the chairman, secretary and other officials had been whisked away to the boardroom. That left Hector and Maureen. Except Maureen wasn't there either.

Hector panicked. He found an extremely well-dressed commissionaire who had more medal ribbons than the average American private and asked him the way to the press box. It was then that Hector realised that he didn't have a pass or a ticket or anything. Just as this officious man with all the grace and civility of a Wembley steward was about to throw Hector out through the doors, Maureen came screeching round the corner with a man in tow waving a handful of passes.

Now complete with enough passes to enable them to get into

Buckingham Palace, Hector and Maureen were led up to the most luxurious press box either of them had ever seen. Not that they had seen many. About the biggest either of them had been in before was at Wandsworth Town when Hector had done the match report for the *Harwood Observer*. That one had been wooden, open to the weather and seated about six people.

This one was all glassed in with space for about a hundred people. Neither of them had seen anything like it in their lives. They were shown to a desk with two chairs about halfway along and two rows from the front. Their guide excused himself but said that their hostess would be along shortly. Sure enough a very pretty young girl in a red and blue uniform appeared about a minute later and insisted on taking the pair of them on a tour of the facilities. Apart from plenty of space to write on, the desk was equipped with two phones and two sockets for their laptops. Hector didn't like to explain that far from having laptops, all they had was one single notepad between them.

Then they were taken along the back of the still completely deserted press room to the hospitality suite. All manner of sandwiches and other snacks were laid out on a long table along one wall. There was a fully equipped bar along the back wall and very sumptuous armchairs in the middle of the room. Around all the walls were TV screens showing just about every channel in Christendom and in one corner stood four PCs connected to the Internet. Hector's jaw dropped. He slumped into one of the chairs and it wasn't until Maureen appeared five minutes later with a pint of Stonethreshers Goldenhammer for him and half of a lager for her that he regained the power of speech.

'How much was that?' he asked.

'Free, gratis and for nothing,' replied the grinning Maureen.

'My sort of place,' said Hector, sipping the froth from the top of the beer.

'Not too many of them,' she said. 'You're supposed to be working.'

Hector mumbled something incoherent under his breath and she slapped him gently in case it was rude.

This is the life, he thought as he slurped his pint. He really felt sorry for Terry O'Booth and Harry Louis, neither of whom could be there that afternoon.

Yeah, right, of course he did. Terry was in Latvia with the Irish national side, as was his major passion, and Harry had been so convinced that Boro's season would be over by now that he had booked his summer holiday and was sitting on a beach on the Costa Packet probably gnashing his teeth. And that left Hector.

This is the life, thought Hector again as he sat in the extremely comfortable chair and sipped his pint. He had been pondering the way his life had changed since he met Maureen. When he had first met her at the railway station one fateful Saturday morning, he had been a devoted groundhopper. The saddest of the sad. His life revolved around nothing but football programmes and train timetables. He'd been abroad only once and hadn't enjoyed that. His flat had resembled the local tip and his life had resembled much the same thing. And then into his life had come Maureen. He was still a groundhopper of sorts. He liked to go to new grounds and still did to a certain extent, although after his nightmare experiences up north a few years ago, he didn't get the urge to go quite so much any more. Most Saturdays he spent with Maureen watching Boro or on an occasional visit to see Arsenal. He did still read the odd science fiction novel, but not with the fervour he once did. There was no need to live in a fantasy world any longer; for him his everyday life was a bit of a fantasy land thanks to Maureen. His flat now sparkled and was so neat and tidy that at times he thought he had walked into the wrong one. They still had their own flats although they tended to spend most of the time together in one or the other of them. He had even been to America, although when he thought about it he still felt a small pain in his leg where he had been shot while he was there. Yes, his life had certainly changed, he thought, unconsciously rubbing the wound. But definitely for the better, he decided as he drained the last of his pint.

Hector dispatched Maureen back to the bar for another Stonethreshers Goldenhammer and just let himself sink deep down into the luxury of his chair. Behind him he could hear a conversation being conducted in hushed tones. He wasn't sure who was talking and he had to strain his ears to make out all the words, but as nothing else was going on and since Maureen was taking an inordinately long time to come back with the beer, he listened intently. He was bloody glad he did.

'Two–nil, no problem; both goals second half,' hissed a voice.

'Great, but how can you be sure?' said another.

'Well, we've got the goalie, two of the back four, the captain and that striker who gets all their goals,' said the first voice again.

'Christ, how much did that lot cost us?' asked the second.

'Oh, only a couple of grand,' said the first. 'I thought it might be double that.'

'Quick, someone's coming,' the second voice warned. 'Meet me downstairs at half-time and we can sort out the details.'

'They're gonna want the money by then,' went on the first. 'I've told the physio that they'll get it by half-time at the latest.'

'You've got it with you, then?'

'Yeah, right here.'

And then it went quiet. Hector turned and peered over the top of the chair in the direction the voices had come from, but there was no one there. Just then Maureen appeared with Hector's pint. *It must have been Maureen who disturbed them*, he thought.

'What's up with you?' she asked. 'You look like you've seen a ghost.'

'Not seen, but maybe heard,' Hector replied. 'It's a fix!'

'What's a fix?' she asked him. 'And what ghost?'

'The game, the final – this,' he said, pointing out towards the pitch. 'It's all a fix. Someone's going to win two–nil, but I don't know who.'

'You'd better tell me what's been going on,' said Maureen as she sat back down.

So Hector told her of the conversation he had overheard. After he had told her they both just sat there for a few minutes looking at each other. What on earth could they do? They didn't know who had arranged the fix and, more importantly, they didn't know whether it was Harwood Borough or Birstall that had taken it. How could they find out without causing a scandal? And, even more important, how could they stop it? It was going to be a very long and difficult afternoon!

They went back to their desk and looked out at the scene that was unfolding before them. It was simply stunning. The press box was situated on the third deck of seating and hung out over the top of the deck below to give the illusion that they were flying over the top of the pitch itself. The seats were gradually filling up with the fans, all dressed in red and white at the Harwood Borough end and in black and orange at the Birstall end (the were known as the Bees).

Out on the pitch the Boro players, all smartly dressed in their new club suits, were poking their highly polished shoes into the immaculate turf and waving at the crowd.

Hector and Maureen turned to each other, but no words would come to either of them. They didn't know what to do.

If it was Harwood Borough that had taken the bribe, Hector didn't know what he would do. The disgrace that would follow when the story got out, as it surely would, would never be lived down. Even if it was Birstall and Boro won the cup, when the truth came out their victory would be trashed.

Hector knew he had to do something drastic. And he didn't have a lot of time. It was gone two o'clock now, less than an hour to the start. Whatever the hell he was going to do, it would have to be done quickly.

He made a decision. He drank the remains of his pint in one swallow, handed his notepad to Maureen and announced, 'I'm not sure how, but I'm going to sort this mess out. If I'm not back by kick-off, you'll have to do the report!'

And with that he walked off, just like Captain Oates at the South Pole. Maureen just looked dumbfounded. She didn't even have the chance to tell him to be careful.

The two advantages that he had, he reasoned, were that firstly he knew what was going on, sort of, but the fixers didn't know that he knew. Secondly he had all sorts of passes hanging round his neck that looked like they would get him access to anywhere he wanted to go.

He was right. At the entrance to the corridor that led to the two teams' dressing rooms the commissionaire guarding it just smiled at him when he saw the passes dangling from his neck and pulled the door open for him to enter.

So far so good, thought Hector. He paused outside the Harwood Borough dressing room. What was he going to do – burst in and announce that he knew all about the fix? That might be okay if it was Birstall taking the money, but if it was Harwood Borough and half the bloody team were in on it he could be in serious trouble. If he burst into the Birstall dressing room he could also be in serious trouble.

No, he thought, *probably better to hang around and see what happens*. It was twenty past two now, only about twenty-five minutes until the teams were led out on to the pitch for the presentations. It was at half-time that something was going to happen. *I might as well go back upstairs*, he thought to himself, *and watch the first half from the press box and then nip down here five minutes before half-time*.

Good plan, he decided, but where was he going to hide when the interval came and the money was handed over? He couldn't just stand around in the corridor. If he did then probably nothing would happen; he had to find somewhere to hide. He tried the handle to the door next to the Harwood Borough dressing room but it was locked. He tried the one on the door next to that, which turned okay, but the door opened to reveal the referee's room with the officials in the middle of getting changed.

'Sorry,' blurted out Hector. 'Er, Press. I was looking for the Harwood

Borough changing room.'

'Two doors down on the left, mate,' came a gruff reply from a half-naked official.

Hector shut the door and moved to the other side of the corridor. The first handle he tried over there was right next door to the Birstall changing room and to his relief the door opened into a store cupboard that had plenty of room for him to squeeze inside.

Better just try it out for size, he thought to himself. *I don't want to get down here at half-time and find I can't fit in.* With that he squeezed into the cupboard and pulled the door behind him. He couldn't see too much through the crack in the door that he left, but he could hear everything being said in the dressing room next door. This would do him perfectly. He just knew that it was Birstall; it couldn't be Boro now, could it? And from here he could burst out and expose the crooks to the world. Well, to the commissionaire round the corner at least. Then what? He hadn't thought of that. What if everyone just denied it or, even worse, dragged him into the Birstall changing room? Maybe they were all in on it by now. Then he would be in a mess. He needed another plan. He listened more intently to what was going on next door.

The door clicked shut as he leant on the other side of the dressing room wall, plunging the tiny space into total darkness. Hector was a bit disorientated and as he turned to try to find the door handle he brushed against something that on reflection he wished he hadn't.

Something heavy hit him on the back of the head. As he slipped into unconsciousness, the last thing Hector thought of was poor old Maureen having to write the match report. Then everything went black, or in this case even blacker.

When he woke up he was surprised to find he was still standing. He was in fact pinned to the wall by some sort of heavy metal easel.

He could hear voices outside in the corridor. He managed to pull both hands free of the thing and pressed the light button on his new watch. It said 15.50. It was half-time. His head hurt like thunder but there was no time to worry about that now. He eased his way clear of the obstruction. As he did he whacked his leg hard against the doorknob. He wanted to yell out in pain but managed to stop himself. At least he had found the way out!

He opened the door gently and could see two figures standing in the corridor just a few feet away. *This is it*, he thought to himself. *I've got them now*. And then all other thoughts left his head.

It was not people from Birstall standing there, but Harwood Borough's main striker, Matt Zanardi, and the manager, Sid Melbourne.

So that was it then. It was Harwood Borough after all. Hector could hardly even bring himself to breathe. He wasn't so much distraught, he was more destroyed. His team, his idols, his life, all gone there and then in that one moment. Why, oh why, had he overheard that conversation? Why had he made Maureen go and get him another drink? If she hadn't then she would have been sitting there with him and whoever the crooks were they would have gone somewhere else. He would have slumped to the floor if there had been room. But he couldn't even do that. As he stood there feeling sorry for himself, he could plainly hear the conversation outside.

'You can't take me off now,' Zanardi was saying. 'I'm doing okay. I know I missed that sitter, but it had a really horrible bobble. You can't take me off; it's the bloody final!'

Hector listened harder. This did not sound like the way you would accept a bribe.

Then he heard Melbourne's voice. 'I don't care, it just isn't working with you and McFraser up front; one of you has got to come off and he looks the livelier.'

'Bollocks!' exclaimed Zanardi's voice followed by the sound of what could only be a football boot colliding with a wall.

The only sound that followed was the slamming of a door.

Hector started to breathe again. He pulled the door almost shut. Then he heard footsteps followed by someone knocking on a nearby door. He pushed the door open an inch.

Standing in the corridor was the Harwood Borough chairman, Tom Richardson. And he was tapping on the Birstall door. Hector thought to himself that maybe everything had somehow been a horrible mistake. Nothing was going to happen now that the Harwood Borough chairman was standing there. He thought he would just push his way out and get going up to the press box. Maureen would be worried sick by now.

Then, just as he was about to throw the door open, a thought struck him. What the hell would he tell the chairman? How could he explain that he was coming out of an equipment cupboard when it was the chairman himself who had got him the job of writing the match report? A job that he had so far miserably failed even to start. No, better to stay where he was until the chairman had gone. It couldn't be too long until the second half started, so surely it would be better to wait a couple of minutes until there was nobody around; then he could sneak back upstairs and maybe nobody other than Maureen would be any the wiser.

He stood and waited. Again the chairman tapped on the Birstall changing room door. The door opened and Hector watched in amazement as what could only be the Birstall physio stepped into the corridor.

'Where the hell have you been?' the Birstall man said.

'I couldn't come any quicker. Our bloody manager was practically holding his team talk out here,' the chairman replied.

'Well, have you got it?' the physio asked.

'Of course I bloody have,' said the chairman.

Hector watched as the chairman then reached inside his pocket and pulled out a brown envelope, which he held out to the other man.

Just then the heavy metal easel that had been pinning Hector decided to observe the laws of gravity and it fell towards the door. As it did so it shoved Hector through the doorway. The door slammed back on to its hinges, the easel crashed to the floor and Hector flew out into the corridor like a cork out of a bottle. The chairman and the Birstall physio froze. They looked at Hector, they looked at each other and then the chairman fled back up the corridor and the physio shot back inside the dressing room, slamming the door behind him. Hector bounced off the far wall and landed on his knees on the carpet.

For some strange reason, probably the after-effects of the blow on the head, Hector stayed on all fours staring at the carpet. And what a carpet it was. Bright red with the Arsenal club crest all along it, it looked absolutely lovely to Hector in his bemused state. His eyes just followed the line of club badges all the way up the corridor. And then his eyes fell on the envelope. It was lying there outside the Birstall dressing room door. Hector was still feeling a little woozy, but he was not stupid. He stood up, he looked around, he walked up the corridor as nonchalantly as he could and stooped down to pick up the envelope. As he did he heard a door open behind him.

He froze in mid-stoop. It was the physio. Now he was in trouble.

But it wasn't the physio at all. It was the referee. 'Are you all right, son?' he asked. 'I heard a crash out here.'

'Er, yeah, I'm all right,' said Hector, although in all fairness he probably wasn't. 'That door flew open and that easel burst out,' he said, pointing at the metal heap on the floor, which turned out on closer inspection to be a blackboard and stand.

'Okay then, as long as you're all right.' With that the referee went back inside his room and closed the door.

Hector was all alone in the corridor. He stuffed the envelope into his blazer pocket and walked as quickly as he could to the door he had initially come through. Dozing in a chair on the other side was the commissionaire, completely oblivious to what had gone on.

Hector rushed up the stairs to the press box and made his way down to where Maureen was sitting.

She leapt to her feet when she saw him. 'Oh, Hector, I've been so worried. Where have you been? What on earth happened? Are you all right?'

'I'm fine, I think,' replied Hector, 'and as for what happened, I don't think you would believe me if I told you. How have *you* got on?' he asked her.

'Not bad,' she answered. 'Nothing much has happened really. Zanardi missed a sitter, but other than that it's been pretty boring, I suppose.'

Just then the teams made their way back onto the pitch for the second half.

Hector patted his pocket. There was still a lump in it. It was nearly as big as the lump in his throat, but there was no time for that now. He had a match to watch and a report to write.

Harwood Borough started the second half like a steam train. With youngster Rick Parcelle linking up with McFraser up front there was more life to their forward line than Hector had seen in the last month. It was no surprise when they took the lead in the fifty-ninth minute through new boy Parcelle. Kumah Nielsen fed the ball out to Lenny Easterby on the left wing and he flew past his marker before sending a stinging low cross into the box. Parcelle met it on the volley and the ball hit the back of the net before anyone else had moved a muscle.

Behind the goal the best part of ten thousand fans exploded in a sea of red and white. The cacophony of noise that accompanied the celebrations mostly escaped Hector and Maureen in the press box but that didn't stop them joining in the celebrations.

As Hector's backside hit his chair he wondered how unprofessional he had looked leaping into the air as the ball hit the back of the net. He patted his pocket again to make sure that the envelope was still there. It was. Hector decided he didn't give a toss about how unprofessional he had looked.

The next twenty-five minutes of the game went past without much incident. Birstall didn't look too bothered about equalising and Harwood

Borough looked as if they were quite happy to hang on to their one-goal lead.

Then with just five minutes left on the clock Boro put the game beyond Birstall's reach. Lenny Easterby got the ball ten yards into the Birstall half and ran towards goal with it. He ghosted past two half-hearted tackles and curled the ball past the goalkeeper into the far corner of the goal from the edge of the area.

The goalkeeper didn't even put his arms out to stop it. It was as if he didn't want to.

The red and white half of the crowd went absolutely bananas again.

Hector just sat in his chair. He thought about the goal again. *The goalkeeper didn't even put his arms out to stop it. It was as if he didn't want to.*

He checked his pocket again. The fix couldn't have been on. He had the money!

Maureen gave him a big hug. She didn't know what had happened and at that moment ignorance was bliss.

As the black and yellow bedecked fans made their way from the ground looking thoroughly dejected, the red and white half just kept jumping and singing and shouting and celebrating. And then the referee blew the final whistle.

It was over. Harwood Borough had won the FA Trophy two–nil.

In the press box it was Maureen's turn to celebrate. She gave a little yelp of delight and stood banging on the window with both hands.

Hector couldn't bring himself to be so happy. He knew that he should be but that last goal kept going round and round in his mind. *The goalkeeper didn't even put his arms out to stop it. It was as if he didn't want to.*

But then Maureen grabbed him and pulled him out of his chair. 'Come on,' she said, 'we've got to go and see the presentation.'

Hector followed her down the press box steps and out into the open air of the stadium. The Boro players were about to be presented with the cup. Everyone was cheering and waving and shouting. Everyone except Hector, that is.

Somebody came up to him and sent him into almost total paralysis by asking him if he had seen the chairman. Hector found his mouth didn't work so he just shook his head.

After the presentation the players went on a lap of honour. Or rather half a lap of honour; there wasn't anybody left at the other end to waggle the trophy at. And then the players left the pitch to go down to the dressing room.

'Come on,' said Maureen, grabbing Hector by the arm, 'let's go and see the celebrations.'

They went back up through the press box where Hector picked up his notebook and other things and Maureen led him down the stairs to the boardroom. Inside there was nearly as much pandemonium as out in the stands. As they walked through the door they had glasses of champagne put in their hands.

Hector couldn't get into the swing of things. He had to know if the fix had been on or not. He told Maureen he was going to do some player interviews and just before he left the room he gave her the envelope and told her to guard it with her life. She smiled and stuffed it straight into her handbag.

Hector left the boardroom and made his way downstairs towards the changing rooms. The commissionaire was still there, awake this time. He waved Hector past and he made his way up the corridor. He noticed that the blackboard and easel had been put away and the door of the cupboard closed. Hector wasn't sure exactly what he was going to do and he stood in the corridor staring into space. Suddenly the Birstall changing room door flew open and a collection of very angry and fed-up players pushed their way past him towards the exit. At the back of the line the physio passed him and just stared angrily into his face. Hector thought he heard him say a very rude word, but by the time he realised what it was the corridor was empty. They had all gone.

Just then the Harwood Borough door opened and out came Lenny Easterby, horizontally. He fell out into the corridor stark naked but holding the trophy in both hands. He was laughing fit to burst.

'Hec,' he said, 'come and join the fun.'

And so he did.

About an hour later Hector and Maureen were sitting on the team bus on the way back to Harwood. The players were still laughing and joking and swigging from champagne bottles and the trophy itself, which now had a bit of a dent on one side, probably from where Easterby had fallen into the corridor with it. Gone were all the club ties and blazers; the players were past caring what they looked like. And from all the giggling that was going on at the back of the bus, it was pretty obvious that their wives and girlfriends weren't much bothered either.

Maureen was rather more than half-cut herself and was clutching an almost full bottle of Moët et Chandon, but Hector was still a little subdued. Wet but subdued. What had gone on in the changing rooms had been nothing more than chaos. There had been champagne flowing everywhere and quite a proportion of it had flowed down the back of Hector's neck. His blazer was ruined.

What had really gone on after he went back up to the press box at half-time? Had the fix been put on or not? If it had, then what had been used for money? By the look of the Birstall physio as he left after the game it was a pretty good bet that it hadn't. The Birstall players had looked particularly angry as well. Maybe the physio had not told them what had happened in the corridor. *That would teach them*, Hector thought. *Would the true story ever come out*? Unlikely, he decided, but he reckoned that it was a fair bet that Birstall would need a new physio for next season.

The big mystery of the celebrations before they left the stadium was that nobody could find the Harwood Borough chairman. It was said that he had left at half-time in one hell of a rush saying that he had a personal emergency and would have to go. The club secretary said he saw him running across the car park like a scalded cat. Everybody was very surprised to say the least, but they weren't going to let it spoil the celebrations.

They were all on their way back to the club where a party was promised that was going to dwarf the one after the semi-final completely. Hector just hoped that there weren't going to be any strippers this time!

Maureen grabbed his arm and looked at him. 'That jacket's ruined,' she giggled. 'We'll have to buy you another one.'

Hector reached into her handbag and pulled out the envelope. He glanced inside it before stuffing it into his rather soggy inside pocket.

'I think we can afford it,' he said and had a long swig from Maureen's bottle.

Maureen's Roots

It had been a very difficult few weeks. Hector and Maureen had decided to go to Lithonia to see her parents. Technically Lithonia didn't exist – it was still part of Russia – and as such both Hector and Maureen would need visas to enter the country. It was this necessity that had led Hector to stand in a queue outside the Russian embassy in London for seven hours in the pouring rain in a vain attempt to get them. They had finally been issued with them and, after about twenty phone calls, the passports, with visas, had arrived at Hector's flat two days before they were due to depart for Moscow and their twelve-hour train trip to Talnius, the capital of Lithonia. From there they were picking up a hire car for the three-hour drive to the small town where Maureen's parents lived, called Zalgev.

Hector had been very surprised when Maureen had told him about her roots. He knew her surname, Mansikevicus, was a bit strange – it wasn't the sort of name that you came across where they lived – but he had never given it a lot of thought. He knew that she had an Uncle Harry, who was the local stationmaster. It was when Harry was off sick that Hector had first met Maureen. What he didn't know was that Harry's real name was Haricosikus. Haricosikus Mansikevicus – now that was a mouthful; no wonder he called himself Harry!

When Maureen had explained her ancestry, Hector had found himself fascinated. He had promised her that if and when they ever had the money, they would go to Lithonia to see her parents and have a look round the country. When he 'found' two thousand pounds in an envelope at the FA Trophy final it seemed the perfect opportunity to fulfil his promise.

They kept the money hidden away for a year or so in case the ex-chairman of Harwood Borough, Tom Richardson, should resurface and demand the money back, assuming it had been his, of course. He had sent a letter of resignation to the club immediately after the FA Trophy success the previous year and for all intents and purposes had never been seen since. But both Hector and Maureen thought it best to be on the safe side and wait before doing anything with the money.

So here they were at Heathrow awaiting their Aeroflot flight to Moscow's Sheremetievo Airport on the first leg of their lengthy journey. Maureen had explained to him that Sarunas, her father, had moved to England in the early 1960s when he had a job working for the Soviet embassy in London. He had met Louise, Maureen's mum, in 1966 and Maureen had been born, shamefully out of wedlock, a year later. When Sarunas had been recalled to Moscow in 1969, he and Louise, now his wife, had moved back leaving Maureen to be brought up by his brother, Haricosikus, who had British citizenship.

After the break-up of the Soviet Union, Sarunas and Louise had left Moscow and moved back to Sarunas's home town of Zalgev in Lithonia where they were now happily retired. Sarunas's only real activity nowadays was as secretary of his local football team, Kalgev Zalgev.

Maureen and her parents corresponded regularly but had not actually met since the day her parents had left for Moscow in 1969 and Maureen had been far too young then to remember that. It promised to be a very emotional meeting when it finally happened.

The flight to Moscow could not have been much better, for which Hector was very grateful. He was not a good flier. They were both pleasantly surprised that the announcements were in English and that the food was edible; they had heard all sorts of rumours about Russian food, not realising that the meals on the plane would be English. It was also very pleasing that the plane landed ten minutes early. What was not so pleasing was the time it took to clear Russian immigration. Hector was not a happy bunny standing in the queue. It had cost the pair of them a hundred pounds each for their visas and now they were left standing there for two hours while the immigration officers seemingly took as long as possible to process each person.

'It's a wonder anybody ever bothers coming here at all,' said Hector in the queue. 'I thought they were desperate for tourists; you wouldn't believe it the way they treat you!'

'Shh,' whispered Maureen. 'You never know who's listening.'

So for the next hour they just stood silently waiting their turn.

But they got in eventually and a minibus took them to their hotel near the airport for a couple of nights' stay. After an excellent night's sleep in the very nice room they had, they spent the next day on a tour of the city. Maureen had said it would be an awful shame to travel to such a famous place without bothering to see any of it, so they booked two seats on a tour bus that picked them up at the hotel, and sat back to see the sights.

The tour lasted four hours in all and they enjoyed every minute of it. They had driven all around the Kremlin walls and had a stop for about an hour in Red Square. They had both been very impressed with St Basil's

Cathedral from the outside, but very disappointed with the plainness of the inside. They didn't have time to queue up for a look at Lenin's tomb, but did a bit of shopping in the giant department store GUM instead. It was quite chilly walking around in the open – it was late October – but at least it wasn't snowing. Maureen didn't like the cold one bit and was no lover of snow except on Christmas cards.

Instead of going back to the hotel on the bus, they got off at the huge Russian space museum with the intention of getting back under their own steam on the metro. Hector loved the Space Museum. He was very big on the science fiction front and he found all the space capsules and rockets quite breathtaking. *He was like a kid in a sweet shop*, thought Maureen. If she hadn't physically dragged him out of the museum he would have stayed there until it closed, but even when they got outside the fun didn't stop for Hector. Not only was there a massive gold statue dedicated to Yuri Gagarin, the first man in space, but there were several full-size lunar rockets to look at.

It was almost dark by the time they made their way down the escalators to the metro, and how Maureen wished she had dragged him down there an hour earlier. She had never seen so many people on one train in her life and although they had a metro map, the station names on the map were written in English. The actual signs on the station platforms were written in the Russian Cyrillic language, which to Hector and Maureen was completely indecipherable.

They were saved from having to spend the rest of their days touring the Moscow metro system by a very nice man who, speaking almost perfect English, worked out which station they wanted and told them when to get off. As they came back up to ground level they were both very grateful to see their hotel only about three hundred yards down the road.

They didn't venture out again that night in case they got hopelessly lost and instead endured an almost inedible meal in the hotel restaurant. They started with borscht, a local soup that appeared to be made from fish bones and beetroot. Then they had steak. Or it was supposed to be steak. Whilst chewing it and chewing it and chewing it, they contemplated that if this was what was being served up in four-star hotels, what the hell were the local people eating? They didn't want to know, but Hector was pretty sure they would find out in a few days' time.

And that was that. They watched TV for an hour or so but couldn't take it any longer; it was awful.

After another early night and another breakfast of hard-boiled eggs, caviar, toast and rancid coffee, it was time for the journey to the station to catch the train westwards.

They went by taxi to the station, which was across the city and cost an absolute fortune. To say that they were ripped off by the taxi driver was an understatement, although it wasn't as bad as it could have been after Maureen had changed a whole pile of American dollars with one of the waiters at the hotel. Their friend Neville from Harwood Borough had been to Moscow and had told them that as long as they were careful, changing money with a hotel waiter was the best way of getting value for money. You had to be careful; changing money on the black market was strictly against the law and could lead to all sorts of custodial sentences. This waiter had been okay though and Maureen had come back from seeing him with so many roubles (or Barneys as Hector insisted on calling them after Barney Rubble in *The Flintstones*) they would hardly fit in her bag.

The train journey was interminable. The train was old, the steam locomotive pulling it was older and most of the people on it were even older still. It rattled along through the Russian countryside at a snail's pace and seemed to stop every mile or so to let people off. No one ever seemed to get on, which Hector and Maureen thought a bit odd, but then on reflection they wondered how many Russians would be likely to be going to Lithonia. Any that did would not be made very welcome by all accounts. Lithonia was in the middle of trying to get autonomy from Russia as its bigger and more affluent neighbours Estonia, Latvia and Lithonia had already done. The Russian government had shown no signs so far of acceding to this request or even taking it seriously. This meant that the Russians were about as popular in Lithonia as the Israelis were in Palestine.

The train trudged on. Hector and Maureen dozed. Then they read. Then they dozed. Eventually the train pulled into Talnius. As far as they could make out, Hector and Maureen were the only two passengers left on the train and in the half-light of an early Lithonian evening they alighted from the train into a scene straight out of *Dr Zhivago*.

They collected their luggage from the goods van, remembering to tip the guard. They had been warned that if they didn't give absolutely anybody who did anything for them some money, they were likely to lose all their possessions.

Hector wasn't sure exactly what he was expecting, but whatever it was, it wasn't what he got. The station was almost completely deserted; the only visible person was behind the counter of a newsstand. There was a souvenir stand, which was closed; there was a small bar, which was closed; there was a food shop, which was closed; there was a ticket office, which was closed; and there were two car rental booths, which looked like confessionals, which were also closed.

Everything was dark and gloomy. There were lights on but it was still very gloomy. Almost everything was made of dark wood: the shops, the doors and even part of the walls. What wasn't made of dark wood was painted some sort of dark cream. Hector could see why it wasn't a tourist centre.

They had arranged a hire car for the following day from Lith-U-Rent, which disturbingly was not one of the car firms visible in the station foyer. But they did have a number to ring. And they weren't due to pick it up until the morning; they were to spend the night in the station hotel, which was apparently next door.

It was! It loomed up out of the gloom as the pair of them walked down the deserted steps outside the station. It looked about as inviting as Count Dracula's castle. It didn't have bats flying in and out of it, but if it had then Hector would not have been surprised.

They walked across the station car park to the hotel and into reception. There was a dark wooden desk inside the entrance at which sat what looked to be a dark wooden woman. But she broke into a warm smile as the two of them approached and welcomed them in English. They were both taken aback by this; they hadn't been sure if anyone would speak any English at all. The rest of the place looked deserted. There was a bar of sorts in the corner of the foyer but that was deserted (and made solely of dark wood). In the opposite corner was the restaurant. It too was completely deserted, Hector noted as he stuck his head inside while Maureen got them checked in.

They rode in the rickety dark brown lift to the stuffy old dark brown fourth floor. They wheeled their luggage down the corridor on the most ragged carpet Hector had ever seen in his life, until they found the huge dark wooden door that led to their room.

It was with great trepidation that Maureen opened the door, but they needn't have worried. Inside it was quite nice. Not up to the standard of the one they had stayed in, in Moscow, but not as bad as they had feared.

There were two beds, both covered in a sort of brown rug that could have doubled as a carpet. There was a writing desk (made of dark brown wood) with a matching chair. There was a dark wooden wardrobe and a dark wooden chest of drawers. On top of the chest of drawers was a television set that had a light brown plastic casing. It was the only thing that wasn't dark brown that they had seen since they arrived and was quite a shock. The carpet was dark brown, the lampshade was brown and the curtains were brown. The walls were a sort of cream colour, or at least they had been the last time they had seen a lick of paint. But it was reasonably clean, to Maureen's relief. The bathroom was not too bad, although the shower arrangements left a lot to be desired. It was all painted in a garish pink colour that clashed so much with the dark brown of everything else as to be laughable. Again, as in Moscow, there was no plug in the sink which they both thought strange. Obviously a local custom. It was only for one night though and Hector said he had stayed in worse B&Bs in the north of England on his groundhopping trips.

Maureen sorted out the luggage while Hector attempted in vain to find something watchable on the TV and then they got ready to go out. The guidebooks they had read, what there was of them, all said that Talnius had a thriving pub scene, and with only one night before they were off to Zalgev, Hector in particular was determined to give it a go.

The woman on reception had told Maureen that the best way of getting into town was by the council-operated minibus that ran from outside the station and took about ten minutes to get into the city centre. It cost the extortionate amount of about ten pence (over double the bus fare) but was much cheaper than a taxi and apparently much quicker than the local bus.

They took her advice and clambered into a rickety old transit van that many years ago was very probably white, but was now six different tones of rust. It backfired almost every hundred yards but dropped them off in front of the cathedral ten minutes after leaving the station forecourt.

Hector headed straight for the nearest bar. They went inside and ordered two beers, one large and one small. It was excellent. Hector knew a thing or two about beer and this stuff, Grodny's, was very good, maybe a bit too 'lagery' for his personal taste, but, all the same, for foreign beer very nice. They had a couple and then moved on to another bar called ironically Maureen O'Grady's, where he was stunned to find his favourite Irish beer, Kilgarvan's, on sale. He sank a couple of them and was just on the point of ordering a third when Maureen suggested they find a restaurant. The guidebooks all recommended a Lithonian one called Zmikle Zmakle and they found it just off the cathedral square. They got a table in the basement where to the strains of a Lithonian folk band they had a very acceptable meal of local specialities for about three pounds a head, including a couple of stone jugs full of local beer. By about halfway through his second jug of beer,

Hector had decided that he rather liked Lithonia. Maureen wasn't quite as convinced, but if Hector was happy then she was happy too.

After two more pubs Maureen hailed a cab and the pair of them arrived back at the hotel around eleven o'clock. Hector would have quite happily stayed out for a few more hours but Maureen had a long drive the following morning and wanted a reasonably early night.

Back in their room Hector took his shoes and trousers off, lay down on the bed under the carpet provided and was asleep before his head hit the pillow. Maureen took considerably longer to get off to sleep, mainly due to Hector's mumbling and snoring, but she too got a good eight hours in before they got up around half past eight the following morning.

A breakfast followed in the restaurant downstairs that at best could be described as interesting. The coffee, as ever, was unbelievably appalling, but it was the bread that was truly remarkable. It was either two weeks old or made out of worn-out shoes – probably the latter. The eggs were rock hard, stone cold and seemingly glued to the shells and the milk was so rancid it must have come from a constipated goat.

They decided to leave it and have an early lunch!

They checked out of the hotel and made their way over to the station. The place was heaving with life – well, comparatively it was. The paper shop was still open with the same girl serving behind the counter. The souvenir stand was still closed, the small bar was still closed, the food shop was still closed, the ticket office was still closed and the two car rental booths that looked like confessionals were also still closed. But there were passengers standing around. *Three of them – a veritable throng*, thought Hector. Worryingly though there was no one who looked like he might be from Lith-U-Rent. They looked around the two closed car rental booths but could find no mention of any Lith-U-Rent. They decided to ring the number they had been given.

This threw up another problem: Russian telephones. Fortunately there was a sticker on the phones in the station that explained their use in English. These instructions were wrong, obviously, but they were in English. At the fourth attempt, the previous three refusing to give back the coins they had put in, they finally got through. The gentleman who answered, Ramunas, explained that he had had a problem with the car that they were supposed to have and he had had to exchange it for another one. He went on to say that he would be outside with their car in five minutes.

True to his word, he pulled up in the station forecourt exactly five minutes later. To their relief the car he had brought them was actually quite reasonable and, after spending ten minutes on a bench sorting out the paperwork, they prepared to drive off.

Maureen had had loads of experience of driving abroad on the wrong side of the road so Hector wasn't at all nervous about this aspect of the journey. It was the navigating side of things that frightened him to death, for he was the designated navigator. Hector had an acute fear of maps. Once unfolded, he could never ever fold them back up correctly. It didn't matter how many times he tried; they just would not go back and end up flat. After Hector had looked at a map and folded it back up it was always three times as thick as it had started, with at least one page sticking out the side. The front and back covers always disappeared too. And it was up to him whether they found the town of Zalgev or not. Scary.

They set off slowly to negotiate their way around Talnius, and to Hector's complete surprise they found the road to Zalgev with very few problems. They did go left instead of right at one set of traffic lights and they did get on the road to Zaunat instead of Zalgev, but compared to the disaster that Hector had been expecting, that was a positive success.

Once on the right road they chugged along merrily, with Hector finding some weird and wonderful local radio stations to listen to along the way. It was around a hundred and twenty miles to Zalgev from Talnius, but the journey went surprisingly quickly for the pair of them, so fascinated were they by the passing scenery.

They stopped after about an hour at a small roadside café for lunch, which turned out to be surprisingly good. The coffee actually tasted like coffee and the chicken sandwiches they had were quite superb. And it cost less than a quid between them.

Back on the road, the towns they passed through got smaller and smaller and seemingly bleaker and bleaker the further they got from Talnius. The road they were on was a dual carriageway so they didn't have to go into the towns and villages, only passing by them at a distance. *It was just as well*, Hector thought; they didn't look the sorts of places he would like to spend very long in, but they were very different to anything he had seen before so he was intrigued by them. Every now and then Maureen had to overtake a horse and cart or even a handcart, but in the main the vehicles they passed all looked reasonably smart and well cared for.

They had already decided that before they attempted to find Maureen's parents, they were going to check into the hotel that was to be their home for the next three nights, her parents' place being too small to accommodate them in comfort, apparently. They had been told that Zalgev was not exactly the hotel capital of Europe, but even so they were surprised by what they found. They had a small street map of Zalgev, which was just as well or they might never have found the hotel.

The first surprise was that it was situated in the middle of a pedestrian precinct, making access by car very difficult to say the least. They parked in an adjacent road and walked through the now persistent drizzle to the hotel entrance. Outside they just stood and stared. If the hotel in Talnius had been like something out of a Transylvanian nightmare, then this one had all the warmth and appeal of Frankenstein's castle. It was a gloomy reminder of all that was bad about Soviet architecture and made the one in Talnius seem positively bright and colourful by comparison. And it wasn't even in the right place. They had a picture of the hotel in a tourist brochure they had managed to get and it looked quite nice. It was on the corner of the street with nice brightly painted yellow walls and a neat-looking tower on the top. And there were the yellow walls and there was the tower on the top. But it wasn't the hotel; it was a nearby restaurant!

The hotel was about a hundred yards down the street and from outside it was quite easy to understand why they had photographed the restaurant instead. It really was so gloomy that had anyone seen a picture of it they would have refused to stay there even if it was the only hotel in town (and there were two others!). It was made of the customary ex-Soviet dark grey concrete that hadn't been cleaned since the day it was built. The only light in the gloom was a deep yellow neon sign that hung above the door announcing the legend HOTEL KALGEV.

Hector and Maureen pushed their way through the huge dark wooden revolving door and walked into the reception area. It was at least as gloomy inside as it was out, possibly even gloomier. And it was completely deserted. Then they heard a chair scrape on the floor behind the reception desk and an apparition of horror emerged to confront them. It was a woman (probably) of indeterminate age, dressed completely in black except for a large silver brooch on the front of her dress. She had long black hair and very pale make-up except for the largest and most colourful lips Hector had ever seen on a woman. Her lipstick was bright scarlet and she looked for all the world like she had been Miss Red Army in 1939. Behind the red lips were yellow tobacco-stained teeth, and all in all her appearance made Hector feel quite queasy.

It was Maureen who approached the desk, saying, 'Excuse me, we have a reservation here.'

'Mansikevicus?' asked the ghastly apparition.

'Yes,' replied Maureen. 'And it's for three nights,' she added, wishing that it wasn't.

The monster from the black lagoon placed the hotel register on the counter for Maureen to sign and she was quite perturbed to find only her name in it.

'Not too busy then?' she asked.

'Wrong time of year for it,' came the hollow reply.

With that Maureen produced her credit card.

'I'll need cash, please,' said the bride of Frankenstein.

'No, you don't,' said Maureen rather angrily. 'You have a sign there that says you take credit cards.' She pointed at the sign on the counter. 'And I quite clearly stated on the fax I sent you that I would be paying by credit card.'

Dracula's daughter smiled gruesomely before hissing, 'We have trouble with the bank. We cannot currently accept credit cards. We will sort it out in the morning.'

With that she put the largest hotel key on to the counter that Hector and Maureen had ever seen in their lives. It was huge, made of brass and had a tag like a small tree trunk attached to it with the number 222 on it.

'I'm surprised it doesn't have 666 on it,' Hector whispered to Maureen.

Maureen picked the key up, just about. It weighed about half a ton. 'Difficult to lose this.' She smiled. 'Where's the lift?'

'No lift,' said Miss KGB 1946.

'What about the car park you confirmed that you had?' Maureen enquired with clenched teeth.

'Down those stairs and out the door,' came the reply, the woman pointing across the reception area to a small flight of steps that led to an old green door.

'Thanks for all your help,' snarled Maureen and she and Hector walked to the steps.

The green door opened on to a small courtyard protected by a barrier from a narrow backstreet. They walked in the drizzle towards a main road that they could see in the distance and then realised that, quite by chance, they had parked just round the corner. Maureen went and got the car, while Hector managed to raise the barrier letting Maureen into the courtyard and she parked right next to the door into the hotel.

They dragged the luggage up the small set of steps, across the reception area, which was now totally deserted again, and up two flights of large and ornate, if very gloomy, stairs to the second floor. They found the room easily enough but stood outside the door for a minute, not quite knowing what to expect from the interior.

For all intents and purposes they might well have been back in the hotel in Talnius. The room was almost identical. The television was dark brown to match the rest of the furniture and was absolutely huge, far too big for the small table it was precariously resting on. The rugs that adorned the two wooden single beds were a lighter shade of brown and the carpet on the floor was a deep red, but other than that it could have been the same room.

The bathroom was straight out of Munster Towers. It was pink, but not the bright pink of Talnius. The sink had a crack running right across it so it looked as though it wouldn't hold much water for long, even if it had had a plug, which of course it hadn't, and the toilet seat was the strangest shape that either of them had ever seen. But it was the shower arrangements that were the pièce de résistance of the whole establishment. It was quite simply a length of old green hosepipe pushed on to one of the bath taps. And that was it. No bracket on the wall, no shower rose on the other end and no choice of water temperature. Hector burst out laughing when he saw it but Maureen had a rather more ominous look on her face.

Twenty minutes later and the pair of them were sitting in the car studying the map trying to figure the best way to Maureen's parents' place. After much discussion they set off in what they thought was the right direction only to find that the road they wanted to turn down was a one-way street going in the other direction. After much toing and froing they arrived in the correct street of small terraced houses and pulled up outside number 56, their destination.

From the outside the houses looked a bit like those in *Coronation Street* with their front doors opening directly on to the street. Number 56 even had a big brass knocker in the middle of its dark blue door.

Maureen knocked on it. The door was opened by what was obviously Maureen's mother. She had a huge smile on her face and Maureen rushed into her welcoming embrace. Maureen's mum burst into tears. Maureen burst into tears. Maureen's dad appeared behind the pair of them and he burst into tears. Hector didn't want to be left out so he burst into tears as well.

Ten minutes later they were all sitting in the front room drinking tea and most of them had stopped crying. All except Maureen's mum, that is. It looked possible that Maureen's mum would never stop crying. She had said that it was the happiest day of her life. About twelve times she had said that it was the happiest day of her life, between blubs. When five minutes later Maureen herself burst into tears again, Hector thought that he couldn't take any more. Luckily Maureen's dad, Sarunas, obviously felt the same and motioned for Hector to follow him.

They went up the stairs and into what was at one time the small house's second bedroom. It was a bedroom no longer. It appeared to be the club office of FC Kalgev Zalgev, the club of which Sarunas was secretary. Whatever it was supposed to be, it was clear to Hector that the reason that they had to stay in the hotel from hell in the town centre was that the spare bedroom at Maureen's parents' house was now some kind of office.

'Welcome to my den,' said Sarunas proudly with almost no hint of a foreign accent.

'Wow!' exclaimed Hector.

Sarunas sat down in an old armchair in one corner of the room while Hector looked around the walls at all the photos the old man had plastered over them. There were old black and white pictures in old wooden frames and some new-looking ones in coloured plastic frames and more just stuck straight on to the walls. There were various club pennants hanging from the picture rail that ran round the room, but Hector had never heard of any of the teams on them. Above the fireplace was a large colour team photo of, Hector supposed, Kalgev Zalgev looking proud and smart in a new-looking red and green striped football kit.

'When we got promoted,' the old boy said helpfully, 'nearly five years ago now. Probably the proudest moment of my life.'

Along the wall opposite the armchair that Sarunas was sitting in was an old roll-top desk absolutely stuffed full with pieces of paper and other items of various colours. On top of the desk stood two battered old silver cups and one reasonably new-looking trophy with a model of a footballer on the top. Above these, on the wall, hung a framed colour photo of Sarunas in a very smart suit and a player in the same red and green kit of the team photo. Also in the picture was a third man, very smartly dressed in a three-piece suit upon which hung a big gold chain, who was shaking Sarunas's hand.

'That's the mayor,' said a voice from the armchair. 'Sit down and I'll tell you all about it if you like,' he went on.

'I can't think of anything else I would rather do,' replied Hector.

They cleared the chair that sat in front of the desk of papers and Hector sat down to listen to the old boy's tale.

According to the story, the rise of FC Kalgev Zalgev had been nothing short of meteoric over the last fifteen years. Over that relatively short amount of time the team had risen from a very minor junior league to a division only one below the Russian premiership, the top level in the whole massive country, which had teams of the calibre of CSKA and Spartak Moscow. Most of the recent-looking photos on the wall were from the day that they had won the local senior division five years ago to earn a place in the league they were in now. And if only they could continue their rise and win this division, they would play at the very highest level.

The old man almost had tears in his eyes as he talked about their promotion. It was the greatest day in the history of the town, he said. The after-match party went on for three days. Everyone was convinced that the glory would continue and they would sail through this new division the following season and the year after they would host the likes of CSKA at their small ground which was just a short walk away from where they were sitting.

But the reality had been far harder than anyone would have liked to admit. They avoided relegation in that first season by just two points and although they had risen to almost mid-table in the following three years, they were having another poor year at the moment. There had still been highlights though. Last season they had travelled to the regional capital to play Talnius, the area's most famous team, who had been playing in the premiership themselves only two years before, and had won three–nil. The party, after the team returned from that game was nearly as good as the promotion one, the old boy said, although it only lasted two days this time!

But as he talked about the current season the old boy's voice got quieter and even seemed to tremble slightly. It appeared that after Kalgev had scored this marvellous victory over their local rivals they had almost immediately lost their three best players. The win had come right at the end of the previous season and as soon as the season had finished, Talnius had made Kalgev an offer they couldn't refuse for the trio. The top scorer from that season, the goalkeeper and the club captain, who gloried in the name of Donatas Karlikanovas, had all moved to the capital for the price of a new stand. It was good business financially, Sarunas admitted, but it had ripped the heart out of the side and they had never recovered. The new season had started badly for Kalgev and they had lost all of their first six games of the league programme. A recovery had got them up as high as twelfth (out of twenty-two) by mid-season, but another slump had seen them fall back down towards the relegation zone. In fact, with one game left to play, they were just one point above their bitterest of rivals, Zhelegnogorsk, who occupied the final relegation place in the table.

By one of those strange coincidences that happen in football, they had to play Zhelegnogorsk to finish the season. The game was to be played in Zalgev in two days' time and Hector and Maureen would be there to see it. It was one, if not *the* main reason, why Hector had been so keen to come on this adventure. Sarunas wasn't particularly bothered by the upcoming game, as he said Kalgev only needed a point and they were at home, where they hadn't lost for three months. *Still*, thought Hector, *it was likely to be a big occasion however much of a foregone conclusion the end result apparently was.*

Before they got up to rejoin the women downstairs, Sarunas gave Hector a club handbook and a couple of recent programmes to look through.

By the time they got back to the front room, Maureen's mum had actually stopped crying. They smiled at the two men as they entered and Louise immediately left for the kitchen where she was cooking dinner. While Maureen chatted happily with her father, Hector had a look through the handbook and programmes he had been given. The first thing he noticed was that they were not written in Russian Cyrillic script, but a language that Hector assumed must be Lithonian. This surprised him and he made a mental note to ask Sarunas about it. The second thing he noticed was that he couldn't understand a single word he read. He wasn't surprised he couldn't understand anything, on reflection he thought he would have been much more surprised if he could! But they were about football and they had line-ups and league tables and things, so he still enjoyed looking through them.

He was pleasantly surprised by the quality of the programme. He hadn't known what sort of programme to expect from a regional Russian football team in the back end of nowhere. In fact, he hadn't been sure that they would produce one at all. But all things considered, it was at least as good as Harwood Borough's production and in many respects better. It had a smart green and red cover superimposed with an aerial shot of their tidy-looking little ground. He could see from the photo that it had a new-looking single tier covered stand the complete length of one side, with what looked like covered terracing on the opposite side of the pitch. Behind one goal was a very small-looking covered seating area in one corner and maybe four rows of uncovered terrace steps the width of the pitch, but the other end was just one large steep concrete terrace open to the elements. The ground didn't look too bad to Hector from the photo, maybe Conference level at best at home, and would certainly do for one afternoon's entertainment.

The inside pages of the programme had plenty of reading, even if Hector didn't know what it was all about, interspersed with a few black and white action photos and tons of adverts. Hector just loved reading the list of players' names. *These Lithonian names were just fantastic*, he thought. He had honestly thought that Maureen had been pulling his leg when she told him her surname was Mansikevicus, and now he was in a country, or at least part of a country, where seemingly all the names were of that ilk. Donatas Karlikanovas – what a great name for a captain. Hector wished that Harwood Borough had a captain called Donatas Karlikanovas; no offence to Barry Johns, the current incumbent. *But Donatas Karlikanovas had a certain ring to it*, he thought. All in all not a bad effort of a programme, he was thinking as he was called into the kitchen for dinner.

Dinner was delicious; Louise had done her daughter proud. *They had bowls of home-made tomato soup for starters followed by roast boar, a real local delicacy that must have cost a fortune*, thought Hector. For dessert they had apple pie and custard, the custard powder having been brought by Maureen from England. For some reason that no one knew, it was impossible to get custard powder in that part of the world and as it was Sarunas's favourite from his time in England, Maureen had brought several packets over for him.

After dinner they all piled into the hire car for the short trip back to the hotel. They parked in the car park and walked into reception. Maureen's parents were not impressed by what they saw. Sarunas even offered to clear his den up so they could stay there and not have to sleep in this rathole, as he put it. But Maureen was having none of it. It was only for three nights and they would cope. They exited the hotel by means of the revolving door out into the street with Sarunas vowing quietly to do something about it.

The reason they had all gone back to the hotel was that Sarunas was taking them to the Kalgev Zalgev supporters' club, which was only a short walk from the hotel. *From the outside the supporters' club didn't look much better than the hotel*, Hector thought, *but once inside it was excellent*. It was basically a large hall with a stage at one end and about two-dozen wooden tables and chairs in the main body of the hall. Above the stage was a giant badge that Hector recognised as being the FC Kalgev Zalgev club badge, in red and green paint. Along one whole side of the hall was a bar complete with about twelve pumps with 'Grodny's' printed on top, behind which hung all manner of photos, pennants, scarves, shirts and other memorabilia. Hector loved the place the minute he walked in. It was not unlike the main hall at Harwood Borough. Not quite as plush maybe, but very good all the same and very functional.

There were about twenty people in the hall mainly sitting at the tables in small groups drinking, and it was to one of these groups that Sarunas headed the moment they arrived. After what was evidently a very brief but heated exchange between Sarunas and one of the people sitting at the table, the other person left in quite a hurry.

Sarunas took his wife and their two visitors to the bar where he introduced them to the two bar staff and ordered a round of drinks. No money changed hands. Hector thought he was probably going to enjoy himself.

He did. But not as much as Maureen did when they arrived back at the hotel about two hours later.

They were met in reception by a man who looked just like the one who had run out of the supporters' club when they had arrived. With a huge grin he apologised to the couple and explained that there had been a mix-up when they arrived and that they had been allocated the wrong room. He said he hoped that they didn't mind, but their luggage and belongings had been moved to the correct one while they had been out. He guided them into the lift that had mysteriously appeared just round the corner from the stairs and up to the seventh floor. The first thing Hector and Maureen noticed on leaving the lift was the luxuriousness of the carpet. It was a rich, deep red and looked to them almost new.

The room they were shown into was not so much a room, more of a suite. It was hard to believe that they were in the same hotel. It was lovely.

After the man, who had introduced himself as the manager, had left, Hector and Maureen just collapsed on the enormous double bed with laughter.

'Looks like your old man carries a bit of influence in this town,' laughed Hector.

'Doesn't it just,' answered Maureen. 'This must be where the head man from Moscow stays when he's in town.'

There was a massive bathroom (with a proper shower), a separate dressing room and even a sort of small kitchen with a fridge and a small cooker. On the elegant mahogany sideboard in the main room was a vase full of red roses and a large bucket of ice complete with a bottle of champagne. 'With the compliments of the management,' the man had said before he left, 'to make up for our little, er, indiscretion.'

'It's bloody Russian,' said Hector examining the bottle.

'I didn't know you were so fussy,' giggled Maureen.

'I'm not,' said Hector, trying to get the top off the bottle. He had not had much experience opening bottles of champagne and in the end it was Maureen who got the cork out, nearly shattering the vase of roses in the process.

Hector slumped into a luxurious large armchair with a glass of the bubbly in one hand and a remote control for the TV in the other.

'I could get used to this,' he slurred.

'Sho could I,' hiccupped Maureen from the bed.

After a lovely breakfast served in their room the next morning, they picked Louise and Sarunas up for a day in the country.

With Sarunas doing the navigating, much to Hector's relief, they went to a small town about twenty miles away where they parked and visited the local market. It was full of life and colour and they had a marvellous hour or so ambling around the stalls. There were people selling all kinds of fruit and vegetables and flowers and clothes and God knows what else. They bought a few bits and pieces, before they went off to see a huge Gothic castle nearby.

On the way Maureen asked her father what on earth he had said to the hotel manager the previous evening.

'Nothing much,' he answered. 'I just told him that unless he gave you a decent room then his tickets for the game on Saturday might go missing. He's a big fan.'

'Obviously,' said Maureen.

The castle was a delight. Unlike the ones back in England, it hadn't been all tarted up for tourists with vast admission charges and red ropes everywhere stopping you going in certain places. It was not exactly a ruin, but not altogether inhabited either. It had certainly seen better days and was obviously very carefully looked after, but it was to all appearances completely deserted.

A man suddenly appeared through a doorway and after a quick discussion with Sarunas agreed to show them around. He was apparently the curator of what was basically a museum and he lived in a small cottage in the castle grounds. He told Sarunas, who then translated, that they didn't get very many visitors and were pleased when they did. He took them all over the small castle explaining what was what and who was who as he went. He explained that the castle had been founded by the legendary (at least in Lithonia) warrior Kalgev, after whom the Zalgev football team was named. He had founded what was then the country of Lithonia in the thirteenth century and had defended most of it from this castle and a series of others dotted around the countryside until his death. His family and their descendants had lived in the castle right up until the Russian Revolution some six hundred-odd years later, but now it was falling into disrepair. The curator explained that he and his wife were both paid a small sum by the local council to keep it in as good order as they could, but it was really too big a job for an elderly couple.

Inside the car it was very quiet as they drove away, all of them sad at the story they had been told. Sarunas was particularly upset, especially as his links with Kalgev were so strong through the football team.

'You'd think that even the bloody Russians could find the money to keep such a historic building in good condition,' he moaned as they drove back to Zalgev.

That evening they ate in a local restaurant in Zalgev accompanied by a folk band that after an hour both Hector and Maureen could have happily strangled, but they didn't want to be rude so they just gritted their teeth. The meal had been excellent and the local wine even better.

Afterwards they all went back to the supporters' club in town so that Maureen could park the car and have a drink herself. There was a band setting up to play when they got there and for a few desperate minutes Maureen though that the musicians were the same ones from the restaurant. But she needn't have worried; they were actually quite good and played all sorts of seventies and eighties music. After a couple of hours they left Sarunas and Louise in the club and made their way back to their hotel where they had another comfortable night in their suite.

The next day, Friday, they were due to meet Maureen's dad at the football ground for a look around, but not until after lunch so they took the opportunity, after another sumptuous room-service breakfast, to have a wander around the town. It was much nicer than it had looked on their arrival, with a big onion-domed Russian Orthodox cathedral in the centre of the main square that they explored at some length. They went into a supermarket and were almost stunned to see how modern it was, with scanners at the checkouts and all manner of nice-looking food available. They bought some tram tickets and got on one until it reached the end of the line; then they simply got one back to where they had started. Hector liked trams, he decided. It was a pity that they didn't still have them back home.

They went into all sorts of shops just looking at the goods on sale and comparing the prices with those back home. Even compared to the 'official' exchange rate most things were a bargain; at the rate Maureen had got back in Moscow it was as if they were practically giving things away. They couldn't buy much though; they didn't have room in their cases.

After a light lunch they met Sarunas and had a good ramble around the football ground. Apart from the new main stand with red seats and a green painted roof, the rest of it was much older and more run-down than it had appeared in the picture on the programme cover. The big open terrace at one end was made of ancient crumbling concrete that looked distinctly unsafe to Hector, and the cover over the standing area opposite the new stand looked as if it would collapse with one decent puff of wind.

Sarunas was very proud of it all as he showed them round, however, and they wondered about the state of some of the other grounds they must play at if he was so enthusiastic about this one. There were, noted Hector, no floodlights, to which Sarunas replied that as the season ran through the summer months they weren't really necessary, but if and when they ever got promoted again they would have to install some. How they would afford them he didn't know. *Probably by selling off all their decent players on the cheap again*, thought Hector to himself.

They walked back from the ground to Maureen's parents' house where they had a quiet evening in watching TV after another delicious home-cooked meal provided by her mum. Three times during the evening Hector quietly asked Maureen if they could go back to the supporters' club, but quite naturally she wanted to spend their last evening in Lithonia with her parents.

They got away about ten and Hector made do by supping a few cans of beer in the hotel that he had bought in the supermarket that morning and had put in the fridge before they went out.

The evening ended in uproarious laughter as they watched TV in their room. They watched a very badly dubbed episode of an American drama series in which all the voices were dubbed into Russian by one person. Very obviously male with a deep gruff voice, he spoke everyone's lines, whether they were male or female, young or old. The effect was quite stunning and absolutely hysterical and rounded the evening off well.

The next morning they had a nice long lie-in before Maureen packed up everything ready for the start of the trip home immediately after the game. Checking out of the hotel wasn't without its problems. Madam Zaza was back in reception and the credit card machine had miraculously repaired itself, allowing Maureen not to have to get a wad of money from the bank.

It was as they were loading the luggage into the car boot outside that the fun started. A large man wandered over to them and asked them for their car parking money. When Maureen asked him what the hell he was talking about he went bananas and started ranting and raving about the money he said he was owed for the car park. Back inside the hotel they went with the man in tow and while Maureen, the car park attendant and Dracula's daughter had a loud shouting match, Hector sneaked out and opened the barrier. He got in the car and waited. Maureen came out soon after with a face like thunder, got into the driver's seat and, with a final tirade out of the window at the attendant who had followed her out, drove out of the car park.

Maureen was not in a good mood; she had steadfastly refused to pay the man and now she drove far too fast to the football ground, where she parked opposite the main gates.

Hardly anybody was about when they arrived at the ground; it was still almost two hours to go to kick-off. Sarunas was there and he showed them around the parts they had not been to the day before. The changing rooms underneath the new stand, the club office, the officials' changing room, and so on. They were also introduced to the official club cat, Jude, a huge fat black creature 'employed' to keep the rats and mice away. He was lying across two seats when they found him, fast asleep in the weak sunshine that bathed the new stand. He yawned at Maureen as she stroked his chin, but spat at Hector when he tried the same thing.

Complimentary programmes were handed to both of them and they were taken into the small club bar, restricted for the use of visiting VIPs and guests, for a pre-match drink. Soon after, the team bus arrived from Zhelegnogorsk and their officials were brought into the same bar and introduced to Hector and Maureen. There was a certain coldness amongst them, mused Hector to himself, but it was only to be expected he supposed, given the circumstances. For a start, at the end of the day one of the two teams would be relegated to a much more local and inferior league. Secondly,

Sarunas had told Hector that the two teams didn't get on anyway. Zhelegnogorsk was not part of Lithonia despite the fact that it was less than two hundred miles away and the people considered themselves to be completely Russian. This always caused friction between the two sets of fans and Kalgev had further upset the apple cart by banning Zhelegnogorsk fans from attending that day's game after serious trouble in the same match the previous season. No wonder the mood in the bar was somewhat cool, said Maureen when Hector told her all the facts.

Slowly people started to arrive for the game and when Hector and Maureen took their places in the main stand about fifteen minutes before the start, the ground was at least three-quarters full. The large terrace behind the goal was awash with green and red banners and scarves and flags, the two colours not only belonging to the football club, but also making up the Lithonian flag.

Sarunas had spent half an hour in the small bar with them explaining the tremendous amount of nationality problems that the local people had. Everyone in the district felt Lithonian but were to all intents and purposes suppressed by the Russians to the extent that the flying of the Lithonian flag in public was technically illegal. As was using the Lithonian language in schools and in any published materials. Hector asked him about the club programme that was blatantly printed in Lithonian, and this brought a wry smile to the old man's lips. He said that when they had started printing their programmes in Lithonian some four years earlier there had been such an outcry from Moscow that all the club officials, Sarunas included, had been threatened with imprisonment. It had taken nearly twelve months and some very hard bargaining before things settled down and the issue was dropped. Technically the programmes were still illegal documents and Sarunas warned Hector to keep any copies he had well hidden in his luggage once they had gone further than Talnius on their way home.

He said that the strangest sight they saw every season was at the away game at Talnius, where the home fans, as well as exhibiting their own colours of blue and white, also paraded the red and green of Lithonia. It made it look as if half of the home fans were supporting the away side!

By the time the game kicked off, the small ground was very nearly full. Sarunas had said it held as many as fifteen thousand but Hector was slightly sceptical. In his opinion there were probably getting on for ten thousand inside but it certainly wouldn't have held half as many again.

Hector had taken several photos of the ground the day before but wanted to remember the occasion as best he could by taking more of the game itself, so he happily snapped away in his seat as the game got under way. They were sitting about halfway up the new stand right on the halfway line. Maureen and Hector sat between Louise and Sarunas and directly behind the mayor (whom Hector had recognised from the photograph above Sarunas's desk) and his good lady wife.

The first ten minutes of the game were very nervous, both on and off the pitch. The tension was eased considerably when Kalgev took the lead in the twelfth minute. And what a good goal it was. Flying right-winger Kestutis Marciulonis sped past his marker and delivered a perfect cross onto the head of unmarked striker Linas Kunigelis, who thundered the ball into the net from five yards out.

The fans went wild both on the terracing and in the stand. For twenty-five minutes the atmosphere inside the ground was marvellous with the crowd singing and waving and cheering as if their heroes were winning a promotion, not fighting to avoid relegation.

Then, five minutes before half-time, disaster struck. Zhelegnogorsk equalised after a bad mistake by the Kalgev goalkeeper, Ivil Grabdeborl, the only non-Lithonian in the team, who completely misjudged a corner letting the away side's big defender Boris Zentraff nod in the equaliser.

The atmosphere at half-time was sombre, but not suicidal; a draw after all would keep Kalgev up and condemn their hated rivals. The weather didn't help the mood either. Gone was the weak sunshine to be replaced by overcast skies and a persistent drizzle. All in all it wasn't the happiest place in the world to be as the teams lined up for the second half kick-off.

Zhelegnogorsk started the second half with real purpose, and it was not really a surprise when they went in front after fifteen minutes. Pacy striker Boris Kikov streaked past a static Kalgev defence to side-foot the ball home from the edge of the box despite a despairing dive from Grabdeborl.

The mood in the ground changed at once from sombre to funereal. All was not lost though and Kalgev slowly came back into the game. With ten minutes to go the Zhelegnogorsk goalmouth looked a bit like a scene from the Alamo with wave after wave of red and green shirts hurling themselves into the box stubbornly defended by the black and white shirted ranks of the away side.

And then it happened. Kunigelis latched on to a half clearance from the Russians and drove the ball low into the net off the far post. The scenes that followed were amazing. The noise, the colour, the smoke from a hundred red and green flares that were let off – just everything was incredible. Everyone in the stand hugged everyone else; everyone was laughing and clapping and singing. Everything was going to be all right after all.

Hector was greatly relieved. He didn't want Maureen's dad's team relegated and he laughed and cheered and hugged along with everyone else. All they had to do was not let in a goal for four minutes, plus any time added on by the referee and they were safe.

The Zhelegnogorsk players, on the other hand, knew that they were beaten. With their heads down low, most of them looked like they had lost the will to live. It was all over for them.

It was almost five minutes later that fate decided to take a hand in the day's proceedings. And it was at Hector that its fickle finger pointed!

It was deep into injury time and the supporters were preparing for another massive celebration when Hector noticed he had just one picture left on the film in his camera, so he thought he might as well take it. At the moment he pushed the button to take the photo, the mayoress, sitting in front of Hector, thought that the game was over as the referee gave Kalgev a free kick on the halfway line. She leapt to her feet and turned round to hug the first person she saw. What she actually saw was the flash from Hector's camera as it exploded right into her eyes. It temporarily blinded the poor woman who fell backwards on top of a large man in the row in front of her.

The force of the mayoress falling on top of him pushed the large gentleman forward and he headbutted the rear of another smaller man directly in front of him. Being struck heavily on the back of the head caused this man to shove his legs out and kick the person immediately in the row in front of him. This person, a young woman, having been violently kicked in the behind, jerked forward and reached out with both arms to stop herself falling off her seat. These arms missed the seat in front and shoved a small boy in the front row of the stand so violently that he spilt the contents of his freshly poured hot coffee from his father's flask.

This would have been okay though, had Jude not been curled up asleep on the floor under the boy's seat. The hot liquid poured over the cat's back and he took off, well, like a scalded cat. Straight between the boy's legs he flew, under the rail of the fence in front of the stand and between the two teams' dugouts. On to the pitch he went and at full steam headed directly towards the home team's goal.

At that precise moment, the Kalgev goalkeeper, Grabdeborl, was positioning himself under the ball, which had been desperately hoofed up in the air towards him by the Zhelegnogorsk defence. Jude, of course, neither knew nor cared of such matters and, head down, was just making for the safety of the small stand in the corner behind the goal.

As Grabdeborl clutched at the ball, the cat flew between his legs, causing him to lose his balance, and he slipped in the mud that the drizzle had turned his goalmouth into and dropped the football over his shoulder.

The ball then serenely and agonisingly slowly rolled gently into the corner of the net behind him.

The whole world went quiet. The only noise in the entire ground was the sound of the referee's whistle signalling the goal, followed a few seconds later by the loud celebrations of the amazed Zhelegnogorsk players on the pitch and their officials in the stand.

Twenty seconds later to the disbelief of the entire stadium the referee blew the final whistle. It was all over. Kalgev Zalgev two – Zhelegnogorsk three. Kalgev were relegated.

It didn't take people too long to figure out where the blame lay for this defeat and almost every person in the entire stand turned to face Hector with snarls on their faces.

Quick as a flash Sarunas grabbed Hector and dragged him to the end of the row and down the steps. 'I think it's about time you left,' he said with a growl.

Maureen and her mum appeared and the four of them ran out of the ground to the hire car. Maureen opened her door and got in while Sarunas bundled Hector – *rather more forcibly than was absolutely necessary*, he thought – into the other side.

'Go quick, for God's sake,' said the old man. 'And ring me when you get home.'

Maureen nodded and took off as quickly as she dared.

She drove out of town even quicker than she had driven to the ground a few hours earlier. And she never said a word. In total silence she drove the hundred and twenty miles back to Talnius in just over two hours and she still hadn't spoken to Hector when they parked the car back at the station, leaving the keys in it as instructed, and unloaded their luggage from the boot.

All the way along the dual carriageway back to the capital Hector had repeatedly looked behind him expecting a mass of red and green bedecked cars to be chasing them. Once, when they overtook a car that backfired, he was convinced that someone was shooting at him! But they got back safely, if silently, and sat waiting on the platform for their train.

Hector's attempts to engage Maureen in conversation were met with a sharp glare and a stony silence. For two hours they waited until finally the Moscow train arrived and they clambered on board to start the long journey home.

As Hector sat opposite Maureen, feigning sleep, he just kept replaying in his mind the awful thing he had done. Single-handedly he had got the love of his life's father's football team relegated and in the process upset an entire nation of people, or certainly half of them. He peeped at Maureen. She still did not look happy. Would she ever talk to him again? It was pretty obvious that he would never be welcome again in Lithonia, but what the hell would happen when her parents visited them the following year as they had arranged? It did not bear thinking about.

It was going to be a very, very long trip back to England!

Hector's Dragon

Hector was worried. Some very strange things had been happening at Harwood Borough and he didn't like them one little bit. It was nothing in particular, just a feeling he got that things were not going in an advantageous direction. And it was all down to the Chinese!

The team had taken on a Chinese assistant manager. Then they signed three Chinese players. The tea hut started serving Chinese food on match days. Several Chinese supporters started coming to matches regularly; some applied to join and were accepted into the Vice-President's Association. A new shirt sponsor was announced, Wun Tun Woks Ltd. They started selling Chinese beer, Gleen Dlagon, in the club bar. Two more Chinese players were signed (although they definitely had English passports, honest). The manager resigned under mysterious circumstances and was replaced by – yes, you've guessed it – a Chinese man. All sorts of Chinese adverts started appearing in the programme. Two Chinese gentlemen were voted on to the board of directors. All the bar staff were sacked and replaced by Chinese ones. All the articles in the programme started to carry Chinese translations alongside them. The club turned the clubhouse hall into a martial arts centre, and all tannoy announcements were preceded by the banging of a gong. Finally four more Chinese players (with Portuguese passports) arrived.

But the worst thing about it all was that Hector seemed to be the only one who had noticed all this!

Hector was worried. All his friends still went to the games, but it was different somehow. For a start there was no tangible atmosphere at the games any more. Nobody yelled encouragement at the players or screamed derision at them when they did something badly. A goal or a good move or a good tackle was met with polite clapping, even from Hector's friends. A poor ball or missed chance or, worst of all, a lack of effort was met by nothing other than a stony silence. It was as if criticism was forbidden. Whereas the previous manager had spent most of the game pacing the sideline haranguing the referee or any of his players not trying hard enough, the new incumbent, Mr Wun Wun Wunce, had a different tactic. He stayed buried deep in his dugout, only appearing occasionally to stare coldly at any supporter brave enough to offer criticism of either player or tactic. The atmosphere at most games never rose above freezing whatever the weather conditions.

Something strange was definitely going on and Hector was going to get to the bottom of it!

It had all come to a head the previous Tuesday evening. Boro had been playing Wibsey Island in a league match and things weren't going so well. The players were having a poor season in general and the team of late had slipped down the table almost into a relegation place. Against Wibsey yet another three Chinese players had made their debut and things had gone from bad to worse. Wibsey had scored with almost their first shot on goal, and, despite Harwood having lots of possession, they could not convert this into shots on goal. With about ten minutes left, one of the new Chinese players had been caught offside immediately in front of where Hector and his friends were standing. The player, Mee Kno Trie, instead of getting the ball that had run ten yards in front of him, just turned round and started walking towards the halfway line, allowing the Wibsey goalkeeper to waste over a minute of valuable time.

When Hector had yelled at the player to pull his finger out and go and get the ball, the player had said something incomprehensible to him in Chinese and carried on walking. Hector was less than pleased with this and suggested in no uncertain terms that if this particular player could not be bothered, then maybe he should catch the first junk back to Shanghai, or words to that effect.

From the crowd's reaction you would have thought that Hector had not only suggested the dissolution of the monarchy, but had started the ball rolling himself by setting fire to the Union Jack – or maybe the Chinese flag would have been more appropriate. Not only did several members of the crowd start to shout at him, but even his own friends started to have a go at him.

Then the head of Mr Wunce appeared from the dugout and the noise immediately stopped. Hector couldn't believe what was happening before his eyes, or rather his ears. The rest of the game petered out in almost complete silence, with Wibsey going on to win two–nil. This result left Harwood Borough deep in the mire, only one point above the relegation zone, but in the bar afterwards you would have thought that they had won. There was no criticism of the manager or his team selection or the tactics or the fact that most of the players quite obviously were not bothered. In fact, Hector thought that the atmosphere was more like it should be at a garden party. Where had all the passion gone? Twelve months earlier and after a performance like that half the crowd would have been waiting outside the changing room with a noose. Now everyone was sipping Chinese beer or herbal tea in the clubhouse and folding the programme into little paper swans with moving wings.

Hector couldn't take any more of it. He drained his glass of diet cola and went home early. He had been drinking diet cola as all the English beers usually on sale had been removed from the bar. If you wanted beer you drank Gleen Dlagon. If you didn't want Gleen Dlagon you didn't drink beer. Simple! Hector was having none of it and settled for a diet cola.

The following Saturday Hector had arranged to meet Maureen at the club at twelve o'clock, some three hours before the kick-off of a league game against Handyside United and two hours before he usually arrived. Maureen was taking Hector into town to buy a new dress for a function she had to attend and he suggested meeting at the club, as she wasn't sure what time she would be out of the hairdresser's. Walking into what he expected to be the deserted car park, he was absolutely stunned to see all the players and all his friends, along with just about everyone else he had ever seen at the Boro, doing t'ai chi in the car park. He was so stunned that he was still standing open-mouthed and staring when Maureen arrived ten minutes later to pick him up.

When Hector told her about the t'ai chi she just smiled and talked as though it was the most natural thing in the world. He told her he thought something was seriously wrong at the club, but she told him not to worry; it was just his imagination working overtime. What really worried Hector was that when he asked her what she thought was behind the influx of all the Chinese players and supporters, she told him that he was talking nonsense and that Boro had no more foreign players at the club than any other team.

What really did it for Hector was when Maureen chose a long red silk dress with gold trim, a split up the side and a dragon print pattern. She looked like the bride of Fu Manchu; Hector had never seen her wearing anything like it in her life. When he mentioned this, Maureen just laughed at him and told him to open his eyes and take more interest. She said that it was just like the style of dress she had always worn. Hector knew he had a big problem. Whatever the hell it was that was affecting his favourite football club, it was affecting his beloved as well. Now he knew he had to do something about it.

Fortunately the function that Maureen was going to was in Birmingham and she was leaving the following morning by train. She was not coming back for five days and Hector made a decision there and then to sort it out by the time she returned. Unfortunately he didn't know what the problem was. Or where to start trying to find it.

They drove back to the ground in silence.

The game against Handyside went the same way as the previous one, more or less, with Boro going a goal down early on and the players not looking particularly interested in getting it back. Handyside got another one before Harwood halved the deficit from a corner. The ball was swung across by one of the few English players left in the team, Barry Johns, and the Handyside goalie with a rush of blood to the head punched it straight at Boro centre half Hym To Tawl. The ball hit Tawl square in the mouth and flew back past the stunned goalkeeper and into the net.

Hector leapt into the air. Almost everyone else was unmoved. A round of polite clapping swept gently around the ground. The players shook hands gentlemanly and trotted back to the halfway line to await the kick-off. Even Barry Johns, once famous throughout the league for his passion and rugged play, just ambled back to the centre as if he was taking an afternoon stroll.

Hector turned round to watch his friends' reactions. Maureen was talking to Billy Smallwood about Chinese food and seemed to be oblivious to the goal. Kevin and Neville were clapping politely but the look in their eyes said that it didn't really matter.

Handyside went on to score two more goals and everyone filed back into the bar at the final whistle. Hector was disconsolate, but nobody else seemed much bothered at all. A look at the teletext on the TV on the bar told Hector all he needed to know. A home win by the team directly below Boro, Blues Athletic, had pushed Harwood into the bottom three. He tried to talk to Neville and Kevin about it but all they were seemingly interested in was finding out what channel *Enter the Dragon* was showing on. Hector took Maureen to one side and asked her if she wanted to go for a meal. She said sure, but it would have to be Chinese.

Hector finished his diet cola and went home on his own. He called in at his local off-licence on the way for some cans of beer. The first thing he saw as he pushed the door open was a huge display of tins of Gleen Dlagon. The bright sparkling sign above the pyramid of cans announced: GLEEN DLAGON, THE NEW DRINK FROM THE ORIENT. Another sign flashed the message 'Half price introductory offer'. Hector bought six cans of Old Nadgers Throatcharmer and a large bag of peanuts, ignoring an offer of a free can of Gleen Dlagon to try, and left the shop feeling even more depressed.

Things didn't improve when he arrived home. Pushed through his letter box was, amongst other rubbish, a leaflet advertising Gleen Dlagon beer, now on sale at his local supermarket at half price. Another leaflet advised him to try a special new pizza at Pizza Place. Called the Chinese, it was covered in sweet and sour chicken and baby sweetcorn. It came with two complimentary cans of Gleen Dlagon. Hector tore the advert into pieces and settled down to watch TV.

He checked through the channels. On the first was an old Charlie Chan film. On the second was a documentary about the Great Wall of China. On the third was the obscure *Oriental Game Show: No Surrender*, while the fourth was showing *Cooking with Ken Hom*. As a last resort he switched to Channel Five, a thing he only ever did in emergencies. He was pleasantly surprised to find that they were showing an old Ealing comedy. Almost as soon as he opened his first can of beer, the film went into an advert break. The first advert was for, surprise, surprise, Gleen Dlagon beer. The viewer was encouraged by a stupid jiggling bright green dragon that danced along a wall of beer cans to 'buy Gleen Dlagon, the new drink from the Orient, now on sale at all good supermarkets and off-licences. Half price while stocks last!'

Hector turned the TV off and switched on the radio to listen to one of the Saturday evening football phone-ins. This was better, he decided. He even picked a station that didn't have any adverts, just in case.

Two hours later he fell fast asleep in his chair. He woke up at three, stiff as a board. But he had had an idea while he dozed. It must be something to do with the beer! That was it: they were drugging the beer. It was obviously some diabolical plot to take over the country.

He sat in the dark for three-quarters of an hour before he dragged himself off to bed. He had cracked it. Why didn't he think of it before? Mind you, he might know what was happening, but what on earth was he going to do about it?

He didn't sleep well for the rest of the night.

The next morning he went round to Maureen's to see her off to Birmingham. He was absolutely horrified to find that she had taken all the pictures down in her flat and replaced them with Chinese rural scenes. And in the kitchen hung a calendar from the local Chinese takeaway! There was a distinct smell of Chinese food in the air too and Hector couldn't get Maureen down the stairs and into her car quickly enough.

After she pulled away, Hector went straight back upstairs to begin his investigations. The first thing he needed was an empty beer can. It was around this time that Hector hit his first big snag. Maureen didn't drink beer!

Well, not very often anyway; she was a white wine drinker and only drank beer when the weather was really, really warm. And then only lager.

Still, he thought, *she could have had the odd one here and there.*

On the way back to his own flat, Hector went back into the off-licence for another few cans of Old Nadgers Throatcharmer. This time he took the free can of Gleen Dlagon. Back home he poured the Chinese beer out into the cleanest glass he could find and stared at it for about five minutes. It kept its head quite well and was very slightly green in hue. Other than that it looked and smelt like any other beer. Now came the big test: what did it taste like?

Hector didn't know quite what to do about tasting it. Did he try to tie himself into his chair beforehand, just in case after a few sips he felt like dashing out for a Chinese takeaway? No, he rejected that idea as he couldn't figure out a way to do it. What about if he shut himself up in the broom cupboard while he drank it? No, that was an even stupider idea.

In the end he just sat at the kitchen table and had a swig. *Not bad*, he thought as he waited for some dire effect to take hold of him. Maybe he would get the urge to grow a very long thin moustache. Maybe he would feel like he needed to rush out and buy a wok.

In the end he needed nothing. He drained the last of the beer from his glass, licked his lips and sat back in his chair. He felt nothing. No effects at all. No craving for anything unusual, not even a particular craving for another beer. He felt a bit peckish, but he hadn't eaten all morning so that explained that one. He made himself a cheese sandwich. Just cheese. Nothing remotely Chinese there, just a bit of good old English Cheddar.

He sat at the table and munched on his sandwich while studying the now empty Chinese beer can. There wasn't too much information on it about where it was brewed, but the address of the UK distributor was actually in Harwood itself. Hector thought that maybe he should pay them a visit.

At work the next morning, the first thing Hector did was book the rest of the week off as holiday. He then spent most of the day on the telephone trying to find out more about the origins of Gleen Dlagon, but he drew a blank. He also tried to find out if the distributors, Ying Tong Yiddle and Po, handled anything else other than Gleen Dlagon beer. It would appear that nobody knew. He couldn't find anyone who had even heard of them. Ying

Tong Yiddle and Po operated from one of these small new out-of-town industrial estates and had only been open a matter of weeks. Hector rang a friend of his who worked on the same estate, but he knew nothing either. Apparently this company didn't use its own lorries to deliver anything, just plain unmarked ones. And he hadn't seen any gangs of Chinese cut-throats wandering around either. All in all they gave the appearance of a normal small distribution company.

Hector didn't sleep too much that night; he just seemed to lie in bed trying to figure out a plan of action. By dawn he still hadn't come up with very much other than that he was going to the distribution company that morning to find out whatever he could about this diabolical Chinese plan to take over the country using drugged beer.

He had convinced himself by now that that was what was happening, and hours and hours without sleep had made those convictions even stronger. But he still didn't know what to do. At one stage, around four o'clock, he decided that he was just going to walk into their offices and confront them. He would walk in as bold as brass and say something along the lines of, 'Okay, I know what you are doing and if you don't stop I will go straight to the police!' And exactly what did he think that would achieve? Did he really think that his threats would bring this obviously desperate and evil organisation crashing down? No, he wasn't that stupid, or at least he wasn't by around half past four.

By five o'clock he had decided to go to the police first. That was it, he decided: go to the police and tell them what was going on and they would charge round to this warehouse and catch all the crooks red-handed. Yes, that was definitely the way to do it; he might even get to go with them on the raid – now that would be something. And think of the publicity! He could ring the local paper before they went to make sure that a reporter and a cameraman – make that two cameramen to be on the safe side – would be there waiting. Except, of course, that by half past five he realised that he couldn't really go and tell the police what was going on as he didn't have a clue what *was* going on.

By six o'clock he was back to square one. What the hell was he going to do?

Around half past six he dozed off and had a dream about himself and Elliott Ness screaming around in an old black police car firing wildly from old-fashioned tommy guns and taking on dozens of crooks single-handed. They shot their way into a huge old waterfront warehouse and gunned down about fifty Chinese pirates all with coloured bandannas on their heads and carrying evil-looking long knives in their teeth.

As the last pirate bit the dust Ness turned to Hector and smiled an evil smile. He pulled off his Elliott Ness mask to reveal that he was really Ken Hom, the Chinese chef off the telly. He withdrew an enormous and very solid wok from behind his back and went to smash Hector across the head with it. Hector instinctively ducked to one side to get away from the killer wok and… fell out of bed, waking himself up as he hit the floor with a large bump.

He decided that he had had enough sleep for one night; it was too dangerous. He washed, dressed and sat downstairs staring at the cooker. He knew that he should make himself some breakfast, but he just didn't feel like it. His stomach felt like someone had kicked it. He felt decidedly queasy.

Eventually he had two cups of tea and watched breakfast TV for an hour before putting his best anorak on and walking to the bus stop. He caught a bus just after nine o'clock and watched the people of Harwood scurry around in the drizzle as he got nearer and nearer to his destination. He had planned to get off the bus a couple of stops before the estate to let his head clear as he walked along, but the persistent drizzle had made him change his mind. He got off at the entrance to the estate and went straight up to the huge map that was positioned right by the road. Ying Tong Yiddle and Po was easy enough to spot; the paint of the company's sign on the map was brand new and almost glowed, even in the gloom of the morning. The unit he wanted was the very last one on the left-hand side and by the look of things was about three hundred yards from where he was standing.

Very slowly he started walking towards it. With every step he took his stomach felt worse. At last he turned a corner, and there was his destination slap bang in front of him. It didn't look much from the outside, he had to admit. It was just a fairly large warehouse, one half of which had a huge shutter open that was big enough to admit an articulated lorry. There was no lorry in it, and inside Hector could just make out huge pallets loaded with red and green cans. There was no mistaking the brand. There was only one red and green beer can on the market: Gleen Dlagon.

Outside the building there was nothing to announce who the company was, just a blank blue wall. Apart from the huge shutter there was also a blue door, and next to the door was a big metal letter box. Above the letter box was a plaque that Hector thought probably had the company details on it. He thought that a good look at that plaque was as good a next move as any he could think of and he strolled across the road to get a closer look.

Two paces into the road he heard an ominous noise behind him, a sort of dull roar. He turned round to see a huge articulated lorry about ten feet away from him and he heard a deep hoot from its horn. His body reacted to the crisis by shutting down. He fainted.

Hector awoke to find himself sitting in an armchair. He could make out a large swaying face staring at him. In his confused state of mind it looked like a beautiful woman. A beautiful Chinese woman. With a long moustache. Hector shut his eyes again. When he opened them again the large face had gone, to be replaced by two smaller ones. One was indeed that of a beautiful Chinese woman, but there was no long droopy moustache. That was in the middle of the other face, which belonged to a podgy Chinese man with small round glasses and piggy little red eyes.

The woman spoke. 'Are you all right?' she asked softly. 'Do you need an ambulance?'

Hector didn't say a word. He just stared blankly at the girl.

'Are you all right?' she repeated.

'Err, yes, I think so,' stammered Hector. He didn't think he had ever seen anyone so gorgeous in his life. He must be wrong about this place, he thought to himself. Surely no one as beautiful as that could be involved in anything underhand.

'You walked out in front of one of our lorries,' she went on. 'You were very lucky. If the driver hadn't been slowing right down to turn into the depot, he would have squashed you flat.'

'I guess I was then,' said Hector, still not taking his eyes off her.

This time the other person spoke. Hector turned to look at him as he started to speak. This one was a different kettle of fish altogether. He looked like the sort of person who had guilty stamped all over him before you even knew what he was guilty of.

'What were you doing outside here?' he asked in a very sharp Chinese accent.

Hector focused on him more seriously. He looked for all the world like the old horror film actor Peter Lorre. Hector decided there and then that he was behind all the problems and was very probably holding the girl hostage. Drugged, that was it; he was holding her hostage and she was drugged. But Hector would sort it out. He knew he would. But as usual he didn't know how. Or when, or where.

'Well? I asked you what you were doing here,' said the evil little man.

'I was, er, I was coming here to see, er, I was coming here to see if there were any jobs going,' Hector stammered. *Not bad,* he thought to himself. *Not bad at all for the spur of the moment.* 'And the next thing I knew I was sitting in here.'

'I don't believe him,' said the man to the girl. 'I think he's spying.'

'Spying?' she said in surprise. 'You have got to be kidding. Have you ever seen a spy who looked like that? And what sort of spy would almost get himself killed?'

'Either a very poor one, or a very good one,' replied the man, staring menacingly at Hector.

'I don't believe it,' the girl went on.

'Well, he's here now; what are we going to do with him?' he asked.

'I'm going to get him a cup of tea,' she said and turned to Hector. 'Unless you'd like a glass of beer?'

That did it. At the mention of the word beer, Hector came back to reality with a bang. 'No, no, no,' he stuttered, shaking his head so violently that he nearly fell off the chair. 'Tea would do very nicely, thanks.'

The girl turned and walked away. Hector was transfixed by her walk. He just stared after her until the man started talking to him again.

'My name is Mr Wu,' he said. 'What is yours?'

Hector didn't answer straight away. He wondered if he should give a false name. A proper spy would give a false name. 'Er, Len,' he replied after a long pause. 'Len Daily.'

'You don't seem too sure.' The small man grinned at him. 'I hope you are telling me the truth.'

'Yes,' said Hector stiffly, 'of course I am.'

'Good,' said the man. Then he sat down opposite Hector and stared at him inscrutably.

Hector felt most uncomfortable with this nasty little man staring at him. He got more and more determined by the second to get this matter sorted out. He wanted this horrible little man thrown in the deepest, darkest prison cell that the country could find. He was just thinking what a shame it was that torture had been abolished when the girl returned.

'I'm sorry I've been so long,' she said. 'The kettle's on the blink.'

She handed Hector a small cup, inside which was possibly the evilest-smelling liquid he had ever known in his life. He stared at it blankly.

'It's Chinese tea,' said the girl. 'I hope you like it.'

'I've never had Chinese tea before,' said Hector. 'Don't you get milk with it?'

The girl laughed. 'No, not usually.'

'He says his name is Len Daily,' snarled the man from the chair opposite Hector.

'Well, if that's what he says it is, then I'm sure that's what it is.' The girl beamed.

'I'm still not so sure,' Mr Wu said. 'There are no jobs here anyway, so you can go as soon as you have drunk your tea.'

Hector had to think quickly; he had to stall him. He needed to stay for as long as it took him to figure out exactly what was going on.

For one of the first times in his life, Hector's brain acted quicker than his body. He had a great idea, or at least what seemed like a great idea at the time. He leapt to his feet and as he did so he spilt the hot tea all down the front of his trousers. And hot it most certainly was. The liquid, having no milk in it to cool it, was not too far short of scalding and about three fifths of a second after it hit Hector's trousers the heat burnt through to his skin. And it was very delicate skin that it landed on. As Hector jumped three feet in the air and started jiggling around like a madman, the thought occurred to him that maybe this wasn't the best idea he had ever had. Certainly not down the trousers. And definitely not down the top of his trousers.

He screamed. Loudly.

Now it was Mr Wu's turn to nearly fall off his chair. Or more accurately to be knocked off his chair as Hector careered around the room like a maniac, whooping and hollering at the top of his voice.

The girl ran to the kitchen and came back with a towel she had soaked in cold water. 'Here,' she said, throwing it at Hector.

Hector grabbed it and applied it to his smouldering groin. The relief was almost instantaneous. He stopped yelling and just went 'Aah' as the burning subsided.

'You poor man,' said the girl. 'Quick, get those trousers off.'

It was the best offer Hector had had all day and he pulled his shoes off and started to undo his trousers.

'I've had enough of this,' said Mr Wu, and he got up and left the room.

The girl took Hector's trousers away into the small kitchen and Hector sat back in the chair.

'My name's Lie, by the way,' came the girl's voice from the kitchen. 'Lie Chee. What did you say yours was again?'

'Hector,' said Hector without thinking.

'I thought Mr Wu said your name was Len,' she said.

'Er, it is,' answered a now thoroughly confused Hector, 'but everyone calls me Hector.'

'Why?'

'Er, it's a bit complicated really,' Hector stuttered. 'It's a long story.'

'Maybe you could tell me some time,' came the girl's voice softly.

Hector hoped she would hurry back with his trousers; he was starting to get very excited. After all, it was not every day that he got shut in an office without any trousers on in the company of the most beautiful girl he had ever seen.

'Are you really after a job?' she asked.

'Yes,' said Hector, or Len, or whoever he was. 'As you are fairly new to the area, I thought there might be something available.'

'Well, there aren't any at the moment, I'm afraid,' came the girl's voice. 'But I'll tell you what; once these trousers have dried on this radiator, I will take you around and show you what goes on here, and if something turns up you will at least know what we are all about.'

Yeeessssssss, Hector thought to himself. *Cracked it*!

Ten minutes later and with a warm if still slightly damp pair of trousers on, Hector was led by Lie Chee out of the office and into the warehouse. Hector could hardly contain his excitement. He was on the verge of cracking a major drugs case and rescuing a beautiful girl in the process. He would be a hero and he could only speculate how grateful the girl would be. He got a sudden pang of conscience thinking about Maureen, but he thought he would worry about that if and when he ever had anything to worry about.

The first thing Hector noticed about the warehouse was that nothing appeared to be happening. The lorry that had almost run Hector down was parked in the entrance, its open loading shutter gaping like a giant dragon's mouth. Inside the warehouse itself there was pallet after pallet of canned Gleen Dlagon beer and many more pallets of other products, all seemingly Chinese in origin and all enclosed in yard after yard of shrink wrap. Hector couldn't make out what all of these products were, but they all seemed to be drink related. Among them he could see things like peanuts, bar snacks and boxes and boxes of crisps. There was one young Chinese boy sitting at a desk reading a newspaper, but other than that the place was deserted. Hector had half expected to see a collection of cut-throats sitting around spooning white powder into the beer cans, or at the very least Mr Wu beating somebody with a bamboo stick. But there was nothing like it. Suspiciously though, there was no sign of Mr Wu.

'Where has that man gone?' asked Hector. 'Mr Wu.'

'He must be upstairs,' Lie Chee replied. 'Come on I'll show you.'

With that she led Hector back across the almost deserted warehouse to where the office door stood open. Instead of going through it she started to climb a metal staircase that led to a door to what appeared to be another office immediately above the one where Hector had spent the last hour.

She walked through the doorway and stood to one side to allow Hector to enter. As he did so, his jaw almost hit the floor. For there in the middle of the room was Mr Wu, sitting at a small wicker table and drinking what appeared to be a cup of Chinese tea. It was not the sight of Mr Wu, however, that made Hector's jaw drop in amazement; it was the sight of Mr Wu's companion. For sitting in a chair opposite him at the table was… Maureen!

Hector was more than stunned; he was on the verge of losing consciousness again. Maureen – what the hell was she doing here? And with Mr Wu, the evil genius behind this entire scam. Hector really and truly was at a loss for words. His Maureen, who was supposed to be in Birmingham at a conference, was sitting calmly at a table with the evil Mr Wu drinking Chinese tea. Wu had obviously drugged her as well as Lie Chee. Was there no end to his deviousness?

'Ah, the supposed Mr Daily, I presume,' said the evil-looking Chinese man.

Hector gulped.

'Have you met Mr Daily, my dear?' Wu asked Maureen.

'No, I haven't,' replied Maureen, rising to her feet and holding her hand out to Hector. 'Charmed, I'm sure,' she said, clutching Hector's hand in hers.

Hector gulped again.

As she squeezed his hand, he felt her tickle his palm with her little finger, as if conveying some kind of message. She looked him straight in the eye and, with Mr Wu directly behind her, she gave Hector a little wink.

Now, Hector might not be the brightest nail in the box, but even he could see that something was going on here, so he decided to play along.

'Hi,' he stammered, 'my name is Hec… er, Len; I'm here looking for a job. Lie Chee was just showing me around.'

'This is our rest area,' interrupted Lie Chee. 'The lorry driver who almost ran you down is out the back making himself a cup of tea.'

With that a small door opened behind Mr Wu and a large man entered the room carrying a steaming mug of coffee. 'Last time I saw you, you were lying in the road in front of me,' said the man. 'I thought I'd killed you.'

'Sorry about that,' said Hector. 'I fainted.'

'Maybe next time you'll look where the hell you are going,' added the man before he sat down on a large settee in the corner and picked up a newspaper.

'I really think I must be going now,' said Hector to Lie Chee, and with that he turned and made his way back down the stairs, ignoring Maureen completely.

When they reached the bottom of the staircase Lie Chee pushed past Hector to open the outside door. He could smell her perfume as she squeezed past him. It was lovely.

'Before you go,' she said, smiling at him, 'if you leave me your address and phone number I will let you know if anything suitable comes up.'

Hector was in a quandary. He would love this gorgeous woman to have his details, but just as he was going to give them to her, he thought of Maureen upstairs with the evil Mr Wu. And he thought what might happen if *he* got hold of Hector's details.

'I'll drop them in to you,' said Hector, pushing his way out into the fresh air. 'Thanks for the tea and the look round,' he said over his shoulder to the girl as he half walked, half ran back up the road to the bus stop.

An hour later Hector was sitting at his kitchen table, grimly holding a mug of English tea. He was desperately trying to make sense of the morning's experiences. 'What had he learnt?' he kept asking himself. And the answer always came back the same: 'Absolutely nothing. Well, that wasn't quite true,' he admitted to himself. He had learnt that Mr Wu was obviously behind this attempt to paralyse the country and that this man would probably stop at nothing to get his evil plan to succeed. He had already drugged at least two women to help him and God knows what other tricks he had tried to help with his scheme.

Suddenly, in mid-thought, he heard his front door open with a loud click, followed by footsteps on the stairs.

Then he heard Maureen's voice coming through the open doorway. 'Oh, he's here all right, trust me,' she was saying to somebody.

Maureen's figure glided round the kitchen doorway and for the first time Hector noticed that she was wearing the red Chinese dress she had bought only a few days before. He was thinking how good she looked in it when he caught sight of the inscrutable Mr Wu.

Hector made a leap for the drawer by the sink and grabbed a long carving knife from it, which he waved menacingly around in the air.

'Don't be stupid, Hec,' said Maureen with disdain. 'You'll only cut yourself. I think it's about time you two met properly,' she went on. 'Hector, this is Detective Inspector Brinklow, from Scotland Yard. He's with the drugs squad. Detective, this is Hector, my boyfriend, who apparently thinks he's a cross between Zorro and Inspector Gadget.'

'Good to meet you,' said the detective, holding his hand out to Hector.

Hector gulped, and not for the first time that day.

Maureen walked across the kitchen and gave Hector a hug. 'Don't worry,' she said, 'he's not really Chinese. And he's certainly not an evil drugs baron if that's what you're worrying about.'

'I think it's about time we had a little chat,' said the detective inspector.

With that he pulled another chair up to the table and told Hector an interesting story.

Two hours later, Hector and Maureen were sitting in Hector's front room watching TV. At least, Maureen was watching TV; Hector was trying to take in all that the inspector had been telling him. If he was indeed Detective Inspector Brinklow. Hector still wasn't convinced, although it had to be said that when he had taken his glasses and false moustache off and stood up straight, there was very little, if anything, Chinese about him.

Between Maureen and this man they had told Hector a strange but quite believable story – or at least to Hector's ears it was a believable story.

Apparently both Ying Tong Yiddle and Po and the Gleen Dlagon Corporation were really a front for a gang of crooks in China intent on flooding the UK with illegal immigrants and narcotics. Mr Wu, or Detective Inspector Brinklow or whatever his name was, had infiltrated this organisation and was in the process, or so he said, of rounding up the ringleaders, of which Lie Chee was one, and making several important arrests.

The illegal immigrants were being smuggled in via the football club as players and supporters and the drugs were rather surprisingly nothing to do with the beer, but one particular brand of snack food, Ply-Cee Prawn Crackers. The beer apparently didn't have any illegal narcotics in it at all; all that it had that normal beer didn't was a Chinese herb that tended to make people hungry, hence the need for snack foods. It was this herb that gave the beer its green hue. The drug in the prawn crackers was a mind control drug, which was why no one at the football club knew or even suspected that anything untoward was going on. The same drug was also in the crisps and peanuts and all the other Ply-Cee brand snacks that were now going on the market.

Brinklow said how desperately they were trying to keep the problem contained in Harwood. So far the only delivery of Ply-Cee products destined for somewhere else had been successfully stopped by the police and the driver detained for exceeding his tachograph limits. The goods were still locked up in the lorry parked somewhere in Manchester.

The inspector had asked Maureen to get involved as it was her who had noticed that there was something going on at the football club in the first place and had contacted the police with her suspicions. She had only really found out by chance after continually refusing offers of the snack in question and noticing what happened to the people who ate it. She hadn't told Hector what she had discovered for two reasons: firstly, the police had asked her to tell no one; secondly, and more importantly, she didn't want Hector to get hurt.

She said that she had nearly fainted herself when Hector had walked into the rest room at Ying Tong Yiddle and Po. The inspector had taken her there to see if she could sniff anything out, while he kept the delightful and apparently extremely dangerous Lie Chee busy. And then Hector had turned up out of the blue and almost blown the entire operation sky-high. Hector couldn't understand why Maureen was being used by the police and not some policewoman and he had to admit that he thought the reply he was given was a bit lame. Maureen said that there was simply no one suitable available and that, as she knew most of the details, the police, or more specifically Detective Inspector Brinklow, had asked her if she would co-operate. She said that although she was quite naturally nervous, she had agreed eventually, thinking it might be exciting.

The inspector told Hector that Maureen had noticed that these Ply-Cee Prawn Crackers were normally available in bowls on the bar at the football club and most people seemed to munch a few while waiting for a drink. Fortunately Hector hated snack food, prawn crackers in particular, so it hadn't affected him either. Certain people at the football club were apparently in on what was going on, but for safety reasons the inspector would not tell Hector who they were.

Both Maureen and the inspector told Hector to keep his head down and stay out of the way. Under no circumstances was Hector ever to go to Ying Tong Yiddle and Po again, or even contemplate seeing Lie Chee. He was also advised to miss Harwood Borough's next game on the following Saturday, as things were apparently expected to come to a head some time during the afternoon.

With these warnings Brinklow had excused himself, refitted his glasses and moustache, and left.

Maureen refused to discuss the matter any more after the detective inspector left and changed the subject by asking Hector what he fancied for tea. Hector said he wasn't much bothered, but nearly collapsed when Maureen asked him if he fancied a Chinese takeaway. He was almost hyperventilating by the time he realised that Maureen was joking, and in the end they settled for good old-fashioned English fish and chips. Hector wouldn't even have vinegar on his chips as he thought it was a bit too exotic given the circumstances and he wasn't at all sure that vinegar wasn't of Chinese origin. As to the suggestion by Maureen that he have a pickled egg…

Hector was back at his desk in his own goods-in area the next morning. He had cancelled his remaining three days' holiday, as there was nothing he could do. Or rather nothing he was allowed to do.

He didn't get a lot done at work though, it has to be said. He spent most of the next few days chewing on the end of his pencil and thinking about what was going on at Ying Tong Yiddle and Po. He hadn't seen or heard from Maureen by Saturday morning, which worried him even though she had told him not to worry. He had seen neither hide nor hair of Mr Wu, Lie Chee or any other Chinese person whatsoever. In fact, it was as if nothing had happened at all. He deliberately avoided going to Harwood Borough, even missing training on Thursday evening, a thing he would never normally do intentionally. At least three evenings a week he would drop into the club for an hour or so on his way home from work, but this week he gave it a wide berth. It didn't stop him from wondering what was going on there. Were all his friends still going and, if they were, what was their involvement in all this by now?

By Thursday he had already decided to go to the game on Saturday, whatever anybody had told him. Apart from anything else, it was another important six-pointer in the battle against possible relegation. They were playing the team last in the division, St Alfreds Town, and anything less than a win for Boro would be nothing short of a disaster.

Hector just had to be there. And he was going to be there early, he had decided!

He didn't sleep properly Friday night, but he had got used to it by then; he hadn't had a good night's sleep for over a week!

He got up early, washed and dressed and spent the morning in his now favourite position of sitting at the kitchen table with a mug of tea in his hands and staring into space. He was so wrapped up in his thoughts about the afternoon that twice his tea went stone cold before he drank it. He forced himself to eat some cold baked beans and a lump of cheese so he had something in his stomach, before he got himself ready for the game. He put his anorak on and tied his red and white scarf round his neck, and at exactly ten past twelve he shut his front door and started to walk the mile or so to the football ground. As he closed the gate that led to the door to his flat, he wondered what the next few hours would bring.

At almost exactly twelve thirty he stood opposite the entrance to the football ground. He didn't know why, but he just stood across the road watching for anything to happen. There was no sign of any t'ai chi going on. In fact, there was not too much of anything going on at all, just as he would suspect at twelve thirty. It looked like all the players' cars were there, although that wasn't many now. Most of the Chinese players came in a small minibus that was getting larger by the week; the local players were now down to about five. He could see the rear end of the minibus poking out from round the rear of the clubhouse. He couldn't see Maureen's car anywhere, which he was very pleased about.

He waited fully fifteen minutes before walking slowly but surely into the clubhouse and directly into the members' bar. Other than a barman, it was totally deserted. He walked to the bar and ordered a diet cola; he wanted to keep a clear head. Anyway, he didn't know what had or had not been tampered with.

He sat at a table in the furthest corner of the bar from the entrance and he waited.

Nothing very much happened for the next hour or so. Around one thirty people slowly started to drift into the bar. First it was a few of the Chinese players, followed by a handful of the Chinese fans. Then a couple of tough-looking away fans arrived. At about one forty-five all Hector's mates arrived, including Kevin Loony. Now Hector *knew* that something strange was happening. Kevin had never turned up for a game that early in his life, even though he lived nearer the ground than any of them. Kevin had a habit of turning up with five minutes to spare on a good day; for him to turn up at one thirty-five was nothing short of spooky.

Kevin and Neville and Billy all stood at the bar and ordered pints of Gleen Dlagon. While they waited they munched on the complimentary bowls of prawn crackers provided. None of them appeared to see Hector sitting in the corner, even when they looked over in his direction. Hector just sat and waited for events to start happening.

Soon after two o'clock, with the bar now about half full with fans, mostly Chinese but with a sprinkling from St Alfreds, Maureen and Mr Wu arrived. They ordered something from the bar and stood in the opposite corner to Hector. It was Mr Wu who saw him first and he didn't look too happy about it. He whispered something to Maureen, who slowly sidled along the wall to where Hector was sitting.

'What the hell are you doing here?' she growled at him through clenched teeth.

'Well, I wasn't going to miss this, was I?' he replied.

'We told you not to come,' she went on. 'It could get very dangerous.'

'Oh, so it's all right for you to be here then,' Hector answered gruffly, 'but it's not all right for me to be here!'

'I've been *trained* for this kind of thing,' snapped back Maureen.

'Trained?' he stammered.

'Yes, trained,' answered Maureen. 'How do you think I got the flat and the car?' she went on. 'You don't get to keep those kind of things by working part-time for the bloody railway, do you?'

Hector muttered that he didn't suppose you did, but in all truth he had never given it much thought.

Since he had first met her, Maureen had always remained a bit of a mystery. Quite often she had to go off for a few days at a time for meetings and conferences and the like, but Hector had never questioned her about it. Now he was beginning to wish that he had. He was starting to get a headache trying to figure out exactly what was going on.

Just then the bar doors opened and in came Lie Chee accompanied by four large dodgy-looking men. They looked like the type of person the word 'henchman' was invented for.

Maureen slid back along the wall towards Mr Wu. Hector lifted his open programme and sat reading it, covering as much of his face as possible. He kept expecting one of Lie Chee's goons to come and pick him up by his collar or something, but in the end nothing untoward happened at all.

At about half past two Hector noticed that most of the Chinese contingent in the bar had left, including Lie Chee and her goons, and Mr Wu and Maureen. Hector relaxed a little. With no one that frightened him around, he wandered up to the bar and made conversation with his friends. Or at least he tried to; it wasn't easy.

They all recognised him and said hello, but that was about it. It was like trying to strike up a conversation with a bunch of tailor's dummies, so Hector left them where they were and made his way into the ground itself.

There were some very strange-looking people standing around on the terraces, Hector noticed as he made his way through the turnstiles, and he was very surprised to be asked by a security guard which team he supported. He was totally stunned by this as in all his life he had never seen a proper security guard at Harwood Borough; there had never been the need for one. But today there must have been at least a dozen.

Hector said he supported Boro and was asked politely but very firmly to go and stand behind the goal at the other end of the ground. He was not going to disagree; this man looked like he knew how to persuade people to do what he wanted.

As he walked around the ground to the other end, he noticed that all the Chinese fans were congregated along the halfway line, while all the away fans, apparently without exception, were standing at the opposite end to where Hector had been told to go. Once in position behind the goal, he noticed that almost everyone he knew from the club was already standing there, including most of the directors and the chairman.

The atmosphere in the ground was quite eerie. As the clock in the corner ticked on towards kick-off time, the atmosphere got even weirder.

Kevin, Billy and Neville all joined Hector behind the goal but didn't seem to recognise where they were. It was then that Hector noticed Lie Chee and her cronies sitting about halfway up the stand opposite all the Chinese fans. In the back row directly behind them were Maureen and Mr Wu, or Detective Inspector Brinklow or whoever the hell he really was.

With ten minutes to go to kick-off the awful Chinese music that had replaced the equally awful 1960s disco records about three months ago stopped abruptly. After three loud crashes of the gong, the teams were read out to polite clapping by the Chinese contingent on the halfway line and total silence from the rest of the ground.

Hector noticed that every single Harwood Borough player was now Chinese in origin; even captain Barry Johns and goalkeeper Damien Line had been replaced. With five minutes to go the Boro team jogged on to the pitch to more polite applause. Thirty seconds before kick-off the away side, referee and linesmen suddenly bolted on to the pitch with the referee blowing his whistle wildly to get the game under way.

It was a bit like a scene from a Keystone Kops film. The St Alfreds team showed absolutely no interest whatsoever in trying to play football and just kicked wildly at the ball every time it came to one of their players. All this meant that even this mess of a Boro team had to look good and they looked as if they might score a goal or two. Hector tried to talk to his friends about all this but they completely ignored him and stared blankly at the pitch.

After fifteen minutes Boro took the lead. Wing Man Wyde slung a long cross into the box that completely eluded the keeper and all the defenders, and Mee Knip Inn slid in at the far post to knock the ball into the corner of the net. Nobody cheered. There was some polite applause, but not even as much of that as there had been in the past.

Five minutes before half-time, Boro got a second when a long shot from Bang Wun Inn, brother of Mee Knip Inn, squirmed under the keeper and into the net. Again, to say that the goal celebrations were muted would be an understatement.

With about a minute of time left on Hector's watch, the referee blew his whistle to end the half and sprinted, flanked by both linesmen, towards the dressing room. The St Alfreds players were not far behind and by the time the sound of the whistle died away the pitch was deserted, other than for the somewhat startled-looking Harwood Borough players.

Suddenly an announcement boomed out from the PA system.

'Everybody please stay exactly where they are,' barked the voice.

This seemed to cause panic amongst not only the players left on the pitch, but the Chinese fans standing along the side.

'I said, please stay exactly where you are. If you do then nobody will get hurt,' boomed the voice again.

At that moment the main gates to the ground burst open and three armoured cars drove on to the pitch. At the same time Hector heard a loud click by his right ear. Mr Wu was standing behind him and was pointing a pistol at his head.

Hector did not seem unduly surprised. 'You're not really a detective inspector, are you?' he said.

'Very clever,' came Wu's voice from behind him. 'Now do as I tell you and maybe I won't have to shoot you.'

Hector gulped.

'*Freeze, scumbag*!' came another voice. A woman's voice. Maureen's voice.

Hector looked up. She was standing right at the very edge of the pitch and it had to be said that she did not look happy. She was holding what looked suspiciously like a sub-machine gun to Hector, and it appeared to be pointing straight at him. One deliciously curved leg stuck out of her red dress and Hector's last conscious thought was that she looked like an exotic Lara Croft.

Then he did what he normally did at such times. He fainted.

When he came round he was sitting in the same chair at the same table in the bar that he had occupied before the game had started. For a few moments he thought he must have fallen asleep and dreamt it all up. It was then that he saw one of Lie Chee's henchmen sitting with his back to him. And standing talking to him were both Lie Chee and a very pale Mr Wu.

Hector's first reaction was to faint again, but he had already tried that trick. His second idea was to get the hell out of there. He knew he was sitting almost next to a fire door and he reasoned that if he could create a bit of a diversion, he could hurl himself through the door and run away across the car park.

He waited for a moment and then he very slowly reached out and picked up the solid glass ashtray that lay on the table in front of him. He gently raised it above his head. Just as he was about to bring it down with a sharp crash across the Chinese man's head, he heard a loud shout.

'*No! Hector, stop*!' It was a woman's voice. Maureen's voice.

Hector stopped in mid-bash. The man turned round slowly with a terrible expression on his face. His arms came out to grab Hector, but then suddenly Maureen was there beside him.

'Okay, Chang, that's enough,' she said rather officially.

'Sorry, captain,' came the reply.

Maureen leant across to Hector and said in a low voice, 'Come with me. I think we need a little chat.'

As Hector followed her across the now sparsely populated bar, he noticed that Mr Wu or whoever he was, was handcuffed to one of Lie Chee's cronies.

Halfway up the stairs to the boardroom, Hector suddenly stopped dead in his tracks. 'That man,' he said, 'he called you captain.'

'Get upstairs and I'll tell you all about it, or at least most of it,' Maureen told him.

And she did.

Slowly but surely she explained to him in the quiet of the unoccupied boardroom that she did not and never had worked for the railway. She was in fact a captain in the SUS, the Special Undercover Service that was even more secret than the SAS. They had been on the trail of Mr Wu, or more precisely Mr Poo Whee as he was really called, for over two years. Poo Whee was really a double agent. He was working for the British police drugs squad but was also the mastermind behind this current operation. His idea was to assist the police in capturing all the illegal immigrants; he had apparently already been paid for his part in bringing them over. He was hoping to leave after the arrests and collect the lorry that had been impounded by the police. The lorry was three-quarters full of perfectly above board, non-drugged snacks, but also had over half a ton of hard drugs hidden inside it. With everyone else in the operation arrested here at the football, he would have got away with around five million pounds worth of illegal narcotics.

Lie Chee, who Poo Whee was banking on blaming for the whole affair, was really Sergeant Agnes Collyer from the Cleckington Lane police station. Her gang of cut-throat cronies were all members of the local Harwood and District Tae Kwon Do and Origami Club. It had taken Maureen every bit of the last two years to infiltrate the gang and set up the phoney Ying Tong Yiddle and Po distribution operation and convince Pooh Wee's suppliers in China to use it to get the drugs and illegal immigrants into the UK. All these weekends that Maureen had told Hector she was on training courses in Birmingham; she had been in China with a bunch of desperadoes. Hector was impressed, very impressed. And not a little smitten with her because of these revelations.

Apparently playing the match that afternoon was the only way to get all the suspects together in one place and both the St Alfreds team and the officials were in on the plan. They weren't keen, but had agreed to do it after various veiled threats were put to them by their local police force. The supposed away fans were all from the anti-terrorist squad and the security guards were all Maureen's men from SUS. After Hector had fainted, Maureen had out-bluffed Pooh Wee and her men had rounded up all the other suspects and taken them away for various types of interrogation and deportation or imprisonment.

Hector went on to ask what would happen to his friends and everyone else at the club. Maureen said the drugs that had been used on them would gradually wear off and they would return to normal. She warned Hector that if he ever told anyone about her part in all of this she would kill him. Having seen her on the pitch with the sub-machine gun, he didn't need any more convincing. She told him that it was okay to tell them all the outline of what had happened and reveal that he himself had had a small part (and she went to great effort to accentuate the word small) in resolving the situation. But to everybody else Maureen had been as drugged as they had and knew no more than they did.

The last thing she told him was that the conversation they had just had had never happened and that what he now knew about her he must totally forget. She peered into his eyes as she told him and, far from worrying about the future of their relationship, Hector knew then that he loved her even more.

As she walked down the stairs back to the bar in front of him, he wondered if she could bring the sub-machine gun home one weekend and put that Chinese dress back on!

Ten days later Hector was sitting in the bar in the club and he was surrounded by his friends who were now fully recovered from their ordeal. Harwood Borough, with all their original players back, had just beaten St Alfreds three–nil in the replay of the match of that fateful Saturday afternoon ten days before. It had not been a hard match, it had to be said. The St Alfreds players had looked haunted somehow throughout the game and they had all seemed quite relieved when the referee, a different one from the original game, had blown the final whistle. None of the St Alfreds players had come into the bar after the game; they had just showered and changed and left.

Hector was supping a pint of Hermnose's Battalion, which had thankfully replaced Gleen Dlagon, and was holding court around the biggest table in the bar. Maureen was sitting beside him holding his hand tightly. If someone asked him a question she didn't want him to answer, she would squeeze it a bit too tightly. Hector got the message, but he was still having great fun explaining to all and sundry exactly what had happened, forgetting of course to tell them that he had missed most of the action as he had fainted.

But the questions were getting a bit boring and Hector was finding it difficult to concentrate. He turned and looked out of the bar window. He could just see the goalmouth at the far end of the pitch. His mind wasn't on that fateful Saturday afternoon though – it was on *next* Saturday evening. Maureen had promised she would stay at his flat for the weekend and she was bringing the sub-machine gun.

And two fake hand grenades!

Hector's Earthquake

Hector was nervous. He was sitting all alone on the top deck of a local bus, but he was still nervous. He was going groundhopping again, something he hadn't done for ages. It had been Maureen's idea. To get away for a bit, she had said. It would do him good, she had said. It would be just like the old times, she had said.

Hector wasn't convinced.

Maureen herself was going away for a while, on one of her special trips. She hadn't told him where she was going – she never did these days – and Hector knew better than to ask.

They had been sitting in the bar at Harwood Borough one evening a couple of weeks ago, when she had suggested he should go away for a few days and maybe do a bit of groundhopping like he used to. At the time, Hector had to admit; it had seemed like a very good idea. He had, after all, been a groundhopper when he first met Maureen and he had loved just wandering around going to football grounds he had never been to before. But all that was in the past.

He had been shot, molested, chased, tied up and God knows what else since then. He had even been involved in drug trafficking and bribery. And he had been all over the place to do it. When he first met Maureen, he had only ever been abroad once and that had been a short trip to Northern France. Now he had been to Ireland, America and Russia. It was all a bit scary when he thought about it. And now he was sitting on top of a double-decker bus on his way to an obscure little football club miles and miles away from where he lived because it had seemed like a good idea at the time.

Hector sighed to himself. *Such is life*, he thought gently and carried on reading his non-league football magazine. He glanced out of the bus window. At least it wasn't raining. Usually when he had been to Lancashire for football it had been raining. He was hard put to remember a time when he had visited Lancashire and it *hadn't* been raining. But this afternoon the sky looked quite bright as the big old bus trundled down a cobbled street that could have been in the centre of any one of a hundred old Lancashire mining towns.

The bus stopped with a jolt.

'Hey, you up there!' came a shout from downstairs. 'This is the stop you wanted.'

It was the conductor. Hector had asked him to give him a shout when they were near the ground. And he had.

Hector clambered down the stairs and jumped off the platform, waving thankfully to the conductor as he did so. As the bus moved away, Hector realised that he had not seen one of those old double-decker buses with a conductor for donkey's years. But Lancashire was a bit like that sometimes. Almost like stepping into a time warp!

Hector slung his rucksack over his shoulder and walked slowly up the road towards the chip shop he could see. As he pushed the door open, he heard a small gong ring in the kitchen. For a few seconds Hector was terror-struck. He had had a very nasty experience with the Chinese not long before and the sound of a gong ringing brought it all flooding back.

Not for long though. A small Chinese head, presumably attached to a small Chinese body, appeared over the top of the counter.

'You want fish-chip, mister?'

'Er, make that sausage and chips, please,' replied Hector.

'You want salt-vinegar?' said the voice again.

'Er, yes please,' replied Hector again.

Hector didn't want to be in a Chinese fish and chip shop in the middle of a small town in northern England, but he didn't really have much choice. He was on a pretty tight budget for these few days away and tea in a fish and chip shop was about all he was going to be able to afford. And if he was going to be in the north of England, then the chip shop he found would invariably be run by the Chinese. As he waited for his food to be wrapped, he wondered when it was that the Chinese had taken over all the northern fish and chip shops in the country. It hadn't been all that long ago, but it had happened very, very quickly – almost overnight, in fact.

Hector wondered if Mandarin Chinese was now taught in northern schools instead of French; it would probably be more handy if it was. Five years ago you were always likely to be offered gravy with your chips up north; now it was more likely to be sweet and sour sauce. Or, better still, Chinese curry sauce, a product so fiendish that it resembled nothing remotely Chinese or Indian at all. *Always a uniformly green-yellow colour, it had none of the subtleties of Indian cooking or the bravado of Chinese cuisine, but it was a fair bet,* thought Hector, *that more of it was consumed each year in the country than milk.*

His concentration was broken by a small arm coming up from behind the counter holding a wrapped bundle of paper. Hector paid the ludicrously small amount demanded and walked back out of the shop.

Three minutes later he was sitting in a bus stop opposite the chippy eating his sausage and chips and pondering his next problem. Where was the football ground? He looked around him. Nothing and nobody. He couldn't very well ask someone for directions; there wasn't anybody to ask, apart from the juvenile in the chippy, and anything more adventurous than 'fish-chip' was likely to be met with stony silence.

This was not the first time Hector had had such a problem. It was all right for fans of big clubs to find professional grounds; most of them were signposted and those that weren't rose up above the local houses like gigantic monoliths. But the average lower non-league ground would trouble Sherlock Holmes to find it. They were invariably tucked away down some dingy alleyway and it was entirely possible to stand outside some of them and not know they were there. Hector knew this for certain as a couple of times in his life he had actually done this. On one occasion he had walked up to an old boy and asked him where the ground was, only to be told that he was standing in the club's car park. And Hector had assumed it was an old bomb site left over from the war! Even the floodlights of non-league clubs tended to be lower than the surrounding houses, so unless they were actually switched on it was often quite difficult to see them from more than a couple of hundred yards away.

And it looked like that would be the trouble for Hector on this particular evening. It was mid-August and Hector was in the town of Shuttleton to watch the local team's first ever game played under their own floodlights. They had been promoted at the end of the previous season to the first division of the Mannington Tramtracks North-West District League and part of the regulations for competing in that lofty division was to have floodlights. They had duly been installed during the summer and tonight the first eleven of Shuttleton Colliery Welfare FC were to play their first home league game of the season against the well-known Potteries side of Timbersfield Town. At least, they were well known in Timbersfield! Shuttleton had brought the game forward a day to the Friday night to inaugurate the lights, which meant Hector had come up on the Friday and would be able to see another game on Saturday afternoon, as well as a testimonial match Sunday lunchtime, before catching his train home on Sunday afternoon. All in all a nice little trip and three new clubs to visit. Hector thought that Shuttleton would be heaving with people coming to see this important occasion, but here he was less than an hour and a half before kick-off and there was nobody in sight.

Suddenly a large white fifty-four seater air-conditioned luxury coach pulled into view at the top of the street. *This looks promising*, thought Hector and, depositing his now empty chip wrapper in the bus stop waste bin, stood up to watch the vehicle's progress. Sure enough, as the coach rumbled slowly past, Hector could see a handwritten cardboard sign inside the front windscreen that announced to the world that it had come from Timbersfield Town FC. And that it was the team bus no less. Hector was impressed.

The coach turned right about halfway down the street into a narrow alley that looked far too small to accept it. With masterly care the driver picked his way up the alleyway and didn't so much as bump his wing mirrors on the side walls. Hector slowly walked behind.

At the end of the alley the bus pulled into a large open area that from the street only fifty feet away did not look like it could possibly exist. But exist it did and there to one side of what was obviously a car park was an archway above which a newly painted sign exclaimed: WELCOME TO COLLIERS VALE, HOME OF SHUTTLETON COLLIERY WELFARE FC, MEMBERS OF THE MANNINGTON TRAMTRACKS NORTH-WEST DISTRICT LEAGUE. Above a very sturdy and obviously well-maintained hedge to the side of the entranceway rose a set of gleaming new twenty-foot high floodlights. *This was the place all right*, Hector thought happily to himself.

The large coach pulled up in front of the gate and the members of the Timbersfield Town team came down the steps as if they were expecting some kind of civic reception.

Now Hector knew when he was on to a good thing and he kept walking by the side of the bus and carried on into the ground along with the members of the party from Timbersfield. He was quite pleased with himself as he ambled around inside the ground having escaped paying his admission money. He would have to remember that trick; it could come in handy.

That was where his luck seemingly ran out. He saw an elderly couple unloading what looked like a box of programmes on to a trestle table and went and asked them where the club bar was. The woman pointed back outside the gates and told Hector that they didn't actually have one yet; the money that was going towards building it had been used for the floodlights. However, she did say that most people who wanted a drink used the bar of the cricket club next door.

With that Hector bought a programme and walked back out of the ground. A man stopped him as he left. Hector thought he was in trouble as the man had obviously seen him enter without paying. Instead of having a go at him though, the man gave Hector a pass saying that if he didn't have one on the way back he would have to pay!

Hector smiled to himself and, putting the pass carefully in his wallet, walked across the car park to the cricket club on the far side.

Inside the gloomy bar, Hector ordered a pint of Gramlington and Hepplethwaite's Nut Brown Mild and a packet of pork scratchings and sat down by the window to read the evening's programme. His peace and quiet didn't last long.

An elderly gentleman wearing sandals, a cloth cap, a string vest and a pair of huge khaki shorts straight out of *It Ain't Arf Hot Mum* bounded over to where poor Hector was sitting and demanded, 'Have Lanky 2nds ever played here?'

Hector peered out of the window and through the grime could see what turned out to be Shuttleton Cricket Club 4th XI bravely trying to withstand the onslaught of Inglethorpe Institute 3rd XI's fast bowling attack.

'I have absolutely no idea whatsoever,' said Hector casually over his shoulder.

'I'm sure they must have,' the refugee from El Alamein mumbled mainly to himself. 'It's such a big ground.'

Fifteen minutes later and halfway through Hector's second pint, the man returned and asked exactly the same question. Hector decided it was time to leave and left the old boy peering out and mumbling that he was *sure* that Lanky 2nds must have played there at some time as, after all, it was such a big ground.

Outside, seemingly half the town had turned out to marvel at the Timbersfield Town team coach. It was pretty obvious that such a vehicle had very rarely, if ever, been seen in the town before and nobody could quite believe how the driver had managed to negotiate his way up the alley without ripping the side off. The driver, wearing a very smart blazer and tie, was standing by the entrance door with a huge grin on his face and twirling a pen around in his fingers as if he was expecting to sign autographs.

Hector hurried past and, handing his pass in at the gate, made his way back inside the ground. It may not have been the best non-league ground he had ever been in, but it was probably in one of the prettiest settings. Along one side a train from the East Lancs. Steam Railway chugged past while behind the tidy, if small, main stand a river quietly meandered along its merry way. On top of the hills that rose majestically behind one goal stood what could only be the winding mechanism of an old coal mine, which presumably gave the team its name. The dominant building of the area was a huge derelict paper mill standing behind the other goal, which gave the whole atmosphere a very austere and definitely northern air. All in all, with the sun slowly sinking behind the paper mill and the new floodlights gradually beginning their luminescent glow, Hector was very impressed. He walked around all four sides of the ground with the knowing look of a man who had seen it all before and decided to watch the game from the end opposite the mineshaft.

By the time the teams came out the crowd had built to quite a size, around three hundred, Hector reckoned, and there was definitely a buzz about it as the teams kicked off. Timbersfield were the first to strike, scoring from a low shot under the keeper in the twenty-fourth minute, but to the great enjoyment of the crowd the home side levelled before half-time. The Timbersfield keeper dropped a harmless-looking cross and the Shuttleton striker, a very young and skinny-looking youth, tapped the ball firmly home. *The celebrations that followed would have done justice to a cup-winning goal,* thought Hector as the goal scorer threw himself amongst his adoring teammates waving his shirt above his head.

There was hardly time to kick off again before the half-time whistle blew and Hector made his way along with most of the crowd towards the refreshment facilities on the opposite side of the ground. Trouble was definitely brewing in the tea hut, along with the tea. They had run out of pies and peas (£1.20p per portion, gravy 10p extra) and the punters were getting ugly. *Well, uglier*, thought Hector smiling at the angry queue of people. *These pies and peas really must be something*, he thought as the mob threatened to engulf the small tea hut along with the two frightened old dears inside it.

He walked out of the now open entrance gates back into the car park with the intention of going back into the cricket club for a swift half, but the appearance of the desert rat outside the doors quickly made him change his mind. Instead, he ambled back towards the football ground passing the Timbersfield team coach as he did so. He was surprised to see the driver sitting on the back seat watching what was obviously a pornographic film on the coach's internal video screen and thought that the players were in for a very interesting and educational trip back to the Potteries after the game.

Back in the ground the second half kicked off with still half the crowd surrounding the tea hut, although the threat of an all-out riot seemed to have passed. The only two real highlights of the second half were a thirty-five-yard thunderbolt shot from a Timbersfield midfield player that the home goalkeeper could only watch fly past him into the net and the antics of two Shuttleton committee members. Basically it is all very nice and pretty having a river meander along the back of your main stand, but if some idiot player whacks the ball into it then someone has to go and get it. And, sure enough, halfway through the second half, that was exactly what happened. At Shuttleton Colliery Welfare that dubious pleasure seemed to belong to members of the club's committee. The biggest cheer of the entire evening went up as two old boys in club blazers pushed and shoved a small rowing boat, painted in the red and blue colours of the team, out through a wire gate behind the stand and into the river. While one wrestled with a small pair of oars, the other bravely stood in the prow of the boat lunging at the floating ball with a giant butterfly net. To rapturous applause from the crowd, that had by now returned hungry from the tea hut, the ball was ensnared, the boat dragged back through the gate and the committee men returned to their seats in the stand in triumph.

To the obvious annoyance of the crowd, there was no further scoring and the game was won two–one by Timbersfield Town. Very quietly the crowd exited the ground and walked back down the small alley to the main road. Hector had already ascertained that his accommodation for the night, the exquisitely named Rat and Wardrobe Hotel, was just round the corner, less than five minutes' walk from the ground and it was to this hopefully pleasant abode that he ambled along with the departing fans.

And very pleasant the Rat and Wardrobe was too, at least from the outside. It was a large old-fashioned pub, just the kind that Hector enjoyed, and it had some of his favourite beers on sale in the saloon bar. There were Ambernorth's Cutthroat Bitter, Werrydale & Strutworth's Antelope Extra and even Bothershead's Bomballerina, a beer so strong it was known as aviation fluid as it was reputed that you could fly a small aircraft on it! And the bar had a large open grate in one corner with a real fire burning in it. *It was not cold at all inside or outside the pub, but the real fire was just so welcoming*, Hector thought as he introduced himself to the landlord.

His room turned out to be lovely. A great big old bed with sheets and blankets and an eiderdown, a little washstand in front of a small bay window that overlooked the road, and an old oak wardrobe opposite a small unlit grate. Hector looked very apprehensively inside the wardrobe just to make sure that it wasn't the one containing the rat that the establishment was named after, but, having ascertained its emptiness, he made his way back down to the bar for a few beers.

The landlady, a large woman with a big smile and an even bigger red nose, insisted on cooking Hector a fry-up for his supper, and armed with a pint of Bomballerina he settled down at a small table by the fire. He was going to start reading a brand new sci-fi adventure he had bought specially for the trip, but a seven-foot tall bright green parrot interrupted him.

Hector thought that the Bomballerina must be stronger than he realised. He looked at the parrot, then he looked at his pint, and then he looked at the parrot again. It was still there. It was still seven feet high, it was still bright green and it was still a parrot. And he had only had two sips of his beer.

This was very worrying. What was even more worrying was that the parrot was trying to rip his own head off. Hector decided that if it wasn't the Bomballerina then it must be stress. That was it; he had been getting far too worked up lately and now he was hallucinating. He must start taking things easier.

He took another glug from his glass. A big glug. But the parrot refused to vanish from his view. And it was still tugging violently at his head. Suddenly, with a large plop, the parrot's head came off in a flare of bright green feathers. Inside was a tall man with little round glasses on.

'Do you mind if I open the window?' said the man. 'I get all steamed up in here.'

Hector shook his head.

The parrot man leant across the table and pushed the window open, knocking a half-full ashtray into Hector's lap as he did so. He slumped into the chair opposite Hector and let out an almighty sigh.

'That's better, that is,' he said. 'People don't realise how hard it is dressed up as a parrot all day.'

'No,' said Hector, 'I don't suppose they do.'

'Hi, I'm Les,' said the parrot man, sticking out a wing.

'I'm, er, Hector,' Hector replied, grabbing the wing in his own hand and shaking it.

'You'll have to excuse my appearance,' said Les. 'The job centre asked me if I fancied birds and when I said yes they gave me this job dressed up as a parrot advertising this bloody new restaurant in the precinct. I've been stuck in this suit for twelve hours a day for three flipping days running. And it's bloody hard work.'

'I've been bitten by two dogs and had another one pee up my leg,' went on Les the parrot. 'And I got savaged by a squirrel yesterday that thought I was some sort of tree! I've had more toffee and sticky sweets stuck to me by small children than I can count, not to mention the two babies that have been sick on my wing,' he ranted, poking out a sticky and evil-smelling feathered appendage at Hector. 'And what one of the little bleeders stuck up my jacksie this afternoon, I just cannot imagine,' he concluded, flopping back in the chair.

'I'm sure I couldn't either,' chipped in Hector, trying not to laugh.

'Look, I don't suppose you could get me a pint while I try to get some of this kit off in the loo, could you?' asked Les. 'I'll square up when I can reach my wallet.'

Hector wandered up to the bar to get Les a drink while the parrot man, in a blaze of colour, pushed his way through the toilet doorway.

'I've never bought a drink for a parrot before,' Hector told the barman.

'Until the other day I had never *sold* a pint to a parrot either,' replied the barman.

'Is he all right, this bloke?' Hector asked.

'Oh yeah, big Les is something of a local character around here; if anything weird and wonderful is going to happen, as sure as eggs is eggs it will happen to big Les,' came the reply.

Just then a large crash-cum-squawk came from the toilet.

'Told you,' said the barman.

Ten minutes later Hector and Les were chatting away as if they had known each other all their lives. Hector was tucking into one of the biggest fry-ups he had ever seen and Les was helping him eat it.

'Been to the football?' Les asked, dropping half a sausage covered in tomato sauce on to the lower half of his plumage, which thankfully he had not removed. The rest of the parrot suit occupied another chair, but the beak had got a bit bent when Les had accidentally sat on it in the loo, hence the squawking.

'Yes,' replied Hector, 'that's why I'm here.'

'I'd have been there myself if I wasn't doing this job,' said Les, 'or at least I would have been if I hadn't been banned from the ground.'

'Banned? How come?' asked Hector.

'Well, it's a long story,' answered Les, taking a slurp of his beer.

It would appear that over the last three years big Les had been solely responsible for destroying the Shuttleton Colliery Welfare FC tea hut on no fewer than two separate occasions and had plunged the entire town of Shuttleton into darkness for forty-eight hours by 'helping' to install the floodlights. He had almost burnt the changing rooms down once and very famously, on the night the team had got promoted last season, he had accidentally set fire to the pitch itself. This he had achieved by drunkenly tripping over the hand roller the groundsman used to level the pitch, which caused Les to fall into the side of the small groundsman's hut. The hut had collapsed and two oil drums full of petrol that the club used to fuel the motorised lawnmower fell out on to the pitch and opened, spilling their contents everywhere. Les had lit a match to see where he was and as he threw it away it ignited the petrol, burning not only the pitch and one set of goalposts, but completely destroying the groundsman's hut and the lawnmower.

It was after this incident that Les had been banned from the ground. It had even been suggested that he start supporting the team's great local rivals, Chattersworth Tuesday, but Les had rejected the idea out of hand. He did still go to as many of the Shuttleton away games as he could, but they refused to let him travel on the team coach after he somehow caused the luggage flap to open in mid-journey and scatter all the players' kit into a lake that they were passing. All this meant that Les did not get to as many Shuttleton games as he would have liked as no one would give him a lift in their car either.

He loved his football though, and delighted Hector with tales of the misadventures he had had all over Lancashire and Yorkshire. By the sound of things he had been banned from almost as many grounds as Hector had been to. The catalogue of disaster that he had left in his wake was absolutely legendary according to the landlord, whom Hector had a quiet pint with after Les had waddled off home dragging two thirds of his parrot suit behind him like a giant scrawny green chicken. By a sheer coincidence Les was planning to attend the same game that Hector was the next afternoon at Pickletown Amateurs, one of the few local grounds that Les was still allowed into. Before Les left the pub he and Hector agreed to meet in the Rat and Wardrobe at eleven thirty the following morning.

Hector was rather apprehensive about going to Pickletown with Les the next day but the landlord had assured him that Les would never do any harm to anyone intentionally and it was probably worth going with him if only for the experience. Yes, that was definitely the right word, the landlord decided; it would certainly be an experience.

Hector slept rather fitfully that night, wondering exactly what he had let himself in for, and he was less than impressed when he awoke at about half past eight the next morning to find that it was raining. The word raining didn't really cover what the weather was doing outside. Deluge would be more appropriate. From his position at the window Hector could see the water pouring down from a dark leaden sky at a rate that would do justice to a full-blown monsoon. It didn't rain like that down south in the middle of February, let alone the second week of August. The main road outside had been transformed overnight into a raging river with torrents of water flowing speedily down to a lake that was forming outside the Chinese chippy.

When Hector commented on this to the landlord as he chewed on his breakfast, the landlord gave a little laugh and said that it was just as well Hector hadn't been there the previous April. The amount of rainwater that had come down was so vast it had flooded the public bar twice. When Hector asked him what they had done about it, the landlord gave another little laugh and said, 'Nothing really, we just put down more sawdust!'

Les arrived just before twelve looking like a seaman who had just rounded the Cape, explaining that he was a bit late due to a car floating into his garden shed 'on the tide' and demolishing it. When Hector asked him if he wanted to call off the trip to Pickletown and sort his shed out, he said no; it wasn't much of a shed anyway after it had been hit by lightning two weeks earlier!

It was only about an hour's bus ride to Pickletown and the bus stop was conveniently right outside the pub, so they didn't have to wait outside in the rain for it to come. The rain had actually eased off to torrential by the time the bus pulled up at the stop and Hector was absolutely astounded by Les's response to his query as to whether the game would be on or not. He answered simply, 'Why wouldn't it?'

Hector pointed at the sky and the lake outside the chippy, to which Les laughed and said, 'We ain't much bothered by a little bit of rain up here, you know.'

A little bit of rain, thought Hector to himself as they boarded the bus; he'd watched more rain come down in the last three hours than had fallen in Hertfordshire throughout the entire previous winter.

On the way up to the top deck the hand rail came away in Les's hand and Hector got an immediate sense of impending doom, but the rest of the journey passed without incident and they arrived outside the ground of Pickletown Amateurs at just about half past one.

The ground didn't look up to much from the outside, it had to be said, but an attendant was just opening up and gave the pair of them a cheery smile as he took their money. They walked along behind a rather dilapidated old wooden stand to what was obviously the clubhouse built on to the back of it and carried on past the changing room entrance and into the bar.

'It's a wonder this place is still standing,' said Les as they walked inside.

'Mmm,' answered Hector. What he wanted to say was that it certainly was considering Les had been there several times, but he didn't want to hurt his new friend's feelings.

The bar on the inside was not much better than on the outside. A few tatty tables and chairs of various shapes and colours were dotted around and the customary football club pennants of foreign teams no one had ever heard of littered the wall behind the bar. Other than that it was pretty bare and bleak. The beer looked good though and Les recommended Fotheringdales Trumpet, so, eventually tracking down the barman, Hector ordered two pints which duly appeared as Les took a seat at one of the tables near the window.

The table Les had chosen was a bit rickety, so while Hector held the pints in his hand, Les attempted to put a folded beer mat under one of the table's legs to stabilise it. Firstly he trapped his finger under the table and then he bumped his head sitting up again. Then, to cap it all off, the chair he was sitting on collapsed sending him tumbling to the floor.

Hector was getting the hang of things now and was only grateful that he had steadfastly held on to the two pints he had bought. He moved to a very sturdy-looking table in front of a solid bench seat that ran along one wall and told Les to sit there carefully. Les did as he was told and the pair managed to avert any major disasters for almost an hour until Les spilt almost half a pint into the large glass ashtray on one edge of the table, which slowly slid off the side and crashed down on to Hector's foot.

'I'm always doing that,' said Les rather ruefully.

'Yes, I bet you are,' answered Hector, rubbing his ankle.

Secretly Hector was rather pleased that he was with a disaster area like Les. He himself had been known to cause a few 'incidents' here and there and his slightly warped mind figured that if he was with an accident waiting to happen like Les, then he himself should encounter no problems whatsoever.

He was, of course, totally way off beam in the thinking stakes.

If Lady Luck, or rather Lady Ill Luck, loves anything more than one mobile disaster area, it is two mobile disaster areas in the same place at the same time! And Lady Luck was lurking just around the corner!

At a quarter past two the pair of them strolled out of the bar to watch a pitch inspection by the referee, who had been held up by the awful driving conditions. The rain quite miraculously stopped the very instant that the referee stepped out on to the pitch and the sun all of a sudden burst through the clouds to brighten the gloomy scene considerably and bathe the ground in warm sunshine.

The referee tried bouncing the ball in the centre of the pitch. It just splattered into the surface water and stayed there. He tried kicking the ball, which seemed to go quite well until it hit a pool of standing water and floated off in the opposite direction with the tide. He moved into one of the penalty areas and repeated the process with just about the same results. He then waded the entire length of the pitch and did the same again, with a depressingly similar outcome.

Hector gloomily said to Les that there was no chance of the game taking place, but Les was far more positive about the situation. He said that at least the referee hadn't sunk into the mud up to his ankles as had happened at one game Les had been to the previous season. And they had still played that game.

Sure enough, the referee, after consulting the groundsman and a couple of Pickletown Amateurs club officials, told them that if it didn't rain any more and if the standing water could be given 'a bit of a forking' then they would give it a go.

Hector stood and waited for the groundsman and his crew to burst into action, but nothing much happened. Over five minutes later the groundsman himself, completely alone and unaided, wandered into the centre of the pitch, stuck a fork in the centre spot and ambled back off towards the clubhouse. With a shake of his head, Hector followed Les back into the bar.

The fork was still sticking out of the centre spot when the teams emerged from the changing rooms five minutes before kick-off, but the important thing was that it hadn't rained any more and the game was on. The old groundsman took an age to recover the fork, but the game kicked off dead on three o'clock in front of a pathetically small crowd of about thirty people.

It wasn't a particularly important match, coming as it did quite early in the season, but Hector had expected a few more people to be there to see it. The away team, Worthingbridge Welding Institute FC, appeared to have absolutely no fans there whatsoever, making Hector wonder if the only welders in Worthingbridge Institute played for the team, leaving none spare to support them.

Les wasn't much help either; he couldn't remember what the crowds were generally like there even though he said he had been there about four times the previous season. He did admit that he had spent one of the games there locked inside a workman's hut, only to be let out after everybody else had gone home. He didn't mention if he thought he had been locked in intentionally, but Hector could guess.

The first half of the match passed by quite without any incident either on the pitch or off it at all and Hector was beginning to believe that his terrible misgivings about going to the game with Les were unfounded when disaster struck during the half-time interval.

Having sunk several pints before the game, Hector went off to the loo, but Les rather quietly said he had to 'go properly, if you know what I mean' and disappeared into one of the two ancient and rusting old cubicles next to the toilet block itself.

As the teams jogged out to begin the second half, there was a sudden explosion behind Hector that caused him to turn round in astonishment. The cubicle, for want of a better word, had simply exploded, presumably with Les still inside it. The corrugated iron roof shot about twenty feet up into the air and crashed straight through the clubhouse bar windows while one of the walls of the toilet just collapsed and sank slowly on to the surrounding grass.

Nobody moved a muscle for a few seconds. Suddenly the door fell off its hinges revealing Les, still groping to do up his trousers, in the doorway. He looked like he had been blown up, which in most senses of the word he had. His hair was sticking straight up and smoking and his face was blackened. Other than that he seemed okay though, and he walked quite deliberately towards Hector.

'I only lit up me fag,' he said, blinking through smoke-stained glasses at Hector as he did so.

'Probably not the best time to do it,' answered Hector through clenched teeth, trying desperately not to burst out laughing.

'No, I suppose not,' went on the still smouldering Les.

As two club officials and the groundsman picked over the wreckage of the latrine, the second half kicked off with most of the players and spectators still laughing at poor old Les.

But had Lady Luck finished with them yet? No, she had certainly not; she was only warming up.

On the pitch the second half was far more entertaining than the first with the match finishing in a two–two draw, the home side snatching a late equaliser when their top scorer and undoubted best player crashed home an unstoppable twenty-yard volley in injury time.

Hector and Les headed straight back into the bar as soon as the final whistle blew. Most of the carnage that the unscheduled appearance of the toilet roof inside the bar had caused had been cleared up by the time the two of them arrived back inside. All the glass had been swept up and the offending sheet of corrugated iron removed, leaving just the gaping hole where the clubhouse window had once been as a reminder that anything untoward had happened at all.

Les went into the internal toilet to clean himself up a bit, with a warning from Hector ringing in his ears; not to smoke until he came back out. Hector himself leant on the bar waiting to order a couple of pints. The barman looked none too friendly as he poured Hector the beer and said that it wasn't the first time Les had caused trouble at the ground. Apparently two years ago he had pulled down the fence along one entire side of the pitch after he tripped over one of the posts holding it up. Right on cue a sorry-looking Les emerged from the toilet with one of the taps in his hand, which he sombrely handed to the barman.

'I think I've managed to stop the flow of water for now,' he said calmly, 'but I would get a plumber in rather quickly if I were you.'

The barman looked as if he would explode and almost ran round the bar in his hurry to get to the toilet to see what disaster Les had caused now.

'I think it's about time we left,' mumbled Hector as he tried to break the beer drinking record for a pint. Finishing his drink in around six seconds, he grabbed Les by the collar and dragged him out, still drinking, into the late afternoon sunshine.

'Hang on,' said Les, 'let me at least take the glass back.'

Hector let him go and he hurried inside the bar with the now empty glass in his hand.

As Hector strolled rather swiftly towards the entrance gate, he heard Les leave the bar and shut the door behind him. Not so much shut as slammed. Violently. About three seconds after he heard the bang of the door, he heard a deep and extremely worrying creaking coming from the same direction.

'Come on,' he yelled to Les, who was scurrying along trying to catch him up. 'I don't know what you have done now, but I think it's time we were as far away from here as possible.'

Less than five seconds after they had got out on to the main road, there was an awful rumbling sound that came from inside the ground, followed by the most terrifyingly loud crash that Hector had ever heard in his life.

A bus pulled up on the opposite side of the road.

'Quick, get on,' yelled Hector.

'But it's going the wrong way,' replied Les.

'I don't care which bloody way it's going,' screamed Hector. 'Just get on it.'

So they did.

The bus trundled off and about four stops down they got off and waited for one going back in the right direction. It took almost half an hour to arrive and they scampered quickly up the stairs to see what they could spot from the top deck as they went back past the ground.

What they saw, from their positions kneeling between the seats with only the top of their heads showing above the lower ledge of the window, was a scene straight out of a disaster film.

Two police cars with blue lights flashing away were sealing off the entrance to the ground, while two fire engines were parked behind them. There was plenty of activity from what they could see, but thankfully there did not appear to be any smoke or flames, and, more importantly, there was no sign of any ambulances.

It was still over a mile further on before either of them stood up and sat on the seats properly.

Less than an hour later the pair of them were sitting, rather shaken, back in the saloon bar of the Rat and Wardrobe. After a couple of pints Les suddenly announced that he had better go home. He finished his pint, shook Hector's hand and wished him well, and left the pub.

Hector heaved a huge sigh of relief. He was sorry in one way to see Les go – he was a very nice person and was good company – but he was a total walking disaster and Hector's nerves couldn't take it any more.

Hector spent another evening in the pub, supping some excellent beer and fighting his way through another special fry-up before hitting the hay early for a good night's sleep. He lay in bed for a while trying to think of ways of politely refusing breakfast the next morning. Any more fat and cholesterol in his system and he thought he might explode a bit like the toilet had done at the ground!

When he eventually dozed off, he slept much more soundly than the night before, safe in the knowledge that he was going to the game at Washburton Rovers the following lunchtime without big Les. Little did Hector know, as he calmly and peacefully slept that night, that Lady Luck and her best friend, the Fickle Finger of Fate, had not yet finished with him. Not by a long way!

In the morning Hector was rather morosely chewing on the huge fried breakfast that he had not been able, despite his protestations, to refuse and reading a couple of the Sunday papers. In one there was a small article about the mysterious collapse of the entire stand, bar and changing room facilities at the small Lancashire team of Pickletown Amateurs FC. It went on to say that miraculously no one was injured in the freak collapse and that the fire chief present after the event said it must have been caused by some unusual form of earth tremor.

Hector was extremely relieved that no one had been hurt and even more relieved that a spokesman for the football club said that, all being well, the insurance should cover all the damage, although it would obviously take some time to sort it all out. Hector gave a little laugh to himself and thought that maybe big Les, or Earthquake as he would always think of him, could hire himself out to clubs needing to replace an old stand or building. The earth tremor ploy would surely be far more believable than the old mysterious late-night fire routine!

Soon after breakfast Hector checked out of the Rat and Wardrobe and began his journey to Washburton Rovers for that lunchtime's testimonial game for long-serving skipper Arnold Clegg, who had played for the club for over twenty years, clocking up over eight hundred first team games. Because of this unusual achievement he had been given the honour of this testimonial match against the professional giants of Warrington West End, who had promised to send as many of their first team squad as possible. There would no doubt be a big crowd at the game – it was rare nowadays to see a top team put a decent side out at a non-league ground – so Hector wanted to get there early.

First he needed to get the bus back to the local station, and then a train to Washburton, followed by around a twenty-five-minute walk to the ground. He reckoned that, if he was lucky, he would get there in a little under an hour and a half, which would give him the same amount of time before kick-off.

As he was standing at the bus stop waiting to begin the first leg of his journey, he heard a car horn sound. Looking up he watched as a small green car attempted to pull up alongside him. What it actually did was splash through a huge puddle left over from the previous day's rain that squirted up and soaked Hector's trousers. The car then bounced up on the pavement causing one of the hubcaps to fly off and bowl down the road like a runaway children's hoop.

Hector did not need to be told who was driving the car and it was absolutely no surprise to him when the now unforgettable face of Earthquake Les peered up at him from the half-wound-down window.

'Sorry, I can't wind it all the way down,' said a beaming Les, 'the handle has come off!'

Hector didn't even bother to look surprised.

'I don't suppose you are on your way to Washburton, are you?' enquired Les.

'I, er, I suppose so, yes,' replied a very nervous-sounding Hector.

'Jump in then; I'm on my way there too,' said Les.

Hector's heart sank. If it had dropped any lower it would have fallen out of the bottom of his damp trousers.

The car's passenger door flew open, but Hector stood where he was, rooted to the spot and staring blankly at the open car door.

'Come on, come on,' said the excited-sounding Les, 'I've got to get there early; I've got a lot to do before the game starts.'

'A lot to do?' said Hector as he reluctantly clambered inside the car. 'What have you got to do with it?'

'It's for Arnold Clegg, you know; it's his testimonial game,' Les answered. 'Arnold Clegg,' he said again, as if Hector should recognise the name. 'He's my brother. The whole family's going today; you'll love meeting them. I'm on the organising committee.'

If Hector had been driving the car, he would have crashed it. He was stunned. He had honestly thought that he was going to get a nice quiet afternoon at the game before catching a train home in the early evening. Now it appeared that he could well end up spending the entire afternoon with the family of the biggest disaster area since the *Titanic* went down.

And Les was organising things!

Hector was so stunned by the news that he didn't notice Les bounce back off the kerb, narrowly missing the bus that Hector had been hoping to catch, or shoot straight through a red light further down the road and coming within two feet of causing a multiple pile-up.

The journey to Washburton was a nightmare come true for Hector. Not only was Les the worst driver he had ever seen, but the sense of impending doom was about five times greater than it had been the previous day. He just didn't know what he was letting himself in for. Lady Luck did though; she had hitched a ride along with them and was sitting in the boot scheming!

Les explained that he had been meaning to ask Hector if he was going to Washburton while they were at the game the previous day, but what with everything that had happened, it had just slipped his mind. He had popped round to the pub on his way, but Hector had just left so he had come looking for him.

Hector couldn't believe that Les's surname had not cropped up the day before. There was no need for it to, he supposed, and there was always the chance that he would not have made the connection, but he might have done and he might have been able to escape. He could have got up early, caught the first bus to the station and been halfway home by now. But he wasn't. He was bouncing along in a battered old car driven by the unluckiest man since the short-sighted Mr Ernest Gribblethwaite of Margate, who mistook his winning lottery ticket worth three million pounds for an old bus ticket and used it to help line his incontinent budgie's cage. And he was going to watch this man's brother play football in the company of his entire family (Earthquake Les that is, not Mr Ernest Gribblethwaite of Margate, although on reflection it would have been better if it *had* been Mr Ernest Gribblethwaite of Margate).

Suddenly Hector did not feel at all well!

In terms of time it didn't take very long to get to the ground at Washburton, but in terms of Hector's lifespan it seemed to take about four complete days. Big Les had more near misses than an American artillery battery but they still managed to arrive in one piece – at least physically they did; Hector didn't think he would ever be the same again mentally.

With Les being on the testimonial committee for his brother there was no need for Hector to pay for admission and once inside he headed straight for the bar. It was not a difficult decision. Firstly it was open and secondly Les had to go to some form of meeting in the boardroom, so Hector could have a quiet drink on his own with no fear of the bar collapsing, or so he thought.

He bought himself a pint of Slapperton's Steamer and a bag of cheese and onion crisps and sat in the most unobtrusive seat he could find, tucked up in one corner, and started to read the programme he had bought.

Less than two minutes later and his attention was snapped firmly into focus as an elderly pair entering the bar proceeded to knock over two chairs and a table while negotiating the doorway. When the male half of the pair knocked an ashtray and a pile of beer mats on to the floor while ordering drinks for the pair of them, Hector just knew that they had to be relations of Les. He was right: they were his parents, as he found out when Les made a quick and disastrous entry to the bar from the boardroom, tripping on the carpet and ripping the lead to the fruit machine out of the wall.

Worse was to follow. No sooner had Les's parents made themselves comfortable than two men in their late twenties knocked the very same table and chairs over as they made their way into the bar. Hector was introduced to Les's younger brothers, twins Bill and Ben, by their parents. Hector nearly choked on his beer. Both these boys were extremely thickset young men just over five feet tall.

The last member of the family Clegg to arrive was the hero of the hour himself, the testimonial man, Arnold. The astounding thing about Arnold was that rather than knocking the Clegg family memorial table and chairs over, he swerved round them like Johann Cruyff riding a tackle. As he approached his parents' table his father knocked the ashtray off as he stood to greet his son. Arnold didn't bat an eyelid; he just half bent and scooped the ashtray up well before it hit the carpet.

Hector was stunned. Arnold was either adopted or was the black sheep of the family; he didn't even bang his head on the table as he stood up. Arnold greeted Hector warmly and signed the front of his programme with a personal greeting, which Hector thought was nice of him.

With the entire family now ensconced in the bar, Hector decided that it would be a lot safer to be somewhere else and made his excuses before leaving for the fresh air and hopefully the sanctuary of the world outside. As he left, he heard a large crash behind him but decided not to turn around to see what it was that had fallen or broken or dropped or shattered. Arnold followed him out and wished him well before entering the changing room to prepare for the game.

Hector headed for the safety of the tea hut on the opposite side of the ground and bought himself some lunch. As he sat on a grass bank behind one goal he watched the crowd assemble as he consumed a very reasonable cheeseburger and chips, washed down with a nice cup of tea. There was no sign of the Clegg family leaving the bar, so there was little point as far as

Hector could see in going back in; he was far too fond of his health. As he sat on the surprisingly dry grass and watched the people arrive, he kept one eye on the clubhouse, expecting any second to see it either collapse or blow up in some bizarre explosion.

But nothing happened. No crashes, no bangs, no window-shattering explosions, no plumes of smoke, no streams of screaming people leaving hurriedly, no nothing. Just peace and serenity.

Hector was surprised. So surprised that twice he got to his feet with the intention of going back inside and seeing for himself what was, or rather wasn't, happening. But common sense prevailed, which made a great change for Hector. *Maureen would be proud of me*, he thought to himself as he queued for another cup of tea.

As Hector started to make his way back to the grass bank, he saw Les standing outside the bar and looking around as if trying to find him. Hector made a decision there and then that he did not want to be found by Les – or anybody else for that matter – until the game had finished, and he ducked around behind the tea hut to hide.

This turned out to be a mistake. Looking back on it later, Hector thought it was probably the worst mistake he made all day, including getting into the car to go to the game with Les, but, as so often happens, it seemed like a good idea at the time.

So concerned was he in not wanting Les to see him that he wasn't really looking where he was going. He walked slap bang wallop into the heavy wooden sign that hung from the side of the hut advertising the day's special offer: CHIPS AND CURRY SAUCE 50P. The sign only gave Hector a glancing blow across the side of his head, but it made him stagger backwards. In staggering backwards he tripped over the thick black cable that linked the hut up to the main electricity supply. Tripping over this cable caused him to fall over, whereupon he bashed his head on the top of one of the large metal propane gas cylinders that supplied the cooking power to the hut. The loud clang of bone on metal rang around inside his head.

As Hector slowly collapsed into the long grass surrounding the cylinders, his last thought was that things like this should only happen to Earthquake Les.

When he awoke he had the distinct impression that he was being slapped around the face by a wet fish. This was not entirely untrue. He was actually having his face wiped by the woman who ran the tea hut, who was using an old teacloth that she had wiped her hands on after making some fish burgers.

'Are you all right, love?' she was saying.

Hector didn't answer. He had no idea if he was all right or not.

'Come on, love,' she went on, 'tell me you're all right.'

Hector groaned.

'How long have you been lying there?' she asked him.

Hector had no idea how long he had been lying there. That was two questions he didn't know the answer to.

The woman started shaking him. Now Hector knew the answer to the first question. He was most certainly not all right. In fact he felt violently sick and had a splitting headache. He groaned again. He managed to prop himself up on his elbow and very gingerly he ran one hand across the top of his head. He winced with pain. Either he had grown another head or he had a bump on the top of his original one the size of an orange.

He stared at the woman. He could still smell the fish. No wonder he was feeling sick.

'I'll go and get someone,' the woman said, adding as she rushed off, 'that's if there is anyone left. I suppose even the St John Ambulance men have gone by now; the game's been over nearly an hour.'

Now Hector knew the answer to the second question. It was after the game; probably about six o'clock. Very tentatively he sat up. His head was swimming, but at least with the exit of the woman the overwhelming urge to throw up all over his rucksack had gone.

He tried to get to his feet and just about managed it. He staggered around like a drunk for about twenty seconds, almost tripping over the same cable that had caused his demise in the first place. But eventually he was walking around okay. He still had this amazing thumping in his head and he sat back down on top of one of the gas cylinders.

He wondered whom the woman would find to come and help him. A few seconds later and he knew the answer to this question too.

A loud crash as someone obviously bashed into something was followed by the woman's voice asking, 'Are you all right, love?' But this time the question was to someone else entirely.

Another crash, two small scuffling noises and the sound of some fabric tearing were followed by a different voice. A male voice. Big Les's voice.

'I'm terribly sorry; I must have slipped,' he said.

'Don't worry about that now,' said the woman. 'Quick, in case he's hurt.'

Big Les skidded round the corner of the tea hut to where Hector was sitting rather uncomfortably on top of the gas cylinder.

'Hector,' said Les, 'we've all been worried sick about you, we didn't know where you were.'

'Well, at least you do now,' replied Hector, rubbing his sore head.

'Quick, we must get you to the hospital,' added Les, turning round and walking straight into the special offer sign. It didn't knock him over though. *Probably used to it*, thought Hector ruefully to himself. He tried to stop him, but Les was gone before he managed to get on his feet.

As Hector walked round the corner of the building he saw Les reverse his car towards him. He would have reversed straight into the hut itself had a large litter bin not got in the way. The litter bin hit the deck, spilling its contents all over the place. The car swerved away from the bin and came to a complete stop as Les steered it into the wall behind the bin. Les half clambered and half fell out of the driver's door as his two brothers came running across from the clubhouse, closely followed by their parents.

Hector tried desperately to bring things under control but the Clegg family had already taken over the proceedings. The two brothers picked Hector up rather forcibly and bundled him into the back seat of the car. At the same time, Les's mother jammed herself into the rear of the car via the door on the other side and started fussing over Hector's head, pulling out a hanky and licking it before wiping the offending spot.

Les and his father scrambled into the two front seats and Les reversed back from the wall, over the top of the waste bin and bounced out of the football ground and into the main road outside.

Les's father turned to Hector and said, 'You're lucky that Les was still there; he was going ten minutes ago but stayed behind as he wanted to see you before he left.'

'Lucky?' muttered Hector under his breath. 'It depends on your definition of the word.'

As he said it, the car swerved violently to the right as Les desperately tried to avoid ploughing into the back of a bus. He missed the bus, but only by steering on to the pavement and scaring the living daylights out of a group of shoppers. The car careered off on its merry way, presumably towards the nearest hospital, with Hector and Les's mum bouncing around on the back seat as if it was a trampoline.

Hector glanced at his reflection in Les's rear-view mirror as he swayed about and was very pleased to see that the bump on his head was nowhere near as big as he had first thought. And it didn't hurt so much now either. He tried to tell Les, but Les was still busy trying to negotiate his way to the accident and emergency unit without putting himself and any other unfortunate road users in there along with Hector.

Five minutes and three near misses later, Les pulled off the main road and into the entrance to the hospital. He nearly ran down an old man in a wheelchair as he swerved through the gates and the car must have still been doing thirty miles an hour as it hit the ambulance ramp up to the accident and emergency department. Fortunately it was only doing about 10 mph when it stopped suddenly outside the doors. It stopped because there was an ambulance in its way and Les bumped straight into the open and mercifully deserted back doors, throwing all the occupants of the car all over the place.

Hector was the first to come to his senses after the collision and flung himself out of the car. As he pulled himself upright, he saw that the hospital was directly opposite the railway station. This was his chance to escape.

As various members of the Clegg family struggled to get out of the vehicle, which was now entwined with the rear of the ambulance, Hector slung his rucksack over his shoulder and ran across the road. As he got to the other side, he glanced back to see a scene of total chaos outside the hospital.

The car was propped up on the ambulance's bumper with Les now arguing with what appeared to be the driver. Mr Clegg was pointing across the road at Hector and shouting something, while Mrs Clegg was rather forcibly being put into a wheelchair by a pair of nurses. Nobody appeared to be hurt as far as Hector could see, and that would do for him.

Ten minutes later he was sitting in a second-class carriage watching the countryside chug past. He had no idea where the train was going, but thought that he would worry about that later. He was away from Washburton in general and the Clegg family in particular. He relaxed as he ran his hand over his sore head. It hurt a bit but not too much and all being well he would be home in a few hours and could bathe it or something then. With a bit of luck Maureen would be home and she could sort it out for him.

He closed his eyes for five minutes, safe in the knowledge that with the Clegg family getting further away from him with every turn of the train's wheels he was safe. At least for the time being.

He didn't see Lady Luck unpacking her knitting and making herself comfortable on the seat opposite.

Hector's Rescue

He just couldn't do it! He thought he could, but when push came to shove he just couldn't do it.

The 'it' in question was throwing out all his old rubbish. The problem was that to Hector it just wasn't rubbish at all. It was things like his old football magazines and his collection of football club coffee mugs. Even the broken ones didn't count as rubbish to Hector. His old anorak had been classified as rubbish, but to Hector it was an old friend. An old friend that he hadn't worn for years, granted, but an old friend just the same. How could he be expected to throw it out? He and that anorak had travelled the length and breadth of the country together for years. It had a couple of holes in it here and there and one of the pockets was badly torn and the yellow furry lining was ripped, but it was his favourite anorak. And there were his books. A collection of the tattiest and most worn-out old science fiction paperbacks in the history of publishing now sat in a box by his front door waiting to be collected by some charity people. And it just wasn't fair.

Hector, you see, had a big problem. It had all started about six weeks ago. The firm that he had worked for as a stock control assistant had closed down. Just like that. One Monday morning all the members of staff had been called into the canteen and the managing director had told them that they had declared bankruptcy and that the factory was closing. Just like that. All the staff were given fifteen minutes to clear their desks and then they were almost physically thrown out of the building by a gang of security guards apparently hired specifically for the job.

Hector stood on the pavement outside and stared at the building. He had worked there since he left school well over twenty years ago. And now he was out. What was he going to do?

And what the hell was he going to do for money? He would get some redundancy payment, eventually, but with the company going bankrupt it wasn't going to be much. And what about Maureen? Would she still want anything to do with him now he was unemployed?

Unemployed. Hector had never thought it was possible. But that was it. He had no job and not too many prospects of getting one. Stock control assistants were two a penny and he was now way over thirty-five. The prospects looked bleak.

It was a very sad and worried Hector who walked the mile and a half home that morning carrying a little brown box. Everything he had accumulated in twenty years of work fitted inside a little cardboard box. And it rattled! He was very sad. And very, very worried.

He need not have worried about Maureen; she was very supportive. She had faith in him even if *he* didn't. They had spent that evening in the pub and she had done her best to cheer him up a bit, but he was inconsolable. He wouldn't have any trouble getting another job, she assured him; he was very experienced. Firms would be crying out for someone with his experience, she was sure. It didn't matter that he was almost thirty-seven years old; it was experience that counted. Hector thought that if he heard the word 'experienced' again he would scream. But it wasn't Maureen's fault; it wasn't fair to have a go at her. It was all his fault.

If he had had any ambition in him, any gumption at all, he would have got himself a better job years ago. All the people who had worked with him when he started now had much better, much flashier jobs; company cars, expense accounts, the lot. The other apprentice who had started at the same time as he had was now his manager. Or rather had been. But Hector? It was all too much trouble. Hector was comfortable with his job. He had always been comfortable with his job. And now all of a sudden he didn't have a job to be comfortable with.

What exactly was to become of him? He was aware that Maureen was still talking to him, but he couldn't really hear a word. He was too busy feeling sorry for himself to take any notice of anything else. Even Maureen.

And now, six weeks later, he was standing in his front doorway surrounded by piles of what Maureen had dismissed as rubbish, and he was waiting for his mate Kevin to arrive with a van he had borrowed to take it all to the local dump. But he wasn't sure that he could go through with it. *She didn't understand*, he thought.

They had decided that he had to get rid of his flat. He wouldn't be able to pay the rent for very long so the sooner he got rid of it the better. He was moving in with Maureen and that was causing him all sorts of problems. Not that he didn't want to live with Maureen. He would have given anything to live with Maureen. He thought he would have, anyway. Now, standing waiting for the van, he suddenly wasn't so sure.

He had had some of this stuff since he was a boy. And now it was going to the dump. It just wasn't fair. He would have cried if he had any tears left. He had spent most of the first week after he had lost his job crying about it, but that had got him nowhere, so he stopped. And now he had no tears left. That made him even sadder.

Maureen had been very good about it all; she couldn't really have been any better. He would have to move in with her until he got another job and they could sort something out, she had insisted. She had made him go to the job centre the day after it had happened and sign on with them. She had made him traipse around town signing on with every employment agency in the place, but it wasn't doing any good. She had helped him apply for almost two dozen jobs from the local paper, but apart from two letters saying that the vacancies had already been filled, he had heard nothing from any of them. And if he waited for any of the agencies to contact him, he would become a very old man.

It was all hopeless. But Maureen wouldn't let him give up. He didn't know what he would do without her. And now he was moving in with her. And he was very sad about it.

It wasn't fair on Maureen, he thought. She had a lovely little flat, he had to admit, but that was exactly the trouble. It was little. It was a studio flat about half a mile away from where Hector lived – sorry, had lived. And even for a studio flat it was pretty small. Just one bedroom, a small little kitchen and a tiny bathroom. It was hardly big enough for Maureen, let alone the pair of them. Hector had stayed there many weekends and it felt cramped then; God knows what it would be like full-time.

It wasn't fair on Maureen. If only Hector had got himself a life. If only he had shown some ambition. He could have been anything by now, anything. Instead he had just become comfortable. And now it had come down to this.

Well, he wasn't having it. It might be a bit late in the day, but he wasn't going to be pushed around by life any more. He was going to do something about his miserable existence. And he was going to do it right now! But what?

He went back inside, closed the door behind him and sat on the stairs with his head in his hands. He had to think of something and he had to think of it quickly.

When Kevin arrived over an hour later and thankfully half an hour late, Hector bounded through the door and down the path to meet him.

'Change of plan!' he yelled as Kevin got out of the van. 'We're not going to the dump. We're going to Billy's place.'

'Why?' asked Kevin, not surprisingly.

'Because he's letting me use his garage for a few months to keep all this stuff in,' Hector beamed.

'Bully for him,' said Kevin. 'He must be madder than Maureen.'

'Shut up and help me get it all in the back,' said Hector, yanking the rear doors of the van open.

It took two trips, all of the morning and about half of the afternoon, to get all of Hector's belongings to Billy's, but at last they were done. Not only was the 'rubbish' stored fairly neatly in the back of Billy's garage, but all Hector's prize possessions as well that he had been going to take with him to Maureen's flat. You see, he wasn't going to move in with her at all. Hector had a plan. His programmes, his dad's football medals, his football memorabilia collection, everything. All stacked up under a very old and very dubiously smelling groundsheet that they had found. The only things left were a suitcase full of clothes and other essential items and a small, quite heavy little case that Kevin had heaved down the stairs from the flat to the van.

'What on earth is in this?' he asked Hector.

'Don't know, I found it under the bed but I can't find the key,' replied Hector. 'Might be something valuable though. Now, if you could just whizz me round to Maureen's for a minute and then drop me off at the station, I would be very grateful,' he said to the perplexed-looking Kevin.

'You wouldn't like to explain what the hell is going on by any chance?' asked Kevin.

'I've got a plan,' said Hector, grinning from ear to ear. And he did have, sort of. 'It's all in here,' he said, pointing to a large envelope in his jacket pocket. 'I hope Maureen understands.'

'So do I,' said Kevin rather ruefully.

Then they were off. The two cases were in the back of the van, the keys had been pushed through the letter box and they were on their way to Maureen's.

Hector let himself into Maureen's flat, having struggled up the stairs with the two cases. He put the envelope on the table and the small case under the bed. He let himself have a long look around and then, wiping a tear from his eye, he went back down the stairs to Kevin and the van.

An hour later, Hector sat on the train as it headed northwards to his new life. He sat back in his seat and smiled to himself. He had done it. He had made a decision. Not only made a decision, but he had acted on it. He was going to be a writer!

What he was going to write, he didn't actually know. But he was going to be a writer. He had written lots and lots of articles for football magazines and programmes and most people seemed to enjoy them. He had done dozens of match reports and other things and it had always seemed rather easy to him. Now he was going to find out how easy or hard it really was. He was going to write a book. It would be very well received, he was sure, and would undoubtedly make him famous. And rich. Rich and famous. He smiled at the idea. He liked that.

He jolted back to reality. The only problem was – what the hell was the book going to be about? Still, that could wait; he would have to get himself ready first.

He had over two and a half thousand pounds in the bank that had come through the week before as his redundancy payment. He had rung his old friend Harry in Newton Aycliffe while he had waited for Kevin that morning and had sorted out where he was going to live for a couple of months. He had it all sorted. More or less.

Harry had an uncle who owned a beach house somewhere north of Hartlepool that he rented out in the summer but closed up in the winter, as nobody wanted to stay there at that time of year. Hector had never been there, but Harry often spoke of it and what a nice place it was. He had practically grown up there. Harry had rung Hector back within ten minutes of his call and said that his uncle had agreed that Hector could rent it for the winter. It was cheap too!

And that had been it. All sorted.

Hector had had a quick look at the train timetable (he was never without one) and discovered he could get into Newton Aycliffe at about seven thirty that evening. Harry said he would pick him up there and take him to the house that night. Hector was amazed at how easily it was all coming together. Harry had bought a car that summer and said that, all being well, they would be there by about nine o'clock that night.

Hector sat with a grin on his face. His only concern was about this uncle of Harry's. He had met various members of Harry's best friend Brian's family and they were all as mad as hatters. Totally barking. Harry's would be okay though, he hoped. They couldn't all be raving bloody mad up in that part of the world, could they?

With these thoughts buzzing round his head, he dozed off.

The journey went well. The train was only ten minutes late into Newton Aycliffe and Harry and Brian were waiting for him as he dragged his case out of the station.

The first doubts crept into Hector's mind as they drove towards Hartlepool.

'I'll be round about ten in the morning,' said Harry. 'We can sort the gas out then. Shouldn't be too bad tonight; it's not got cold yet.'

Gas, thought Hector, *what gas*?

They left the bright lights of Hartlepool behind them and then they started to leave any sort of lights behind them as the roads they went down got narrower and narrower.

'It's lovely here in the summer,' said Harry over his shoulder as the car bounced down a dirt track that seemingly led to nowhere.

But it's bloody October, thought Hector, now starting seriously to wonder if he was doing the right thing.

Then the car pulled to a halt and they all got out.

'Here we are,' said Harry.

Yeah, but where? thought Hector. He couldn't see anything. There was nothing to see. Except blackness.

If there was a house there, it wasn't exactly apparent. Hector could hear the sea pounding away reasonably close by but still couldn't see much at all. Slowly a dark black building seemed to loom out of the night and then suddenly the darkness was pierced by a beam of light. Then another one.

Harry had switched on a couple of torches. He walked over to Hector and put one of the torches in his hand.

'You'll need this,' said Harry.

'I was afraid I would,' gulped Hector.

They moved round to the front of the single-storey building and Harry opened the front door. Hector followed him inside and trained the beam on the wall by the door.

'What are you looking for?' asked Harry.

'The light switch,' said Hector sarcastically.

'You'll be bloody lucky,' Hector heard Brian mumble from behind him.

Hector's heart sank into his shoes.

'No point of having a light switch,' Harry's voice floated across the gloom. 'No electricity to connect it up to.'

Hector just stopped moving. 'No electricity,' he stammered, 'How will I…' His voice trailed off.

'That's what the gas is for,' said Harry. 'Its propane; works a treat. When we've got some anyway. That's why I'm coming round in the morning,' he went on. 'For tonight you'll just have to make do.'

Twenty minutes later Harry and Brian had gone, leaving Hector sitting in an armchair with his torch beam focused on the floor in front of him. *Christ*, he thought, *what have I done*?

A short while later he lay in the big old brass bed with two old blankets pulled around him for warmth and quite frankly wished he was dead. He had set off far too hastily with this grandiose plan of becoming a famous writer and now everything was coming crashing down around him.

His plan was to buy a cheap second-hand computer on which to write this epic tome, but now there would be no point. It wouldn't bloody work if he did. Harry had said that his uncle had been thinking of installing electricity the previous summer, but had not got round to it. He would definitely get it sorted out next year though, he had said brightly.

'Great,' Hector had replied. *Very bloody helpful*, he thought to himself.

At least there was running water. He had not wanted to ask, but the relief that swept through him as water gushed out of the taps in the sink of the bathroom was almost staggering. It was stone cold, of course, but it was running water. Hector had had visions of having to go out and buy a bucket!

As he lay in bed he started to wonder what he was going to write about. It had seemed such a good idea at first. Write a book, find a more than willing publisher, attend a few book signings, buy a big house for him and Maureen, and live happily ever after. Maybe another book or two, the odd public appearance, supermarket opening, that sort of thing, and that was it. Easy-peasy.

Now, lying in a freezing cold bed in total darkness with only the roar of the wind and the crashing of the sea to listen to, he was not a happy bunny. What was he going to write about? He simply had no idea. What did he know about? *Stock control. That would be exciting*, he thought. *Get well rich off a book about stock control. What else do I know about? Nothing. Stock control and football, nothing else at all, just stock control and football.*

Football. That was it. Of course. He had been all over the place watching football. And had had some very, very strange experiences on the way. All his mates had laughed and laughed at the stories of his adventures; why not put them all together in a book? Hope started to creep back into his mind and he somehow felt physically warmer. 'Football, what about that, eh?' he mumbled. He even managed a little chuckle.

Eventually, some hours later, he nodded off to sleep.

He woke up to bright sunshine flooding the room. As he lay in the big old bed, he smiled to himself. It was going to be all right. He knew it would. He wondered what the time was. *It must be getting on*, he thought; it was pretty bright. He must go and find a phone box before Harry arrived; he had to ring Maureen. He knew she would be worried stiff about him.

He threw back the blankets and swung his legs over the side. He pulled himself lazily to his feet and rubbed his eyes. As he opened them he stopped dead. He very nearly fell back on the bed in shock.

There in the corner of the room was a little old man sitting on a chair.

He smiled warmly at Hector. 'Awreet?' he said.

'Er…' said Hector.

'I'm Uncle Norman,' said the old man. 'Thif if my plafe.'

'Er…' said Hector again.

As the old man pulled himself up and out of the chair, Hector could see that he was no more than five feet tall at the most. He had a completely bald head save for a ring of pure white fluffy hair round the top like a very old and unkempt monk. He had a huge purply-red nose and his face was generally much the same colour. As he smiled, Hector saw that the old man seemed to have just one tooth. *That would account for the speech impediment*, he thought. But he was smiling; that was a good sign. *He must be nearly ninety years old*, he thought.

'I juft came down to make fure you fettled in awreet,' the old man said. 'And I've brought you a preffent!'

Hector just stood looking at him. The old man was dressed in an ancient and threadbare light blue shirt over which he had a darker blue sleeveless jumper. He had on an old and very worn pair of grey trousers and a pair of what appeared to be slippers, with the toe of one of them worn through.

He shuffled towards the door. 'Come on, I'll fyow you,' he said.

Hector dumbly followed him out into the main room of the house. In the daylight the place looked a whole lot better than it had the previous night. Not brilliant, but better. It was obviously very old and largely made of wood. Different people had seemingly repaired various parts of it over the years in different ways. All in all it was a very odd-looking building.

There was an old and battered settee along one wall and two armchairs that matched neither each other nor the settee in the centre of the room. Under a big window that appeared to be almost the whole width of one wall stood a dark old folding table. And on the table stood the biggest and oldest typewriter Hector had ever seen in his life. The old man was proudly pointing at it, his mouth split into a wide grin that highlighted his one large yellow tooth.

'You're a writer, ain't cher?' he asked.

Hector nodded, still speechless and not a little confused.

'Ay, 'Arry faid you waff.' The old man cackled. 'I thought thif might come in handy,' he said, gesturing at the typewriter.

Hector just stood and stared.

Suddenly a voice came from behind him. 'I see you've met Uncle Norman then?' said Harry. 'Lovely bloke; deaf as a post. *All right, Uncle?*' he shouted.

'Ay, lad,' came the reply. 'I waff juft fyowing the young feller me lad here me typewriter. He can youffe it for hif book if he likef.'

'Don't knock it, Hec lad; it's probably the best you're going to get around here,' said Harry laughing.

Hector's heart sank. Not quite into his shoes this time – he didn't have them on – but pretty far down all the same. He stood in the middle of the room with his mouth open. Fortunately he was fully dressed apart from his shoes; it had been far too cold to get undressed last night. In fact he had put an extra jumper on before he got into bed to be on the safe side.

'Nife to have met you,' said the old man, still grinning like a demented cat. 'If there if anything you want, juft talk to Harry here.'

And with that he shuffled out of the room. A few seconds later Hector heard the front door slam.

It was some time before Hector could move. He just stood staring at the old man's typewriter. How the hell was he going to produce anything legible on that?

Later that day Hector fed his first piece of paper into the ancient-looking machine.

It had been a strange day all round really. Everything looked so different from the night before. The single-storey house stood all on its own about fifty yards from the sea and about five yards back from a nice clean sandy beach. The nearest house was about two hundred yards away in one direction and in the other there was nothing much at all. The small beach seemed to fade out and merge with some grey and menacing-looking rocks. Behind the house was a narrow road made of a mixture of shingle and other assorted stones. It was down this road that they had come the previous evening.

At the end of the road stood a phone box. One of the old red ones. With a door. It didn't quite have a 'press button B' type phone in it but it was pretty ancient. But it worked. He had rung Maureen and she had answered it before the end of the first ring.

She sounded very upset and was obviously very worried. What did he think he was doing? Was he completely mad? How could he go off like that, and so on. He did his best to calm her down but it was several minutes before her voice had slowed down enough for Hector to talk sensibly to her.

Yes, he said, he probably did know what he was doing. Yes, he was completely mad. No, he was not coming straight home and, more importantly, no, he wasn't going to tell her where he was. Not yet. He had visions of her appearing in the middle of the night and physically dragging him back to Harwood. And he wasn't ready to give up yet. He was more determined than ever to make it work.

He said he would ring her every evening and let her know how he was getting on, and in a week or so, when she had calmed down, he would tell her where he was. Until then he was going to write merrily away and see how it went. In the end she agreed; after all, she didn't have much choice.

Hector promised he would ring again the following evening and he clambered into Harry's car (there was no Brian this time) and off they went to find civilisation.

There was a small town about two miles away that seemed to have everything Hector needed. Not really a town, it was more a parade of shops. In the summer it was probably a hive of activity but in the middle of October it was only just about alive. There was an old-fashioned hardware shop that supplied them with a large gas cylinder that would give Hector heat and light. He bought food from a small convenience shop, most of it tinned or in packets as he didn't have a fridge or a freezer. He even managed to buy a ream of paper for the typewriter, on the off chance that it worked. This had come from a newsagent's and had cost a small fortune, but was vital if Hector's plan was going to work. He had bought three nice bottles of wine and a very cheap bottle of whisky (for warmth, he kidded himself, if I can't get the heating right) and headed back to the house.

Back inside, he explored everywhere that he could, with Harry's help. There might not have been a fridge, but perched on the back step was a small blue metallic box with 'Osokool' written on the front. Inside, it was lined with polystyrene and apparently, so Harry said, if cold water was poured into the top, would keep milk, butter and cheese cool and fresh for days. They found quite a respectable eiderdown in a cupboard which would keep Hector warm at night and even an old hot water bottle with a furry cover that resembled 'Dougal' out of *The Magic Roundabout.* At least he was not going to freeze.

Harry connected the gas and showed Hector how to use it. They had arranged with the shop that someone would come every week and change the cylinder as they did in the summer unless Hector rang them and told them not to. And suddenly things started to warm up. There were two heaters, one in the main room and one in the bedroom, and they both rather surprisingly burst into life. Hector thought that it was a pity that there wasn't one in the bathroom, but it would just have to do. The kitchen would keep warm with the cooker. All in all it could have been worse.

Harry left soon after, promising to be back on Saturday morning to take Hector to the football with him and Brian. After he had gone, Hector had a good look around all by himself and poked and peered in every cupboard and drawer to see what was lying about. There was just about enough to get by on. Some plates and cutlery and mugs in the kitchen. Various items of linen in an airing cupboard in the bathroom, and he even found six bottles of Mudthorpes Jubilee Ale under the sink. *I'll have them tonight with my tea*, he thought.

And then it was time to start the novel. He turned on the living room light as it was just starting to get dark and sat down at the typewriter. The light gave an eerie sort of brightness to the room and made a hissing sound that Hector didn't like at all.

Having spent a few moments exploring the keyboard, he fed in his first sheet of paper. 'Th Lif and Tims af Hctar Blnkinsap,' he typed.

Great start.

The 'e' didn't work at all and the 'o' came out as 'a'. *Bloody marvellous, it looks like it's written in Bulgarian*, he thought.

He ripped out the sheet, put in another one and started again. 'Hctar's Truvls.' *Even bloody worse*, he thought.

He ripped that sheet out as well and threw it at the window. He was thinking about throwing the typewriter after it, when he noticed there was a face staring back at him from outside the window. It was a boy. And he was staring blankly in at Hector.

Then the boy's face disappeared. Hector looked again. Nothing. Had he imagined it? He went outside to look. As he walked round to the beach side of the house he thought he heard voices coming from the sea. As he peered into the early evening gloom, he could see a boy running away from him towards the rocks. And he could see a boat, about the size of a life raft, bobbing up and down in the sea by the rocks. And he could quite plainly hear a woman's voice screaming.

He ran towards the boat. It had started to rain and the wind had risen suddenly. He got level to where the boat was rocking and rolling in the surf about ten yards out to sea at the same time as the boy. The boy was dressed very strangely and was crying.

'Mama, Mama,' he was crying.

Hector could see a woman standing up in the boat and waving. She was yelling and screaming for help. The boat made a big leap and crashed into the rocks before being sucked further out to sea. As Hector stood on the beach totally confused, the boat lurched back into the rocks again. He couldn't see the woman now; she must have fallen back into the boat. Or at least he hoped she had. If not she had fallen overboard and that didn't bear thinking about.

Hector could see a rope hanging from the front of the boat and, without thinking he ran into the water and dived into the surf after it. He swam as hard as he could and eventually he caught the rope in his left hand and started back to the beach away from the rocks.

He was very relieved to feel his feet touch the bottom and as he dragged himself up the beach, he heaved the rope behind him. The boy was running alongside him and he heaved on the rope too for all he was worth. He was saying something that Hector couldn't understand. He heaved and heaved with all his might and slowly the small boat responded until it beached itself on the sand in front of an exhausted Hector. He leapt inside it and saw the woman lying on the bottom. It looked like she had knocked herself out. Quickly he picked her up and carried her up the beach to the house. He had only had a quick look but there didn't seem to be anyone else in the boat with her, so he left it just where it was halfway up the beach.

The boy ran alongside, jabbering in some strange language, but Hector didn't have time to worry about that now. He reached the house, pushed through the open door and went straight into the bedroom. He gently laid the woman on the bed and took a step backwards.

This was not the same bedroom he had slept in last night. He didn't know where it was, but it definitely wasn't the same room. It looked like the same bed, much cleaner and newer, but probably the same. Gone was the old tatty eiderdown; in its place was a very neatly embroidered old-fashioned bedspread.

And the light had changed. There was an oil lamp hanging from the ceiling. That had definitely not been there earlier. He had come into the wrong house by mistake. So whose house was it? The boy was sitting on the bed beside the woman who was apparently his mother and he was crying again. The woman was starting to stir. Hector thought he had better get some help. He rushed back outside and looked around him.

There was no mistaking it; it was the same house all right, but it had changed. He wasn't sure how or when, but it had. Still, no time to worry about that now. He ran up the road to the phone box, but it wasn't there. He ran back to the house. He was in a state of near panic when he saw that the house further up the beach had some lights on. He ran off towards it. He skidded round the corner and felt his legs give way as he slipped and crashed to the ground. He leapt to his feet and banged rapidly on the door.

There was no answer. He banged again, but nothing happened. He walked round to the front and then noticed that there were no lights on now. It was all boarded up with shutters on the windows. He took a few steps back to the beach.

This is crazy, he thought, and he turned and ran back to his own place. He ran straight through the doorway and into the bedroom. It was deserted. No woman, no crying boy, no oil lamp, no bedspread, just his threadbare eiderdown. He went into the living room. Nothing, just the soft hiss of the gaslight.

I do not like this, thought Hector to himself.

He went back out on the beach. The rain had stopped and the wind had died down completely. He walked to where he had left the boat. Again nothing. Not only no boat, but no marks in the sand where it had been. And it had only been five minutes ago he had dragged it there. *Where had it gone? And where were the woman and the boy? Come to that*, he thought, *where was the bloody phone box?*

He ran back to the house, round the side and up the path. The phone box was there in front of him. He opened the door, went in, picked up the receiver and listened. It was working, the soft purr echoing inside his head.

He walked slowly back to the house. He must have somehow imagined it, he thought. But he was still dripping wet!

He didn't sleep much again that night. He had drunk almost two of the bottles of wine by the time he turned in. And all six of the bottles of Mudthorpes Jubilee, but that hadn't helped. Every time he closed his eyes he saw the boat, or the woman, or the boy, or some combination of all three.

It was almost dawn before he drifted off.

The next day, he tried the old typewriter again. The first line he wrote said: 'Hctar Blnkinsap wus u sud mun.' He gave up again.

After that he spent most of the morning on the beach. He walked up and down where he had been the night before, or at least where he thought he had been the night before. He stood looking out to sea for ages. Then he went back inside and dozed for a couple of hours on the settee. Then for some strange reason he stood on a chair and clambered up into the loft.

He could see all sorts of assorted junk. Bits of furniture, boxes, old clothes and a big pile of newspapers. Hector picked up the top few and clambered back down. The top one was dated Wednesday, 15 October 1908. *Over ninety years ago*, thought Hector.

When he read the headline across the top he nearly stopped breathing.

UNKNOWN LOCAL MAN SAVES COUNTESS AND YOUNG SON. Below it was a picture of a beautiful young woman in a flowing ball gown. It was the same woman he had dragged from the boat last night.

Forcing himself to breathe, he read the story.

The German-registered steam ship *Nordved* ran aground on Blackhall Rocks last night in the teeth of a raging gale. On board were not only the players and directors of the famous German football team from Bad Klunzenberg but their illustrious patrons, Count and Countess von Heizenhofferhoff. The players were on their way to take part in a prestigious friendly match against Newcastle United to celebrate being crowned German champions for the first time in their history last season.

As the ship struck the rocks, apparently Countess Catherine, together with her young son Willie, was put into a lifeboat in case the ship should start sinking. Somehow the lifeboat became detached from the ship and floated off into the storm.

Some time later a heroic local man dived into the sea and rescued both the countess and her son from certain death. The man then carried them to a deserted beach house and raised the alarm with neighbours before disappearing into the night. Police searching for the man could find no trace.

The countess is recovering in hospital and Count von Heizenhofferhoff would like to reward the man responsible.

The Bad Klunzenberg team, who were later rescued when the local lifeboat towed the ship to safety, are to play a friendly against the local Blackhall Welfare team next Wednesday afternoon. The match will take place at three o'clock at the Welfare's Ditchwater Lane ground.

After the game, if the man responsible for the rescue has not been found, Count von Heizenhofferhoff will make a presentation to the mayor of

Hartlepool in appreciation of his gratitude. It is hoped that Countess Catherine will be fit enough to attend the event.

Hector read the story three times. Then he read the rest of the papers. Right up until the very day of the game itself the papers went. The story ran and ran as the search for the man continued. But try as they might, the authorities could not find him. Hector couldn't wait to read the outcome of the match and the story, but the paper for Thursday, 24th October was not there.

He went back into the loft but it wasn't there either. The next paper was from 1933 and the story was totally dead and buried by then.

Hector sat and thought about it after he returned from the loft. This was all a bit spooky. He had had a somewhat similar experience happen to him a few years ago in Somerset. Could the same thing be happening to him again?

Suddenly he knew what his book was going to be about. It was going to be the story of the events that happened on that Saturday in April in Shepton Mallet. It wouldn't fill a whole book though; still, it would do for a start. Then he could write about all sorts of other adventures. Like when he had been to Ireland and broke his leg. And when he had got shot in America. And the Trophy final at Highbury. There really was a lot he could write about when he got going. If only the damn typewriter worked properly.

But what about this mystery with Countess von Heizenhofferhoff and the shipwreck? If he could make some sense out of that, think what a great ending to the book it would make, he told himself. He owed it to himself to try to get to the bottom of it, he decided.

He rang Maureen again later and told her what he was going to write about. He didn't tell her about the countess though. He had told her about Shepton Mallet once but she obviously didn't believe him. She had thought it was a good story though and now she agreed that it might be worth trying to get it and the other adventures published. He told her about the typewriter and he said he would try to find another one. He even told her reluctantly where he was and she said she would come up soon for the weekend if Hector could get Harry to pick her up at the station. He was sure Harry would and he whistled to himself as he walked down the path back to the beach house.

He lay in bed that night much happier. Now he had a real plan. And the next day he was going out to look for a new typewriter. But first he had to find Blackhall Welfare's ground. He had never heard of them and they weren't listed in the non-league handbook, but he did have an address: Ditchwater Lane. He would try to find it first thing in the morning.

He slept much better that night.

Next morning he was up bright and early and was for some reason really keen to get on with things. He walked back to the parade of shops he had been to with Harry the day before and to his delight he found that the small road running down the back of the shops was called Ditchwater Lane. He asked in the shops if anyone knew where the football ground was, but unsurprisingly he found that no one knew of a football ground anywhere in the area, let alone in Ditchwater Lane.

Down the lane he went, which was not easy. It was obviously very rarely used nowadays and was very uneven and overgrown. About two hundred yards down it, Hector came to almost a complete stop. A tree had blown down across the lane and he had to clamber through the branches to get past. But it was worth the struggle. About fifty yards further on, to the right-hand side of the lane, was what must unmistakably have once been a football ground. Not a very big one, but an ex-football ground all the same. It was all so overgrown with weeds that it was difficult to get in over the broken fencing, but he was not going to give up now. There were no goalposts still standing but he could definitely make out the remains of an old iron stand along one side of the weed-choked but still vaguely open space that had once been the pitch. *It had obviously been derelict for donkey's years*, thought Hector, as there were no signs of any floodlights anywhere and no trace of any dugouts or terracing, but this had to be the place he was looking for.

He hunted for ages for any old signs or painted pieces of wood but found nothing that gave any clue whatsoever as to the origins of the team that used to play there, but Hector was not surprised. This was what he was searching for and he would bet his shirt that if he turned up here the following Wednesday afternoon then things would be rather different. He just somehow knew that they would.

He scrambled back up the lane and caught a bus into Hartlepool, where he managed to buy quite a reasonable, fairly new and, more importantly, portable typewriter for fifty quid in a second-hand shop. He replenished his wallet from a cash dispenser and splashed out on three little luxuries. He bought himself a nice mechanical alarm clock – the one he had brought with him was useless as it was an electric one – and a new duvet. He also bought a battery-operated radio.

That afternoon back at the beach house he finally started his novel. And it went surprisingly well. It took him time to get used to using a typewriter again as he had been using a PC at work for the last ten years that had things like spellcheck and auto-correct on it. The one thing he hadn't thought to buy was some correction fluid, so the pages he typed were all a bit messy. But as he sat down for an evening meal of beans on toast with a lump of cheese (for the second night running) and his last bottle of wine, he was rather pleased with his efforts.

He had typed seven pages, covering about two thirds of the story of his fateful trip to Shepton Mallet. Strangely enough, although it had been more than three years since it happened, he had almost total recall of the event as if it had been yesterday. *If only I could remember things connected with my work as clearly as that*, he thought to himself, *I might have been able to get another job*!

And for the second night running he slept soundly, snuggled up as he was in his brand new duvet.

Friday dawned clear and cold, and after a trip back to the shops for more milk, beans, bread and cheese (and correction fluid), he sat back down at the typewriter and started bashing away at the keyboard. He finished the story about Shepton Mallet and then started another one about meeting Maureen for the first time.

He worried at times that he couldn't remember exact details or times and dates, but it suddenly occurred to him that, as he was the only one there at the time, nobody was going to argue with him about the finer points. This cheered him up no end and he just typed and typed and typed until he started to get cramps in his fingers.

He went for a stroll along the beach (it was totally and utterly deserted) made himself some more beans on toast (with cheese) and then sat back down at the typewriter. He typed late into the evening until his fingers wouldn't let him continue. Then he sat back on the settee and reread his manuscript. It was amazing that every time he read it he found things he had missed or that were not quite right and in the end there were almost as many handwritten notes on the pages as there were typed words. It didn't really bother him as he assumed he would have to enter it all into a word processor before he sent it off for publishing anyway.

He must remember to keep the pieces of paper though, he reasoned. When he was famous these original manuscripts would be worth a fortune!

When he awoke on Saturday morning his arms and hands ached like he just couldn't believe and he was glad that Harry and Brian were coming to take him out, as he didn't think he would ever be able to type again.

They arrived about twelve and were delighted when Hector told them how well he was getting on. Harry told him to hide the little typewriter away when they went out in case Uncle Norman popped in and was insulted by the fact that Hector wasn't using his old one. And so, with the new typewriter safely hidden away under the bed, they set out for the afternoon's entertainment.

Harry had chosen for that afternoon's game a match between Hetton-le-Hole Harriers and Leadgate Colliery Welfare in the Dreadnought and Cutler's Iron Foundry North-Eastern Junior Combination Division Three (East).

Hector was excited for two reasons. One, he was still basically a very sad man and got excited easily; two, this was one league he had never seen a game in before. He was even more excited when he found out that the clubhouse sold Old Wally Bates's Gutbuster, a legendary northern brew that he had only ever had once before in his life. He wasn't sure how many of them he sank before the game but he seemed to miss about twenty minutes of the first half through having to go to the toilet every five minutes.

The game was pretty good, probably, he thought to himself back in the bar afterwards. His recollections were all a bit sketchy due to the extra two pints he had crammed in at half-time and the ones he was now sinking happily back in the clubhouse.

He didn't remember much about the drive back to Blackhall, but he did remember ringing Maureen from the phone box when he got back. He had no recollection whatsoever of what they talked about, but when he woke up lying on the settee at almost one thirty the following morning, he was very glad that he had phoned her. He had been so wrapped up in the typing he had forgotten to ring her on Friday and he had a very vague idea that she had had a right go at him about it. *Never mind*, he thought, *I'll make it up with her tomorrow.*

He dragged his body, with the driest mouth in Christendom and a thumping headache the like of which he had very rarely had before, into his bed and slept soundly until nearly half past eleven on Sunday morning.

When he woke up he felt worse than he had done the previous night. It took him almost an hour to get out of bed and then another hour sitting on the settee to get the strength up to make himself a mug of tea. He tried walking outside to see if the sea air would make him feel any better, but all it did was make him nearly sick. He sat on the settee for another two hours before he found the courage to get dressed, walk up to the phone box and ring Maureen. He soon wished he hadn't.

Maureen gave him a right mouthful. How much had he drunk the night before, what was all this about a woman in a boat, who or what was Count of Heizerwoof and what on earth was all this about a reward?

He was too ill and tired and scared and unable to explain most of it, but he told her he loved her and was looking forward to the weekend when she was coming up, and he put the phone down just as she said the words, 'And another thing…'

He hoped desperately that she thought they had been cut off, otherwise he was in for another mouthful the following night, and he strolled back to the house very slowly and dejectedly, suddenly full of apprehension.

Monday and Tuesday followed exactly the same pattern. On both days Hector got up around nine, had a piece of toast and a cold can of beans, walked for half an hour or so to the shops and back for a paper and spent the rest of the morning typing.

In the early afternoon, as his hands started to ache, he would sit down and read the paper he had bought from cover to cover before doing another hour or two's typing. He would then phone Maureen; she had calmed down now and was quite pleasant on the phone. He would end the evening by listening to the radio. The first night he listened to a football phone-in, until he got so angry he was tempted to walk up to the phone box and ring in. The second night he tried a current affairs programme, but got so wound up by the idiot politicians he was listening to that he went back to the football phone-in.

And that was about it.

On both nights he gave the beans a miss, instead going for spaghetti on toast the first night (with a lump of cheese, naturally) and spaghetti hoops the second. Then off to bed he went, having read back through the day's typing as the last job of the evening.

Wednesday was different. This was going to be the day of the match, or at least he hoped it was, and after finishing the fifth chapter of his book, about the first time he had visited this part of the world, he sat down for some quiet contemplation.

He still got the odd nightmare about that huge woman in the pink frills he had encountered on that fateful trip and he noticed the palms of his hands starting to sweat at the mere thought of her. He went for a long walk along the beach to get the old hag out of his mind but it didn't really work. He tried to concentrate on what the afternoon would bring, but all the time his mind wandered back to that awful night in Newton Aycliffe and gave him the sweats.

In the end he got changed ready for the match and walked towards the shops. He kept waiting for something to happen, but much to his chagrin nothing did. He even walked down Ditchwater Lane to the fallen tree, but nothing changed. He sat on the tree, he stood on top of the tree, he clambered through the tree and went to look at the old ground, but it was all still the same as it had always been.

After three-quarters of an hour he gave up. He walked back to the shops, went back into the convenience store and bought some sweets. He was a very disappointed man as he walked outside. He had really expected to find a football match happening and the realisation that it wasn't was proving very hard to take.

He obviously wasn't concentrating very hard on where he was going as the next thing he knew he was sitting on the ground in the middle of the road.

'Watch where you're bloody going,' came a voice from above him.

He looked up and stared straight into the slimy nostrils of a big sweaty horse.

'Are you all right?' the voice asked.

'I, er, I guess so,' said Hector, struggling to his feet.

He looked at the horse again. It was pulling a carriage. And there was another one behind. He smiled to himself as he dusted himself down. He could hear a brass band playing somewhere behind him. He knew what had happened.

He put his hand into his jacket pocket to check that the disposable camera he had bought was okay. It came out of his pocket in about twenty pieces. He said a rude word out loud that shocked a passing couple. The man was done up like a dog's dinner complete with tall black hat and the woman had a long black coat over a huge billowing white dress and a bonnet securely tied to her head with a big white ribbon. They gave Hector a wide berth as they hurried round the corner.

Hector waited for the carriage to move before scuttling off after the couple.

The lane was totally awash with people, mostly all done up in their finery. The lane itself was about twice as wide as it had been earlier and was lined with trees and hedges. Carriages were backed up almost to the main road and as he walked past them Hector could see that the occupants were all done up much like the couple who had thought he had sworn at them.

As he approached the ground, he hit his first major obstacle. How was he going to get in? The fence he had scrambled over the week before was now proudly blocking any entrance to the little ground. The only way in was through a gate at which two large gentlemen in leather trousers, cloth caps and open-necked collarless shirts were collecting what looked like tickets from people as they entered.

Not all of the people going in were dressed like those in the carriages, now that he came to look more closely; most were dressed more like the ticket collectors, and Hector stood and watched for about ten minutes until he suddenly got an idea.

He pulled a tie from his anorak pocket and tied it round his shirt collar. He marched forcefully up to the gate and said, 'I want to see the count, please; I am the one who saved his wife!'

The man just stood and stared at him, but a policeman standing nearby had overheard him and hurried off in the direction of a pink and yellow striped marquee that had been assembled by the entrance to the main stand. A short time later the policeman returned accompanied by another bobby and a man in a top hat and tails.

'Can I help you, sir?' the man in the top hat said. 'I am the mayor.'

'Blimey,' said Hector under his breath. 'I would like to see either Countess Catherine or Count von Heizenhofferhoff himself, please. It is I who dragged the good lady from the boat!'

The mayor looked him up and down. Both the policemen looked him up and down. The gateman looked him up and down. Several of the people who had overheard him looked him up and down. Hector just stood there. There wasn't much else he could do.

He was wearing what he thought were the most inconspicuous clothes he could find. And for the early twenty-first century they probably were as conservative as it was possible to get. Sensible brown shoes, sensible tan trousers, sensible cream shirt and sensible green anorak. It was the anorak that was causing the problem. As Hector looked around him he could see that nobody else had anything like it. He didn't panic; he just took it off, rolled up his shirtsleeves and smiled at the mayor.

'Better come with us, I suppose,' the mayor said and he walked off back towards the marquee. Hector followed with his anorak under his arm and the two policemen brought up the rear. Another two policemen guarded the entrance to the huge tent but Hector and his escort whisked straight past them without so much as a pause.

Inside the marquee it was like a different world. It was packed with people, the male half of which were all dressed like the mayor in long frock coats, waistcoats and high collars. The women all wore the most elegant long gowns Hector had ever seen in his life. *It was like a scene out of* Upstairs, Downstairs, he thought as his little procession pushed their way through the throng.

Suddenly the wall of people parted and Hector and the mayor stood alone in front of a small podium. On the podium were two red padded armchairs and in the chairs sat Countess Catherine, whom Hector recognised from his first encounter and a small dapper man Hector assumed must be Count von Heizenhofferhoff himself.

Hector felt acutely embarrassed as he stood in front of the podium. He could feel the eyes of everyone in the tent on him and he didn't like it. He started to sweat even though without his anorak on it was distinctly chilly in the marquee.

He looked at the count. He looked at the countess. He turned sideways and looked at the mayor. He felt extremely nervous. The countess leant towards her husband and said something quietly in his ear.

Suddenly the count leapt to his feet and jumped off the stage. He rushed towards Hector, his arm outstretched, and grasped Hector's hand in his.

'My boy,' he exclaimed, 'how good it is to meet you at last. I cannot sank you enough for vot you did to save my family,' he went on in perfect English but with a very clipped German accent.

He was much smaller than Hector with a waxed moustache and greased back hair. He had a monocle over his right eye and a scar down his left cheek. Round the white tie at his neck he was wearing a large gold Maltese cross, with an enamelled centre, on a green and gold ribbon. Hector had terrible trouble stopping himself from laughing out loud. He was standing next to what could almost be described as a parody of a German count. *I bet this guy's first name is Wolfgang*, he thought to himself as he managed to turn his laughter into a beaming smile.

As Hector grasped the hand offered by the count, the crowd inside the tent spontaneously burst into fervent applause.

'It is an honour to meet you, Count,' said Hector, smiling.

'Please, please you must call me Volfgang.' The count beamed back. 'Please come and meet my vife. Oh, of course, you haff already met her before. I almost forgot.'

As Hector and the count moved towards the podium, the countess rose to her feet and smiled broadly at Hector. *She definitely looked familiar*, Hector thought as he stepped up on to the stage, but not much like the half-drowned woman he had dragged from the boat. She was dressed in a black ball gown and had more diamonds around her neck than Hector had ever seen in his life. She had two large brooches on the front of her dress, one that appeared to be made of rubies, with a diamond centre, the other shaped like a large spider made entirely of emeralds.

The countess held out a hand; Hector didn't know whether to shake it or kiss it. He chose the latter and it seemed to go down well. She was not the best-looking woman he had ever seen in his life, he had to admit. Not too bad, but she looked just a bit too much like Morticia out of *The Adams Family* for comfort. As she smiled, Hector could swear that two of her teeth were longer than the others, but he told himself that he must be hallucinating.

She leant forward and whispered to him, 'I vont to drink your blud.'

Hector stood rooted to the spot.

The count grabbed his arm and pulled him to one side. 'I must apologise for my vife's English; it isn't vot she vood like it to be,' he said.

It sounded good enough to me, Hector thought, the blood draining from his face.

'Bring anuzzer chair for our guest,' the count barked at a flunky standing nearby. From his tone of voice Hector could tell that the count was used to getting exactly vot he vanted.

A chair was brought up on to the stage, but before Hector could sit down, the count dragged him to the front of the podium and whispered discreetly in his ear, 'Vot is your name, please? I haff an important announcement to make.'

'Er, Hector,' stammered the man of the moment. 'Hector Blenkinsop.'

The count beckoned the mayor towards him and said something in his ear.

The mayor stepped up to the front of the stage and in a deep booming voice announced, 'My lords, ladies and gentlemen, it is my pleasure and privilege to present to you this afternoon... Count von Heizenhofferhoff.'

Christ, thought Hector, *it sounds like he's introducing a boxing match.*

To thunderous applause the count stepped forward. 'As you all vill know, last veek my vife ze countess and my young zun Villie were rescued from ze sea by a brave Englishman,' he started. 'I am very pleased to introduce zat man to you today. Ladies and gentlemen, I give you ze saviour of my family, Mr Hector Blenkinsop.'

Even louder applause echoed around the tent as Hector was pushed to the very edge of the stage.

'Say something,' the mayor said to him.

'Er, I, er, I don't know what to say,' stammered Hector. 'I only did what anyone else would have done in the circumstances.'

That did it; the applause got even louder.

Hector didn't know what to say next, but the count came to his rescue and announced, 'For zis brave act of courage, I present you viz the Star of Heizenhofferhoff. I shall be forever in your debt.' With this the count took the golden cross from around his neck and to Hector's surprise hung it around his. Hector was stunned.

The count went on with his speech and suddenly the crowd started singing 'For he's a jolly good fellow' with gusto. Hector just stared at the cross. *It must be worth some serious money*, he thought.

The count guided him back towards the chair, which was just as well as Hector was on the point of collapsing.

'Zere iz a reward az vell, of course,' said the count. 'Zey are just getting it from my carriage. Tell me, vear did you get zese strange clothes? I haff never zeen anysing like zem.'

'I... I've been abroad,' said Hector, and then, realising that the count had come from abroad, he said, 'France, I've been in France.'

'Typical of ze French,' said the count. 'Zey vear zese strange clothes all the time. I cannot see zem catching on, eh?'

'Oh, I don't know,' said Hector, 'one day perhaps.'

To Hector's enormous relief the conversation was cut short by someone tapping the count on the shoulder and saying something in his ear.

The count looked at Hector and said, 'Apart from the trinket, I vant you to haff zis; it's not much but it is, I sink, a reasonable reward for saving my family.'

With this he pushed a bag the size of a packet of crisps into Hector's hand. It might have been the size of a packet of crisps, but it weighed more like a bag of nails. Hector pulled the drawstring and peered inside. It was coins. Gold coins. And there were dozens of them in there. He pulled the drawstring shut and stuffed the bag into his anorak pocket.

'And now for ze game,' announced the count, rising to his feet.

Hector got up and went to walk away, but the count grabbed his arm. 'Come vis us,' he said. 'You are ze guest of honour.'

Hector smiled ruefully and accompanied the count and countess out of the tent and out on to the pitch.

The two teams were lined up before them. After posing for various photos with the count and countess and the two teams and facing all sorts of questions from the press which he answered as non-committally as he could, it was time for the introductions to the teams. The players from Bad Klunzenberg were all standing to attention, immaculately turned out in white silk shirts, black silk shorts (or they were supposed to be shorts; they reached down to their knees) and black and white hooped socks. Hector was introduced to all of them in turn by the count, who at the end of the line said to Hector, 'What do you sink? Vun day ze Germans vill be ze best footballers in ze vorld!'

'I think you could very well be right,' answered Hector.

The team from Blackhall Welfare could not have been a greater contrast from the Germans. Some were trying to imitate their visitors by standing to attention, but most were either jogging up and down on the spot or just standing still staring into space. They were, from a distance, all wearing identical red and white striped shirts and white shorts and socks. Close up the shirts were all slightly different, with some having the colours running together while on others the stripes were of different sizes. The shorts were even more of a mishmash. Some were white, some were cream and one was a light shade of tan. The socks were all identical though and the players seemed genuinely pleased to meet the 'hero'.

At least the players were glad to meet him. As Hector took his seat in the stand between the count and countess, he could see the mayor in the row behind. And he did not look amused. In fact, he looked as if he was going to burst with rage. Hector had obviously ruined his day, if not his life. If Hector hadn't shown up, then not only would the mayor have been getting all the plaudits, but very probably the reward as well.

The game passed Hector by. In the first half the Germans were seemingly taken aback by the physical tactics of the local players and it was

Blackhall that took the lead ten minutes before half-time, the home team's centre forward, Philip Neviks, thundering a cross from the left wing high into the net.

At half-time Hector was less than happy to see the mayor leave his seat and chat with a group of local men all built like the proverbial brick outhouse. When the mayor pointed at Hector and the men all started nodding, the blood started to drain from his face again. To make matters worse, the countess twice started to talk to Hector, but fortunately he couldn't understand a word she said. Her smile made him very nervous though. There was just something odd about it.

The second half started much better for the visitors. Their higher level of fitness and skill began to tell and inside right Hans Neesan volleyed home the equaliser ten minutes into the half. Five minutes from the end six-foot blond German captain Fritz Schlitz headed what turned out to be the winner from a corner.

Hector just couldn't concentrate. What with the grinning countess on one side of him and the mayor's henchmen waiting at the foot of the stairs, he didn't feel good at all.

At the end of the match everyone started to file out of the stand and back into the marquee. As Hector and the countess rose from their seats, the countess pressed something into his hand and said in absolutely perfect English, 'If you are ever in Germany, you simply must look us up.' And she winked.

Hector froze. It was only when the crowd behind him started shoving that he made his way down the stairs. At the bottom, the mob of men that had talked to the mayor moved menacingly towards him, but he just followed everyone else inside the tent to safety. He could see that the men were standing just outside the entrance and it didn't take a genius to work out their intentions.

What could he do? Suddenly he remembered the countess's gift and when he looked in his hand he saw the emerald brooch she had had on her dress earlier. He carefully pulled out the bag of coins from his anorak pocket and slipped the brooch inside. He put the bag back into his pocket and walked slowly towards the podium.

Suddenly he was face to face with the mayor.

'I would like a word with you,' the mayor said coldly. 'I believe you have something of mine.'

'Not that I know of,' said Hector, backing away.

'Maybe afterwards then.' The Mayor grinned. 'When this little charade is over.'

What the hell am I going to do now? thought Hector. This is turning into some sort of Mack Sennett comedy. All we need now are the Keystone Kops and we've got a full set.

Right on cue four burly policemen marched into the tent and approached the mayor. The mayor spun around and pointed straight at Hector and a shiver ran down his spine. *Time to go*, he thought and, pushing the three nearest people out of his way, he made a dive for the canvas flap of the tent. He scrambled his way out and leapt straight to his feet.

He heard a shout of 'Oi, stop!' to his right and saw the mayor's henchmen charging towards him. With a look of horror he saw two policemen's heads appear under the canvas where he had come from and fear and panic took over.

He ran towards the fence and threw himself into the bushes. He smashed his way through the tangle of branches and jumped at the six-foot fence. Somehow, and afterwards he had no recollection of how, he scrambled up and over the fence and hit the ground in the lane outside running.

He ran back up the lane but disaster loomed. As he got to the corner of the lane and the main road he stumbled and hit the deck. He dragged himself to his feet and tried to get his breath back; he was not used to running, especially from a mob. But there was no mob. There was nobody. He was back where he had started outside the modern convenience store.

It was all over. And he was rich. He thrust his hand into his pocket for the bag, but it was empty. He clutched at his throat for the cross, but that had gone too; lost in the scramble, he supposed. He was distraught. He made his way back down the lane, searching left and right but found nothing. He went back as far as the old ground and searched for hours, until it was dark, but he still found nothing.

It was with a very heavy heart that he made his way back to the cottage by the beach and he lay on his bed for ages bemoaning his luck before eventually he fell asleep.

He awoke with a start. Uncle Norman was sitting in the chair at the foot of the bed. And he was grinning, the sunlight glinting off his one enormous tooth.

'What do you want?' stammered Hector.

'Got fumfink to fyow you,' said the old man.

Hector hoped to God it wasn't another typewriter and pulled his dressing gown on as he slid from the bed.

The old boy held out a photo in a deep brown wooden frame. 'My nephew tellf me you like football,' he grinned.

'I do,' replied an intrigued Hector.

'Fought you might like to fee thif,' the old boy went on, handing Hector the picture.

Hector nearly dropped it on the floor. It was a picture of the two teams from that day over ninety years ago that Hector remembered like it was yesterday. And Hector was standing in front of them!

'That'f my daddy,' said the old man, proudly pointing at one of the Blackhall players. 'It waff a very famous match in thefe partf.'

'Waff it?' asked Hector. 'Why?'

'It waff a game againft the Germanf that were fwipwrecked. There waff fum twuble too appawentwy.'

'Twuble, what twuble? I mean, trouble, what trouble?' asked Hector.

'There waff fum wocal hewo there too – he had faved them or fumwun – but he waff kidnapped and never feen again,' went on Norman.

'Kidnapped!' exploded Hector. 'What the hell happened?'

'Fteady on, fun,' said the old boy. 'Maybe thiff will help.' With that he pulled out two sheets of very old and worn cardboard, which he carefully prised apart. Inside was a yellow and ragged newspaper cutting, which he also very carefully unfolded.

> LOCAL HERO IN KIDNAP DRAMA screamed the headline. Hector carefully took the paper from the old man and read the story.
>
> There was drama after the football match at Blackhall Welfare's Ditchwater Lane ground on Wednesday when local hero Herman Bloominsock was kidnapped by bandits following his award of the Star of Heizenhofferhoff by Count von Heizenhofferhoff before the match.
>
> Mystery still surrounds the whereabouts of the man following his abduction. It was expected that a ransom note would be received from the kidnappers for the return of Mr Bloominsock but by the time this paper went to press no such ransom had been demanded.
>
> The Bad Klunzenberg team, Count and Countess and son Willie are due to sail back to Germany today and they are all said to be very distraught at the disappearance of the man who saved the countess's life only two weeks ago.
>
> If anyone knows of the whereabouts of this brave man can they please contact

either this newspaper or the local police where a very generous reward is awaiting them.
For the full story see page twelve.

But there was no page twelve.

Hector read the paper twice, then he very carefully folded it up and slid it back between the sheets of cardboard.

'Can I borrow this and get it copied?' he asked Norman.

'Yeff, of courfe,' he replied. 'Do you want to copy the photo af well? My old dad waff vewy pwoud of it.'

'If I may,' said Hector. 'I will guard it with my life.'

'Juft leave them on the table when you've finifhed wif them,' said Norman and then he turned and left.

Hector read and reread the clipping and stared at the photo for ages. There he was standing next to the count and countess in front of both teams as plain as daylight. And around his neck was the Star of Heizenhofferhoff. He got sad again thinking about how much it would be worth. If only he still had it, he could forget about writing books and he and Maureen could live in the lap of luxury ever after.

Oh well, no use crying over spilt beer, he chided himself.

Several hours later he was sitting at his typewriter trying to think of another story to write. He had been into Hartlepool and made several good copies of both the photo and the newspaper and had phoned Maureen on the way back and tried to explain without success what had happened. Maureen just thought he had gone completely mad. Never mind, she would see him on Saturday, she had said. This cheered Hector up immensely; he would be seeing his Maureen at the weekend. He felt good. He still couldn't think of anything to write about so he had a quiet evening with a couple of cans of beer and just read and reread the old newspaper clipping.

Friday morning he awoke full of inspiration. Why not write about what had happened with the countess? Even if Maureen didn't believe him, which she obviously wouldn't, it would make a cracking ending for the book. Maybe in his story he could write that he found the jewels and coins buried under the old fence when he had gone back to look for them and they had lived happily ever after. He spent the whole day writing, only stopping for ten minutes to ring Maureen and check that she had rung Harry and arranged for him to pick her up at Newton Aycliffe the following lunchtime.

She sounded very excited on the phone and said that she couldn't wait to see him, which sent Hector back to the cottage feeling happier than he had since he had left home.

He didn't finish the story until very late that evening and although he was pleased to finish it, he was sad that he had had to make up a happy ending.

He was seeing Maureen in a few hours though, and he slept soundly that night.

He awoke very late the next day and he could hear voices. It was Harry and Maureen.

He leapt out of bed, grabbed his dressing gown and stumbled to the door. As he wrenched it open he could see Harry reversing back up to the main road and Maureen walking towards him with a huge grin on her face.

They hugged for about five minutes before Maureen pulled away from him and looked him straight in the eye. 'How could you?' she asked him, but he didn't answer. He just avoided her stare and looked at the threadbare carpet.

'You run away with some half-baked story of becoming a writer, then ring me with some cock and bull story about a shipwreck and a countess and a football match and some jewels,' she ranted. 'Do I look stupid?'

Hector just stood and stared at the floor.

'And just what the hell do you think you are doing leaving this junk in my flat?' she carried on, slamming a small red case on the table. It was the case that Hector had put under her bed; he had completely forgotten to tell her about it.

'I found it under my bed. I can't find the key but I didn't want to throw it away before I knew what was in it. I meant to tell you but…' His voice tailed off. He didn't think that their reunion would be like this. He couldn't understand why Maureen was making such a fuss over such a little thing.

'Key, key, what key?' she said and then she burst out laughing. 'You don't need a key; it hasn't got a lock!'

'Yes, it has,' said Hector. 'Look.'

He turned the case round to where it had had a small brass lock, but in its place was just a simple clasp. He opened it carefully. Inside was a little bag, about the same size as a crisp packet, but as he lifted it out he thought it weighed more like a bag of nails.

He emptied the contents out on the table. It was mainly coins. Gold coins. But there was one other thing – a brooch. It was the shape of a large spider and was made completely of what looked like emeralds.

He started to cry.

Maureen moved beside him and put her arms around him. 'There's something else in the case, under that newspaper,' she said.

And she was right. Under a newspaper with the headline LOCAL HERO IN KIDNAP DRAMA and a photo of Hector standing with the count and countess was the Star of Heizenhofferhoff, still on its green and gold ribbon, and it gleamed in the light as Hector took it out.

'Now exactly what the hell is all this about a drowning countess?' said Maureen, squeezing him tightly.